ELECTRA

ELECTRA

GLADYS SCHMITT

HARCOURT, BRACE & WORLD, INC. NEW YORK

In Memoriam
L.S.
1909–1964

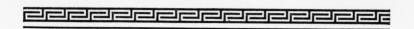

I

ONE

THE TOWER stood on the peak of the Holy Mountain, and there were those among the ignorant who held that the Holy Mountain was the top of all the world. From its narrow windows the eyes of a man could see as much as the eyes of a hovering eagle. To the south the Argive plain rolled out beneath it, and those who labored in the fields and orchards had the look of laboring ants. To the west the Arcadian hills, high as they were, lay below it, their valleys like bowls of light at noon. To the north were the barren stretches, their rocks turned into pebbles by dizzy height, their scrub oak and wild olive trees mere handfuls of twigs and foliage. And to the east the eye passed quickly over the great Citadel, as though a child had built it out of rubble, and leaped on a clear day to the shifting, quivering line of the sea.

Men said that the one-eyed giants had built the tower, as they had built the Citadel, for Perseus the Mighty. How many centuries ago they had laid the enormous stones one upon another with their monstrous hands, nobody knew: that work had been finished in a past beyond remembering. But there were some of the very old among the folk of Mycenae—already half drained of their blood and willing to join the thirsty ones in the country of the dead—who could recall how hard a business it had been for the mortal King Atreus to fill up, without the help of giants, the gaps that years uncountable had made in the walls. Men—the race had declined lamentably since the reign of Perseus—had not been willing to sweat at the task, even on double rations, for more than eight or ten hours between sun and sun. Beasts had burst their hearts straining to drag up the prodigious yield of the quarry; and ten times at least one of the stones had jerked out of hold before it could be wrestled into place, carrying shrieks and blood and battered flesh with it into the gorge below.

But now there was no more building in Mycenae. Agamemnon son of Atreus had been encamped before Troy on the other side of the eastern waters for almost three years, and in these meager days there were neither riches nor men for raising new palace wings above the earth or hollowing out royal tombs beneath. The court was shrunken and deprived of its ceremony and brazen splendor: only those needful for the carrying on of state business had remained within the walls. As for the fighting men, almost all of them had passed in martial order through the Lion Gate with their king; and those that tarried in Mycenae were the sick, the aged, the veterans crippled or outworn by earlier campaigns— men who could not hope to endure the hardships of a sea journey or a siege, men hard put to it, in fact, to guard the folk and the

4

Citadel that Agamemnon left behind when he took up arms for Helen's sake.

In the tower on the top of the Holy Mountain lived one of these, a lean and leathery veteran who had been given this post of honor in return for bitter months before the gates of Thebes and repeated expeditions against the wild highlanders in the Arcadian hills. He was the one who would know it first when Troy went up in flames. As soon as the invaders laid their torches to the besieged city, a beacon would be kindled on the west side of the water, and then another further inland, and then still another— this last so close that the red tidings would actually spring up in his sight. But now there was no promise in his watch: it was winter and no decisive battles would be fought on the windy Trojan plain until spring. Still he slept by daylight and kept his vigil in the dark, looking dutifully every now and again out of the tower window, scanning the vast eastward roll of the land as soon as the prospect below him was shadowy enough to show a signal fire.

Sixty-odd winters had come and gone over his bald and sun-darkened head, and of late he found himself needing less and less sleep. Sleep lay over his wrinkled eyelids as lightly as the most delicately woven piece of linen, scarcely veiling what was in the waking world around him: the mud-plastered walls of the place of his long exile, the spider web in the upper corner of the window, the little portable hearth, the pile of twigs, the great amphora of water, the smaller jars of wine and honey and milk. His ears, too, were no longer sealed when he stretched himself out on his leather pillows: the flapping wings of a passing partridge, the dry crackle of a stag breaking through the brush at the foot of the tower, were enough to shatter his rest. If there were winds about, he woke before the sun had reached its zenith. The mourning sound of the blasts breaking against the solitary tower and the fact that the mountain on which it stood had long been a poor man's cemetery reminded him of the speed with which his own life kept

5

running past him, of the fearfully small number of years still left to him, of the difference between his present fitful sleep and the unbroken sleep of the dead. In the middle of the afternoon, when the long stretch of useless watching lay bleak before him, he welcomed anything that could distract his attention—a fox digging in the dry earth, a woman gathering berries on the slope, a goat strayed from home. So he considered himself lucky when— long before he could hope to be diverted by the lights that would come on in the houses of the Citadel at dusk—the air before him was suddenly filled and agitated with a rare fall of snow.

He felt less solitary with the flurry moving around him: the flakes peopled the vacant atmosphere and their wild whirling blotted out the awesome breadth of his view. He held out his hands to them over the stone window sill and watched them melt away on his old dried skin. He caught one of them on his tongue and took pleasure in its evanescence and tastelessness. The storm thinned a little, and he could make out the over-familiar wall of the Citadel transformed: white lines lay thick between the Cyclopean stones. Then, as if some divine being had gestured for attention in front of his face, the feathery whiteness paused in its dizzying dance, floated instead of whirled, and ceased to fall. The sky changed from leaden grey to purple parting against pale blue, and through a rift in a swollen cloud came a keen shaft of wintry sun.

The return of motionlessness to the wide air around him, the sense of his isolation above the brightening prospect of hill and gorge and plain, the weight of time still to be worn away before he could eat a meal or hope to see any lights—these had barely begun to close in on him when he saw in the long ray that shone through the torn cloud a single figure starting up the slope from the Citadel. That he should have a visitor was strange enough: the men who brought up his supplies from the palace would not be coming back for another nine days, and his friends had tired long since of all he had to draw them with—the novelty of the view. Any break in his watch would have been a dispensation, and this was one he could scarcely have hoped for: it was the princess Electra who was coming up to him through twigs and brush outlined in white—he knew her by the boyish straightness of her body and by her hair. That hair, piled high on her head and fastened there carelessly by one long gold pin, could not be mistaken for any other: it was very thick and the tawny gold color of a lion's mane.

In the seven years before he had been assigned to his present post he had served as a guard in Agamemnon's palace, stationed in the north court where the royal children played, and he had come to know them well. The youngest daughter Iphigenia had been wary and skittish with him: a man is a man to a beautiful girl aware of her beauty, even if he is a commoner and old. But with Electra and the boy Orestes he had found himself at ease; they had taken him from the first as a sage and serviceable companion. It had been possible for him to accept from them what he could never have taken from the Steward of the King's house— fruit from the royal trees and delicacies from the royal table. When the two ran away, as they often did, it had been he who had brought them back; he could still feel their hands, soft and defeated in his grasp. Not that he yearned for them overmuch in his solitude. His connection with them had lasted, after all, for no more than a tenth of his life, and that the swiftest tenth, gone past him too swiftly to have left much sediment. Yet it was good to be remembered and visited by a friend from less desolate days, and he leaned far out over the sill to watch her climbing up, sure of foot, straight of back, her brown cloak flapping behind her and showing her plain blue dress. Sallow though she was, she did not try with barley flour or chalk paste to whiten her dusky skin, but he for one took pleasure in a contrast that was rare enough to be attractive—bright rough locks brushed up from a clear dark brow.

7

She could not have been coming to him on any ordinary visit. Something must have drawn her out into the snowstorm; some urgency must lie behind the speed with which she took his dark and unfamiliar stairs. And as soon as she was in the room, standing before him with the bleak light from the window upon her, he saw trouble—trouble in her set mouth, deep trouble in her straight contracted brows, desperate trouble in her wide-set sea-colored eyes. "It is good to see you again, father," she said, gracious in spite of whatever had brought her; and he remembered that she and her brother Orestes had always called him "father" as easily and familiarly as if they had been the children of peasants or artisans.

"And you also, my lady."

"I am sorry not to have come to you before this."

"You would have been welcome. It is lonelier here than you can guess."

"I can believe it. But look, now"—she seated herself on his stool, not with her sister's soft sinuous sinking but with the definite impact of spare haunches on wood—"have you seen anything of my brother? Has he been here to visit you? Lately, I mean."

"No, my lady, not for two or three moons. Not since he came—I think it was during the Feast of the Horse or a little thereafter—to look at the place where they will light the beacon fire."

"Not yesterday? Not the day before yesterday?"

"No, my lady. Why?"

She shook her head and did not answer. In spite of her courtly bearing—she had learned to hold herself less like the child he had known and more like one of her mother's highborn companions—her face seemed queerly disordered to him: the lips suddenly fell apart, and her eyes were unable to meet his look.

"Has something gone ill?"

"I do not know, father. Perhaps it has. I cannot tell. So he has

8

not been with you? Well, then, he has not been with you. I mean, I do not doubt what you say, I know well enough that you would tell me the truth—"

"But what reason would I have to lie to my lady?"

"No reason, father. None under the sun. And since you assure me that he has not been here, I will go my way and leave you in peace."

But, though she rose from the stool where she had barely settled herself, she did not go her way. She walked over to the window from which he had watched the snow and looked down, lowering her head, not at the wide unfolding of rolling country but at the poor little cemetery on the slope directly below the tower. Few gravestones thrust themselves through the snow-powdered brush, for those who buried their fellows there had little to give away to the dead, and he could not understand what she could be straining to see.

"Are there burials here often, father?"

"Now and again, my lady. In the course of a moon, maybe three times, maybe more."

"Have there been any burials in the last two days?"

He started because she had drawn in her head, had straightened, and was staring at him with the cold demanding look of one of the court ladies who hovered around her mother's chair.

"No, nobody has been buried here for many days," he said. "But, if I can ask it without offense to my lady, why should she concern herself over such a thing?"

"Because . . . because I had a strange dream last night. . . ." A thick cord, like a rope made of the finest hemp, bound her cloak in at the waistline, and she pulled and twisted the ends of it until they began to fray. "I dreamed that somebody was buried down in that graveyard—buried secretly, as if after a murder, and shamefully, too, without funeral gifts or funeral bread and wine.

I dreamed I was on my knees down there where the gravestones are, trying to find the place where the new grave had been made, trying to open it so that I could put my offerings in."

She is growing murky, he thought, withdrawing his eyes from her somber stare; she is of an age to be married, and now she will not be given in marriage until her father comes back from Troy, and girls of her age who lie too long in empty beds are a prey to evil dreams. . . .

"But you tell me that there have been no burials, and that, too, I will take for granted—unless, of course, they came and went, as they might well have done, while my father slept."

"Would that were possible!" he said, dourly smiling. "My sleep is so light that a hare in the brush is enough to break it. I cannot sleep through a lover's tryst, much less a funeral."

"Truly?" She looked at him slantwise, with courtly lightness. "Then I must bring you a box of herb tea to strengthen your sleep. I will see to it at once, I will come again soon, I will not forget." She started for the top of the stairs, holding herself erect; then suddenly she turned again, gone limp, as though some steadying force in her had collapsed, her head down, her hands hanging open against her thighs. "Father," she said in the child's voice that he had known in the north court, "my brother Orestes is gone from us. We woke and he was simply gone. I do not know where next to look for him. Nobody has seen him or heard anything concerning him these last two days."

The few hairs left on his balding skull began to creep. Rumors had been carried up to him these many moons, rumors that he doubted she had heard: the children of the royal pair were kept innocent of the follies of the court and the sins of the world. "But you must not distress yourself over that," he said, counterfeiting calm. "You know how it has always been between him and his mother—it was so in my days there and I have no doubt it is the same thing still. Your brother has surely taken himself off for no

10

other reason than to frighten her. He will come again, as soon as he has given her an uneasy day or two."

"Yes, I also have thought of that."

And dismissed it, he told himself, as I dismiss it now. Did not see him sitting before the hearth, gloating over his doings, in the house of a friend. Saw him dead and in his grave. And is that to be dismissed as the fruit of evil dreams? If a queen takes a lover while her husband the king is across the waters, is it beyond thought that the paramour should cut off the true-born son and stuff his body away in some secret place? . . . The creeping in his scalp was so strong that he thought his hair must be moving in her sight, and he put up his hand and scratched his head.

She went back to the stool and sat down again, no longer a conscious imitator of a lady of the court, turned now into a taller and more sorrowful version of what he had known when he had been a palace guardsman—her shoulders sloping forward, her hands clasped and thrust between her knees. "Yes," she said as if there had been no silence between them. "I also thought of that, father, but it seems unlikely. For the last moon there have been only the usual little quarrels, nothing, surely, to make him want to frighten her so much. And furthermore, if he went away to frighten *her,* how is it that he should have taken no thought of *me?*"

It was a question that deserved the asking. Though there were two years between them, they had been—and for all he knew they still were—like two plums growing from a single divided stem: her shoulder forever against the boy's shoulder, and their sunbrowned hands, so like that it was almost impossible to tell them apart, forever intertwined. They were at one with each other for their father and against their mother; they were at one with each other for freedom and against ceremony; they were at one with each other in a kind of unannounced aristocracy against the rest of a less high-strung and responsive world. It had always been

11

"our horse," "our corner in the courtyard," "our dovecote," "our swing in the pear tree." Even their hair was alike, though nowhere else in Mycenae was such hair to be seen, and their voices seemed always to be the same instrument playing, hers high and his low. "Yet he is a young man now, my lady Electra," he said, willing to challenge even their immutable fellowship if he could deliver her from fright. "It is possible that he went on an errand of another sort, one which he could not speak of even to his dear sister—"

"Oh, you mean to a woman. No, I do not think he went to a woman. You see, father, he took his tutor with him. His tutor, too—the husband of my nurse—has been gone these last two days."

In the blank stillness that hung over the little chamber he played with the notion of asking her outright: Have you heard that your mother has taken Aegisthus to her bed? But it was plain from her eyes that she knew no such thing, and he did not mean to be the one to tell her: if she must be told, her nurse would serve her better in that than he. "Have you searched his sleeping chamber?" he asked, trying to keep his voice even and untroubled. "Perhaps he left something for you there—a message or a sign."

"No, father. I looked, but I found nothing." Her hands moved among the folds of her blue dress. Her fingers were laden with rings, and one of these she turned round and round, staring at it solemnly and without hope. "This ring," she said, "is my father's seal and signet. He gave it to Orestes—before he went out through the Lion Gate toward Troy, he gave it to my brother to keep for him until he comes again. And the night before my brother went —wherever he went—he asked me to wear it while he played a game of chance. It's very large, as you see, and it kept falling off while he played. When a person is afraid he lets himself make much of little things. I would like to take hope from the fact that he left the ring with me that night, but I have held it for him many times before, and many times before he has forgotten to ask me to give it back."

"Nevertheless, perhaps he intended it to be a sign of sorts."

She slowly shook her head.

"And furthermore, why should you be afraid for him? Is he not the sole heir to the domains of Agamemnon? While Agamemnon lives, who would dare to touch a hair on the head of his only son?"

She nodded and sighed deeply. "That's true, father. I have thought of that, and it gives me some comfort," she said.

But the doubt remains with you nevertheless, he thought, as surely as the doubt remains with me who could answer myself with the name of Aegisthus, could even imagine that Aegisthus somehow knows that the king my lord is dead . . . The hairs on his head began to stir again, and there was a strange crawling up and down his spine. It was sacrilege even to think of such a possibility. To brush the living with the black wing of envisioned death was to bring them a step closer to their graves. He saw Agamemnon's dark face, expressionless as the face of a corpse, as he rode in his chariot through the Lion Gate. "Let him return soon!" he said and forced his eyes to meet her inquiring look, though he had spoken not to her but to the gods. "His son cannot remain away from the Citadel beyond the hour of his return. When the king comes to us again, that and all else that goes ill in Mycenae must go well."

"Ah, must I wait as long as that to see my brother?"

"No, no, I did not mean it so. I mean only that Orestes will come then at the latest—"

"And perhaps that too is not as far off as we think." She said it ruefully, without confidence, only as if she wished to give some reassurance to her friend. She stood up then and walked back

13

to the window, her cloak trailing along the floor, gathering dust. "Show me the headland where you will see the beacon, father," she said.

He came and stood behind her in the chilly air at the window. Here and there, over the whole wide landscape, spatterings of snow remained, powdered over the brown and purple rock and the dull winter green of foliage. The jutting headland where they would light the fire was white at its edges and easy to discern. "There," he said, stretching his arm over her shoulder and pointing to the vastness. She stared long and then nodded, and the fragrance of saffron came to him out of her hair.

She turned then and stepped back, and he saw her head drawn sharply against the domain of the house of Atreus. In the days before Perseus the Mighty, the domain would have passed not from father to son but from mother to daughter, according to the will of the Lady and the old law. But the times had changed and she would take no land with her—would take only jewels and copper talents and ointments and double webs of fine cloth to the prince who received her as his bride. Nor would any prince be likely to slay a lion or run a foot race or ride over a hazardous course in a chariot for her sake: her skin was sallow, her sea-colored eyes were not large enough for real beauty, and her narrow nose was arched at the bridge as though some of her blood had come to her from across the eastern sea. But even though her sister's face was more likely to come floating into a man's dreams, hers, he thought, had the greater power to stand sharp in a man's memory.

"Thank you, father. I must go now—I must, this time. I will have to dress, and do it quickly. There is feasting again in the palace tonight." And with that she gave him her sun-browned hand and was gone.

Feasting again at the palace tonight . . . He seated himself on his leather pillow and thought of that, staring down between

14

his knees at floorboards worn smooth by the feet of generations of watchers and covered with the fine yellow dust that the winds were forever filching from the domain of Agamemnon. Feasting in the palace . . . When he looked for lights in the Citadel at dusk, he never looked for them in those high and lordly windows. In Pylos, in Phaistos, in Corinth such royal lights might bring warmth to the hearts of the folk, but not in Mycenae, not since King Atreus had spread in that same palace a hideous feast for his brother Thyestes.

That, too, had come of love—fierce love, illegitimate and almost incestuous. The wife of a brother was somehow itchingly needful to the men of the house of Atreus. It was as if only the wife of a brother could give easement, satisfying in one dark spasm lust and pride and bitter spite. Take a brother's wife and triumph between her thighs over a brother; so it had been between Thyestes and the wife of his elder brother Atreus. Thyestes had a comelier wife of his own, and dear young children, and peace and half a kingdom; but even so he was only half a man and could not complete himself except by mounting Atreus' wife in Atreus' bed. . . .

Feasting in the palace . . . A feast set out by Atreus for his beloved brother Thyestes . . . There were those among the ancient living who remembered that feast and found in the remembrance of it one more reason for going willingly into the dry country of the dead. For the vengeance of the house of Atreus was always as prodigious as the deed. It was not enough for the shamed Atreus to put away his faithless wife and exile his brother and salve his own wounds with all the lands of his father and another bride. He must make a savory stew in a great copper cauldron and add to it pieces of the infant sons of his brother— shoulder meat, thigh meat, belly meat. Unsuspecting and princely, the adulterer sat down at his brother's table, washing his hands in water fragrant with cumin and celery seed, tasting what was ladled out for him, complimenting the sauce, praising the meat. And then, at a word from Atreus, the dish of dishes was carried in: on bronze inlaid with silver, two round, bloody heads. "This is what you have taken into your mouth, adulterer. Dog, brother and dog, this is the meat that crawls in your guts." And he who had eaten his own little ones vomiting on the table, and goblets and dishes and bowls overturned, and dog facing dog, howling in the night, one in preposterous triumph, the other in superhuman pain. . . .

Feasting tonight in the palace . . . Queen Clytemnestra turning her large grey eyes to that lord whom Agamemnon had left in charge of wife and children and palace and Citadel. Dear friend, so dear as to be almost a member of the family, addressed by king and queen as "our dear cousin" and by the children as "our Uncle Aegisthus." Aegisthus of the goat's beard and the narrow shoulders sitting tonight in Agamemnon's chair—and how had he come by the bond that united him to the royal house, since all men took him to be the son of an exiled Corinthian merchant? Yet there were those in Mycenae who whispered that he had come baseborn out of the loins of Thyestes; that the gods and his dead begetter looked to him to carry out the curse on the house of Atreus in his generation; that he would be the man to avenge the hateful feast that had come out of incestuous loving; that he was already avenging it in the ancient fashion—with more incestuous love. . . .

And again, all over his skin now, there was the crawling and the creeping. He thought it an evil omen, too, that the spider should again be showing itself in the web in the corner of the window—a black and hairy presence which he had not seen for many days and had come to think of as dead and rolled up in a rough ball somewhere on the dusty floor. Evil was not easily destroyed, evil was persistent, evil passed down like a harelip or a purplish mark on the face from generation to generation; and though he was not one to question the gods, it seemed to him a bitter business that the meal which Atreus had served up to Thyestes should taint such gracious and inoffensive beings as the two who grew on one stem and leaned against each other—the missing boy and the sorely troubled girl.

TWO

ALL THE WAY BACK from the watchtower to the palace, the princess Electra had told herself that the cold in her bones would be dissipated as soon as she found herself inside the walls of home. But now that she was there—out of the wind, out of the dampness—her chill was not diminished in the least: it was not the cold of winter but the cold of fear, and its seat was not in her flesh but in her soul.

She walked with her head lowered under the sounding galleries where each of her footsteps echoed repeatedly until the place reverberated with a chorus of footfalls. Her brother had not been shoved away in the poor man's cemetery, no, but that was small comfort; he could be lying elsewhere, in one of six or seven cemeteries or under a heap of brush at the bottom of a gorge; and, now that she was alone and unoccupied with searching, what had been the stuff of a dream became too real—she chewed at her knuckles and closed her eyes against an image of his lifeless face.

Her fright and sick-heartedness turned into anger at the entrance of the great hall. She stopped there on the broad threshold and stared at the unseemly doings within, caring nothing about the slaves who looked in amazement at her drab clothes and her disordered hair. More of the everlasting feasting again tonight—in spite of her father's absence, in spite of her brother's disappearance: on the round hearth in the middle of the room they were laying the wood to make a festal blaze; on the marble table they were putting out silver and copper and crystal for the meal; and she could not shake off the thought that her brother's hands might never again warm themselves before fire, that her brother's mouth might never again take meat and wine. A slave, an old man, was polishing the bronze casing of one of the tall pillars that marked the area of the hearth as a sacred square separate from the rest of the room. Against that pillar Orestes had propped his narrow back when she had last laid eyes on him; and she was hard put to it not to call out to the old man, not to forbid him to rub away whatever invisible exudation of that dear, gone body might remain.

Oh, no, she thought, it is impossible. It was a dream, and not all dreams are true, and nobody here believes that he is dead. . . . It was late, and she should have gone straight to her own chamber in the upper part of the palace to dress, but instead she turned due east toward his, past the open bronze-and-scarlet splendor where the king her father had taken his rest when he was not sleeping among his warriors on the ground. The door of

19

Orestes' room was not standing wide, and her heart leaped like a dolphin to know that some soulless fool had closed that door. As if nobody awaited him, as if nobody expected him to return, as though he were gone forever and there were some under this roof who found it better so. . . . She pushed with all her strength against the slowly yielding wood and found herself in the middle of his chamber, staring at things which she had seen too often in these last two days.

She had sought repeatedly for some sign, some message. To look again was useless, would yield her nothing, would only taint his possessions with her desperation and her bafflement. She would not open his jewel box again and be enraged at his agates and amethysts because they told her nothing. She would not rummage through the cloaks and tunics in the carved chest. In fact, now that she put her mind to it, she felt encouraged by the fact that he had left her no message: it could mean only that his absence would be brief, that he had seen no need to reassure her since he would be coming back so soon. . . . Twice yesterday she had searched his couch, running her hand between the coverlets, into the interstices of the ornate wooden legs, under his pillow covered with embroidered cloth. Now she felt no urge to repeat the futile and monotonous pattern of that search, longed only to lie down where he had lain.

She resisted the pull of that, reminding herself that she must go to the feast tonight to watch and listen, to find out whatever she could. Snatching up one of his bracelets and pushing it up on her thin arm almost as far as the elbow, she went back into the corridor, leaving the door standing open behind her. Let them all take heed of that, she thought; let them see that there is at least one in the palace who believes he will lie on his couch again, and soon. . . .

They were lighting the lamps in the north wing when she came out. They bowed, the silent slaves, and gazed at her with respectful, empty eyes; and she knew that the moment her back was turned they would shake their heads and exchange significant glances: See what a state she is in, notice that cloak and dress, look at the muddy footprints she has left on the floor. . . . All the rooms that opened into the north hall—her mother's, the one reserved for visiting women, and the one belonging to her nurse—were closed, all save one. For the first time since her brother's going, she was aware of the open door of the chamber of her absent sister Iphigenia and was moved to perform a ritual of family piety. She had neglected her sister; and now, as if the discharging of the forgotten obligation would get her the good will of those divine beings who took it for granted that sisters always loved each other, she stepped in and tried to give herself over to solemn meditation.

Forty moons and more had waxed and waned since her father had sent from Aulis for Iphigenia, saying that his fleet lay becalmed in the harbor there because Poseidon would give him no winds to carry him to Troy until he gave his dearest possession at the Aulian shrine. For all those moons this chamber had remained sacred and unchanged, and a melancholy orderliness lay upon it, as if its former tenant had not gone to serve as a priestess in Aulis but to sit mute among her ancestors in the country of the dead. The slaves who kept it spotless had been ordered to disturb nothing, to leave her powders and ointments and bright scarves exactly where she had left them, to dust her beads without moving a one of them, to keep the tarnish from her silver mirror and the cobwebs from her twelve little pairs of doeskin shoes. For the first time, her sister shrugged at the ritual. All this reverence for one who had not descended into darkness! All this tenderness for one who had only gone to live in fine quarters behind the shrine, to choose her own husband and order her own slaves about and arrange her own feasts and ride abroad in a scarlet chariot, her dark hair set off by a crown of gilded laurel, her curving body draped becomingly in the saffron of her new holiness!

On the glistening fleece that covered her sister's couch she saw three indentations. Here, this morning and many another, the queen their mother had mourned—two hollows for her elbows and one for her head. Here on her knees with her honey-colored hair disordered and tears washing the black coloring from her eyelashes down her cheeks in streaks, she was forever repeating the same lament with undiminished intensity. "My little one, my lamb, my most dearly beloved! The gods are cruel, cruel! Of all men, my husband has the most unjust and ruthless heart! That he should have taken her from me—the fairest, sweetest fruit of my womb—for the sake of Helen, for the sake of a whore!" Often she left some sign of her grieving on the fleece: a scarlet thread from her jacket, a crushed petal from a flower, a speck of golden powder from her hair. Today there was the faintest trace of the orange berry juice that she wore on her lips; and a cold smile pulled at the corners of the girl's mouth, a smile that she permitted to grow as it would.

For over Orestes' going there had been no such weeping: the grey eyes had remained unfilmed, the brows above them had arched in a mockery of worry, the white and well-fleshed hand had waved the matter away as though it were a bothersome fly. "Where is he? And why, my daughter, are you asking me? If anybody knows where he has hidden himself, you are the one to know. Me he tells nothing, you he tells everything." And later, bored with too much talk of it, grown petulant: "Where is he gone? To find the Golden Fleece, like Jason. To kill the Nemean lion, like Heracles. Give him nine or ten days and he will be back again, dragging home some atrocious girl or some moth-eaten old hide."

The light-minded words sounded in her ears and made her sneer outright. What was she doing in this mawkishly sacred chamber? Why should she mourn the favorite of gods and parents? Why should she take a single instant of solicitude from one who had always had too little and add it to the store of one who had always had too much? With deliberate impiety she took up the silver mirror that had lain face down since Iphigenia's going and looked into it at her own face. Not milky white, not the face of a mother's lamb or a father's dearest possession, but an honest face, a decent face, and very like her brother's face. . . . She laid the mirror down, face up, among the jars of ointment and the scattered beads, and stepped into the hall, smiling as she shut the door.

And suddenly she knew how late she was, how callously she had forgotten the troubles of her nurse Aglaia. The woman's husband had disappeared from the palace on the same day as her brother; and to add to that large concern the petty worries of her own unreported wandering was selfish and unkind. Yet there on the stool on the other side of the threshold her nurse sat quiet in the light of the flickering fire in the tripod, her hair so orderly as to seem painted onto her knobby brow, her bony hands on her knees. "Look at you. Look at your hair. Look at your shoes. Spare the carpet, you'll ruin it with your mud," was all that Aglaia said.

"I went up to the watchtower."

"Yes, and fine weather it was for taking a walk to the watchtower." The slave rose and went, not like a grieving widow but like one who is alert and waits, to the marble-covered chest on which the basin and the ewer stood—rich treasures, gifts from Helen and Menelaos, copper inlaid with tin, the spout and handles in the shape of lion heads. Deftly she poured the water. Sharply, with a flap, she undid the linen towel. . . . Here is no mourner— so the young woman thought, shedding her cloak and dress and going about the business of washing and adorning herself and

23

combing the wind's wild snarls out of her hair. Aglaia is sane and waits in sanity for her husband and my brother to return. I am mad to think that either of them could be dead.

It was not until she stood completely transformed—stiff as an ivory image—that Aglaia kindled a pair of lamps so that she might see her splendor in a steady light. From her narrow waist to the toes of her embroidered shoes she was covered and weighted down with a blue-green skirt studded over with golden trinkets in the shape of coiling snakes, a skirt so tucked and pleated that it could have stood alone. Above the waist, it was otherwise, and she hated it. Dress for the court called for a display of womanhood—the short red jacket covered her arms to the wrists but completely bared her pointed, insufficient breasts. All her necklaces had been made as if in malice to stop before the slight and sorry curve began. She looked down ruefully at her bosom and remembered Orestes saying, "It is a pity you must show yourself like that. They want the udders of heifers here, and all you have is two poor little buds."

"A touch of berry juice?" said Aglaia, bringing a mirror and holding it up to her face. "With the green of your skirt and the red of your jacket, your mouth looks pale." She shook her head and turned away from her reflection. She loathed herself in her splendor, loathed the dragging weight of the skirt on her hips and the galling pull of the chains around her neck. She wanted air and looked toward the window, still uncurtained; breathing seemed a laborious business, and under the heavy dip of hair on her forehead sweat had begun to gather, though her hands and feet were still cold.

Out there night was coming down grey-blue upon the Citadel. In the house of her Uncle Aegisthus—a pillared mansion not more than a hundred paces from the palace—the lamps had been lighted; and she thought how he too must be preparing himself for the feast, loading the usual excessive adornment on his negligible

24

frame. The thought of him at the business of dressing heightened her distaste for the evening: whenever she had seen him walk naked in one of the processions of the Lady or the Horse, she was disagreeably aware of some flaw in him—his belly was limp in spite of its thinness, his shoulders were narrow and sloped forward, his ribs showed through the skin of his slack sides. But tonight he would appear in the great hall dressed in a priceless robe dyed some fantastic color, and would move as confidently among the guests as though the gods had given him her father's soldierly dignity.

Aglaia came up behind her, holding out a little jar carved out of green stone. "Not even a little berry juice?" she said. "Believe me, you stand in need of it. Besides, Asterion will be at the feast."

"No, I told you." She pushed the jar away rudely. She had not thought of Asterion once in these two days of trouble, had not once called up the image of his eyes, flat and brown like the eyes of some innocent domesticated animal, or his forehead, low and half covered with thick dark curls. Aglaia was deceiving herself if she thought of him as a husband for her nursling. Agamemnon, describing him to the queen her mother, had said he was "of baser stock than ours and nothing in himself to wonder at," and her brother had said he was "handsome and pleasant enough, but nobody to match *your* wit." If it seemed good to her that he would be there tonight, it was only because he would serve as a refuge from the rest. She could not wander through an evening of feasting alone, and she supposed it was better to have Asterion than nobody at all. . . . She put her arms down on the window sill and fetched up a long sigh.

"Watch," said Aglaia, "there are seeds for the pigeons on that sill and you will get them on your sleeves. Besides, it is late, it is no time to stare out of the window and dream."

It was late indeed. Down in the street below her the doors of

25

the pillared mansion had swung open and her Uncle Aegisthus was stepping out, with a torchbearer behind him, in a hyacinth-colored robe bordered with a design of silver laurel leaves, his thin brown locks combed carefully over the bald spot on the top of his head. He started for the palace, glancing casually over his shoulder; and she drew back from the window, not wanting his look to rest upon her, though it was unlikely that he would have seen her without offering his usual show of affection—a smile, a blown kiss, a wave of the hand.

"There, the first guest is coming, you have waited just long enough to make your lateness a public offense," said Aglaia.

"He is scarcely a guest. He is forever in the great hall."

"Nevertheless, he should be properly greeted."

"Why should I greet him? My mother will be there to greet him."

Aglaia turned away and took up the brown cloak, still damp with the melted snow. "So she will," she said, looking at the dried mud on the hem and rubbing it hard, "so she will."

THREE

IN THE GREAT HALL, in firelight and torchlight commingled, Queen Clytemnestra gave welcome to her twenty guests. Like a gilt and ivory image of the Lady she stood between entrance and pillars near a red marble table—her skin and robe all white, her ornaments all gold. The fingertips of her left hand barely grazed the marble, and she held out her right in measured cordiality to each new visitor, with a jingling of bracelets and a shining of rings. She never turned sidewise to see in the high polish of the stone whether her dignity had suffered anything from the gusts that blew in at the entrance and whipped the torch

27

flames into fiery manes. Chalk powder had filled up the small lines of her weariness; berry juice had painted out the pallor of worry; charcoal had added to a face turned into a mask just such lines as would restore it to an unchanging aspect of pleased humanity. The Cretan slave who attired and painted her was a marvel; and what had been done could be depended upon to last until whoever tarried longest stepped into the torchlit court and left his queen to rub her aching eyes in peace.

If only, she thought, I could do for my spirit what the Cretan has done for my face. If only my spirit could be simplified and pacified. . . . From the day she had come into the palace as Agamemnon's bride until some seven moons ago, she had endured a hard life by dividing it into segments: one thing to be suffered at a time and all the others to be put aside, each for its own hour. Must she sit by her sister Helen on a visit from Lacedaemon to the Citadel, so that the folk of Mycenae who had found her comely enough could see what a poor thing she was side by side with peerless beauty? Then she would put up with that and think of nothing else, not of Orestes' careless bearing or Electra's cold formality when they came to kiss their mother's hand. Must she somehow manage to unlock her body to her husband—harsh, peremptory, willing to waste no more time on her than the bull has for the cow? Then all her will would be gathered up for that, and she would not think of Iphigenia lying feverish in the next chamber: there would be time for a daughter's troubles later, when the hard, dark weight of a husband had been lifted from her crushed breasts. . . .

If only it could be so with me again, she thought, smiling at the Keeper of the King's Archives and saying such honeyed things as have no meaning but pour with ease. If only there were again a time set aside for everything, with everything walled into its proper place. . . . But tonight the walls were down, and longing leaped within her like the hearth fire between the columns, and fear streamed before her like the flames of the torches held by the slaves. "What workman has done such wonders in setting your amethyst?" she said, touching the pendant on the necklace of the Steward's wife. But all the while she was thinking, "How can I live through this evening without making it plain that I am afraid?"

Still she stood by the red marble table, her left hand unstirring, her heavy earrings unshaken, though questions ran like incendiary invaders through the citadel of her mind: Where is the boy? Safe, or come to some harm? Gone to rid himself of the yoke of my rule and the sight of my face? Or gone—knowing more than I thought he knew—to give an evil account of me in Lacedaemon? If so, to whom? Menelaos lies tonight encamped with Agamemnon before Troy, and Helen sleeps entwined with Paris on the other side of the wall. Who is in Lacedaemon to hear Orestes complain of me? Nobody but Hermione, nobody but another helpless child. . . .

Over the shoulder of the next visitor coming up to receive her greeting, she could see on one side of the broad doorway a strip of fresco innocent enough in daylight: a meadow where a slave bent forward to place a garland on the forehead of his lord. But darkness, firelight, and fear had played cunning tricks with the painting. The laurel had been blotted out, the flowers and grass had turned a brownish yellow, the sky had darkened, and what had been flecks of rosy cloud were now swollen and baleful stars. As she greeted the Overseer of the King's Copper Mines and asked after his lady's delicate health, she almost shuddered: the slave in the fresco had become her son bending forward to whisper her guilt into her husband's ear. So they stood transfixed, caught in the awful instant of revelation, with the barren stretch of the Trojan plain under their feet and sickly stars over their heads.

"Ill health is the worst of all human afflictions," said the Overseer's lady, smug with admiration of her own sufferings.

And the queen was hard put to it not to gainsay her, not to

argue that no wasting disease could be as bitter to endure as stark
fright. Fear of Orestes, fear of Agamemnon—yet it was madness
to think the boy could cross the eastern waters in the wild winter.
No ship would put out of port until the winds were gathered up
in the hand of Poseidon, and today there had been snow upon
the walls of the Citadel, and Poseidon would not reach for his
winds until the Cyclopean stones were softened by the waxen new
vines of spring.

The line in front of her had dwindled to three: the withered old
Chief Priest, his plump wife who seemed to wax on his waning,
and their only daughter, married for five years to the King's Messenger to Egypt and now happily and at long last great with child.
As these three stood in the cloud of cedarwood that the Cretan
had added to the queen's person, the other guests who had already been greeted wandered over to the hearth and took their
places around the fire, the younger ones on embroidered cushions, the older ones on carved chairs. She sensed rather than saw
their movements, sensed rather than saw that slaves walked and
bent among them, offering shellfish in great silver bowls, holding
out salvers with goblets of wine. The eyes of the young matron
were directed over her mistress's shoulder. "There is your daughter
Electra," she said. "I had forgotten how tall she has grown."

She did not turn to look: she knew the erect and uncompromising figure well enough and had so little pleasure in it that she
cared not at all whether it had been draped for the occasion in
scarlet or violet, turquoise or white. "Yes, she is as tall as I could
wish," she said, smiling. "Would she might grow a little in the
other direction—she could do with more flesh on her bones."

"Ah," said the flowering wife, looking down in mild depreca-
tion at the lump that thrust itself out beneath the tucks in her
splendid pink skirt, "when a woman carries as much weight as I
carry now, she thinks of thinness as a blessed state."

"Indeed, indeed." She remembered how it had been bearing the heaviness of each of her own through processions and banquets, to hunts and foot races and sacrifices. "Go and sit down," she said, knowing what disorder worked in her spirit when tears of pity—by no means called for, since the young woman was marvelously pleased with herself and her state—stung in her eyes and blurred her sight. "Go and sit down, little cousin, and see to it that you find a comfortable seat."

Now that they were all properly greeted, she went to her own chair—dark wood with stags and lions inlaid in copper and ivory. As soon as she had seated herself, two slaves came to her, one with a goblet, the other with a large bowl of mussels. The goblet she took, but the mussels she rejected, feeling qualmishness stir in her stomach as the dead creatures must have stirred at the bottom of the shoals in the tide. Fear sprang out of fear: before the birth of Iphigenia a mouthful of shellfish had been all that was needed to set the room turning. No, no, she told herself, I have not eaten and grown sick, I have only thought how it would be to eat and grow sick. I am not with child, I am surely not with child. . . .

Two of the better men in the sorry lot came and occupied the cushions on the floor on either side of her. For a sorry lot they were, with the flower of Mycenae encamped with Agamemnon on the Trojan plain. Yet at every feast there were a couple of young men to give voiceless testimony to the pretense that she was in Mycenae what Helen had been in Lacedaemon: eternally wanted by those who were barely half her age, everlastingly desirable though placed by her diadem beyond desire. Talk rose, and a mingling of scents drawn out by the fire, and she talked along with the rest: of the news from Rhodes and Cyprus, of the fresh stucco and paint laid down on the floor of the great hall, of the snow, deceptively gratifying in a bone-dry year but so quickly over that it had scarcely dampened the packed and thirsty crust of the earth.

31

And while she talked and sipped numbness and warmth out of her goblet, she was compelled to look at the daughter her husband had left to her—the other one that her heart brooded upon having been taken from her, put forever beyond her sight. Thin as a boy and too like her brother Orestes, she sat on a cushion as far as possible from her mother, near one of the pillars on the other side of the fire. Shoulder and head rested against the gleaming copper casing, and the firelight made a metallic brightness of her hair. Beside her and talking earnestly sat the boy Asterion, but she did not listen: her unblinking sea-colored eyes stared straight into the blaze. Seeing Orestes, yearning after Orestes, fearing for Orestes? Hers were innocent eyes, guileless in their trouble—she did not know, she could not have such eyes and know. But if the brother had known and fled the palace in his knowledge, how long would it be before the sister—searching without rest, turning every stone, considering every word and glance a clue—would stumble upon the truth?

I must put a guard on my tongue, I must keep a watch on my eyes, I must by no means look at *him,* the queen told herself, and added her voice to the voices of her attendants, who were talking maliciously about the Chief Priest of the Lady: it seemed he was losing his memory and had to be cued with certain key words in order to get through the ritual; it seemed he had carried a basket of fruit to the altar in senile carelessness, leaving apples and stalks of barley strewn behind him and bringing the goddess only two thirds of her due.

Two slaves went to another table, long and draped and set against the east wall, lifted the embroidered cloth that veiled it, and revealed the feast. She nodded to indicate her approval of what the Steward of the House had provided: four carved pheasants, ten large fish cooked brown and boned, onions, a sauce of oil and fried herbs, a mound of moist cheese, a pyramid of dried fruits.

"Ah!" said those of the guests who were not otherwise occupied.

"Ah!" said the younger of the queen's attendants, but his admiration was not strong enough to distract him from something he was pointing out to his fellow. "And look at him again tonight," he said, gesturing in the direction in which she had promised herself not to look. "For all his spindle shanks and bald head, he dresses as if he had not yet passed his twentieth year. Day before yesterday it was saffron yellow, and now it is hyacinth blue."

She looked, in spite of all her vows to the contrary. She looked, and her heart made a palpable leap in her breast. Dear image—bald and meager and draped in hyacinth—but dear none the less: she could have brought down her fist on the becurled head of his detractor in rage and pity for *his* sake. "Go, the two of you, and bring me food," she told them, and her tone was the tone of one who says "Be taken off by a pestilence." When they were gone she looked at her own clenched hands through damp lashes and dug her nails into her palms. So it is with youth, she thought—strength without power, confidence without knowledge, lust without the capacity for delight. Which of the two of them could have awakened what was crushed by insensate service as *he* had awakened it? Which of the two could have sweetened the bitter waters of a queen's life with his seed? Which of the two would have self-mastery enough to give once what he has given night after night: the slow gathering of everything into the spinning whorl of darkness, the spasm that loosens what has been taut as a bowstring for twenty-odd years, the love that comes when need is gone, the quiet folding into sleep?

But she had looked, and she raised her eyes to see whether her daughter had followed her reckless eyes. Not likely. Not at all likely. The girl was busy with a friendly service to Asterion. The Chief Priest's wife, who had upset his plate in passing him and was standing by to make apologies, looked with raisin-eyed misery at the stain of herb sauce spreading on his robe while Electra drew her kerchief from her sleeve and worked assiduously to rub out the spot.

The two young men came back to the royal chair with food she had no desire to eat. They did not stay by her. Being of the court, they had been quick to note her displeasure, and doubtless thought—or so she hoped—that she had only been wearied by their empty chatter. Others came now to do her small services: the Captain of the King's Guardsmen to replace the footstool that had somehow been pushed to one side of her chair, the Overseer of the King's Herds to put a particularly fine dried plum on her plate, the wife of the Master of the King's Slaves to spread a linen napkin over her knees. It was that time in the feast when ceremony gave way to ease: the torchbearers went with their torches in orderly procession into the dark courtyard and left the hall to the kindlier and ruddier light of the hearth fire; the tormenting fresco —indeed, all the frescoes—disappeared into blackness; and she knew that she could permit herself, while she chatted with an old aunt and a guardsman, to look covertly toward the distant spot where *he* sat in a tall chair. At once he felt her glance and returned it, but with so much discretion that it was as if their looks had brushed in flight like moths going through the dark. And before she had her fill of seeing his thin hands—conjurers of passion, bestowers of peace—he raised one to his mouth and turned the wiping of a moistened lip into the blowing of a kiss.

With the torches gone, there was more motion in the great hall. She thought in her guilt that each of her guests had some shadowy secret, some dusky soul's intention like her own and was drawn to it as soon as the food was consumed and the slave carried away the empty plates. The two who had played at being her hopeless lovers in the beginning of the evening had vanished now into the dark, doubtless with fair young women or untried girls;

34

the Chief Priest of the Lady had come close to the blaze, alone and glad to be alone to rest his addled mind and warm his old bones; a new bride was standing before the pregnant wife, actually touching the quickened belly and gazing at the bared, swollen breasts. Electra and Asterion—not hand in hand, only side by side—were wandering around the square marked off by the four pillars, and a thought came into the queen's mind that made her catch her breath: Suppose she dared to arrange a marriage in her husband's absence. . . . Suppose this boy, whose father was encamped with Agamemnon and whose mother was malleable as the wax of the honeycomb in the queen's hands, could be encouraged to press his suit with means a little more urgent than walks around the pillared square. . . . Blind childish passion, heaped gifts, a fine house adorned with laurel and smelling of new paint and stucco—would such things be enough to draw a virginal mind away from a brother lost?

There was a time after the second filling-up of the goblets that the court called the Time of Asking. Slowly, with a pretense at aimlessness, they began to gather from the pillars, from the corners, from the tables, from the hearth, and converged around the royal chair. Like leaves of the forest in a wan wind they came, less eager to ask than in the days of Agamemnon, since one could ask more of a king than of a queen. Those who had nothing to ask came in a kind of autumnal fellowship with those who wanted something; and the bright robes and the pale trailed toward her and stopped around her, and the bodies beneath them shed the scent of warm ointment upon her, and she smiled in answer to their shamefaced smiles while the slaves tipped the bowls of crystal and silver and replenished their drinks.

He was close to her then, since custom not only permitted but actually required his presence. Their dear cousin Aegisthus, whom her husband had left in charge of city and Citadel and wife and

35

children, did for her now what she had done during this ceremony for Agamemnon: he stood by with a stylus and a soft clay tablet and kept a tally of the granted gifts.

"Ah," she said, beginning the ceremony herself as delicacy and protocol demanded, "how I wish I had some of the green myrtle like the sprig that is fastened in my blossoming cousin's hair."

The young woman snatched it from its place and laid it in Clytemnestra's lap.

"And you, little cousin, what do you wish?"

"Nothing," said the flustered wife, "except your prayers for my childbed, and perhaps, if you wish it, a kiss."

While her lips brushed the warm, moist forehead, she could see over the tumbled hair the thin, bearded face of Aegisthus. "Prayers for childbed. One kiss granted and paid to the lady of the King's Messenger to Egypt," he said. "A wise and fortunate young woman indeed." And the queen took pride in the wit that taught him to pay her a ceremonial compliment in a voice that put off all suspicion, yet stirred her to the quick.

"How I wish," said the Captain of the King's Guard, "that I might have nine green shoots from the grapevines of the king my lord to add to my vineyard in spring."

She nodded and said nothing, wanting to make way for that faintly twanging voice to announce the gift.

"How I wish I had the services of the talented craftsman who painted the frescoes in the bedchamber of the queen my lady," said the wife of the Overseer of the King's Armory.

It was an audacious request, and it was fitting that in time of war largesse should be limited. "Have his services," said Clytemnestra, "but let him stay with you no more than three days."

She noticed then and throughout the three askings which followed that Electra was moving through the little crowd, had separated herself from the others, was placing herself in the empty space between the footstool and the blaze. But surely she could

36

not mean to take part in the askings. And if she did, what in the name of all the gods did she mean to ask? As she gave away—too freely in a time of war—the fruit of a pear tree in the royal orchard and the services of an excellent stud horse, terrible questions sounded in her mind: Mother, will you return my brother to me? Will you send my Uncle Aegisthus forth from the Citadel? Will you give me your royal and parental leave to go myself out of this place of black shame?

Fear was the stronger because of the spot where the girl had stationed herself. With so much flickering light behind her, the darkness upon her was thickened so that sometimes she seemed not to be there at all and sometimes she was featureless like a figure covered with a black veil of mourning. A stillness as cold as snow had settled on the group around the royal chair. But I must speak, I must speak to her, the queen told herself. Whatever terrible thing she says will be no more dangerous than this awesome silence in which I and he and she and all the others wait. . . .

"Pardon, my lady." It was his twanging voice, in no wise shaken. "Here is our dear child Electra, whom you overlook."

She opened her mouth, but her tongue, gone dry as a stone, would not move.

"Even a princess may ask," he said lightly, "when the giver is a queen."

She straightened and forced herself to look directly at the figure edged in glimmerings of yellow and red. "What do you want of me, Electra?" she said at last.

"How I wish that my cousin Hermione might come out of Lacedaemon to bear me company in my loneliness."

Oh, but it was such a mild wish—so simple, so childish, so innocent! She let herself sink against the back of her chair. She let her hands trail over the curved arms. She felt a disintegrating ripple of laughter rise and settle again in her throat, unspent. As if all were well—and all was surely well—she addressed herself to this guileless daughter condescendingly, as she would have addressed herself to a troublesome child. "Hermione? Let her come to us then," she said, and caught through the moving shadows the almost imperceptible shake of his balding head. "But let her come to us a little later, darling." She saw the reason now for his unwillingness: *two* of them to hide from and outwit, two children to be sure, but two nevertheless. "Let her come when Orestes, her betrothed, is here to greet her. Let her come when Orestes is home with us again."

"And when will that be, my mother?"

The voice did not demand or accuse. The voice was only desolate and hopeless, but it put its dangerous torch down among the others and they kindled and took fire. "Yes," they said, some in whispers and some aloud, "when will that be?"

"Asked and granted," said the calm, twanging voice, "a visit from the princess Hermione to her cousins Electra and Orestes, whenever the latter returns to us, which will surely be soon, seeing that he is gracious enough, though he has gone on some errand of his own, not to keep his mother and sister and all of us waiting and wondering too long."

It was quenched, the frightening fire. The others talked a little, jesting, about young men and their adventures; the princess Electra bowed and kissed her mother's hand with dry shut lips and went off to rejoin Asterion; the asking was over and *he,* too, was gone, carrying away tablet and stylus as though nothing of the smallest significance had threatened to come to pass. There was nothing now between the queen and the large warmth that the fire poured out, there was no danger any more, but she could scarcely keep her knees from knocking against each other and her teeth from chattering in an accession of bitter chill. Oh, to lie under comforters and hides and rugs, she thought. Oh, to lie on his couch with warm things heaped on me. Oh, to lie and shake

38

against him, my forehead against his forehead, my feet against his feet, my fingers tangled in the wild and living growth on his chest. . . .

She did not see him again until the end of the evening. The time passed in as much empty geniality as though no veiled figure had stood between her and the hearth, as though no murmur had arisen among the guests. Yet she could not rid herself of the mortal chill—all flesh that she touched was warmer than her own— nor could she resign herself to lying alone on her couch tonight. And when the time for the general departure had come, when the slaves with their torches had arranged themselves in a long line to light the visitors across the main court and down the great stone stairway, she signaled to him to come to her last and exchanged with him the formula of assignation that they had arranged between them:

"My cousin Aegisthus will have little sleep tonight."

"My lady the queen also goes late to bed," he said.

FOUR

IT WOULD BE at least an hour—so he told himself—until she came to him. In all respects she was a remarkable woman, as clever as she was beautiful, as circumspect as she was passionate; and she would not go veiled and softly stepping out of her house until every light was quenched and every slave asleep. Usually he was satisfied to be passive and anticipate, to spend the empty time lying on his couch and calling up visions of what always proved better in the performance than it had been in his dreams. But tonight he could not merely wait; tonight a restlessness was on him that made him want the open sky and stirred him to move about,

40

a restlessness that was more than desire in the flesh, though it certainly encompassed that urgency. At the foot of the long stairway where the guests took leave of each other and the line of torches came to an end, he looked up and saw that the moon, pale though she seemed above the red and streaming knots of fire, stood high and bright enough to light the darkest byways of the Citadel. To walk about in moonlight in his festal clothes, to wander past sleeping houses and massive buildings sacred to the king—this seemed to him a fitting prelude to their night, and he dismissed his torchbearer and went on by himself.

The images that he evoked while he walked were sharper goads to his ardor because they came to him in streets where he had never called them up before. He went sure-footed down the Avenue of State, envisioning the queen of Mycenae dropping her cloak and veils and loosening with a shake of her head her honey-colored hair; he stopped in the shadow of Agamemnon's granary to give due thought to Agamemnon's woman's eyes. Grey eyes they were, and very large, and intent; once he had dreamed that he was lying on his bier, that she had come to him and was looking upon him, and that those large and begging eyes of hers had got their answer from his member even though the rest of him was lying in the grip of death. With such eyes as those, her mouth scarcely mattered, except for kissing. Three times around the ancient cemetery of the royal ancestors he went, remembering varieties of kisses: lips brushing lips over and over until the delicate contact became an unbearable torment, tongue exploring tongue until their throats grew tight and there was hardly room for breath, mouth pressed on mouth until the lips were cracked and the kiss was salted with the taste of blood.

He stopped to look over the round enclosure at the gravestones and at their shadows lying long on the turf, long and black in the whiteness of the moon. "I have your woman, she is mine," he thought and yearned to say it aloud so that it might be heard under the grass, might echo through the sealed chambers where golden ornaments lay among scattered bones and dust. He had their woman, knew night after night the ample body that carried the elixir of their majesty; and pride sprang up in him as hot and hard as passion, and the two intermingled until he could not tell passion from pride. He smiled and went on toward the north wall, through the impenetrable shadow cast by the bastion of the Lion Gate. *"Your* woman, too—I have *your* woman," he thought, staring at the ruts in which the wheels of the king's chariot had clattered out of the Citadel—dark ruts undulating like serpents across the whitened paving stones. . . . "Tall in the skin of a lion and sure in his manhood he went. . . ." So sang the bards concerning Agamemnon. But if he who rode forth in the lion skin could stand tonight in the chamber of one he had left behind and see what came to pass there on the couch, he might not be so sure in his manhood. . . .

He walked more swiftly past the gate itself, through the shadows of the copper bars that cut athwart his feet. He thought of her aromatic armpits, of her hardening nipples, of the pale hair of a royal race in a triangle below the mound of her belly, of the precious slippery ointment that waited for him between her thighs. Open, come open. Open to one who was left at home because he was not man enough to bear a shield or wield a sword. Open and receive the member of one who is too frail to march and yet is strong enough to give a woman three spasms to every one of his own, to stir a woman who has lain for twenty years unstirred beneath a king of kings.

But it had risen so wild in him now that he was hard put to it to draw it back, to save it. Call for a guardsman to unlock the gate, and go out. Go out past the shut booths of the traders and past the inn where there will still be lights, go up into the barren place on the northern slope where nothing but uncaring hares and foxes move in the brush under the stunted trees. Go into some black thicket up there and spend it unseen, and hope to have another surge of it in good time—after all, she will not be wanting it at once, she will need comforting, she will come in fear. . . .

The remembrance of her fright was enough to turn back the tide so that he could walk briskly, as if no climax had threatened him, in the shadow of the moon-paled Cyclopean stones of the north wall. If she was afraid, it was not wise to make light of it: she was not one to start at nothing, and even a nameless fear on her part deserved his consideration. That she was not afraid for the safety of her son he could have sworn: she had never loved the lad as she had loved Iphigenia, had felt him as the most dangerous threat to the secrecy of their alliance, and plainly did not believe that any evil had come to him—otherwise she would scarcely have jested about Jason and Heracles. He shook himself and shuddered not because he had any fear of whatever it was that could have made her hands so cold, but at the unnatural and unmanning pull of the inward recession: to save it was better, of course, but the withdrawing tide left a painful knot in a man's guts. She could be fearful only because she thought the runaway knew and was gone elsewhere to carry damaging tales. But that was foolish—womanly foolish; nobody knew, no lovers had ever been more circumspect than he and she. Three lordly houses under whose blanched façades he walked gave him chill reassurance, stared at him unseeing, their lightless windows like blind eyes. As for the boy's accusing them elsewhere—he would relieve her mind of that as soon as she crossed his threshold: in Lacedaemon there would be nobody to listen to his story; he could not find a boat to take him across the dangerous eastern waters to Troy until spring; and at any other court his hosts would think twice before charging a queen on her throne with sins blabbered by a helpless boy whose father and whose father's friends were all abroad at war. . . . Besides, if such an occasion should arise, she had the man to deal with it. He was, if he must say it of himself, a con-

43

summate courtier, adept with the weapons of words—he nodded in self-approbation at the recollection of how offhandedly, how masterfully he had dealt with the business of Hermione at the "asking" tonight. . . .

High above him, on the north wall, he saw torchlight feverish against the serenity of the sky: a guardsman walked there and would see him, but there was no harm in that, that was all to the good. What man in Mycenae, except himself, knowing that the queen was coming to his bed, would stroll as he strolled now past the tall, blank front of the King's Treasury, past the mansion that belonged to the Master of the King's Slaves, past the smaller house where her old aunt—too old to watch and wonder—often called the queen and the queen's dear cousin to the same lively little feasts? Any other man, expecting such a visitor, would be bathing and anointing himself—a fool's mistake, since she loved the smell of his body as she loved all natural smells: turned earth, pressed olives, pressed grapes, the woolly smell of fleece, the smell of twigs and leaves being consumed in flames.

The guardsman on the wall—himself seeming afire because the red of his torch glared back from his helmet and his cuirass of jointed bronze—stopped above him, recognized him as the dear cousin of the king, and said, "A peaceful night, my lord Aegisthus, Master of All the King's Messengers to Foreign Lands," and then went on like a comet, trailing his stream of scarlet fire behind him.

Master of All the King's Messengers to Foreign Lands. . . . One who could, if the fancy struck him, stir up expectation in Cyprus and terror in Crete, make the king of Paphlagonia walk the floor in anxiety for a night or two, put an itching bug into the ear of the Pharaoh of Egypt, keep the fleets of the Rhodians close to their deep-harbored shores. . . . So far he had come, beginning with little or nothing. The soles of his sandals beat assertively now in the quietness. No rank, not even the rank of his merchant "father" who had brought him from Corinth to Mycenae: he was

44

no son of the old man's, the old man had found him in his seventh year wandering dazed and starving on a beach, the old man had taken him in and treated him well enough and made little if anything of the fact that what tugged at his robe was no true-born heir, was probably the issue of some careless lord and some enterprising whore. . . . No health—aches in the winter and fever in summer; joints that went out of their sockets if he lifted more than a minor weight; a nagging cough that often seized him in the morning and racked him all day long, letting the whole world know how moist and hollow it was inside his narrow chest. . . . No beauty, either, certainly no beauty; in every pool and every polished surface he forced himself to look at his own image; he knew what he was and told himself no lies concerning himself. Yet Master of All the King's Messengers to Foreign Lands— that much he had gotten for himself in spite of many things, because the gods had given him two gifts that most men did not get: a tireless member and an unflagging cleverness. The rest had not mattered: possessing something that all women want, able to provide something else that all men could put to profitable use— ill-born, sick, and ugly though he was, he had done well enough.

At the northeast corner of the wall there was a jutting complex of buildings where the guards on duty for the night were always stationed, and he found them there doing exactly what he had expected: taking their ease, enjoying themselves. A cloud of reddish light hung all around them, showing the black alley of the sally port, the huge stones of the wall, the brown earth pounded hard to give them a footing in case they found themselves face to face with an enemy. They sat on the ground in a circle, some ten of them, surrounded by their torches thrust deep into the earth, and between their torches stood the long shafts of their ashen spears. They were playing—silently, grimly—at a game of chance: they did not even shout, they only shrugged or grunted as the little marked squares of stone were shaken out of the wooden

45

cylinder and fell into the circle bordered by their bare and dusty knees. At the sight of him they started, ashamed to be found away from their posts, but he only smiled. It was not *his* affair, it was the business of the Captain of the Guardsmen to watch that they did not neglect their duties. It was not *his* Citadel, it was Agamemnon's that lay naked in the white night, vulnerable to any band of highlanders who might steal from the Arcadian hills to the foot of the unguarded wall.

Not his Citadel . . . Not hers, either, though she would have had it and divided the rule of it with whomever she chose if the land had held fast to the old law. Before the reign of Perseus the Mighty, the women—rulers of the hearth and nourishers of the seed of life—had owned everything and shared it as they pleased; the husband had been no more than a paramour, and the paramour had remained enthroned or had perished according to how well he served the body of the queen. If the old law had held, Agamemnon—harsh and willful and peremptory—would have gone his way long since, not toward Troy but into exile or a burial chamber. Had the old law held, seven moons ago *he* would have found himself in Agamemnon's place and he would have kept it, too, for he was sufficient and she was grateful and loyal. Not to the son Orestes but to any daughter she might bear out of their fiery pleasures would have gone Citadel and town and rolling countryside, mines and slaves and palace and jewels and gold, according to the old distribution. . . .

Not his Citadel . . . And he had resigned himself to that, since he had the woman. The woman and the secret power, the right to sneer at those who vaunted their courage and their spurious manliness, the knowledge that when the dust raised by the royal chariot wheels had settled down again, *he* would fare better than the king of kings—all this had seemed enough. Oh, now and again, starting from a dream, he had asked himself how it would be if Hector's spear or an arrow from the bow of Paris brought

46

her husband down, how he would feel to watch her walking proud and unveiled out of the palace into his house, leaving the vast domain for his sake and not so much as glancing back over her shoulder at what she had surrendered to her son. Yet wait, wait. . . . Suppose the husband fell at Troy and the son came to his death on some foolish adventure or some futile attempt to carry tales abroad? It was too much to hope for, that someone who had always looked through him as though he were a piece of crystal—with eyes as grey as hers but narrower and cool and arrogant—might be lying tonight at the bottom of a chasm in Arcadia, stripped of his splendor by a highland robber or mauled by a lion or gored by a boar. But still, still . . . He stopped short, far beyond the circle of torchlight, alone between the house of the Governor of the King's Store of Ointment and the east wall, and saw the Citadel naked and beautiful as a woman under the steady and solemn gaze of the moon. And what rose within him now was as powerful as the other tide that had made him consider escape through the Lion Gate, only this could not be gotten rid of, this could not be spent in the haunt of foxes and hares. . . .

Not his Citadel, but beautiful, beautiful . . . He exulted in it as he took the curve of the wide avenue that brought him round to the south and showed him at a distance the gleaming bronze discs that studded his own door. For a reason beyond his understanding, the strength and beauty of what was hers by right of the old law kindled again in him the yearning for the strength and beauty of her person. It was as if all primary desires had one seat in him: he thought simultaneously of the king's slaves and her hardened nipples driven back into the mounds of her breasts by his tongue, of the king's copper mines and of the soft down on the inner parts of her thighs, of the limitless power of the king of kings and of the instant of penetration which she never failed to mark with a short cry of wonder and gratitude. . . .

Red light again, and another guardsman approaching him in

front of his mansion, bowing and saying, "May you have a deep sleep this night, my lord," and then, over his shoulder in passing, the formula: "Victory to our lord the king in Troy."

"Victory to our lord the king in Troy," he repeated, making the reservation within himself that our lord the king could be both victorious and dead. As he passed the tall pillars that guarded his doorway he slapped one of them hard, as though it had been a knowing companion, with the flat of his hand. "Look," he said— he who had always kept his own counsels and never had a friend —"though I started with nothing, who knows what I may receive as a free gift from the gods?"

FIVE

ALWAYS AFTER A feast her sleeping chamber looked beautiful to the princess Electra. Always it was as if she had escaped some catastrophe, an earthquake or a storm by sea, and had come weary and thankful to safety in this room. At such times the things that were her own—the tall chest carved with a design of leaping deer, the drawn purple curtains, the couch covered with the lion skin—were like friends she loved the more because it had entered her thoughts that she might not see them again.

She stood alone in her linen night shift in the small warmth of the fire in the tripod. Aglaia had made the fire anew for her before

49

leaving her for the night, but it had already burned down to a slowly pulsing, almost translucent residue. She meant to stay by it until it had utterly died, brooding on her brother, praying to the Lady for his safe return; but the chill outside was seeping through the warp and woof of the draperies, and already she was cold. I will be warmer with my lambskin robe next to my skin, she thought, and she rid herself of her shift with a shrug and kicked it to one side and went to take up her robe from the foot of her couch.

It was a gentle robe, a kind robe, a present from her father, such a thing as a baby might be wrapped in on a winter night. The hide on the outside had been scraped and pounded into softness and dyed the color of a ripe blue plum, and the fleece inside was woolly and warm and faintly oily to the touch. She did not close it at the neck and waist; instead, she let it slide against her as she went back to the fire. And at the soft and stroking touch of it two things sprang up in her at once: a drowsy creeping in her body at the touch of the fleece and the recollection of a purely formal kiss set for the sake of courtesy and policy on the inner part of her wrist where the pulse trembled and the blue veins crossed.

One of the two who had attended her mother at the beginning of the feast—a tall young lord known for the rippling muscular beauty of his person—had remembered on departing that he had taken no notice of the princess during the entire evening, had sought to remedy his neglect by being very gallant on the threshold, had turned her proffered hand around and kissed the inner part of the wrist, stirring something uncalled for in her, stirring her to her shame. . . . The robe hung open, gently moving, softly sliding; and she surveyed her body, long and dusky against the curled greyish white. Had the young man seen her so, he might have put her out of his thoughts less quickly—so she told herself, looking down at what was far fairer than her face. In the whole slender length of her there was only one flaw: a large brown mole between her navel and the triangle of rough and tawny hair. Her waist was narrow, her thighs were firm and covered with a down that shone like finespun threads of gold. Unclothed and free, she seemed to herself—and supposed she might well seem so to any man—like an excellent horse that had been delivered from ridiculous harnessings.

The sleepy stirring of her flesh went on: it was as if her skin had a life of its own. *That* again, she thought, moving out of the warmth, sitting down on the carpet and resting her forehead against the side of the carved chest. *That* again, and what a fool I am to let it come upon me because a wary courtier thought a day might come when he would find himself in need of a good word from me. . . .

The warm brushing and the delicate creeping—she knew enough to know that they were connected with doing the unimaginable thing. She had also learned piecemeal what the unimaginable thing consisted of, partly by watching the beasts in mating season, partly from hints that Aglaia threw out because she believed that kings' children were put at a disadvantage by ignorance, partly by forthright explanations furnished by Orestes because he could not bear that her womanhood should rob her of the knowledge of any mystery which he had come to understand. But she did not wish to think of such matters tonight, she had meant to think of him and nothing else, and furthermore there was nothing to be gained from thinking further about fitting together those two crude and unlikely parts: she had already thought too much about it, and had never been able to decide whether the process was so obvious that it should be taken for granted or so violent and unnatural that it was downright hideous. . . . She rolled her forehead back and forth against the carved and hurting surface of the wood. She closed her hand on her father's ring until the edges of the seal cut into her flesh and helped her to put the stirring down with pain. And, having made an end of *that,* she belonged again to her brother, wanting nobody else, asking for nothing more than their breathless talk and the intertwining of their hands.

Oh, the days of their childhood, the blessed world in which they two had been children—for it seemed to her that the world itself had changed, had lost the intensity of its hues and the sharpness of its edges; and she turned and rested her forehead on her knees and shut her eyes to close out the shabby habitation that remained. The Holy Mountain and the Mountain of the Eagle had been loftier and more majestic then; gods had visited those peaks by night and left the trails of their garments glittering in the dust; gods had sprinkled beads of crystal on the grass, the anemone, and the hyacinths; one prayed and one was heard— always nearby there was a god. On the pure greenness of the southern pasture, the pony that their lord and father had given them had run as white as milk, tossing his mane and glorying in his strength and his youth. And they had told each other that this was no ordinary horse but an incarnation of the Horse, that the unearthly fire could be seen in his eyes, that his coat turned silver when they went to their couches, and that the gift of speech came to his tongue while they slept.

It was her brother who had created these fantasies. She could not create; she could only take what came fresh from his mind and embroider on it womanlike, helping thereby to make it still more fair. It was he who said that the white oval stone in the granite was the eye of a Cyclops imprisoned in the rock; it was she who had covered it in pity with sprigs of myrtle so that it might sleep. It was he who prayed that a griffin—body of a lion, wings of an enormous eagle, a being at once terrible and benevolent—should be sent to them by the gods as their special guardian; it was she who imagined how it would be to fly on a griffin's back from Mycenae to Cyprus, seeing the white clouds from their upper sides, looking between them at Argos and Tiryns and the marshy coastland and the wine-dark sea. The griffin . . . They had made more of the griffin and kept it with them longer than any other creature of their fantasy. Once, when they had been chasing each other up and down the splendid stairway of state, her brother had collided with a vase and smashed it to bits—a very large and precious vase decorated with iris and cuttlefish and sent to their mother by one of the priest-kings of Crete.

"What will become of us now?" she had asked him in a terror that was also somehow a delight.

"We will be beaten. We will be beaten with a switch—on that you may count absolutely, my dear sister," he had said, standing slight and gallant and appalled over the pink and scarlet fragments and trying to turn the business into a jest. And then he had added, tenderly, reaching for her hands across the ruin, "Unless, indeed, a griffin should arrive to carry us out of this."

How long was it since he had mentioned a griffin? Not very long, only a few months ago—he had changed less than the rest of the world, had somehow kept the early untarnished brightness, and felt no shame such as other grown boys would feel to cherish what was left them of their early fellowship. Only last autumn during the Festival of the Grape Harvest, he had been sitting behind her on the balcony while the Captain of the Guardsmen marched by in procession, crowned with grape leaves, carrying a spear tipped with fruit in one hand, and leading a spirited mare with the other. The mare had balked and capered, the spear had lost its cluster of fruit, he had shaken his head in aggravation, and the garland had fallen down over his eyes. Whereupon Orestes had leaned forward, very grave of face, and had whispered into her ear: "Unless the gods send him a griffin, he is lost."

All things perpetually worsened. Last year had been better than this one, and next year the heart would say: "You did not know how fortunate you were when you sat against the carved chest and bemoaned yourself. Matters have grown more mournful for you now, and still more mournful matters are to come." There had been a time when those who had their habitation in the great meandering palace had seemed more like those who lived in the little houses and huts of the lower town, more like a family of peasants or artisans. She saw her mother—her face still fresh and glowing, unspoiled as yet by the arts of the Cretan slave—walking back and forth and singing while the little Iphigenia sucked life and the savor of life from her bared and swollen breast. . . . Fierce as a stab in the chest, fierce as though her mother had been long dead and buried, she yearned to go quickly down the dark corridor and open the door of the queen's sleeping chamber and lie in the curve of that ample arm which had harbored her only seldom in the old days and which never harbored her any more. "Oh, my mother, I am sick with yearning for such a one as the gods will never give me, seeing I have an uncomely face. Oh, my mother, I start out of my sleep every night, thinking how now, even now, one may be stealing toward my father where he lies helpless in his dreams. Oh, my mother, where is my brother? Where are all the good and nourishing things that were with me in the clear-edged, deep-hued past?" And she was on the point of going, she had started up and was gathering the lambskin around her when she remembered the white mask of a face and the petulant voice that had said, "Gone to find the Golden Fleece, like Jason. Gone to kill the Nemean lion, like Heracles."

Nobody, nobody . . . It would be cruel to waken Aglaia. If she could have gone into the slave's bed without disturbing her peace, she would have done so. But the woman's love was like the strings of a lyre, so stretched to the needs of affection that the lightest touch would set her jangling, and she would sit up through the whole of the night and go with bluish marks under her eyes to her customary tasks at dawn. With the weird unreason of a mind that hangs between sleep and waking, she thought of going under the sounding galleries to her brother's room and

waking him—she could envision his slight, inoffensive body starting up from the couch, the coverlet clutched against his still hairless chest. She thought senselessly of asking him where he had
gone, whether he missed her greatly, whether he was hungry or
well fed, cold or close to a fire, alive or dead. . . . Then, shaking
her head to throw off the daze of oncoming sleep, she went over
to the window. Poor Io is out tonight, she thought. Poor Io is
solitary—she also—wandering the weary way from Mycenae to
Paphlagonia and back again, and in her loneliness she may listen
to me in my loneliness. Therefore I will pray.

She pulled back the purple curtain, wondering at the vast bowl
of the sky and thinking how much there was that she did not
understand. The Lady—so it had been told for a thousand years—
had been bitterly angered at poor Io, though how the occasion
could have given rise to anger instead of a stricken heart and an
aching sense of loss, she did not know. Io had been a girl—a
virgin like herself, but fairer of course—serving in the sacred
grove at the Lady's shrine. And the Lady's beloved paramour had
seen the girl and loved her and called up in her flesh the tender
creeping, and had taken her out of the temple into the shadow of
the plane trees, and had done with her there on a bed of ivy the
unimaginable thing. And the Lady had been outraged and had
transformed the girl into a snow white cow with silvered horns,
and had set a gadfly on her flank to sting her forever into restlessness, to drive her forever across the sky from east to west in a
foredoomed pilgrimage in search of a never-to-be-granted peace.

There she stood, white and tormented, high above the Citadel.
Everything beneath her—the little court with its silver tubs filled
with dark laurel, the street with its serpentine ruts, the blank façade
of the house of Aegisthus—all this was washed in her light. "Io,
hear the solitary in your solitude. Io, look upon the helpless in
your helplessness. Turn back the years and give me a father and
a mother. Send my brother back to me, let the two of us fall upon

55

each other's neck, laughing. Let us kiss and join hands. . . ." And then it was as if the prayer had been answered, for she heard distinctly the grating of a latch and the slow groan of a carefully opened door, and thought, "He has returned, he is come."

But immediately she knew—since the latch had grated before the door had creaked—that this was a going forth, not a coming in, and fear took hold on her: Who else could be going from her? Had not the beloved ones already departed, her father to face bitter battles, her brother to a destination known only to the gods? Who else, except perhaps . . . She stood behind the curtain and saw what appeared between the tubs of laurel—veiled and softly stepping in the still, white light of the moon.

It was a woman. It was her mother. The royal bracelets, covering the round arm from elbow to wrist, could be worn by nobody but the queen. But why veiled? Why softly stepping? If the lady of the palace chose to come out and pay her respects to the wandering Io, it was not only her right but an admirable act of piety. And pay her respects to Io she did: she drew the veil aside and raised her face—pale, lax, with the marks of age and sorrow upon it, yet beautiful and a begetter of tender remembrances without its powdery disguise—and looked up at the silver horns and made the customary sign, putting her fingers to her unpainted mouth to signify a kiss. "Guard her and sustain her also, Io, for she is lonely in spite of her feasting and her wine-drinking and her bitter jests and her petulance. Comfort her, Io, since she has not seen her husband's face these forty moons and more, and the one child she loved has been taken from her and given to a god." Then the veil came down again over her features, and the ample body began to move covertly. Instead of walking back between the black clumps in the shining tubs, she went forward—why, in the name of all the gods?—setting her white embroidered shoes into the rutted, moon-blanched street. Where? Why? And while the eyes watched unbelieving the heart knew and raced and stopped and struggled feebly like a fish pulled up out of water, like a fish dying in a welter of tangled net and sand. Where? To the pillared house of Aegisthus. Why? To do there, with him, the unimaginable thing.

But if honor lay in the palace and shame lay on the other side of the street? If one face was somber with the hard burdens of rule and the other was empty of everything except cunning and lust? If the voice of one was a brazen command and the voice of the other was a mocking or ingratiating twang? If the body of one was as hard and brown as though the gods had chiseled it out of sandstone and the body of the other was like beeswax—lax and meager and flabby to the touch? Was the itch so strong, was an empty couch so galling that one who had known an Agamemnon could part her thighs for an Aegisthus?

Standing behind the curtain and holding the crazy movement of her heart with one hand and the disintegrating surge of her stomach with the other, the girl thought suddenly of the anguish of Thyestes. He had vomited the hideous feast; she wished she had the courage to pluck out her eyes. And, most horrible of all, as the veil trailed past the pillars and into the blackness of Aegisthus' house, her flesh began to creep at the thought of what was to come about there—crept with a sickening and tormenting persistence, crept so disgustingly that she tore off the sheepskin robe as if it had been smeared with poison, and stood naked—sweating hot and shaking cold by turns in the raw air of night.

Flanks, buttocks, the smells of excretion . . . Secret hair and slippery wetness and the member swollen and purplish and arrogant . . . Those two, stuck together, become one beast by joining their bestial parts . . . It seemed to her then that they, in their loathsome transport, were at the core of the world, that the world was rocked by their thrustings and strivings, made putrid with their exudations, made rotten enough to fall apart.

A wan hope kept her standing a little longer at the window—

57

it was possible that her own evil heart had led her to believe what was not so. Perhaps all that went on behind the shadowed façade was an exchange of urgent words: some message newly brought that must be transmitted, some matter come to a head that called for midnight counselling. . . . But it was not so, and she had not believed for an instant that it could be so. Until Io had moved far to the west she waited behind the curtain. No light had been kindled in the pillared mansion—there was only darkness there for the dark doings of the couch. Aching at the back of her neck, dizzy, sick at the stomach, afraid that her heart would stop altogether if she did not lie down, she stepped over the lambskin robe as if it were a scorpion and flung herself onto her couch and slept.

SIX

IO HAD WANED and come again, and with her that tide of blood
for which Queen Clytemnestra waited in anxiety whenever the
wandering goddess reappeared above the Citadel. Those six or
seven days which most women dreaded, she welcomed. While they
lasted—and only for so long—she could be certain that no lawless
seed was sprouting in her womb, that the gods still favored her,
still shielded her from punishment. Those six or seven days in
which other women languished and pined after more than ordinary attention, she was moved to action and experienced a re-
surgence of vitality. In the times of uncertainty she was weak

enough to deceive herself because she was unable to bear any burden other than her fear; but while her body gave blood as freely as it gave milk and the ointment of passion, she was strong enough to tell herself the truth.

She told herself that her son Orestes must have taken flight from the palace because he had learned in spite of all their circumspection that she and Aegisthus shared one bed. If he had gone on some childish adventure he would have returned by now or would not still be keeping himself in hiding. Aegisthus in his role of Master of All the King's Messengers stood at the middle of the realm as a spider stands at the middle of his web; and Aegisthus had inquired everywhere, at the remotest provincial courts and the most distant harbors, and had not turned up a single trace. Very well, then, Orestes had departed in knowledge, possibly because he had felt the repulsion of the innocent, possibly because he had feared—fool that he was—that she or her lover might cut him down. Wherever he sojourned, he would probably tell tales, but there was a great difference between hearing such tales and believing them and an even greater difference between believing and taking action against a queen on her throne. So much for Orestes, she told herself, rubbing with satisfaction the softened curve of her belly and the loosened tendons at the back of her neck; she could do nothing in his case but wait and pray. But it was another matter with the girl.

Whether the girl knew or did not know, neither she nor her lover could make out, though they watched her constantly, like a pair of eagles circling over a hare. What signs had she given them? None, really. Since her father had ridden forth, she had eaten barely enough to keep her alive, so nothing could be made of the fact that she was thin. That she kept herself apart could not be considered peculiar either: she had always thought herself a lesser light among the merrymakers of the court; the strangeness of her beauty—for beauty she had, though it was of a subtle and unu-

60

sual kind—had led her to see herself as unbeautiful. Except with her brother, her father, and Aglaia, she mistrusted herself and kept herself remote, so nothing could be taken from her present preference for solitude. Since her early adolescence, she had been given to long brooding and hard judgments; so the scornful line of her upper lip, the cool lift of her chin, the austere and level look of her sea-grey eyes were habitual and could not be taken for signs.

Yet she was certain sooner or later to discover their bond. In the days of respite, when the queen's fear ebbed and her strength returned according to the time of the moon, she and Aegisthus, meeting by night for speech and companionship, agreed that it would be best to see that the girl was otherwise occupied. It was unfortunate that the most tempting suitors should be under the walls of Troy, but there was always Asterion. And whatever drawbacks that young man brought with him—shyness, the plumpness of one who had been sick and pampered as a child, a distaste for either magnificence or exercise—could be made up for by regal generosity.

Ten bronze talents, a house newly adorned, a goodly piece of the royal orchard, ten fine mares and two superb stallions, a small herd and a large flock, jewels, tripods, rugs, chairs and tables inlaid with tin and ivory—Clytemnestra grew more certain that her daughter would accept the match with each new item that they added to the list. From the other side, of course, there was nothing but enthusiasm: when they went to the boy's mother, she was thrown into a transport of delight at the prospect of so close an alliance with the house of Atreus. For a day they pondered whether it would be well to invite her and her son to sit with them when the subject was broached to the princess, but in the end they decided otherwise. The boy's mother was over-eager and might press too much; and the boy himself, self-conscious and retiring, might not seem as eager as he really was. So the

61

queen and Aegisthus decided that the subject had better be introduced in private, at a little supper—the three of them only, around a small and tempting table set near the hearth in the great hall. It rained, but that was no ill omen, that was all to the good: they would be the more intimate and comfortable close to the roaring and fragrant fire. Ease and closeness—such was the mode they had chosen for the evening, and it was in this mode that the queen sent a slave to her daughter to say that it would be unnecessary to dress for the occasion: any plain dress and the purple sheepskin robe would do well enough.

The slave came back while the queen was tasting the barley broth, and her dear cousin Aegisthus was taking a fine piece of venison off the spit. "Did the princess send any answer?" she said.

"Yes, my lady and my queen. She said that, with your permission, she will leave her sheepskin robe in her bedchamber. She said that she never wears it anymore. She said it gives her an itching in her skin."

"Really? Now that is a strange business. She had that robe as a present from her father"—she was addressing Aegisthus; the slave had taken himself off at a wave of her hand—"and I told her to wear it only because I thought she would be more at ease in it than in anything else. Ah, well, how can one tell what will give her pleasure? She is a bundle of whims and itches, itches and whims. For all I know, merely *because* we have done what we could to give her a quiet family supper, she will come down to us in her best jacket and skirt, decked out in every ornament she owns."

The prediction was exaggerated but not groundless. When the young woman came into the great hall, she came in her own barbaric version of splendor, the knack for which she seemed to have gotten with the shape of her nose and her arbitrary temper from those of her ancestors born across the eastern sea. From neck to ankles she was encased in a narrow robe the color of a poppy.

Her hair was piled on her head in three irreproachable diminishing tiers, the highest of which was ornamented with a gold pin in the shape of a dove. On her left arm was a single bracelet—her brother's. On her right hand was a single ring—her father's seal and signet. Under the scarlet linen her body showed long and so fearfully thin that Clytemnestra wondered how a bridegroom could possess her without bruising himself on her bones.

"Who else will sit at meat with us tonight?" she asked, pausing ten paces away from the table.

"Why, nobody," said the queen, startled by the arrogant scarlet, the provocative bracelet, and the still more provocative ring, which, if it belonged on any other hand than Orestes', belonged on her own.

"Truly, my lady and my mother? That is strange."

"And why should it be so strange?" She heard in her own voice a conciliatory softness that she regretted but could not control. "Why should the three of us not sit down to meat now and again, ourselves only, without other guests?"

The wide-set sea-colored eyes fixed themselves upon her but did not seem to be taking her in. "Without other guests?" The voice was as ungiving as the eyes; it addressed her no more than it addressed the bronze plates and the embroidered tablecloth. "But there has scarcely been an evening since my father rode forth when my mother has considered us sufficient unto ourselves. When have we not had guests?"

"Is it a fault to be hospitable, my daughter?" She asked it earnestly: she had always known that neither the elder girl nor her brother had any taste for banqueting, but it had never occurred to her that her little feasts had seemed to them a downright offense against her absent lord. And while she pondered it, she saw to her confusion that her intentions for this evening were being pulled awry: there stood the girl, apart from them and above them as if she were standing in judgment upon them, and her own

63

voice had neither motherly ease nor queenly authority, and the broth was already tepid, and the meat was growing cold.

It was then that he moved with his usual self-confidence to mend whatever had gone amiss. "Come, sit," he said, pulling back a chair and motioning the young woman toward it with wry, casual gallantry. "However it has been on other evenings, this evening we three are alone." She sat and turned her face toward him, but she might as well have been looking at the dimmed frescoes or the blazing fire on the hearth. Nor did the fact that she was seated reduce her dignity in any significant measure: her straight back, her thinness, and the diminishing coils of her burnished hair still gave her an uncompromising height. She kept her silence as though she were waiting in some impatience for him to get on and be finished with whatever he had begun; and he also offered conciliation, though in a voice that was not self-effacing. "Surely," he said, "you cannot think ill of your mother because she does what she can to wear away a weary time of waiting with a little cheer and a little grace. What banquets she spreads, she spreads for your father's sake as well as for her own. It is no kindness to a man to make his house a place of mourning while he lives, nor is it praiseworthy in a queen that she should be niggardly with such hospitality as her king would dispense if he sat beside her on their throne. What better service can she do him here than to give comfort and pleasure to those who serve him well?"

"Ah, yes." She had not touched her plate, though he had heaped it for her. Her elbows were set on either side of it, her hands were joined above it, and her chin rested on her intertwined fingertips. "My Uncle Aegisthus is entirely right." She said it to the silver goblet that stood in front of her; she said it gravely and without malice. "What could be more gratifying to the gods than a woman who gives comfort and pleasure to those who serve her husband well?"

Oh, but it would be foolish to strip away the offhand tone in which the words were clothed and burn with anger or go cold with fear at the naked words themselves. A tender conscience will find hard edges on which to injure itself; and Clytemnestra curved her mouth into a smile and saw to it that she tipped the jar that held the barley broth with a steady hand.

"Not so much of it," said Electra.

"She is right," said Aegisthus, perfectly serene. "Let her stint on the soup and save her stomach for the venison."

"And very good venison it is, I can assure my cousin. An excellent piece of meat—properly aged and well spiced—"

She stopped with her over-amiable voice still sounding in the air; she stopped because the cool grey eyes had fastened on her at last. "Whatever my mother serves up"—it was uttered slowly, so that no word of it was blurred or lost—"is bound to be properly aged and well spiced."

The queen set the jar of broth down with a thud. She asked herself whether the red tide of rage and fright could be showing through the chalk-white mask, whether the loose folds of her robe were being visibly stirred by the fierce speed of her heart. "True, true," her lover was saying in a twanging workaday voice; and she did not know whether to wonder at him or at herself. At herself, surely. The girl was eating as calmly as if nothing more exceptionable than last night's thunder had been alluded to, and the girl had never been notable for her poise. If what the girl had said was to be taken as *she* had taken it, then the girl was coarse and worldly-wise, and anybody at court would swear for her delicacy and her innocence. "Eat, child, you are much too thin," she said, fatuous in her relief. "I was saying to Aglaia only yesterday that every moon finds you thinner than the last. And that is not well, that is not well at all, considering the business we will be speaking of tonight."

"What business is that, my lady and my mother?" She was

afraid—her upper lip had trembled for all her seeming carelessness. Darkness lay beyond the circle of agitated light thrown
round them by the fire, and she had lifted her proud chin and
was staring into the dark.

"No business to give you an instant of distress," said Aegisthus
in spite of a mouthful of bread. "It is only that your friend Asterion
has asked for you."

"Yes, Electra, Asterion has asked for you." As she said it, her
white and well-fleshed hand came down on her daughter's bony,
dusky forearm and lay where it had fallen, though the arm was
as unresponsive to her touch as a severed bough. Tears smarted
in her eyes nevertheless; an unexpected and incomprehensible
surge of tenderness rose over her uneasiness. Whether it was genu-
ine or false—whether she truly felt what she thought she felt or
had only brought herself to feel what a mother was expected to
feel on such an occasion—she could not tell.

"Asterion has asked for me?"

They smiled and nodded at her both at once, and the queen
saw on the floor near the table the swollen, grotesque shadows
of their two bobbing heads.

"I beg my mother to forgive me. I trust that my Uncle Aegisthus will excuse my blunt speech. But there is nothing in me to
make me believe that what you tell me can be so." Her voice rose
and shook; her hand flung down her napkin; she turned quickly
from one to the other, with cold eyes fixed and unmoving in
her turning face. "Whoever tells me that Asterion has asked for
me, tells me a lie."

"Ah, come, now, ease yourself a little," said Aegisthus, as if
he were soothing a skittish mare. "You rear too quickly, you take
offense at nothing. Why should either of us tell you a lie?"

"I do not know. I do not know—as yet. But this I am certain
of: *Asterion* would never ask for *me*. Asterion is a child and would
have neither the need nor the courage for such asking. You—

66

or you"—the keen grey look flashed first at the one and then at the other—"or perhaps the two of you together went to Asterion's mother and told her that I was to be had for the asking. And, after he had been duly goaded and reminded that I was Agamemnon's daughter, poor Asterion agreed."

Ah, blessed Lady, what a blunderer the gods have made me! thought the queen, slowly exhaling her long-suspended breath. If the girl knew anything, all she knew was that marriage business had been done behind her back. If she was affronted at anything, it was only that she thought they had dealt lightly with her pride. Poor thing, tricked out in poppy-red (I am not a lamb to be led by a ribbon, I am knowing and bold). Poor thing, with her hair piled up in three coils and topped with a golden dove (If I take proper pains with myself, I am not so bad a bargain as you think). Poor thing, flaunting her brother's bracelet (Not everyone will be glad to see the last of me, there is one who will weep to see me go). Poor thing, exhibiting her father's seal and signet (Remember that it is the daughter of Agamemnon whom you give to a green boy with small skill in love). . . .

And, knowing these things as only a woman can know them, Clytemnestra shook her head at Aegisthus, who had opened his mouth to speak, and let her fingers slip down her daughter's meager arm to lie on her cold long hand. "If we have put it to you in an awkward and roundabout fashion, I and your Uncle Aegisthus, then you must excuse us," she said. "It is true, we went together to the mother of Asterion. It is true that the mother spoke to the son and that the son agreed. But believe me, my daughter, not one grain of your dignity was thereby lost. We went only after we had seen with our own eyes how it was with Asterion—we knew without asking that his desire was all toward you but that he could not find the courage to tell you so. And to speak the truth it seemed to us that you were drawn to him also—you have walked and talked with him and no other, you have distinguished him by

67

making him your sole companion, and, seeing that you are maidenly and chaste, you might not even know it yourself if your desire had answered his desire."

"I have no desire after any man, my mother—"

"As I have just said, you are chaste and would not know. It is a dreary life you lead here in the palace, with your father encamped before Troy and your sister at the shrine in Aulis and your brother gone heedlessly from us on some affair of his own. Only the gods know how long it will be until this place is changed for the better, and we thought to send you to a happier place, a house of your own, in which you might have the consolations of love."

She drew her hand from under her mother's and laid it in her own lap. It was clenched and it trembled. The knuckles showed white through the sand-colored skin. "My mother exalts the consolations of love too much. They may be for her, but they are not for me," she said.

"Not for you?" said Aegisthus, bantering. "Not for you indeed." He turned upon her such a kindly, half-jesting, half-knowing face as the dour Agamemnon could never have shown her. He held his head to one side so that he could look into her averted eyes. "Are you not, then, a woman, child of the king my lord and the queen my lady? Have the gods made you according to some new mold, without a woman's needs and a woman's parts?"

Like some wild red bird out of Egypt she started up and turned upon him. She thrust her small breasts forward until they protruded out of her thinness. "My uncle sees that I have these," she said, striking them with her fist. "Let him take it also as a given thing that I have this—" she smote herself again, and her brother's bracelet rang, colliding with the golden cross pinned at her hip. "But it betrays me not. It works me no such havoc as runs wild in others I could name—"

Blessed Lady, let me not go white, Clytemnestra prayed. She

means my sister Helen. She means the wife of the Captain of the King's Guardsmen. She does not mean me.

"—It drives me not to lie and to connive and to make filth out of my body and to deceive the blameless and put shame upon my house—"

He also had risen, and for an instant it seemed to Clytemnestra that he would go at her daughter for her sake, would strike the dusky taunting face with the flat of his hand. Then the dark tide that had risen in his eyes washed back, and he flung up his arms and fetched up an impatient sigh. "All this," he said in a voice at once reasonable and aggrieved, "all this because your mother and my most unfortunate self have foolishly sought to do for you what the king would have done long since if he had been here. You are too long unmarried. Are we in need of anything more than this mad talk to know that it is so? Long since, you should have lain down under the same coverlet with another."

"Let my Uncle Aegisthus so lie down when and with whom he will. As for me, I want it not—"

"Why? How so?"

"Because it is hideous to me. Because it chokes me with loathing. Because I have come upon that which makes it seem to me the occupation of flies and scorpions. I would rather walk in dung up to my chin. I would rather lie dead in a gully and be eaten by dogs—"

"No, now," said the queen, raising her hand in a trembling parody of authority, "we have had enough."

"Have you, truly, my mother? Then let us speak of it no more, lest both you and my Uncle Aegisthus have too much."

The sickness of certainty rose in her stomach like vomit. The girl knew, and her knowledge was in her mother's mouth like the green-brown taste of bile. "Hold your tongue or I myself will strike you," she said. But she said it in a tone so sickly faint that a child could not have feared the force of her hand.

69

"Sit down, my girl," said Aegisthus, pointing to Electra's chair. "Whatever grievances you have against us, you are a princess of Mycenae, not a screeching she-fiend out of Libya. Sit you down and put a bridle on your voice, unless it is your intention to share the counsels of the house of Atreus with the slaves."

She sat, but her shoulders heaved and her clenched hands pressed together between her knees. After a long silence, in which the noises of the hearth fire seemed as loud as the roar of a great conflagration, she said quietly, like a pained child, "Add this to all the other ills you have brought upon me: you have robbed me of Asterion, and I had no other friend." Whereupon she laid her head against the table, disordering her hair, and wept.

The queen looked across her sobbing daughter at Aegisthus and got no consolation from his eyes. His hand made an almost imperceptible gesture of resignation; if he smiled ruefully and nodded at his lady, it was only to entreat her to close the scene—shameful and futile as it had been—with her customary dignity.

"Do not weep, Electra. What is there to weep for?" she said.

"Everything, everything—"

"If you will not have him, then you will not have him. No great harm has been done."

"I will not have him. Go to his mother and tell her so."

"It will be done tomorrow. What would you have me tell her?"

"What is it to me what you tell her? Tell her he is too fat. Tell her I will not marry until Orestes takes Hermione. Tell her I have a mortal sickness—that would not be a lie. I am mortally sick. I am mortally sick of myself and the world."

"That," said Aegisthus, with pity in his twanging voice, "will be remedied by time." His loose-jointed fingers fell, in real compassion, on the young woman's shoulder, but she started back as though he had touched her with an ember, and struck at his hand.

"Never touch me," she said, glaring at him with wild, wet eyes. "Never come near me, never touch me." She got up in a confusion of rumpled scarlet linen and left the table, moving out of the firelight into the dark. And there, safe in the shadow, she raised her voice again, mimicking with murderous accuracy the voice of the beloved. "That will be remedied by time," she said out of the blackness. "Shall I tell you when it will be remedied? When the walls of Troy are down and the beacon fire is lighted. When Agamemnon—my father and the husband of your woman —comes back to what he is fool enough to call his home."

SEVEN

THE PRINCESS ELECTRA fell into the black gorge of sleep that
night at moonrise and did not clamber out of it again until some
four hours after dawn. Fright and the sweat of fright and the smell
of that sweat were upon her when she awakened. She sat up on
her couch and ran her fingers through her drenched hair. After
the rending of spirit that had come about in the great hall last
evening, she could not understand how it was that no change had
taken place in the world. It seemed to her inconceivable that the
rest of the human race should be going about its petty daily affairs
and making its petty daily noises: the ring of pots, the calls of

criers in the streets, the grinding of mortar and pestle, the rattle of wagon wheels over the stones.

What shall I do, what in the name of the Lady shall I do? she asked herself, and could envision nothing but walking up and down, back and forth, like an imprisoned and terrified beast in the small confines of her room. Through sticky eyelashes—she had been too exhausted to wash away the stuff with which she had made herself brazen yesterday—she saw that Aglaia had left a brown robe of mourning on top of the carved chest. But how could she have known when I told her nothing? she thought. Then she remembered that the robe could have nothing to do with what had come about last night. Aglaia had laid it out only because today was one of the nine days in the year set apart for mourning the dead; and—since Clytemnestra loathed cemeteries and all the rest were gone forth—she was the only member of the house of Atreus on hand to pour wine and ointment over the graves in the round cemetery by the west wall.

"But how can I do it?" she said aloud. How can I walk in the public streets? How can I show this ravaged face to the folk? . . . She stood and found that her knees were as weak as water under her weight; she stretched out her hand in the clear sunlight and saw that her fingers shook. But once she had rid herself of her damp shift and drawn the coarse dry cloth over her head, she found that the shaking had begun to subside. Yes, she said to herself as if she were speaking to a sorely troubled child, first I will wash this sticky sweat from my hands and face and armpits, and then I will take a bite of bread and a little milk for strength, and then we will go down to the graves of the ancestors, Aglaia and I. . . .

The mere performance of the ceremony seemed as much as she could hope to manage, and when difficulties arose in connection with it she felt the shaking of her hands and the weakness of her knees like threats of disintegration. Orestes had always gone with her on these pious visits, carrying the heavy amphora; Aglaia had carried the stirrup jar in which the Cretan oil had been infused with Mycenean saffron, cumin, and powdered cedarwood; and she herself had carried the garlands to be wound around the stones. The discussion in the west court concerning which of them was to carry what drove her almost as wild as the talk around the table yesterday; she wrested the amphora from Aglaia, saying with pointless bitterness that she trusted she had enough strength to carry a few measures of wine; she shouted her refusal at the slave boy who offered to come with them; she flung the carefully made garlands over her nurse's head and pulled them down around her shoulders so roughly that many of the myrtle sprigs—fragile and precious in a year of drought—fell onto the paving stones. For the first half of the walk she felt a questionable and angry pride in showing herself to the folk as a bearer of burdens; but a few paces away from the enclosure, where their passage was blocked by a wagoner and his stubborn mule, rage boiled up in her against the stupid peasants who were forever dragging their unwanted goods and unruly beasts into the Citadel, and she could not answer the man's apologies with even a semblance of grace. The amphora was indeed too heavy for her: the sweat came back and her shoulder ached. The gods are looking upon me, she thought, walking at last between the two great slabs of rough stone that stood at the entrance. The gods gaze at me out of the peaceful firmament and know with what an unseemly heart I come to bring my offerings to the dead.

Yet the aspect of the place—the green turf, the tan stone, the blue sky—wrought upon her anguished spirit strongly enough to permit her to perform the ceremony with the required dignity. Her mind departed from her mother and Aegisthus while she anointed the tombstones of the nameless notables with the sad, aged fragrance of the ritual oil; she forgot her anger when she drenched the turf with the wine that bubbled out of the amphora; not tenderness itself, but at least the remembrance of tenderness came upon her when she wound the injured garlands around the half-obliterated likenesses of those who lay below. She had thought with hot pleasure of the ceremonial smashing of the vessels: to hurl them against the wall, to reduce them to a heap of potsherds had seemed to her a way to relieve her heart. But when the pieces lay neatly brushed together against the inner wall of the enclosure, she felt nothing but exhaustion and emptiness.

"Shall we go back now, my lady?" Aglaia said.

Back to what? There before her, as palpable as the rough wall and the broken pottery, lay the day of torment. How would she murder the hours? What would she say if she came suddenly upon her mother? How could she sleep? Where would she eat? "No," she said, giving way to the quaking and letting herself down to sit cross-legged on the damp turf. "Let us rest a little first. I am too tired for the walk back home."

"I told you not to carry the amphora. The slave would gladly have—"

"It was not carrying the amphora that made me tired."

"No? What, then?"

Her nurse sat down and faced her, after kissing her old hand toward the concentric circles of memorial stones.

To answer briefly was impossible: there was no help for it— she was forced to recount the whole hideous business. And, when she had delivered herself at last of the dreadful revelation, her stifled anger was not allayed by her nurse's steady stare. Whether or not it was dreadful to Aglaia, it was certainly not a revelation; and it was galling to the girl to realize that she had been so late to learn what others had come to take more or less calmly.

"How is it that you and your husband knew it, and every slave in the palace knew it, and I knew it not?" she said.

"Look, now, Electra, think a little. Would it not have been better if you had never come to know of it at all?" She laid a bony hand on her mistress's knee, but the girl struck it aside.

"Am I a baby to be fed with a spoon whatever you decide is my meat? How is it that slaves, whispering behind my back, should take it upon themselves to judge what shall be told and what shall not be told to a member of the house of Atreus?"

The woman had flushed when her touch had been rejected. Now she turned white, and the bones of her face stood out hard in the brightness of the sun. "It was not slaves, it was not my miserable husband and my even more despicable self who settled upon what you were to be told," she said. "My husband sealed his mouth and I sealed mine at the bidding of your brother Orestes. It was he who gave the order—perhaps that will be an ointment to your pride."

Oh, but it was not. That *he* should have known and kept his knowledge from her, that he should have gone forth and left her behind to discover the dreadful business for herself, to stand sick and solitary at the window, to retch at the unbelievable thing and struggle with it—that was the sharpest wound of all. "How long did he know before he departed? How long did he keep it from me?" she said.

"No more than two days, my lady. My husband heard it from a guardsman but said no word of it even to me until he himself had seen it with his own eyes. After that he brought the matter to me, and we two went to the prince with it because it seemed to us that he was in great danger—"

What danger? She saw it, yet she would not see it. She tried to shut it out as her blinking eyes strove to shut out the pitiless sun. "How should the sole heir of Agamemnon come to harm? Who would dare—"

"Look, now, my lady, surely you understand. Surely you see that, if anything evil befell the king our lord—which all the gods forefend—the queen's lover might cut off the king's son, inasmuch as Orestes alone would stand between him and the throne. And even if all goes well in Troy and the king returns whole and laden with spoils and glory, so long as the queen and her lover know that Orestes may have knowledge of what has passed between them, how can they risk what he might whisper in his father's ear? No, he had no choice, your brother. There was nothing for him to do but what he did—go forth in secret, taking only my husband with him, to journey to some safer place."

"And leave me behind in ignorance? Leave me behind, in their hands, to suffer whatever I had to suffer and face whatever I had to face alone?"

"But my lady's dangers are not the dangers of her brother. The old law is gone from the land—no woman is a stumbling-block on the way to the throne. Nor did Orestes think that his sister would come upon the knowledge that put him in jeopardy. He thought—yes, and my husband and I were fools enough to think it too—that you might remain safe in your ignorance until your father came home."

She did not answer. She stared at the barren scene around her and saw—sharp and clear as the memorial stones under the blue sky—the hard shape of her brother's dilemma, and behind it the stony actuality of her own. No matter what they had thought, the three of them in their secret council, she too was now in mortal danger, had flown careless into it last evening like a light-crazed bird. The two over whom she had foolishly exulted at the table— they were her enemies. Henceforth, day and night, they would stalk her, their nets would be out to drag her in. How could it be otherwise since she had vaunted her knowledge before them and they would be certain that whatever she knew she would reveal to her father and her lord? "How could he leave me here alone? How was it that he did not take me with him?" she said at last.

The nurse spoke reasonably and soothingly of the impossibility of that: How could a woman, gently bred from the day she was taken out of her swaddling clothes, climb down into gullies and up the sides of mountains, struggle with wild boars and lions, go hungering and thirsting from one city to another to beg unwilling princes for a hiding place? It was all sane enough, but she did not listen; her thoughts went up in a senseless but utterly blessed fantasy. Why was she a woman? What had she to do with womanishness after what she had seen from the window on that loathsome night? In her thoughts she put her womanliness from her: she chopped off her hair, she dressed herself in a tunic, she slung a great bow over her shoulder, she fastened a quiver of clanking arrows at her side. Hand in hand with him she strode down the long dry roads and through the thorny thickets. She ate begged or stolen bread with him in the shadow of a plane tree. Her head against his shoulder, she slept beside him under the stars. And he and she were so alike that those who encountered them took them for twins—two lads, sun-browned and tawny, not entirely mortal, born of some reluctant nymph on whom they had been begotten by a god. . . .

"He would have taken you with him if it had been possible. Surely you know as much, surely you see how sorry a business it was for him to leave you behind," Aglaia said.

She shook herself out of her high dream. "Sorry and dangerous —for now I, too, am scarcely safe, seeing that my mother and that other one can no longer believe that I am in ignorance of what I have told them I know."

But, by the very fact that Aglaia continued to sit cross-legged and motionless on the turf, she minimized the girl's dilemma, she refused to give due importance to yesterday's perilous encounter in the great hall. And when she spoke her voice was quiet and even, as though she were speaking of a torn skirt or a pair of soiled shoes. "You must not take these present troubles too much to heart," she said. "Nothing came about last evening that cannot be undone before you go to your couch tonight."

"Undone? How can it be undone? They know what they know. Who can make them forget?"

"Nobody can make them forget, of course. But that will not be needful. All that is needful is for you to show them that this business is of little concern to you—"

"Of little concern to me? Of little concern to me that my mother is deceiving my father with a he-goat?" She tore, at the turf, ripping up the frail winter blades by the roots.

"Yes, that is what I said. You are young and chaste, it is true. It is also true that what you learned is a distress to you in your youth and your chastity. Yet to my mind—do not fly in my face until you have heard me out—to my mind, it concerns you too much."

"Too much?"

"Listen, and tell me the truth out of your heart: Do you honestly believe that your father has lain womanless, night in, night out, since he left the Citadel?"

She could not say that she thought so. Before the host of the Achaians had settled down to the siege of Troy, it had engaged in many victorious encounters with the Trojan allies, coming into possession of much spoil and scores of captives, including the wives and daughters of the highborn families that lived in the unwalled cities of the eastern coast. Her father—king of kings and pre-eminent over the host—would have had first choice of the booty, and she could not doubt that he had sometimes chosen a woman and taken his prize of war to his tent to deal with as he pleased. "Certainly he has had his captives. But what has that to do with my mother and Aegisthus?" she said.

"Little, plainly, to your way of thinking. But to my way of

thinking, much. If your father has taken to himself three, four, five of the eastern women, how is it that your mother is a she-dog in your eyes because she has taken one man?"

Always she had seen the dispensing of the captives as a formal, even a gracious procedure: a fair woman was taken by the hand and led from among a welter of beautiful weapons and rich ornaments, fresh and smiling, to her new lord. Now for the first time she saw how it must be in reality, and her heart sickened. These women were in bitter grief—the bodies of their brothers and fathers and husbands lay behind them in the ruins of their smoking towns. Some of them had breasts swollen with milk clotted there for slain children. All of them were in a state to tear their garments and beat their heads—none of them could think of love. To take such a woman into a tent, to wrest from her grieving body a victor's due . . . She turned from the thought of it in anger and disgust. "That is the way of warriors," she said nevertheless. "They take what they can."

"Warriors only?"

"It is a different matter with men. A man may choose what he will."

"Truly? And does it never seem hard to you that the same right to choose does not hold for you and me? Does it not seem to you that we suffer more than we should for the lack of a little extra tail of flesh in front—"

"You talk like a whore out of the tavern—and in the presence of the holy dead."

"You talk like an aged virgin or a man, and those who sleep under the sod here know as well as I that you are neither. If you do not have aching breasts and a hungry mouth as yet, you will get them in good time."

"Never speak of that to me. In that, I have no part. Ever since I have seen what I have seen—"

"Oh, come, now, what have you seen? A woman in the ripeness of her years—a woman, too, who has been little loved and sorely ill-treated—going to take her pleasure with one who likes her better than captives or power or gold stored up in a treasury. You have seen nothing you would not see in any other court if you happened to look out of the window at the proper hour."

She thought of Helen. She thought of the queens of Phaistos and Knossos. So many came crowding into her thoughts that she could not protest. "Little loved?" she said instead, and knew as she uttered it that this also was true. Sharp in her memory she saw her father—a black-bearded and shaggy-chested presence—seated on the hearth in the great hall, with the little Iphigenia on his knee, and she herself seated on one side of him and her brother Orestes on the other. And while they jested together—for with the three of *them* he was always warm and free—she saw with undeniable clarity her mother lay by her whorl and come up to the little company, with an uncertain smile on her face. No, Clytemnestra had not stayed by them long, not on that occasion nor on any other. Whatever she sought, stopping before her lord on the hearth of her home, had not been there. The bearded visage, so open when it turned itself to the children, had been transformed on her approach into a mask—sullen, shut, impervious. "Perhaps one thing or another came between them," she said. "Perhaps he loved her in the beginning, and afterwards his love began to wane. But Aglaia lies when she says that my mother was ill-used."

"Not publicly insulted, no. But he never gave with joy—whatever he gave to her, he gave at her asking and with a tight fist. Two of her children—you and your brother—learned early enough to bear themselves toward her after his manner, with carelessness and coldness and pride. The third—she was too soft to be cut to his pattern—the third he took from her and gave to a god. When has a queen in Achaia been more wretchedly used?"

"She was always well served, and I never saw her without a score of ornaments—"

"She was well served because she was his wife: if she had been ill served, that would have affronted his dignity. As for her jewels, they were her own. No, now, if you had lived her life, you might see why she should be going to one who at least gives her a 'By your leave' before he mounts her. If you had lived her life, you would understand how much comfort is to be had with one—a goat, if you choose—who has the grace to give thanks for his pleasure with a good word and a kiss."

But how could anybody speak of such matters in this holy place at this desperate hour? Had she not kept staring steadily at the austere gravestones, her flesh might well have come to life again with all this coarse, unseemly talk: the pale down was actually beginning to rise on her skin. She felt impelled to jump up and walk the circuit of the wall, looking over the parapet at the blank and innocent sky; her exasperation, as palpable as an itching scab, drove her to cruelty. "Your husband, too, is gone forth," she said, "and doubtless he will take a woman somewhere along the way. Because of that, will you go sneaking into another man's bed?"

Aglaia laughed and looked at her with blank and level eyes. "I? No, not I," she said. "I am as chaste as you would wish, but let me tell you why. I am growing old, and no guardsman stands behind a pillar watching for me to come out when the lamps are being quenched, no slave is driven into the court to look with longing up at the windows of such a one as I. I am proud, and pride is a thorn to carry in the heart, and my lady Electra has just such a thorn and tends it as if it were an anemone or a hyacinth. But I must tell her this much, though she will be deaf to it: In the latter days it is a hard thing to be as I am now—

too proud to reach out to any of *them,* and too old to have any of them reach out to *me."*

But the world Aglaia called up for her was unendurable. Its ground was as uncertain under her feet as ground cracking in an earthquake; its sky was a chaos of comets and careening moons in which no sun would rise or set again. In this world her aging nurse had a writhing womb and spoke of it. In this world her serene and imperious mother lay under a he-goat and gave and experienced obscene transports, and those who knew of the horror merely shrugged or snickered behind their hands. No, she would not live in it, she rejected it utterly. She got up, as rigid and unsure as if the turf were actually heaving under her feet; she turned her back on the woman and went to the parapet and looked over it at the clean, sane mountains, filling her clogged chest with long draughts of blameless air. "If only he had taken me with him—then I would never have seen it. Then I would not have heard what I have heard from you. If the world is as you say it is, what am I to do?" she said.

"Why, marry."

"Marry?"

"Certainly." The nurse had not moved; the voice was speaking calmly behind her. "Go to your mother this afternoon. Go early, before the hall fills up with guests. Speak to her humbly—whether you *are* humble or not makes no difference. Tell her you have put such childish things as you said last night behind you. Say that, on second thought, you see you could make a happier marriage than the gods gave her in her day if you took Asterion."

She could not answer. She could not even think of it. The boy, their promised possessions, their proffered house, the very couch on which they would lie down together had been flung into the portentous confusion of the unendurable world. She stared at the peaks—blue and cool as sea water in the light of noon—and

83

bruised her clenched hands on the stones of the parapet and whispered her brother's name.

"Why should you reject him? I thought there was always a great fondness between you two."

"Fondness is not love."

"There are times when it serves better. We have gotten on well enough with it these twenty-odd years, my man and I."

"He did not ask for me. They went to him and asked him—"

"Well, he cannot have been averse to it—otherwise the matter would not have been brought to you."

"I will not have what was chosen for me by a lecher and a whore, to seal my eyes against seeing and to stuff my mouth against carrying tales. I will wait until my father comes home and chooses a husband for me—"

"Pure and righteous as your father is, dragging his captives behind him."

"Righteous or unrighteous, he has not dealt with me in such a way that he deserves to come home and find me married—"

"It might gall him somewhat more to come home and find you dead."

"Dead?"

"You yourself have pointed out the danger. You yourself have said that nobody can make the two of them forget what you have told them you know. And how can they risk your telling it to the king unless you give them reason to believe that you have accepted a covenant with them and will hold your tongue? Come, go to your mother and tell her that you will marry Asterion."

"I do not want him. He is a child."

"That is a matter time will mend."

"He will never go forth to do the deeds of a man."

"It will be no grief to you to have him at home to bring you gifts and set pillows behind your back and warm your feet on a winter's night."

"I do not want him." An eagle hung for an instant suspended in flight, black against the luminous noonday whiteness, black above the blue ridges that seemed to stretch forever toward the west. Could the eye of that eagle see, on some bleak rock, the fair and supple body of her brother Orestes lying down to sleep away the heat of the day? "I do not want him and I will not have him. He is too fat," she said.

"That last," said Aglaia, "is the first sane argument that has issued from your mouth. He is too fat, I admit it myself. But his bones are very good, and his skin is as clear as a peeled almond, and his flesh will dwindle soon enough, seeing that he will be living with such a hard judge as yourself."

It was not the impertinence, it was not the implied insult that goaded her into rage. It was the pair of words "living with," which, in court parlance, whispered behind raised fingers, meant doing the unimaginable thing. More threatening because of the envisioned loss of his childish plumpness, peremptory in his role as husband, endowed as he was for the first time in her mind now with "a little tail of flesh in the front"—and that swelling and purpling—she saw Asterion standing over her couch in unacceptable nakedness. A wildness came upon her, so that she beat with her fists on the parapet, and said far too loudly, "Aglaia, I swear—"

The woman leaped up, white in the face. "Do not swear, not here," she said. "Utter no oaths. Those oaths are terrible and binding that are sworn above the holy dead."

"Let them be terrible. Let them be binding. Let the thirsty ones listen and hear."

"The gods seal up your mouth. You are as wild as a colt—wild and mad. Utter no oaths in this place—"

"In this place, or at the shrine of the Lady, or in the holy cave of Poseidon I swear, and I will swear—"

"Do not say it—"

"That I will not marry Asterion."

85

"So? Enough then, enough of it—"

"That I will not be given in marriage to any man while my brother and my father are gone forth from home—"

"Enough. Be satisfied."

"And that whatsoever evil I have learned I will make known to my father and my lord."

EIGHT

IT WAS NOT prudence that kept the Master of All the King's
Messengers this long while from his solitary meetings with his lady
and his queen. Ever since their exchange with the princess Electra over barley broth and venison, the very idea of prudence had
become laughable. They had never been prudent, they had only
thought themselves so; it was not that nobody knew about their
connection, it was only that everybody—with the exception of the
daughter—had pretended not to know. And this discovery, which
should have undone him, begot in him a strange sensation of relief, as when a laugh that has long been tickling inside bursts out

at last. It exhilarated him, it filled him with an inexplicable good cheer. He found that he actually had more time on his hands these days—he had spent so much of it before trying to convince himself that their doings were unguessed by everybody from her old aunt to the slave who came to waken him from a sleep that he had not slept.

No, now that the girl had come at them raging, now that there was plainly no way to gag the girl except an unthinkable one, he had grown bold and even exultant on public occasions. He had addressed the queen of Mycenae by her given name, had carried dainty bits of food to her during a banquet, had gone so far as to fasten a button on the front of her jacket with his own hand. The white foal, the pride of his stable, which she had loved from its birth, he sent her as a gift—let her groom think whatever he pleased. The first anemones that blossomed in his garden he carried to her in a silver vase, and she set them on the long marble table in the great hall for all her guests to see. Even his likeness, which he was having carved for her in intaglio on an onyx, she would not keep secretly in her room; she would no sooner have it than he would see it hanging between her two superb breasts.

It was not prudence that had interrupted their assignations some ten days back, before the first curled leaves and tendrils showed blood red on the walls of the Citadel. They had been forced to get on as well as they could without each other because he was entertaining an unexpected visitor: a cousin, a second cousin, an only-the-gods-knew-what—at any rate, some relative of the old man who had fostered him—had arrived from Corinth and robbed him of the privacy of his home and had taken from the two of them the only place where they could make love. For this relative, this Polydamian, was an aging night-wanderer, given to sleeplessness or bad dreams, either of which was likely to drive him out of his room in search of a slice of meat or a goblet of wine and a little conversation in the bedroom of his host.

The cousin, like the old man, was a merchant. The old man had been forthright and crude; the cousin—as a person would expect in one who had inherited wealth instead of wresting it out of the fist of fate—was a not altogether savory mixture of formality and vulgarity, candor and guile. His very errand carried a kind of taint: he had come to buy in Mycenae certain small ornaments—butterflies, cuttlefish, wheels, laurel leaves, stars—that the craftsmen of Mycenae pressed out of dark clay and covered with gold leaf; and he neither admitted nor denied that he meant to sell them in his native city as solid gold. His appearance was disconcerting, too: sometimes he looked like a reverend priest about to bless and sometimes like a mule about to bray. He was very short, and his legs were even shorter than the rest of him; his nose was long, with grey hair sprouting from the nostrils; his eyes were enormous, with black pupils and a yellowish cast over the white parts; his head was bald except for a wreath of hair running back from the temples, a wreath so carefully combed and set that it looked like an inappropriate tin crown. And his mind was as equivocal and changeable as his person: most of his talk was made up of vapid jokes, old and ridiculous jingles, vain and pointless plays on words; but when the listener took him for a fool and answered him as a fool, his tongue lashed out as sharp as a snake's and made his mocker more inane than himself.

With such a one Aegisthus had been yoked for ten days. There was no avoiding it: the old man had taken him up, starving and nameless, from the beach on which he had been abandoned; the old man was dead; and he was bound to show hospitality to the old man's kin. Nor was he niggardly in the discharge of his obligations. Ten times a day he could have picked up a vase and smashed it over the cousin's bald head, but he made himself entirely available, walked and talked to his guest in the garden, took him to court and wherever else he himself was invited to dine, offered to find him women—an offer he rejected—and kept the wine-jars constantly open, the table amply spread. Nor did he once permit himself the questions that threatened to leap out every time that Polydamian came back from the pottery kilns in the lower town outside the walls: How many accursed ornaments have you still to buy? How much profit do you mean to make out of the foolish wives of the scribes and city accountants of Corinth? When in the name of all the gods do you mean to go home and leave me in peace?

It was close to the end of the visit—though at the time Aegisthus had not known when the visit would come to an end—that Polydamian had made the unbelievable revelation, the revelation which had turned the renewal of lovemaking into an impossibility even after the guest was gone. They were sitting—the Master of All the King's Messengers and the relative of his dead adoptive father—alone at midnight in the bedchamber of the host. The visitor had been repeating all day that he knew he was not going to be able to sleep, and he had decided half an hour ago that he would not even try. He looked even more ridiculous than usual with his short-legged, almost malformed nakedness showing here and there through a loosely fastened robe of linen dyed a violent green. He sat cross-legged on a sheepskin carpet in front of his host; the gods had never fashioned him for chairs—the seats, the legs, the arms of them always proved too long. He leaned his draped elbow on his flexed knee and rested his yellowish cheek against the palm of his little hand.

> "A sleepless man may be a bore,
> But still you will not hear him snore"

—so he said, and winked one cloudy eye, and smiled.

Aegisthus did not answer. Instead, he tried to broaden the vista. He had a troubling sense of being boxed in with the little creature and took reassurance from the wideness of his view. The walls of his room—grey stucco studded with brazen nails—were set well apart; there was space enough for a couch, a tripod, three beautiful chairs, and four rugs scattered like islands on the painted floor; the windows were large, and the diaphanous saffron-colored curtains streamed in on a wind that suggested the vastness of the spring night. Yet, once he had looked at all the lamplit openness around him and brought his eyes back to Polydamian's face, he still felt shut up, held down, in need of a breath of air.

"What are you looking for? Not moths this early in the year. Do you see a god or a daemon or something of that sort?" the cousin said.

You have been master of my hours these last ten days, he thought. You have directed my feet, managed my mouth, deprived my member; you have decided where I will go, when I will eat, what I must do without. Then have the grace to leave my eyes in my own charge—let me look at what I please.

"Aegisthus is silent."

"Is that a fault? How should I know what I was looking at? A man thinks, and his eyes rove about."

"And what was it that a man thought about?"

"The curiosity of my cousin is insatiable. So that it will have something to gnaw on, let us say that I thought of a woman—a woman naked except for an onyx pendant and a bracelet."

"A woman Aegisthus desires? Plainly, he has only to reach out his hand for her and he will have her. The gods are with him in all things. He could not have been more fortunate if he had been given his own from the hour he was born. . . ."

He did not listen closely. The image he had evoked in order to torment his visitor was tormenting him instead: the blown curtains were her drapings falling away, his face ached to press against her belly and her thighs.

". . . And indeed it may be better as it is. Had my cousin Aegisthus been in possession of what was his own from the start,

91

he might have taken less delight in it than it gives him now, when it has been rendered back to him in his middle years. If he had not lived a while with the old man in a meaner house, would he take so much pleasure in this one? If he had not once thought himself the inheritor of no more than a merchant's modest means, would he consider himself so blessed in the heritage of Thyestes?"

"Thyestes?" He put down the generative stirring; he blotted out the image of her body; he forced himself to see nothing but the yellowish eyes with their ebony irises—candid yet full of guile. "What has Thyestes to do with it? What is my cousin Polydamian talking about?"

"But surely Aegisthus knows his own parentage. Surely the old man did not keep him in ignorance of what is generally known in Corinth—"

"And what is generally known in Corinth?" He felt an unreasonable impulse to grasp the wrinkled, discolored throat and press his fingers into it: whether to make it deliver its news more quickly or to choke it into eternal silence, he did not know.

"Why, that my cousin Aegisthus is the sole surviving son of Thyestes—a bastard, yes, but the sole surviving son nevertheless—"

"What?"

"They say, too, that the gods have seen to it that he has gotten his inheritance, even though his father did not live to bespeak it for him. Does he not have the finest house in Mycenae, second only to the palace? Is he not Master of All the King's Messengers? Has Fate not seen to it that, though he came here as a stranger, he is addressed as the dear cousin of Agamemnon and Agamemnon's queen? . . ."

And now no room, no palace, not the wide night itself could have been big enough to relieve him of the smothering conviction that he was boxed in. Certain sounds that he had heard recurrently in his dreams: Wild sobbing—his own. A fierce scraping and roaring—the sea going out and coming in. An awful soft gurgling, like water bubbling up through loose earth—a man's breath and voice bubbling up through torn vitals, coming up on a surge of blood. Words—what words? Oh, he had heard them, he had heard them in actuality and afterwards in nightmares, coming out of the foam-flecked stiffening mouth along with the blood: "Blood-vengeance, son of my flesh. Blood-vengeance on Agamemnon, son of Atreus . . ." Had he repeated that while the eyes grew lusterless? Had he sworn it on a sword as he was bidden, and cut his fingers on the blade? The yellow curtains blew across his dream, bellied inward, placed him in the present; and he saw himself as if he were another man, saw himself staring at his own lifted fingers, looking for a scar. The old man had found him on the beach and had taken him thence, knowing well from what regal, bitter seed he had sprung. And when matters had not gone too well with the old man in Corinth—perhaps he too had tried to peddle clay for solid gold—he had brought his foster child back to this place where Fate could use another counter in the game. It was as if his coarse, shrewd face—long buried in a respectable tomb—was nevertheless here in the room. He chuckled, he nodded knowingly, he chewed on the corner of his lip. "Was I not clever?" he said. "Did I not do well to set the son of Thyestes down, well endowed with copper talents and dressed in fine cloth, in the very courtyard of the son of Atreus?"

That night—the last that the guest spent under the roof of the splendid house of the pillars—yielded Aegisthus little more than he had kept stored in some closed chamber of his being since he had been a child. He asked, and he was answered: Yes, the old man had found him on the beach beside the body—bloody and still warm—of a warrior whose shield and cuirass had identified him more or less solidly as Thyestes. Yes, the little lad had cut the fingers of his right hand, probably playing with his father's sword. Yes, the old man had spoken of his origin to others, all of them gone down now to dwell among the thirsty ones. Yes, the

cuirass and the sword were stored in some chest in Corinth—
where, only the gods could say; but if Aegisthus wished them looked
for, he, the cousin, was the man to track them down:

> *"Over the ground or under the ground,*
> *If I cannot find them, they'll never be found."*

He rejected the offer with thanks, not because he did not want
further reason to communicate with and be grateful to this queer
being, though there was some thought of that in the speed of his
rejection. Actually, he knew more, far more, than any blade or
breastplate could give him: knew the red line of sunset over the
sullen and leaden sea, knew the whitening face and the words
that gurgled out of the dying mouth, knew from whence he had
come and what oath he had sworn and where he was destined
to go.

Polydamian took off next day for Corinth in a lumbering chariot,
his gimcrack collection loaded onto three dull mules. But the
heaviness, the dank and unclean oppression that his person had
brought into the mansion was not drawn out with it, was so powerful that—for the first time within his remembrance—Aegisthus in
health used sickness as an excuse and went without fever to his
bed. There he lay, unvisited because he had sent a servant about
to all his friends, even to her, saying that he wanted no visitors,
though in her case the servant had carried the onyx engraved
with his portrait as an assurance of love. All things stopped, and
there was one thing that should not have stopped: he should have
been preparing the mansion for the Spring Festival. Some time
ago she had suggested to him that he open *his* house to the folk
for the celebration this year: by dispensing meat and wine, by
walking sociably among the lesser scribes and the artisans and the
peasants from the surrounding countryside, he would build up a
store of favor that he might need when the tightfisted and dour

official celebrant of the Feast had sacked Troy and come back home.

Two precious days he lay on his couch, neglecting the getting of garlands and the preparation of food, rising only to see to the needs of his body, which in themselves had strangely dwindled, as though the cousin had stricken bowels and bladder with sluggishness. The recollections let out of the dark room in his brain were bad, to be sure; but it was not in them that the worst of it lay. The worst of it was hard to define. He groped after the worst of it in black, smothering night, when dawn showed stone-grey through the weave of the curtains, when sunlight quivered like water or faded and lay pink like a mixture of blood and brine on the stucco wall. And as the definition of the worst of it became plainer and plainer, a strange sort of love, a strange sort of longing imposed itself like a shadow across his reason: he saw, not her whole body and not the moist and tangled triangle of hair that gave promise of the clinging and hospitable cleft, but her breasts. Warm white mounds with the wrinkled nipples of a nursing mother, they lay across his speculations. He shuddered with longing, he was hollow in the chest with an anguished yearning to lay his cold face between them and weep.

On the night of the second day he started out of his sleep like a man who has received a dagger thrust in the back. Knowledge of the worst of it had been given to him in his sleep, and he sat with his legs over the side of the couch and his feet on the cold floor—he sat without moving until sunrise, putting it into words. Fate had used him, he had been used. All that he had believed he had done for himself—rising from abandonment and bastardy to own this house and be the queen's lover and Master of All the King's Messengers—Fate had done to him. He who had thought he had made a subtle pattern of a thousand tied strings—he himself had been only a little piece of string tied passive in

95

Fate's hands. It was not his wit that had pulled him up through the ranks—Fate had pulled him. It was not his member and the charm that he had nurtured in spite of his unfortunate body that had made it possible for him to bind himself to the most magnificent of women—Fate had plunged him into her and knotted the two of them together in order to serve the old curse on the house of Atreus. It would not be by his own power that he would move—if, indeed, he ever moved, he or his bowels or his bladder —to do what must be done considering what had already come to pass: it would be Fate moving him like any other useful piece of human trash to work out the undoing of Agamemnon and the avenging of Thyestes.

And when the understanding was sharp within him—clear and accepted, for when had he rejected a hard actuality?—the inward hollow, the insatiable emptiness, the obsession with her breasts were upon him again, so strong that he was hard put to it not to moan aloud and rouse up the slave who slept on the other side of his door. Where is my manhood? he thought, and tried helplessly to summon it into hardness down there between his legs: it was limp, it would not stir. And how will it be between her and me if it never leaps into life at the sight of her again? he asked himself, and answered himself that there was compassion in her, that she had yearned to be a tender and consoling mother, that there were on her nipples the white scars left by mouths that had sucked too eagerly, that she had said once that she could never have enough of nursing, that even when the milk was gone she longed to nurse and dreamed often that an infant clung there, sucking away, giving itself and her indescribable bliss. . . .

Such unnerving conjectures, since they had nothing to do with the matter, ought to be put away; and he had put them away by the time the sunlight was visible on the wall. He asked himself: Shall I tell her? and he answered himself: No, by no means, and he felt his sick mouth curving into the usual secret and knowing smile. Not to tell her would be the wise way, of course; yet immediately he fell to mocking at his own circumspection. Keep his own council or spread it abroad—it was all one. Whatever he did, however he conducted himself—like a man or like a stricken child—it was no doing of *his*. Fate opened his mouth or clamped it shut according to Fate's will. And that mouth of his, so ready with apt words, stammered as it called the slave. That mouth of his was full of the taste of bile or the taste of a terrible savory stew or the taste of the blood that had bubbled up into Thyestes' mouth and stained the sand.

He resorted to action then simply because inaction was unbearable in the company of such thoughts. He flung himself into his preparations for the Spring Festival as a warrior would fling himself into a battle. He tried to outdo Fate, to be more prodigal and preposterous than Fate could wish in his ordering of flowers to be plucked and woven into garlands, sheep and kids to be slain and flayed and spitted, wine—old and stored for some great never-quite-attained occasion for celebration—to be brought up from the dark cellar under his lordly hall. Fate had designed that he should feed the folk: well, he would feed them until their bowels hung heavy, he would wine them until their bladders ran like everlasting fountains, he would bedazzle them with flowers until they thought they were demigods and went at it—a he and a she coupling in every room, on every hillside, in every doorway, in every patch of shadow cast by the Cyclopean wall.

A morning of hurrying about in the supervision of such duties put his own sluggish body to rights—how far to rights he was not certain because he did not try again to call manhood into fiery hardness: he did not dare, he was too fearful that the limpness would persist, he preferred to sustain himself upon the hope that matters down there had undergone the same happy change which his vitals had profited by. And by noon—when the garden was deflowered and heaped with the bleeding bodies of small beasts

97

still in their skins, when the great hall was almost oppressive with the smell of plucked flowers being bruised and manipulated into crowns and festoons—by noon he felt that he could look her in the face.

"Go to my lady the queen of Mycenae," he said to a little slave girl, "and tell her to come and see what we have done here whenever she can."

"But shall we not first rid the garden of the blood and entrails before we invite my lady the queen?"

"No, no, that is not necessary. My lady is not like you—afraid of a little guts and blood."

"No, surely, but she might pity all the poor lambs."

"True enough. Tell the men to flay them and get them out of the way, and then go and tell her. You are right, my girl. My lady the queen is compassionate."

NINE

THE LITTLE slave girl was welcome at the palace. Clytemnestra, who had been sitting idly with a silver mirror in her hand and contemplating her unmasked and marred beauty before the arrival of the child, gave her a vial of saffron-flower ointment out of sheer relief and said that she would be with the Master of All the King's Messengers early in the afternoon. Such questions as would have probed into the reasons for his neglect she stifled; whatever she wanted to know would be revealed to her in good time; and perhaps, knowing all, she would have no cause to feel herself neglected anymore.

Her morning had been harrowing, and the large sea-green and shrimp-colored chamber had a ravaged look, though really there was little disorder—only her scarlet woolen robe flung across the bottom of her couch, her jewels in a heap on the table before her, and three rejected skirts lying stiff over a carved chair. Her daughter had been here while she was dressing—*that* added to all her other worries. Her daughter had come in, as arrogant in simple white as she had been that evening in poppy red, standing in the middle of the room, refusing to sit down, making a great stir over the celebration of the Spring Festival.

"Is it true, my mother, that you do not mean to feed the folk here in the palace this year in the king my father's name?"

"Certainly it is true. How could I? It is a heavy business arranging and giving such a feast, as you should know from the endless troubles we had with it last year."

"Yet last year we survived the feast, and the palace did not go up in smoke, and everything was in order again in two days' time."

"You forget that your brother was with us then, overseeing the distribution of wine and meat. This year he has chosen to take himself off and hide himself away. I cannot do it alone."

The girl had not countered with the soft thing, the loving thing. The girl had not said, "Let us share this heavy burden and give the feast together, you and I." In her white, enigmatic beauty, with two red stains of anger on her high cheekbones and contempt tightening her untinted lips, she had gone to the window and looked out over the court, as if all her care were for the pigeons feeding there. Her questions she had flung over her shoulder, never turning her face, simply tossing her words in her mother's direction.

"And for that reason the merrymaking that has blessed the house of Atreus these many generations is now to bless and honor the house of Aegisthus?"

"Who told you so?"

"What does it matter? I know that it is so."

"Your uncle and my dear cousin has offered to take this heavy burden from our shoulders, seeing that we are two women alone."

"Had he asked me, I would have rejected his offer."

"He did not ask you. He asked me. So long as Agamemnon is before Troy, *I* am the one to be asked. *You* will be asked only when I am dead and gone."

There had been silence then and long gazing at the pigeons and one thin hand thrust backward so that the ring crowned with the seal and signet had flashed in the morning sun. "My father would wish us to hold the Festival here. My brother would wish it also," the girl had said.

"It will be held in the house of the Master of All the King's Messengers."

"My mother has agreed to that?"

"Yes, surely. I have accepted his generosity."

"Then there will be two feasts—one there and one here."

Protests, complaints, quarrels—these she had expected. But open rebellion and such a counter-proposal she had not anticipated, perhaps because she had not dared to envision it, aching as she had been these many days with the unexplained division from her lover. "I will not celebrate the Spring Festival in my house this year," she had heard herself saying, and had felt herself guilty of a certain mulelike stupidity, had known herself unstrung by her first sharp realization that her daughter's wit was nimbler, keener, more pliable than her own.

"If my mother will not set out a feast, then I myself will set it out."

"Truly? And with what? I will give you nothing. Where will you find the means to buy meat and wine?"

"I will sell some of my trinkets. I have no use for trinkets."

"A fine price you will get for your trinkets in a year of war! Nobody has the wherewithal to buy."

"I will get what I can."

101

"And let us say you get it." Her spirit and her voice had both drawn strength from a sudden upsurge of spite. "Let us say you get some wretched furnishings-forth from what is yours to sell. Say you get half a dozen amphorae of sour wine and a few bedraggled sheep. You can scarcely think that I will let the slaves help you with the preparing and the serving out—"

"If the slaves will not help me, I will do it myself."

"What—slit a sheep's throat? Flay a lamb?" The girl had always been tender and delicate. The girl had always refused to go on the hunts, had been unable to bear the death agonies even of a wild boar.

"Yes, my mother. For the king my father and for my brother Orestes, I will slit and flay with my own hands."

"I would like to see you do it."

"My mother may watch if it gives her pleasure."

"You are a fool, Electra. You count too much on the love of the folk. What did your father give them that they should love him? And if Aegisthus serves fat meat and you serve lean and scrawny cuts, where do you think the folk will take their fare?"

"I do not know, my mother." The hand that flourished the seal and signet had dropped, limp, like a bird transfixed in flight by an arrow. "I do not know whether the folk will choose good or evil, but I will give them the time and the place to choose."

"You will do nothing of the kind."

"I will do what I must."

She will indeed, the queen had thought, watching her straight back moving—regal in its frailty—through the door of the bed-chamber and down the hall. She will indeed. . . . And that worry had been added to all the other ill-assorted things on the rubbish heap of her torment: Is the cousin gone? Is the beloved sick? Now that spring is come, will Orestes cross the eastern waters? What stirred under my girdle? A seed stirring into life? Suppose he has not called me because he no longer desires me. Suppose the very

102

violence of his appetite was bound to turn into distaste. Suppose he already loves me not and I am with child and must stand big-bellied when my husband comes home, with my body and my children to accuse me and none to shield me, my one friend sick of the sight of this marred face. . . .

So she had been thinking when Aegisthus' little slave girl came to invite her to inspect his preparations; and thereafter her happiness on one account was enough to engulf the other tormenting matters. It rose around her like warm water in a bath; it soothed her dry and itching skin; it loosened her tight muscles; it allowed her to shed a few easy tears. And when these were dried she called her Cretan wonder-worker to her and was as fair as ever in purple and white by the time they had dragged the last slain lambs from his garden. At the last instant, before she left her room, she changed her white shoes for black ones. Why mar good doeskin with blood?

She found him, much as he had always been, standing in the great hall of his mansion and directing the slaves who were making garlands out of hyacinth and anemone. It was the overpowering smell of spring flowers rather than the sight of him that oppressed her. If he was somewhat pale, if there were dark markings like bruises under his eyes, she had often seen him so: he was a man frail of flesh, and she had learned not to fear for him, to fix her attention and nourish her pride rather on the will that invariably overmastered the frailty. He kissed her hand with lingering tenderness, allowing his lips to move over veined wrist and full forearm in spite of the presence of the garland-weavers, who kept their eyes on their cloyingly sweet labors with admirable consideration. She was about to make the rounds of the room with him, commending his taste and his servants' skill, when a slave of her own— an old man thin and bald and out of breath—came through his open portal and addressed her with an urgency that excused his waiver of ceremony. "My queen and my lady," he said, stopping

103

between two young girls whose laps were filled with flowers, "one has come to us from the eastern coast with news from Troy."

"What news?" She stood against her lover's side and shoulder. Though she was heavier than he, though this afternoon he looked more than usually slight, pale as he was and carelessly dressed in a short grey tunic, she set her weight against him as if he had been a tower.

"News that Hector has been slain."

"Hector has been slain?"

"So says this traveler, my lady."

"No, truly?" Her agitation came partly from the terrible fact that news which would call up rejoicing in the whole city could call up in her nothing but dread, and partly because she had felt the faintest of tremors in the body of him whom she leaned upon.

"The traveler is certain of it. It was seen by the eyes of his brother and told to him very circumstantially, my lady. The Shield of Troy went down at the hand of the hero Achilles, and this same hero vented his anger upon the corpse, dragged it in fury nine times around the Trojan walls—"

"Then Troy will fall and the war will be over—"

She had not been able to keep the mournfulness out of her voice. The flower-twining slaves had all looked up, less in wonderment than in comprehension and pity. As for the old man, who had belonged first to Atreus and then to Agamemnon—there was a tinge of reproof in his tone when he said, "Indeed, my lady and my queen, Troy *will* fall and the war *will* be over and my lord the king will ride back into his Citadel crowned with the laurels of victory."

"Is the word of the traveler to be depended upon?" Her question hung plaintive and futile over the silence that neither maid nor man dared break with a triumphal shout or a clapping of hands.

104

"If my queen and my lady harbors doubts, let her examine him. She need not come at once. He is weary, and we should keep him through the night."

"Yes, surely. Feed him well and prepare a couch for him under the galleries. Has my daughter spoken with him?"

"Yes, my lady. The princess Electra saw to his needs with her own hands, thereby giving him honor in return for his news. She sits with him now while he takes meat and wine and bread."

"Good." The tower was firm again behind her. Her voice was capable of cheer, false in her own ears but convincing enough to permit the listeners to nod and smile. "Tell him I will come before sundown to set his evening meal before him. Tell him he will have gifts from me, a crimson cloak and a young roan stallion. Go now and bid the Steward of the House give every slave of Agamemnon's a double ration tonight at table and three measures of wine. Here is my ring: take it to the Steward with my word."

For some incomprehensible reason—perhaps bodily feebleness, perhaps the dullness of an old brain—the ancient slave did not come to take the ring but stood where he had stood from the beginning, his white and knotted hands hanging loose at his sides, close to the lustrous hair of the flower-burdened girls. It was Aegisthus who took the ring and carried it across the room to him; and for the moment while she was without her prop it seemed to her that either she or the floor on which she stood was reeling and pitching, that she must surely fall. But then he returned and was there to be rested against once more, and the old man was on his way back to the palace, and the young slaves had made the proper happy murmur and were again absorbed in their fragrant business.

"Step into the garden with me and see how I have robbed my flower beds for the delight of the folk," Aegisthus said, and took her by the hand, and led her past heaped blossoms and lowered

105

eyelids and young bent heads into a garden robbed indeed—stripped of flowers and trampled by flayers and vacant and hot in the afternoon sun.

There was a bench new-coated with white stucco in the as yet scanty shade of a leafing plane tree—a bench so white as to assail her eyes, so glaring that she felt relief in blotting out its brightness by sitting down on it with the shadows of the wind-turned fresh foliage moving over her hands and knees. She did not wish to look at these fluttering shadows or at the trodden turf with its brownish stains. She did not wish to raise her head and look at the sky either—to look up was to invite dizziness, and to be dizzy might mean to be with child.

"Come, take heart," he said, seating himself beside her. "What is, is. What will come, will come. And when it comes we will meet it together. And until it comes there are yet many more nights when I can lie with my head on your breasts."

Something in that undid her spirit: it shivered like the shadow of the shaken leaves; it ran all to talk, wild talk, loud enough to make him lay his finger over his lips. She told him how there would be no more lying together—none of that, none of that. She told him how, if his seed had not already taken root within her, it was no doing of his or hers but only because some god had persisted in saving her from her own heedlessness. She asked him what he meant to do if Agamemnon's homecoming found her with the proof of her madness as big as a melon in her belly. Electra knew, Orestes knew, the slaves knew, every potter and muleteer in Mycenae knew. No more of that, no more, no more—

And with a gentleness, a willingness to listen to reason that he had never shown before, he took her hand and held it to his face, he kissed it in mute hunger as if he could feed his mouth on it, he told her that she was wise, that however she would have it, so it would be. "You speak," he said, "as if there were only one pleasure and I were demanding it of you at the risk of your life.

106

Have I demanded it? Am I myself a potter or a muleteer that knows only one means of delight: to spill my seed into your womb? There are other ways whereby I can be blessed and you can be satisfied, and every one of them is as gratifying to me as the way that has been our use. May the gods undo me if I do not see that it is even better with you than it has ever been."

She barely had time to wonder at him—she was so taken up with wondering at herself. Stricken as she was by the terrible triumphal news, harried as she was by Electra's open arrogance, sick as she was with the imagined smell of flowers and with the sight of a bit of lamb's entrail that lay like a long pink worm half covered with flies near the toe of her shoe, she could not keep herself from thinking of those new pleasures that he proposed: With what strokings, what kissings, what light searches and slowly increasing pressures did he mean to fill their nights? "Ah, blessed gods," she said, letting herself rest languid against the trunk of the plane tree, as if his hands and mouth were already at her, "ah, blessed gods, I would rather die on your couch before he comes home."

"I also."

"Truly? Then let us find some numbing poison and die even so."

"No, no. Dead, we do not have each other. Dead, we are clods of earth and neither touch nor tremble. The death-spasm is not the love-spasm—that is a dream."

"Then what will we do?"

"Let me think of it. Give me time for thinking. My brain has been hammered first by a foolish visitor and then by sickness and now by this word of the slaying of Hector. I am dull in the head. I can think of nothing but what a carnival we will make of the nights that are before us—"

"I too can think of no other thing. Except—wait—I have jewels and talents of copper and bronze. You have them also. We

107

could take whatever we could carry and go forth from this city—"

"Where?"

"Anywhere. To Paphlagonia, to Egypt. To some small place in Crete or in Cyprus where there is no palace and no citadel. There we might find ourselves a little house and say we are exiles from Tiryns or Pylos. Who would know?"

"Yet I do not think we will flee."

"What?"

"I said I do not think we will flee. Something—Fate or one of the gods—will hold us here—"

"I never knew that you believed in Fate." She had been staring through all their talk at the length of entrail, and was inordinately appalled now that no part of its pinkish slickness could be seen, for it had vanished completely under the squirming swarm that buzzed audibly in the stillness of the spring afternoon.

"Whatever I believe, what good would it do to flee?" he said in weariness. He, too, was resting his back against the plane tree. He, too, was saving his eyes from the glare: his eyelids were almost shut, his face was pale, and she thought that so he would look, drained and discolored, in death. "Do you think he would leave us in peace?" he said, incongruously smiling. "Do you think a son of the house of Atreus could receive such an affront and let it rest? Atreus answered such an affront by serving up two babies in a stew. We have no children, and we will have none—as I have told you, I will see to that. It is our own flesh, then, that he will have for his vengeance, and he will find it no matter where we carry it. No, it is useless, it is foolishness to think that we can flee."

They sat silent then for a while, she with her eyes upon him, watching his lifeless face. Then suddenly his eyelids quivered, the corners of his mouth stirred, and he leaped up and shook himself as a dog will, and took her by both her hands. "I have a thought— a different thought," he said.

"What thought?"

108

"Come inside and I will tell you. Why should you sit here? There is an abomination near your foot—why should you sit and stare at it and sicken yourself?"

She let him pull her up and went with him into his mansion. The great hall was empty now of slaves. The garlands draped the four pillars surrounding his hearth and hung over the doorways, and he stopped to look with admiration at the finished work, and she could not bear to tell him what was on the tip of her tongue: that her daughter would set up another Spring Festival to outface his, would do whatever could be done to draw the folk away from this prepared room.

"Sit down," he said, drawing two chairs close together beside the blackened, empty hearth. Spring had come, and the ashes looked pale and incongruous in the strong sun of spring. When autumn is here again, she thought, who will make a fire on this hearth, and who will sit and whisper by that fire?

"Look," he said, sitting close to her with his elbows propped on his parted knees and his long hands hanging down loosely between, "what I have thought of is no light matter. The slaves are nearby. Say yes or no, but do not raise your voice."

"Must you warn me? Am I a wild girl given to weeping and laughing fits?"

"No, not commonly. But you were wild enough in the garden a moment ago."

She remembered it and accepted his chiding. Indeed, it was somehow good to be chidden. If she had missed anything in him today, it was his easy man's assumption that she recognized and even feared the vigor of his will.

He kept his head down and seemed to address himself to the design painted on the stucco-covered floor, a zigzag pattern done in orange on white, one of those dizzying patterns at which she was afraid to stare. She did not dare to sit at her ease and breathe deeply, either: though the flower smell was not so strong now—

the blossoms were no longer being bruised and broken and had stopped bleeding an excess of fragrance—she found the air still a little heavy, still oversweet.

"Why should we die?" he said, cracking his loose knuckles. "Let another die instead."

"Agamemnon?"

"Who else?"

She closed her hands over the carved arms of the chair so hard that she knew her palms were taking on the print from the chiseled ivory. "The gods may yet see to that for us," she said. "The war is not yet over. The city is not yet taken. The fact that Hector is slain does not mean that the Trojans will open their gates. There will be battles. There may yet be many battles. Not all those who are encamped in the Trojan plain will board their ships and come home."

"We must not trust to that. Kings have other men's chests to shield them."

"But who would lay hands on—"

"The sacred scepter-bearing issue of Atreus? I. I myself."

"How? Where?"

"That is no great matter. Wherever and however seems best. At a festival. At a banquet, somewhere and sometime when he and those who attend him are gathered so that we can take them all together. He is for my carving. The rest can fall at the hands of those who will profit by it when we sit on the throne."

It seemed to her that what he was saying he spoke by rote. Now and again, at the Festivals of the Horse and the Lady, boys and girls would run through ancient ritual lines, speaking at each other in a language so often repeated that everybody caught the meaning of it though there was barely a word in it that anybody but a priest could understand. So this exchange seemed to her, going on in muted and unexpressive voices—foreknown, obvious,

110

and meaningless. She sighed and drew her hand across her face. "Go on. I am listening," she said.

"What is there to go on to? I have said it all."

"What of the folk? Will they sit by and gape at it and then go peaceably about their daily business?"

"Will they rise up in the first month of peace and make a new havoc for the sake of Agamemnon? He has starved them and bled them and dragged the best of their sons across the eastern waters to fetch Helen home. Do you think they love him with a consuming love?"

"No. You are right. But what of the children?"

"The children are children. Once we have the throne, we can do with them what we will."

"One of them—the most dangerous one, the lad—one of them, Aegisthus, is gone beyond our reach."

"I will find him. I have looked, but I have not looked hard enough. Over the ground or under the ground, if I cannot find him he cannot be found."

"What?"

"Nothing. My foolish guest, my cousin Polydamian, was forever making rhymes, and I too seem to have fallen into that foolishness."

He laughed, still hunching over and staring at the floor, and for an instant this unimaginable conversation took on for her the shape and color of actuality. Loudly—loudly enough to make him glance up at her in warning, rolling up his eyes without raising his head—she said, "You would not touch the boy? You would not do away with the girl?"

"Not if they bear it as the folk will surely bear it. Not if they marry as they should, and take themselves and their portions off to other citadels. Is he not bound to Hermione? Let him inherit from Menelaos."

111

"And she?"

"What can she do?"

She thought, and did not say it, that she could sell jewels and buy small beasts and wine to make a Spring Festival in her father's name. She envisioned, and did not mention, the grey eyes, level and hard, under the straight blond eyebrows. "Nothing. You are right. She is a woman," she said.

"Oh, as to that"—he laughed again, senselessly—"you too are a woman. And if it is predestined that we sit side by side on the throne, I will be more than content if the land is ruled again according to the old law. I am weary now, and after such doings as we speak of I will be yet more weary. It is not that I wish to rule. It is not that I wish for anything. It is only because—no, now, you have your reason, and I have my reason, and we two together, we have our reason. Can you come to me tonight?"

She did not answer at once. For the first time, she had been incapable of reading what lay behind his words, and it was unaccountably frightening to her, it was as if her life were cracking up like an ill-made piece of pottery between her hands. "How can I come to you? Have you forgotten that there is a traveler with us?" she said.

"The traveler is probably weary and will long to sleep. Sit with him while he eats the evening meal so that he can boast to his grandchildren that he has been at table with a queen. But afterwards, I beg you—"

When had he said: "I beg you"?

"—afterwards come to me. I will not give you children. I will give you only those other pleasures we spoke of in the garden. Come, for otherwise it will be a very heavy night for me."

"Yes, and for me also," she said, and heard with wonder that there was contempt in her voice. "Be sure of it, I will come."

TEN

THOUGH ELECTRA had shown a joyful face at the news of the slaying of Hector, she had been as appalled to hear it as her mother and her mother's paramour. Those threats which she had been pushing off into the far future had come close enough all in a moment to breathe upon her; the noose was lying slack about her neck, and it was no longer a matter of years, it was barely the matter of a season until the knot might be jerked tight. "The closer the day of my father's return"—so she thought, serving the traveler—"the less time will be left before the two of them try to stiffen my talking tongue in death."

Had the tidings not come, her move to outface her mother in the business of the Spring Festival would have seemed to her prudent and courageous, the first in what was to be a series of attempts to win the folk to her cause. But now that the queen and Aegisthus were warned of the imminence of the king's arrival, this Spring Festival had become a reckless piece of gambling, a risk of everything on one throw of the dice. She had set up an occasion which could be her undoing: a few days hence the folk might well show her enemies that her death would scarcely provoke a public murmur. And very likely they would furnish just such proof, drawn away from her meager fare by the savor of Aegisthus' spitted lambs, the thought of Aegisthus' fine old wine.

For why, she asked herself for the first time, should they honor my father? He has taken their sons and dragged them away to war. He has bent their backs with the mining of copper and the beating out of armor and weapons. He has leveled their groves for the fashioning of chariots and ships. Never in twenty years of drought did he forego his king's share of their thin harvests. Never when the men of the Arcadian hills came down against the vulnerable lower town beneath the Citadel did he speak of enlarging the circuit of the wall. Nor can I think that the folk will come to my feast out of fear of what he will do when he returns. What more can he do in vengeance than he has already done in indifference? Nothing much, since he cannot kill them: when he comes back he will need them still to hammer and chop and carve and weave and dig the stubborn ground.

It was true that certain signs in her favor had been given to her when she went bartering on the day before the Festival, taking her leather bag of jewels into the sprawling, slanting lanes of the lower town. No man, even in a year of war, had tried to take advantage of her need, her haste, or her helplessness. Every man with whom she had dealt in the selling of her trinkets or the buying of her provisions had dealt with her generously. "So you, too, will give a feast, my lady?" they had said; and she had answered, "Yes, a poorer one than that which will be given by the Master of All the King's Messengers, but the Lady has bidden me give it in my father's and brother's names." Whereupon, out of their poverty, they had over-reached what she had expected, adding a lamb here and a kid there, letting the measure of flour flow over the brim, striking the amphorae to make certain that only full ones should be sent along after her. "Add that for your father's sake—he has been a harsh king but a just one," said one of them. And another said, "Take this also for the sake of your brother Orestes, who was never niggling when he dispensed barley to the poor."

It was true also that she had found two partisans among the officers of the court, where she had expected to find none. As she passed through the royal meadowland with her unruly prizes around her, the Overseer of the King's Herds had recognized and saluted her, though she wore just such a short brown tunic as a peasant or an artisan might have worn on such an errand and had knotted a kerchief over her hair. "Here, add these to your flock," the old man said, releasing five of her father's kids and three of his lambs. "Consider them a gift from me. Say they are what the foxes or the eagles might have carried off if I had not been about your father's business day and night." His kindness had sustained her, had given her the courage to drive her findings into an empty killing-pen behind the palace, had even endowed her with the strength to look at what milled around her feet and butted against her bare shins as though they were not living creatures, but things. For I will have to take the knife to them, she thought, and if I come to know them by their spots or their sprouting horns or the marks on their moist muzzles, I will surely weep.

She had shut them in and was feeding them household prov-ender when the Steward of the House had come out of the back entrance and vaulted lightly over the wooden gate into the pen. He was a man who had seen forty summers, but he was lithe and tall. In the house, as befitted his office, he went about in long robes, white or crimson, holding his head high, setting his hawk-face in a look of perpetual preoccupied disdain. But here he too wore a tunic like a peasant's, and his hard face was angularly and sardonically merry, and she was not afraid to look at his long legs, shaggy with dark hair—they seemed less like a man's legs than like a centaur's.

"I did not think you would do it," he said.

"Neither did Aglaia. But I have done it. Flour and wine will come after me in a wagon. I myself must unload and store and knead and kill and flay. My mother says she will not grant me slaves."

"Your mother," said the Steward, "is gone forth to spend the day and the evening with her old aunt."

That he had omitted the titles, that he had spoken of mother and old aunt as if the women of the breed of Atreus were to him like other women—this was disrespectful, but it was somehow promising. She looked at him with a boldness born of her enterprise. She looked straight and without uneasiness into the black eyes under the dark and jutting eyebrows.

"You did well with your dealings," he said. "I would not have thought that your jewels would have brought you so much."

"Some added a beast in recognition of my father's justice. Others let the measure flow over because of the kindness of my brother Orestes."

"And none because of the courage that sent you out trading, my lady and my mistress?"

"I do not think so. They did not tell me so."

"Then let me say what they did not dare to say: You are a brave daughter and a loving sister. Because of that, though your mother has strictly forbidden it, I will send two slaves out here to kill and flay tonight and cut and spit tomorrow, and I will take the matter entirely upon my own head."

116

"The Steward is kind."

"Also, I will send three slaves to knead and bake."

"The Steward is very kind indeed."

"Also, from my own household I will give raisins and prunes and figs, and such garlands as my garden will yield—"

She had begun to grow hot, standing bare-armed and bare-legged under the steady black gaze. A drop of sweat had risen under the kerchief and was coursing down her nose, and she was glad to hide her face behind the hand that wiped it away. "Will you not be in my mother's disfavor for what you do for me?" she said.

"Yes, doubtless. And before the traveler arrived I might not have been so heedless. But your mother will dispense her displeasure a little less openhandedly now—since Hector is slain, she will want more friends and fewer enemies."

"And the slaves that help me—will they not be beaten?"

"Very probably. Therefore I will send men."

"Do so, good Steward. The men can bear the lash better than the girls."

"I will do so, but not entirely for your reason. Sending men will give me less trouble, for it will be a small matter to find a few lads in this household who will be willing to take the lash for the princess Electra." His eyes hid themselves behind their lids. His face took on a courtly mask, and his centaur body in its tunic stood as formally erect as if it had been draped in the usual crimson or white. "Not only because she has a courageous heart," he added. "Also because there are many who find her very fair."

Having so said, he bowed and left her dazed by her surprise and by the bright sunlight shining on the backs of the moving beasts, and agitated by something—she knew not what—that dimmed her eyes with tears. She had wished with a great hunger to believe him. For a brief time she *had* believed him and had wondered which of the slaves would give their backs to be bruised

117

because bruises carried for her sake would be sources of sweetness and reasons for pride. Then she had remembered how it had always been at the Spring Festivals, how the eyes of men had fastened on her mother and Iphigenia, how her face had been pelted only by flowers badly aimed, how the shouts that had sent up her name had always been isolated and weak. He uses me, he flatters me, she told herself. He ingratiates himself with me—to my shame because I am fool enough to believe him—since Hector is slain and Troy will fall and my tongue will serve him better with Agamemnon than the tongue of my mother. And who stands in need of his flattery—he with his hairy legs and his beaked nose? Who would want her body stripped and handled in the minds of slaves?

Then the spring day had seemed less lovely to her and her morning's triumph less gratifying. Walking through the pen to the back entrance through which the Steward disappeared, she had vented her bitterness on the beasts, had shoved them this way and that. All tender and tear-evoking thoughts—even the thought of how these dumb creatures lived and enjoyed their provender and were soon to be slain and skinned and turned into meat—she had put from her. I did not go trading and herding this morning to buy myself the admiration of the Steward or the love of slaves, she had thought. I went for the sake of the king my father, I went for the sake of my brother Orestes. What I did I did to challenge a traitor and his wanton, not to be lied to, not to be told that I am fair. . . .

So, during the remainder of the day, she did not tally up her gains. Her gains were drowned, and remained so until the evening of the Festival, in the old soreness and the old shame. In the end she was not even glad that the heaviest labor had been lifted from her: in laboring she could have spent her fear; and fear had invaded her, had taken over her whole body, had made her hands unsteady and incapable, her ears so alert that any sound struck

118

them like a slap, her pulse so undependable that it hastened and halted and trembled, her head numb within and given without to a crawling as of countless ants in and out among the roots of her hair. Early on the evening of the feast she had so convinced herself that Aegisthus' mansion would be peopled with servants and her own home utterly emptied of them that she did not believe what she saw when she went up to her bedchamber to dress. The Steward of the House was standing erect in crimson in his usual place at the door, a score of male and female slaves were laying out food and putting the last touches to the garlands, and the wife of the Captain of the King's Guardsmen—a hard, lean woman in a blue and green skirt that shimmered darkly like the skin of a snake—was being covertly directorial about the restoration of a toppled pyramid of fruit. Something had come to pass, some change had come about, but she was too agitated to wonder at it. In her mind, she had seen her Spring Festival as poor and unpatronized, and nothing could rouse in her the faintest hope that it would be otherwise.

The day had been warm and sultry, and the sun was going down in a mist, dispersing a dull redness like fever through the streets and over the roofs of the Citadel. Her bedchamber was invaded by it; the drawn curtains were pinkish, with streaks of red showing through where the weave was thin; Aglaia sat like an idol with the glow upon her; everything copper in the room burned like fire. She stopped at a small low table and drank a tall gobletful of wine, more than was her habit, but she felt the need of it to nerve her for the Festival. On the couch, on top of the tawny lion-skin coverlet, lay what her nurse had chosen as the proper dress for one who celebrated the Spring Festival in the names of absent ones: a stiff white skirt, a white jacket embroidered with a fine gold tracery of iris, and a modest crown.

Modest—subdued and modest—such to Aglaia's mind was her proper attitude, and she rebelled against it from the start. She went over to the couch, picked up the jacket, and flung it down again. "How is it that you did not choose a brown mourning robe for me while you were about it?" she said.

The slave did not answer to the point. She sat unmoving, her hands clasped around her knees, the knotted veins showing purple, their knuckles shining white in the strange glare. "Did you stop long enough to see what was afoot down in the great hall?" she asked. "Did you understand that your mother seems to have relented? At any rate, she has left you the Steward of the House and some twenty slaves."

"How do you know they stayed at her bidding?"

"The Steward told me so."

"Why would she give such an order?" She took up the stiff skirt, looked at it in scorn, and dropped it to the floor. "She told me she would give me nothing—whatever I did I was to do alone."

"And are you sorry that she has changed her orders?"

The question maddened her. She was, in all truth, very sorry, and the wine almost permitted her to say so. She had liked it better, much better, when she and the Steward and a few slave boys had stood ready for open rebellion. She did not speak, only cast a disparaging look upon the unimpressive crown.

"Your mother is quick to rage—not so quick as you or my lord the king, but quick nevertheless. She is also—unlike the two of you—quick to cool and to listen to the voice of reason. Doubtless she has said to herself that she will not make open war with you tonight. Bear yourself circumspectly, hold your feast as one who does a duty rather than as one who fights a battle, and tomorrow you and she will still be able to speak to each other. While there is speech and decency between you, you are safe, and you and she may yet make peace."

"I want no peace."

"That is plain enough."

"I will not wear these suppliant's rags that you have laid out

120

for me. Besides, I do not mean to walk among the folk with bared breasts."

"You will wear what you will wear. You are Agamemnon's daughter—and if there is a noose for your neck, I have no doubt that you will wear that, too. What shall I lay out for you now?"

She had intended to wear green, an inoffensive color—neither the yellow of unseemly happiness nor the red of royalty and revolt. But now a poisonous anger, spawned of terror and bafflement, made her say, "That poppy-colored thing. That, and gold shoes and a tall crown."

Aglaia crossed the room in stiff rage, gathered up the white things with one angular sweep of her withering arm, and carried them over to the carved chest. There was silence while she laid them by and got out the others, silence in which the wine tingled and the day's heat seemed to grow more thick and oppressive. The slave dragged up the scarlet robe and held it in front of her, so that it looked shameful and ridiculous with her veined and calloused feet below it and her bony, world-weary face above. "This?" she said.

"That."

"If I remember rightly, you wore this the evening when you came to swords' points with your mother and your Uncle Aegisthus—"

"So I did."

"It is neither seemly to wear red to your Spring Festival nor wise to wear this particular robe, considering what remembrances it will call up. If your mother makes a gesture of peace in your direction, why should you wave this red rag in her face?"

"Because I choose to wear it. Bring it here."

Aglaia brought it, handling it as charily as though the cloth had been smeared like Medea's gift to Creusa with a poison that would break into flame at a touch. "Take it then," she said, thrusting it toward her mistress. "Take it and put it on, you poor witless fool."

She stripped, breathless with agitation and hot with the wine, eager to feel the coolness of the air on her dry skin. But the air was not cool, nor was the tepid water with which Aglaia sprinkled her, nor the sun-warmed linen towel with which she dried herself. Like some stupid line, some obsessive musical phrase, a single thought kept repeating itself in her numb head: Summer, like the death of Hector, is with us a little too soon. . . . "Get me a better crown, a very high one," she said, once she had girdled in the red robe and stepped into her golden shoes.

"Has my lady forgotten that she sold most of her crowns? She has no crown higher or better for insulting her mother than this."

She looked appalled at the top of the narrow table where the poor remainders of her splendor lay—was she indeed losing her wits that she could have forgotten so weighty a matter? If she were, or if the wine were working in her, she would not falter for such a reason, would not let Aglaia guess her state. "Then get me a proper crown from the chamber of my sister Iphigenia. She has one that is very high," she said.

"From the chamber of Iphigenia? Are you drunken with wine?"

"If I am, it is no affair of yours. On my fifteenth birthday, my father gave me permission to drink as I choose. Go as I told you and bring me the tallest crown."

"Why should I ask for a lash on my old back?"

"You will not be beaten." Her tongue was a little thick. "I will take the matter upon my own head."

And when Aglaia had returned, when the tawny hair had been built up in three tiers and the crown had been bound fast to the highest tier with leather thongs, when the lips had been stained with berry juice and various small ornaments had been pinned here and there—an octopus, a spiral, a butterfly—there was yet one more argument.

"Surely," said Aglaia, "you do not mean to go among the folk wearing that ring."

122

"What ring?"

"Your father's seal and signet."

She looked at it and drew her other hand across the back of her neck where the tightness of heat and wine and fear and anger had made a knot as big as the egg of a bird. "How can I take it off? I never take it off. I cannot leave it lying here in the bed-chamber," she said.

"Give it to me. I will carry it for you."

For an instant the blur lessened and it seemed to her that it might be well to put the ring into Aglaia's keeping. To wear it was to say to the folk: Royalty is with me, power is with me; those who celebrate the Spring Festival at the pillared mansion are usurpers, and their hospitality is illegitimate, and their prayers and sacrifices are mockeries in the sight of the gods. She was playing with the ring, she had gone so far as to slip it over her knuckle when she saw through the weave of the curtain Aegisthus' festal torches being carried into the street. "My father gave this ring to my brother, and my brother gave it to me, and I will hold it so tight that even in death those who want it will be forced to cut off my fingers," she said, and went without further speech into the narrow sun-reddened corridor and down the broad, hot stairs.

There was a certain sweetness to the first hour of her Spring Festival; it would have been sweetness untainted if she had not defied Aglaia and dressed herself outrageously, and she knew as much. Those who came early to the formal court of reception— a paved area that stretched under the murky rose-red sky from the palace to the very edge of the southern gorge—came not to make themselves drunken nor to join a rebellion nor to find themselves partners for the wild spasm of loving for which the Lady granted license that night. They were the very old and the very young, come with small presents for the reigning house whose harshness they either wished to forget or had not yet experienced; and she was aware that the barbaric splendor in which she had decked herself worked against their need to transform her into a cool and gentle dream. Before the heat of the day had subsided, they had walked a long way uphill from their little houses in the lower town; the clothes on their backs, their poor best, were soaked with sweat, and their gifts of flowers wilted in their hands. They wanted water chiefly, and she ordered the Steward to see that three great copper cauldrons were brought out and filled with the sweet and holy water of the spring Perseia; but the water soon grew warm and its surface reflected the hot sky, so that they drank without much satisfaction.

In addition to their drooping blossoms they carried up to her samples of the crafts by which they lived: small and sorry jars made of thick pottery or roughly carved from soft stone, kitchen knives, wood boxes, mats of plaited reeds, single beads of glass, balls of linen thread dyed yellow and purple and green. Thinking how ill these offerings would fit into the grandeur of the palace, thinking how vast a breach there was between their lives and hers, she flushed and felt her forehead dampen. A kind of fierce pathos entered into the gifts and made them vulnerable and precious, so that she was tormented all the while she talked with them by a fear that something they had brought might be carelessly destroyed or treated by a servant with contempt.

"Now that Hector is fallen," said a very old man, "my princess need not fear for her father much longer."

"How beautiful my lady's hair is," said an ancient woman. "It is just as they say—the very color of the royal beast of the house of Atreus."

Children, less rigid in their Festival manners than their elders, crowded in upon her. One, a brown lad emaciated like the rest of them after years of war and drought, took a fold of her scarlet skirt and held it against his face as if he could draw magic and nourishment into his drab, starved life out of the cloth.

124

"Come here, you little dog," said his grandmother. "You may not touch the princess."

"Oh, but he may, he may," she said, feeling the sting of tears in her eyes. And she bent over him quickly and kissed his sweaty curls so fiercely that she frightened him with her need to give and receive some show of bodily love.

They were a diffident and orderly crowd, taking only small slices of the lamb, dividing among three and four out of politeness a piece of bread intended for one, asking "May I have it?" before they put their fingers to the dried fruit. They wandered in small groups into the palace—the aged ones staring in awe at the garlanded pillars, the children touching such surfaces as their palms had never known: carved ivory, polished marble, bright bronze and crystal, alabaster, unbelievably delicate cloth. Watching them from the doorway, she remembered an old prophecy: the offspring of Heracles were fated to come down out of the hills some day by the thousands and to avenge the wrongs that had been done to their heroic ancestor so thoroughly that no child would be left alive in its swaddlings, no stone standing upon another stone. It came upon her then like a stab under the ribs that her father's absence was no private grief; she was not the only one whom he could shield from a violent death. And in a passion of concern and tenderness for these his neglected flock, she went about among them serving them food that they could not reject in their shyness or mannerliness since it was pressed upon them by a royal hand; she put slivers of meat into the moist mouths of children. "If you cannot eat it tonight, take it home and have it tomorrow," she said to many an ancient artisan and peasant; and her poppy-colored dress was dribbled with drippings and her fingers were sticky from the fruit.

In the space of an hour all these first-comers had departed. They did not pass through the side entrance of the great hall and cross the smaller court where she had seen her mother walk veiled under the moon. They did not go to eat the good meat and drink the aged wine of the Master of All the King's Messengers in the house across the cobbled street. When she asked them—for their own sakes, since she wished them to be filled at any cost to herself—whether they would not honor the second feast, they shook their heads and started toward the ramp up which they had come, all of them making the same excuse: the Spring Festival was really a feast for those in their prime, who could drink and roister through the night; the old ones were weary and the young ones must be put to bed so that their mothers and fathers could walk up in turn and receive their share at the princess's hands.

She saw when they were gone that others in splendid clothes had come in through the side entrance—doubtless from Aegisthus' feast—to lend their presences to the Festival being given in the names of the absent ones. In addition to the wife of the Captain of the King's Guardsmen, there was the Captain himself, burly, ruddy, and somewhat drunken; since his lady was noted for her infidelities, he plainly saw no reason to subdue his own whims and was laying hands on every comely slave-girl that got into his path. There were the doddering Chief Priest of the Lady, half a dozen gallants, the Keeper of the King's Archives, two young wives without their husbands, the son and daughter-in-law of the Overseer of the King's Herds, and five or six others whose names and titles the wine and the heat and the sudden accession of grief for the folk had driven out of her head. So they had come to her. . . . She stopped near a marble table and examined her reflection; she straightened the tall crown, put a loose strand of hair into place, and permitted herself a malicious smile.

It occurred to her then that she might cross the great hall, step into the smaller court, and see what sort of crowd had gathered in the house of the pillars. If it was a large crowd, then the adulterers might do what they would with her; if it was a small one, they might distrust their power and stay their hands. The issue—driven out of her thoughts earlier by her first visitors—was so plain to her now, the urgency of her case was so sharply upon her, that she stopped on her way to draw some steadying dullness from another long draught of wine. As she set the goblet down she saw in the mingled red of the evening and the yellow of the newly lighted torches an image of her brother so immediate that she believed for an instant he actually stood before her: he looked at her sternly, sighed deeply, and shook his head. In the matter of drinking, he himself was abstemious, and twice within her remembrance he had wrested a goblet from her, saying, "No, now, you have taken enough." His image also she outfaced, though it was dear. You have left me alone, with evil and the threat of death on my hands, she thought. I must take my strength where I can find it, and where can I find it except in wine?

When she came into the lesser court, followed at a distance by the Steward of the House, she saw that the red sky was paling, though there was still more than sufficient light for seeing and being seen. She took no measures to hide herself. She came clear of the clumps of laurel and the massive columns and found herself looking, across an empty street, straight into her mother's face. Only courtiers stood behind the ample figure in its pale drapings —only courtiers and a few of the fifty scribes in the king's service; *that* group was not roughened and darkened by the poor clothes and leathery faces of the folk; and in her joy to see it her body stiffened and straightened and her look turned level and arrogant. The queen half raised her full white arm in greeting, then let it fall and shrugged and turned aside. She had seen the haughty look, the seal and signet, the poppy-colored robe, and Iphigenia's crown—she had seen enough. Laughing as it was her way to laugh whenever shame was put upon her, she laid her arm around the back of one of her ladies and disappeared into the shadow of the columns, her veils fluttering behind her—fled into that vile cav-

127

ern of evil, ran to her goatsbeard, her spindle-shanks, her fellow-coupler, just as she had done on that other sickening night.

"Come back into the main court, my lady and my princess," said the Steward of the House. "More of the folk have come to greet you." And he held out his hand to her, so that she knew she seemed to him neither safe in her isolation nor steady on her feet.

Others had come indeed. The great hall and the reception court were milling with them, and they brought no sweetness with them. These were of the middle generation who knew the house of Atreus for what it was and laid their bets as men lay bets on runners and wrestlers, after a shrewd comparison of muscle and bone. The first one to address her was a hearty peasant, and he looked at her—looked through the thin scarlet fabric—with narrowed eyes. "The goat eats well tonight, eh, my lady and my princess?" he said. "They tell me there are fifty spitted lambs over there and wine both red and yellow, none of it less than seven years old. But no matter how the goat stuffs himself, the lion will be stronger in the end, I know it well. For that reason I have chosen to eat with the she-cub, though the Lady knows that the house of Atreus was never too squeamish about what sort of fare they offered to the poor."

"I have offered whatever I could out of my own poverty," she said, and stared him down, and heard his rough commendation of her pride behind her—he laughed uproariously and slapped his thigh.

Now in the great hall it was all noise and heat from the bodies and torches, and she knew that the Steward of the House was staying by her to discourage the folk from reaching out in their abandon and their growing drunkenness to lay hands upon her royal and sacred person—a person made the more tempting and available by the scarlet robe and the bared arms which, since they were seldom to be seen, were more inviting than a pair of formally bared breasts.

"Look, she goes in flame color," said a woman of the tavern at the top of her voice.

"It is time," said a tanner stinking of his trade, "that we saw her in a proper crown."

And it was hard for her to remember that these too were the folk, that they had once been hungry children and would come in time to walk about with shattered spirits, mild and rejected like the rest of the old. It was hard for her to speak to them graciously and to watch them tear off great chunks of meat and stuff their mouths with fruit and bread. It was hard for her to move slowly, constantly stopping, through the springtime reek of them: they smelled seminal, they smelled animal, they smelled of the only reward of their labors—the unimaginable thing that happens in the dark.

Nor were these visitors, like those who had come before them, easily wearied. Their appetites and their curiosity were insatiable; the more they ate, the more strength they had for exploring the palace; and the more they saw, the more they took unto themselves. In the rising surge of noise and movement, they stripped the carcasses on the spits down to the white skeletons; they snatched the wine bowls from the slaves and drank without troubling themselves to use the goblets; they pulled the flowers from pillar and doorway and vase, smelling them avidly and then casting them aside. They sang raucously, pitting one song against another in maddening cacophony; they stumbled over footstools and against chairs; they lurched into their hostess, the Steward, the courtly guests. And though most of their eyes were bleared with drinking, they stared ravenously: she felt their stares upon her naked arms, her hair, the lines of her body shadowed forth through her robe—she saw that some of them even pointed at her ring.

As she walked among them, striving to talk with them serenely, obsessive fantasies went through her mind. What would it be like, she asked herself, to have her hair undone by a sickly-seeming

129

weaver who stood behind her, breathing on her neck and staring at the three tiers and the tall crown? How would it be with her, she wondered as she watched the black-nailed, gesturing hands of a brawny peasant, if those hands were to tear the cloth away from her breasts? The Steward, who followed her like a lean and devoted hound, had been a comfort to her in the beginning; but now as the heat and the noise heightened, he too became a part of her obsession. She imagined his sun-browned hands searching her body, his sardonic mouth set cruel on her lips. "Orestes," she thought again and again in the generative smell and the tormenting press. Once, standing against a pillar and trying to catch her breath, she found herself looking—in vain—for the mild, low forehead of the rejected Asterion.

"Forgive me, my lady and my princess," said the Steward, "but you are very white in the face. Perhaps you should step into the *main* court"—by putting a light stress upon the word, he made it plain that it would be senseless for her to go back to the lesser court and stare again across the street—"and take a drink of water and have a breath of air."

The part of the formal court closest to the palace entrance was occupied, was like bruised fruit on which flies have settled. It was squirming with a snake dance in honor of the Lady—a long twitching line of the folk in which, here and there, some gallant, some young wife, some officer of her father's had taken a place. But beyond that wriggling line—it broke respectfully to let her go through—there was blessed openness and emptiness. Io was up and cast her light upon the paving stones and the waist-high parapet that divided the margin of the main court from the sheer drop of the southern gorge. The water that ran at the bottom of the gorge could be seen as a glistening, serpentine line of black, but the sound of it could not be heard; its babble was lost completely under the shouting and the shrill music of the pipes that accompanied the dance.

130

I am on the edge of a precipice, she thought. If it were not for this parapet—she was dizzy with wine—one false step would be enough to send me hurtling down, and it might be better so. And, as she had been obsessed by the thought that the encroaching hands and eyes were closing in upon her, so she imagined herself climbing over the moon-gilded parapet, rolling over the black and soft-seeming furze down the steep declivity, cracking like a doll or an idol against this rock and that stunted tree, splashing un-heard into the glistening water, lying on her back among pebbles, in an attitude of abandonment and rest, with her dead face to the moon.

There was a sound within that over-rode the other sounds: the guests were smashing pottery goblets against wall and floor; they were drinking high and holy toasts and were shattering whatever they had taken to their mouths so that it could not be put to ordinary use by less god-driven men. What were they swearing? No need to go again among them to find out—the Steward would come and tell her in good time. . . . There was a general shout within, so loud that she thought she could feel the paving stones vibrating under her feet. Thrice there was that thunder inside, and then the shout was taken up by the snake-dancers between her and the door—they were simply shouting her name, doubtless in gratefulness for her meat and bread and wine.

She turned and saw the Steward approaching her in strangely even haste. Her thoughts were still drenched in the water at the bottom of the gorge; her vision was watery with wine; and he had taught himself, in order to combine dignity with speed, to walk so smoothly that he seemed to be floating toward her over the pale paving stones. Having come up beside her, he laid his hand over hers on the parapet, not in a man-gesture but as if to steady her for some piece of fearful news. "Now my lady and my princess suffers not from a sparseness of partisans, but from an over-abun-dance of them," he said.

131

"What do you mean?"

"You see how it is in the house of the pillars across the street. You see also how it is here. They will not move from the palace this night. Furthermore, they are making toasts and swearing oaths—"

"Why?"

"If my lady wanted it otherwise, she should not have worn this ring." He uncovered her hand and then covered it again at once, and sighed.

"Why not, good Steward?"

"Can my princess be so innocent as never to have thought what her father's ring would signify to the folk? Did she not know in her heart that to wear the ring was to say to them, 'I and not my mother hold the power'? And if she herself knew it not, did not her good nurse Aglaia enlighten her ignorance?"

She could not lie—both he and Aglaia had shown her too much kindness. She brought herself to look straight into his hawk face, moonlit below, dark above under its celebratory laurel crown. "Aglaia warned me and I did not heed her. But I never thought it would be as it is," she said.

In the stillness that fell between them there was another crash of smashed pottery, and he shook his head.

"Do they swear that they will stand by me until my brother or my father comes home?" she asked, and knew that there was something false in her voice and in the modesty of her claims.

"More. Much more. More, I think, than my lady would wish. If she appears among them now, they will lift her up on their shoulders and carry her round the hall and seat her on her father's throne. And thereafter they will also take up whatever weapons they can find, and make her way sure and clear for her by removing whatever stands counter to her reign—"

"No!"

"Yes, truly. Am I to take it then that the desires of the folk

132

outrun my lady's desires? Shall I go inside and tell them it is your will that there be no more toasts and oaths?"

"Yes, oh, yes. Go and tell them. Go and tell them at once." Again she had the sickening sense that she was about to go over the parapet. The vast landscape, rolling downward to the sea, opened up before her clearing eyes. The hills of her father's domain reproached her; the white, close stars fixed their admonitory stares upon her; death in the shallow water at the bottom of the gorge would not be enough to atone for such monstrous doings—she felt herself rolling and rolling down an endless steep toward the bleak, chalky edge of the world. . . . "I told Aglaia that I would wear the ring, no matter what came to pass. But let the gods bear witness that I never thought it would come to this."

"Nor I. The folk are angry and hungry. Your father's disregard of your mother has been shown to them repeatedly, nor is Aegisthus such a one as can kindle much fear or much love. You, too, are angry and hungry, though in a different fashion. And you are young and untried—no man in his senses would expect you to know revolt even when it stares you in the face."

Weak tears came up out of her gratefulness. Her fingers stirred under his, and he pressed down on them hard and then lifted his hand.

"I will go then," he said, "and let them know that they outstrip your wishes. I will say that you neither accuse your mother nor plead the old law that could set you up in her place. I will tell them that you are a worthy daughter and a loyal sister, and wish nothing to be settled until such time as your brother or your father comes home."

"Yes, surely."

"Only do not show your face among them."

"Must I stay here then?" She looked in fright at the downward sweep of the land and at the accusing stars.

"No, not if it troubles you. Go through the low door into the little room where the court petitioners wait. I will come for you when they are gone."

He had made a child of her, and in the small, closed, dark reception room she remained a frightened child. She knew the place well enough—had known it from her early years when she and her brother and sister had come here to meet some lord from Cyprus, some prince of the royal house of Egypt, some priestly messenger from Crete and to entertain them while they waited for their audiences with the king. It had been a fine ritual, redolent of the flowers they had carried to the waiting ones, rich in a sense of self-importance, and richer still with dreams of faraway lands; and the recollection of such occasions made the present seem more harsh and raw even than it had seemed in the vast and admonitory night. There was no reason for her to trip over the lion-skin carpet as she did: she knew it was there, had sat on it countless times, chatting and laughing with some alien dignitary. There was no excuse for her bruising her shins on the stucco bench that projected from two of the walls: on that same bench she had laid many bunches of summer flowers, many pottery toys to be carried across wide waters, with her greeting, to lordly children in other palaces. Of late she had not been here often, since it was the Master of All the King's Messengers who helped the visitors pass their time while they waited for a word with her mother; but she still knew the room, knew even the strange close smell of dried plaster and foreign ointments as well as she knew the palm of her hand.

She sat down on the stucco bench and waited for the return of the Steward—in anxiety at first, then in heavy consciousness of her bodily weariness, then in languor, then in something between waking and sleep. Shouts, songs, the shrilling of pipes, the thud of dancers' feet blended peculiarly with senseless images that crossed her thoughts: a doll with a noose around its neck, a dolphin spouting above a wave, a fox pursuing a goose that dragged a mangled wing. The sounds took on the quality of visions, and the visions took on the quality of sounds. Now and again she would come out of her half-sleep with a jerk of her whole body; but then she would hear that the noises were subsiding, would think that the Steward of the House was getting matters in hand, would sigh and sink back against the cool smoothness of the bench and give herself up again to the queerness of her semi-dreams. . . .

So, when the door that opened into the little room from the great hall swung wide and the light of a torch burst painful upon her eyes, she could not know whether she was drifting in sleep or sitting upright on the bench face to face with an actuality. It was the Captain of the King's Guardsmen who stood before her, dressed in a short festival tunic, his arms and chest covered like a beast's with swirls of thick curling hair. His behavior was as strange as any of the matters that had come to pass in her half-sleep: he set his torch in a bronze holder, fell on his knees in front of her, and began to press wet, hot, eating kisses onto her hands. "My lady," he said, "my love, my queen!"

All she could summon up against him was a nursery whimper. Besides, she could not yet be certain of his reality—he seemed to her only a sharper instance of her earlier obsession.

"Put your faith in me, my princess. Your Steward is playing you false. We had a fine blaze for you out there, and he has thrown water on it. Who would serve you as I can serve you? I am the only man that you can trust."

She could not answer. Her tongue stuck to the roof of her mouth in fear, and what little strength she had went all into her wild and useless effort to drag her hands out of his grasp.

"I have my guardsmen. My men will stand with me," he said, still assaulting her wrists with his slippery lips. "Promise them to double their miserable rations. Say that you will give them one day in ten for rest. Indulge them only a little, and they will cross

135

the street with swords. Accept me, wretch that I am, and sit on the throne beside me, and none—not even the Achaian host come back from Troy—can strike us down. You would be doing no more than is your right according to the old law, now that your mother has brought shame upon herself."

Mad as it was, it was no dream. She opened her mouth to shriek and saw that the Steward of the House, sardonic and serene, was standing at his ease on the threshold. "Who told the Captain of the King's Guardsmen that he might enter this private room?" he asked. "Who gave him permission to lay hands in his drunkenness upon the sacred person of the daughter of Agamemnon, my lord and my king?"

Like a bull, the Captain snorted and straightened and turned upon the newcomer. "Get hence," he said, "or I will run you through." His voice was thick and low, and his broad fat shoulders bulged with power.

"What will you run me through with?" the Steward said, and rightly: the Captain was unarmed, it was sacrilege to come with weapons to the Festival of a divinity.

"My bare hands will serve me well enough."

"I think you will not use them. Your accuser sits behind you. What will you do when she speaks of this tomorrow to her mother, who is still a queen upon her throne?"

The Captain lurched forward at the Steward, stumbled and fell short of him, and made a great thud as he hit the floor, face foremost, knocking the wits out of his head. But in his fall he had jarred the torch out of its holder, and it lay burning on the carpet, its flames eating quickly into the lion hide.

"Go to the court, my lady," said the Steward quietly, as if the spreading flames were no more to him than the contents of an overturned amphora of wine. "I will see to this one"—he looked down at the sprawled Captain—"but go out into the court. This

136

is no small matter. There is enough oil stored under this floor to burn us all to crisps."

Unstrung, incapable, she stared at him without moving, and he ran past her through the door to the main court and came in again at once, with the weight of one of the tremendous cauldrons dragging down his arms. "This will take care of it," he said, and poured the water here and there across the little runnels of fire that rippled toward the curtains. Smoke and an acrid smell rose from the lion skin and eddied slowly through the door and into the great hall, where somebody shouted, "Is there a fire?"

The Steward ran by her again and returned with the second of the cauldrons. This time he walked on fire, at once trampling and spilling water onto the little licking flames. "Him I can afford to anoint now," he said, for the blaze was out, and he splashed the last of the water over the Captain, who barely stirred. There were more cries of "Fire!" from the great hall, and womanish squeals, and the noise of running feet. He sighed and flung the empty cauldron from him to the floor, where it set up a hollow, rolling clang. She saw then that his feet were blistered, that the bottom of his robe hung in blackened ribbons, that the hair had been singed from his hands and arms; and great shame and pity made her weep.

"No, now, do not shed tears over it," he said, picking up the quenched torch as if he had no other thought but to set the room to rights. "Your guests are going—that at least is a piece of good fortune. I will remember henceforth that the best way to end a troublesome Festival is to start a little fire. As for this one here, I will drag him forth, so that the air in the court can revive him and his comrades-at-arms can find him, if they are sober enough to notice that he is missing. Then I will come back and watch a while to make certain that nothing kindles here. You had best go to your couch and sleep."

137

She did not go at once. In sorrow for his burns and for the little room in which she had once been happy, in terror of the coming day, in sick-heartedness at what she had set afoot with a ring and a scarlet robe, she flung herself upon the weary Steward and cried fiercely against him, laying her head on the ruined crimson that covered his chest. She wept long, and he long supported her, not scanting his pity, though surely he was exhausted and in much pain. "Henceforth," he said, "since you have neither father nor mother to order you about, look to your nurse. Listen to your nurse, like a good little maid." Having so said, he put her from him, kissed her on the forehead, and led her through the ravaged and abandoned great hall to the foot of the stairs.

ELEVEN

THE FESTIVAL NIGHT was almost spent when Clytemnestra crossed the vacant street and the smaller court and entered the great hall of the palace, where one burning wick floated in oil and the Steward of the House sat in a tall chair close to the flame, erect and formal still, although he was asleep. The clutter that her feet discerned on the floor—torn flowers, scraps of food, puddles of wine—did not surprise her. She was not surprised either by the acrid smell of a smothered fire, or by the blisters that showed on the hands and arms of the sleeper once she had come up to his side. Nothing could have stirred her, not curtains torn to rib-

139

bons nor piles of smashed pottery nor the bronze and crystal throne cracked in two. Exhaustion and sick-heartedness had benumbed her; and if she had found the palace itself in ruins she would only have said, "As the gods will, so it is," and gone to look for some other place to sleep.

She had suffered much tonight; she had suffered for two beings, for *him* and for herself; and in her suffering she had told herself repeatedly: This is how it is with lovers, this is the penalty for a great love. When few of the folk had come to his feast and none had stayed, she had felt an annihilating pity for his fine wine despised and his flowers unadmired and his lambs slain and roasted in vain. When some of the court, seeing which way the wind was blowing, had gone to make themselves safe by ingratiating themselves with her daughter, her own anger had been doubled at the realization of his shame. When his hall had been emptied and he had ordered his torchbearers—casually, with a jerky cheerfulness —to quench their lights, she had felt twin fists of terror beating inside her chest, one for him and one for herself. And—strangest and most sorrowful of all—neither he nor she had found the heart to put the balm of passion on their mutual pain. On this night of the Spring Festival when the Lady would have given license for lawless ardor to anyone, even to a queen so long as she looked to the purity of her womb, he and she had done no more than sit almost speechless in his hall for hours, her hand over his damp and unstirring hand. The failing of their desire on this one occasion when desire was sanctioned had made her feel that they were no longer a part of humanity, that they had been cut adrift from the rest of the world.

Never before had she known such weariness as she had known sitting in his empty and torchless hall beside him. It had been as if the wine of her blood were drying in her veins, the marrow of her bones were melting away, her body itself were growing malleable like beeswax, to be bent and molded by Fate, to have henceforth no will of its own. He had made no move to touch her, had only fetched up three or four sighs and asked several times, without expecting an answer, what he was to do with all that bread, all that meat. She had seen how his unused abundance would be a dilemma to him: to dispense it in the streets tomorrow would be to call attention to his failure, and to throw it away in a year of war and drought would bring down upon him the accusation of outrageous wastefulness. But she could imagine only preposterous solutions: set the house afire so that what had been rejected could be consumed in flames; call in the slaves and order them to devour it all before dawn; dig a great trench in the northern wilderness beyond the wall and bury it there. . . . And finally, when these thoughts had begun to turn into dreams—when, nodding, she had seen herself at the bottom of a pit and had felt the weight of roasted carcasses upon her—she had risen, kissed him on his moist bald forehead, and come over to her own house, where nothing could rouse her from a torpor that was like a waking sleep.

The Steward stirred in his doze, made as if to rub his eyes, and winced at the pain he had given his blistered hands. "Forgive me, my queen and my lady," he said, rising and bowing before her. "I remained here to tell you that there was a small fire—nothing to distress you much, merely a matter of a burned rug. It was in the little waiting room, but now it is quite out. I think it has been out for some time. Otherwise, all is well."

All is well. . . . So in Lacedaemon, in the country of her birth, the watchman had called now and again as the night advanced. And she had wakened out of untroubled rest at the sound of his call and had sunk again into even deeper, safer sleep. . . . "But your hands are burned—yes, and your feet also—"

"It is nothing. I have put ointment on the burns." He held up his hands and they showed raw and slick with oil in the light of his lamp. "Does my queen and my lady wish to know how the fire broke out?"

141

She did not care; but, since he had beaten and trampled flames to save her property, she owed him her attention. "Yes," she said with a poor semblance of interest. "How did it come about?"

"Many were drunken, and one of the young women was pursued and took refuge in there, and a fool followed her in his drunkenness and dropped his torch and set the rug afire."

He went on, but she did not listen. She was thinking with remote regret how her husband had told her proudly once that no fire had been set to the palace since the time the followers of Thyestes had made a futile attempt to take vengeance on Atreus. Under the Steward's night-hushed voice, she could hear her lord recounting how, after the fearful banquet, twenty men had come and put torches to the splendid stair. . . . "As to your daughter, the princess Electra, she went to her bedchamber very sorrowful, much chastened in her heart."

Very sorrowful? Much chastened? She wondered if in her dullness she had heard him aright: the words had nothing to do with the scarlet figure that had flashed malicious triumph at her half a night ago. "Truly? And what could have chastened her heart?" she said.

"She is young, my queen and my mistress. She did not know beforehand how it would be to stand alone among so many of the roistering folk. Though she put a bold face on it at first, in the end I think she was afraid."

Afraid? The queen—standing in the wretched leavings of the feast, breathing the acrid residue of smoke, guessing from such ravaged garlands as showed within the area of the wan light what riot had run rampant around the rest of the room—saw that her daughter might well have been afraid. And in her fear, she thought, did she once look toward the house of the pillars with other eyes than those I saw? Did she think the name of "mother" along with all the other shameful names she has heaped upon me? It is possible: the young, too, know themselves sullied by the ordure of the years; the young, too, for all their insolence, sometimes hold out their arms toward a cleaner, safer past. . . .

"Perhaps she is not yet asleep," said the Steward. "It is not long since she went upstairs."

Whereupon a strange thought came into her head: if the girl was not sleeping, she could follow her into her bedchamber; if the girl was remorseful, she might take upon her own crowned head her full measure of blame; if the girl harbored even the smallest love for her, she herself might ask for pity and offer love. Never once—she realized it now with wonder—had she pulled the veil of pride from her face; never once had she spoken to her daughter in a nakedness of spirit, laying before her the sorry, pitiable truth.

Yet, when she had asked the Steward for a light and he had kindled one for her at the lamp beside him, she went very slowly to the foot of the broad stairs. At no time since the bond had been established between her and Aegisthus had she made a move without his knowledge and his counsel, and she considered going back to ask him, "Shall I sit humble on the side of Electra's couch and tell her how it has been with me and ask her earnestly to hold her peace?" But she knew that he would have no more strength for her question than she had had for his: he would sit staring at her in a daze, he would tell her to do whatever she thought best, he would sigh and ask her again how he could dispose of the shaming plenty he had prepared in his foolishness. . . . Perhaps it is some god who directs me, she thought, and, warily picking her way upstairs through the clutter, she passed her own room and Aglaia's and pushed open Electra's door.

The young woman lay face up with her hair spread out over a scarlet bolster. Her right hand clutched the back of her neck as if some pain gnawed there even in her dreams, and her left arm trailed naked and thin over the tawny coverlet. Her eyelids did not quiver at the encroachment of the lamp's pale glow; her spare

143

cheeks had the stiff and shining look of flesh on which tears have dried, flesh that would taste of the dried salt of tears if it were kissed. How long is it—so she asked herself as she stood staring—since my lips have touched her? And it seemed to her then, she could not tell why, that a spasm of grief had closed her womb for all time while she was sharing the futile feast with him tonight. Three I brought forth, she told herself, and one was snatched away, and one has fled, and here lies the third, the last. . . .

She knew then that she too was weeping. Tears streaked her face, so that when she dragged her hand across it her palm was smeared with white from her cheeks and black from her eyelashes and red from her mouth. Yet she had no thought of wiping her marred visage clear with her veil. Let her see me as I am, she thought. Let her waken and see me even so.

As if her thoughts had passed through the shifting stuff of dreams, her daughter sighed, tugged at the back of her neck, and wakened. Her face went slack in helpless, mortal terror; her look flew to the hand that did not hold the light. A dagger—she plainly believed that her mother had come to her with a dagger, and still looked for the murdering blade although her awakened eyes must surely discern that it was not there. "Mother!" she said in the voice of a sick child; and what she revealed was so terrible that it tore through the torpor, shook the exhausted body, made the lamp tremble in the shaking hand.

"Gracious gods—most blessed Lady—" She held out the smeared palm, she exhibited its emptiness and innocence.

At which the grey eyes lost their wildness, went blank, and gathered out of blankness the known level look. "What does my mother want of me?" Electra said.

"Nothing—nothing—"

"To chastise me because my feast was too riotous, considering that across the street—"

"No, Electra—"

144

"To call me to account for setting a fire in the waiting room?" She sat up and took upon herself the old rigidity, the customary arrogance.

"No, scarcely that. As things stand with me, I can scarcely concern myself over a burned rug—"

"Then wherefore has my mother roused me up?"

"Is it so strange," she asked, fighting a great sob that swelled like a bubble in her chest, "is it so strange after such a night that a mother should come to her child's couch to assure herself that all is well with her child?"

For the space of a few breaths the young woman seemed to be considering the question in good faith. She sat upright like an idol made of dark sandstone and brooded with her long hands laid in her lap, one over the other. Then whatever had begun to open in her heart was slammed shut. "I am grateful to my mother that she is concerned for me, even at this late day. Let her know that all is well with me—as well as it can be with one who has seen what I have seen. Let me wish my mother a renewing sleep—if it is possible for one who has done what my mother has done ever to be renewed by sleep."

The insult troubled her no more than the preposterous waste standing on the spits in the house of Aegisthus. I am numbed with the little death that I have suffered tonight, she thought, and set her lamp on a low table near a goblet stained with the lees of some wine. "You think to dismiss me. You think to drive me forth with bitter talk," she said. "But I will not go from this room. I will speak, and you will hear."

"Because you are the queen and I am nothing?"

"Because I am a woman and you are a girl." Though the couch was so narrow that her haunches must press against her daughter's leg if she sat, she let her weight down upon it. Not in weariness— her weariness was so deep that it could not be relieved by sitting or lying—only to indicate that she meant to remain. The young leg stretched as stiff as wood against her; the small breasts under the lion skin heaved in an impatient sigh. And the orderly procession of thoughts, the sane arguments that she had expected to have at hand were not there to serve her need. Wild as pigeons her thoughts flew up, reasonless; and her mouth opened and let whatever had been shut up within escape. "I myself was once a child in Lacedaemon," she said.

And perhaps it had been best to begin so; perhaps this utterance too had been given her by a god. Her daughter looked at her long as if the grey gaze could strip off the mask and the splendor and the years, as if it could see her as she had been, hearing between sleep and sleep the watchman's cry that all was well.

"Like you, I was the daughter of a king. Like you, I was innocent. Like you I was closed away—fools that we are to close away our children from the world. I too had a light mother—and I charged her harshly with her lightness. Would the gods could raise her up to me now"—the thick bubble swelled in her again, big, uncontrollable, bursting this time into an audible sob— "would I might kiss her hands and say 'Forgive, forgive.'"

The girl looked at her in puzzlement, saying nothing with her lips, saying only with her eyes: What next? and How so? Tears for a light mother? To her they were curiosities, she could not understand them—anemones on a dunghill, butterflies on carrion. . . . Then she dismissed them, either as lies or as foibles. "I doubt my mother would be coming at midnight after a day of feasting to tell me the tale of her life," she said. "Therefore I ask again: Why has she come?"

"To tell you the truth."

"What truth?"

"More than you see in your innocence."

"My innocence? I have no innocence." She spread her palms and looked at their emptiness. "My mother and her paramour have taken away my innocence."

146

"Truly? Can that be so? Before you learned that I lay down with Aegisthus, is it possible that you did not know a man lies down with a woman?"

"I knew that the bridegroom lies down with the bride."

"What are you, what kind of spirit is in you that a few words out of a priest's mouth and a banquet and a procession with torches should turn what is loathsome to you into a high and holy thing? I went in a procession, after ritual and feasting, to your father's couch, and there I was mastered and used and consigned to separate, solitary sleep. I went unblessed and without torches to the couch of Aegisthus, and—"

"Do you say it? Do you boast of it? Do you thrust it in the face of the daughter of Agamemnon?"

She disregarded the unripe righteousness. Tears rose where rage should have sprung, and she let the tears fall, slow and almost audible, onto the lion skin. "You are *my* daughter also," she said. "He sowed his seed and turned his back on me, yes, and on you in me. It was I that carried you and fed you on my blood. It was I that labored and screamed while he rode out to the hunt. No, you must allow me to tell you only this much of the tale of my life: When he came to me in an ill humor after bad hunting or troubling news, he looked at you as he might look at dried prunes set before him when he had no appetite. His heart was bitter because I had given him a girl."

"No man wants a daughter as the first fruit. Doubtless it embittered him. Doubtless I was another sorrow added to the many in his heart—"

"You credit him with too great a heart and stuff too many sorrows into it. He is a man and fortunate—a king among kings—and his wish and his satisfaction are one. What he lost to Aegisthus is a thing that he valued no more than the lees in that goblet."

"He lost his pride."

"His pride, his pride! How is it that you never think of me?

147

Why should I go loveless to my grave in order to coddle his pride? Troy will be sacked, and he will bring home whatever delights him, and she will sit at the board and stare at my aging face. Such slights are hard to bear—you find them hard to bear yourself. As I remember it, you took it ill enough when your brother neglected you for a while to play with the little Hermione. You sulked in a corner, you did not eat, you would not lift your head. His pride and yours—these are weighty matters to you. How is it then that you never give a thought to my pride?"

"Is my mother certain that he will bring a woman with him?"

It was not the question itself that turned back the queen's anger. It was some hesitancy in the voice, some faltering in the grey look—the first faltering that she had seen tonight. She leaned forward, bringing her unmasked, smeared face close to her daughter's. She let the tears fall shamelessly; she shamelessly encouraged the welling up of more tears. "Certain, certain," she said on another sob. "Her couch will creak by night—not mine, not mine. Surely you know I would have waited"—she lied as shamelessly as she wept—"if there had been anything for me to wait for, anything but disgrace. He will come back happy in some Trojan woman, so occupied with some Trojan woman that he will forget I have lain with him and given him children. He will take so little thought of me that he will never ask himself how I have spent the years between his going and his return. Nor will he think to question for his pride's sake whether the worthless vessel he used half-willingly has been kept pure for him on the shelf. Unless the slaves tattle—and why should they tattle, have I not been a kind mistress?—he will never know. Unless my enemies betray me— and my son and daughter are my only enemies—he will suffer no hurt, not even in his pride."

"Some one will speak of it—"

"No, believe me." Her hand fell on the spare thigh under the lion skin, and the thigh did not pull away, but suffered her touch. "There has been too much—who would want more of it?—too much murder, too much war, too much blood. If every man and woman in Mycenae knew of it, they need only see that you had sealed your own lips, and they would keep silent for your sake and for the sake of peace."

"I could not go to my grave with such a secret."

"Tell it later. Tell it when I am gone and he that was so rash and foolish as to love me is gone after me—tell it and satisfy your strange heart, and let my husband and the folk be satisfied with cursings and mockings of skeletons, with desecrations and spoilings of graves. Only let him live his life, keeping his powers and his honors. Only let me live mine, second in my husband's sight as I was when he came to Lacedaemon to speak for me, and saw that Helen was fairer than I, and hankered after Helen, and scorned himself and me that he—the eldest of the house of Atreus —should be forced to couple with what was second best."

The muscles in the thin thigh stiffened. The eyelids came down over the eyes, and the eyes opened again to show the old level look. "Did my mother find it so hard to have a fair sister?" said Electra. "And has she forgotten that I also have a fair sister, beside whom I have been as nothing in my mother's sight?"

It seemed to Clytemnestra then that she had two choices. They came to her sharp and visible, in the shape of a forked road going off in two directions, one toward the sea and the other toward a clump of pines. She could tell the truth—she could say "I loved in Iphigenia what I lacked in myself"—or she could lie. Then all at once it was as if she had no choice, as if she had taken her course earlier, when she had presented her smeared face and released the second sob and encouraged and multiplied the tears. "I loved you —thorny as you were, the gods know that I loved you," she said. "How could it be otherwise? You were my first-born. But even in

149

your childhood you turned from me to him, you and your brother both. His scorn of me was a thing that he passed on to the two of you."

"That is not as I remember it."

"How should you remember what came to pass when you were still a little child?"

"It *is* a mystery. But I remember nevertheless."

"You remember what you wish to remember, and you wish to remember only such things as blacken me and make me monstrous. I tell you, I loved—"

"Iphigenia, and then Aegisthus. No other in this world."

She caught her breath under the impact of it. Even as a child in Lacedaemon, whom had she loved? Not the loose mother or the vain and heedless father. Not the sister who dazzled mother and father and brothers. Not the brothers either, not with Helen's image standing in their eyes. Her spirit flew back through many years and into many chambers, and suffered in each a slight that left her as shaken as if she had been slapped across the face. And here she sat—wordless, aging, undone, offering her marred face to be slapped again, asking again, and again vainly, for pity and love.

"My mother did not come to tell me the truth. She saw how it was with the folk, and she came to ask me to conceal what I know from my father for her sake. If the folk had gathered like flies in the house of the pillars, she would not be sitting on the edge of my couch to console me for my wasted lambs. She would be staying late across the street, making merry over me with her paramour."

That too was so, and she was too weary to dispute it. The wick of the lamp that she had carried with her was beginning to fail for lack of oil; the feverish moon had set long since; and if she closed her eyes she felt herself slipping again toward the bottom of a pit. "Then you will not listen?" she said.

150

"I have listened."

"Without mercy? Without any changing in your heart?"

"I have no heart—it departed out of me with my innocence. My mother presses her breast as though a stone lay under it. I also carry a stone."

"So I have come to understand." She rose, swaying a little, and took up the lamp, knowing how its light would bring out the smudges and the wrinkles and the raw shine under the dried tears. Without more useless speech, she crossed the room and walked through the doorway. In the dark corridor she thought briefly of going back to him, of the dull quiet that would come upon her if she lay against him through the remainder of the night. But her reason told her that he had not gone to his couch, that he was sitting now as she had left him in the dark hall, that he would continue to sit among the leavings of his calamitous feast until his slaves awoke at dawn. And she was glad to have another worry to lay over what she had left behind her in her daughter's chamber: what would he do with them, how would he dispose of them— all those lambs, all that fruit, all that bread?

TWELVE

IT WAS NOT that the Master of All the King's Messengers had any fears for his cause. The success of his cause was foreordained, recorded in the archives of Fate as if it had already been accomplished. The comings and goings of the common crowd could make no difference: Fate was concerned only with the doings of those of lordly blood, and took no account of the doings of the folk. Aegisthus son of Thyestes was invulnerable—he had been steadied by that knowledge through the most threatening stages of the feast on the other side of the street—invulnerable behind the bronze shield of Fate at least until he had shed his cousin's

152

blood. But Aegisthus the adopted son of the Corinthian merchant —what little there was left of him—still carried about with him a vulnerable heart. His largesse had been rejected and his feelings had been hurt, and morning and a pearly morning mist had invaded the ravaged hall in which he sat before he could swallow the impulse to put his head on his knees and weep as bitterly as a chidden child.

His steward, a sleek young Cyprian whom he had made a party to his cause, came to him early, bringing him his morning meal from the kitchen. The great bronze serving plate that he carried, heaped with fresh bread and honey and clotted cream, was ridiculous; to bring eatables into this room was like strewing salt onto the sea. He took the plate nevertheless, set it on the bench beside him, and began to eat a rusk dipped in honey, addressing to the bringer meanwhile the usual morning questions and getting the usual answers: No, there had been no fire lighted on the watchtower during the night; no, the queen of Mycenae had sent him no word; no, no messenger had come with any information concerning the whereabouts of Orestes.

"And what are we to do with all this that is left over from the Festival?" He managed to ask it lightly, making an offhand gesture as though there was no more reason for concern than if a pet hound had relieved himself on the floor.

"It can be disposed of, my lord. I can send some to the city garrison and some to the priests at the shrine of the Lady. The rest we can portion out among the household slaves."

It was a sane solution, such a solution as he should have seen for himself last night instead of plaguing her with the question. "Certainly. See to it at once," he said.

"At once, of course. Only, there is a matter I thought my lord might wish to know of." He walked up to one of the pyramids of dried fruit, laying the pieces carefully in a basket. He presented his master with his back—smooth and somewhat full, but mus-

153

cular—and Aegisthus knew that he was about to deliver some piece of information concerning the conspiracy. The Cyprian was modest and never forgot that he had come into the household as a slave; the Cyprian always flung such statements over his shoulder as if he wished to indicate that he did not presume upon the honor of being a conspirator. "The Captain of the Guardsmen is gone, my lord." He continued with his task, his back still turned, his heavy black curls falling forward to hide his face.

"Gone? Where? Why?"

"It seems he made himself both treasonous and foolish over at the palace. It seems he was carried away with devotion to the princess Electra. It seems, when all of them were howling at their loudest, he pursued her into some little room and offered to do her the honor of marrying her then and there—"

"But he is married—"

"Drunk as he was, that seemed of small importance to him. There was a scuffle, it seems—I believe the Steward of the King's House was involved in it. At any rate, a torch was knocked over, and the Captain was knocked over, and there was a little fire. When he came to his senses—what senses he has, I mean—he took himself off in a chariot, heading east."

"He ran away?"

"Precisely. So now there is no Captain of the King's Guardsmen until my queen and my lady names his successor. I thought my lord might wish to know of it. Shall I go to the garrison and bring him Leontophon?"

His own mind had leaped to Leontophon before the Cyprian had uttered the name. Leontophon—second in command of the few and feeble warriors who had been left to hold the Citadel—was the most capable of the six who had been sworn to the service of Aegisthus and the queen. "Yes, go and send him," he said, dropping the rusk back onto the plate and licking the honey from his fingertips. "But wait—go straight in among the men and say to him in their presence that he is welcome to come to me and choose what food he wants for him and his companions."

"Certainly. At once. It is a happy chance. Is there any other thing that I might bring to please the palate of my lord?" Now that he could speak of matters other than the crucial ones, he turned and smiled. His face was soft, with a catlike kind of blankness. His smile affected only the corners of his mouth—did not change either his smooth cheeks or his dark, almond-shaped eyes. "A bit of cheese? Some nuts? A slice of pheasant's breast?"

"No, nothing. I have more than I can eat. It is indeed a happy chance." He tried to make the Cyprian look at him, but it was useless: the young man bowed his oiled head almost to his knees, straightened, turned, and was gone.

He stood up then, stretched, and walked into the garden. Though every flower had been stripped from it to be twined into the futile garlands, though it was misty and dull in the early light, it was still a more acceptable place than the great hall with its clutter and its smell of roast meat. His shoulders and haunches ached from long hunched sitting, and the sinews behind his knees pulled painfully. He walked up and down among the bloomless stalks, stretching and loosening his tensed muscles and trying to cheer himself with the thought of the favor he was about to do for Leontophon.

For, strange though it was, his chief interest in the business of the Captain's disgrace and flight arose not from the fact that it was highly advantageous to the cause but from the minor consideration that now he could bring about the promotion of this disabled warrior. Not that he was particularly fond of the man, an embittered and aging petty officer who had lost an eye before the gates of Thebes and who was never finished with pointing out the differences between those who sat at home and those who advanced through arrows and spears. Nor did he hope to bind a valuable conspirator more closely to the conspiracy—the fellow would

155

be no more faithful if he were named to the post than he had been before. What was comforting, what warmed him against the morning chill and loosened his stiff joints, was simply the prospect of pleasing somebody, of wresting for himself out of the general disapproval one sign of gratefulness.

The folk had no use for him—the folk had turned their backs on his excellent food. She was impatient with him—he had not played the man with her, had offered her no support, had nagged at her endlessly in her distress about the wasted provisions. And however he looked at the matter, he cut a wretched figure in his own eyes—he himself had small use for himself. For these reasons, rather than for the much more significant reason that the whole garrison had fallen into his hands by what the Cyprian called "a happy chance," he waited in impatience for the moment when he could break the gratifying news to the embittered Leontophon.

Yet he took no pleasure in the brief interim. He filled it—indeed of late he had been filling all inactive spaces in his days—with a peculiar kind of trivial worrying in which he weighed two alternatives, both of small importance, as if his life depended upon which of them he chose. Now it was: Shall I go into the hall, or would it be better for me to meet him here in the garden? Last evening it had been: Shall the two of us—she and I—greet the guests together, or would it be better if I stood in one place and she in another? And on many occasions that had no significance and could have no consequences, he had been stricken motionless by: Shall I try to undo this knotted sandal-thong, or shall I throw it away? Shall I put on green or purple? Shall I nod to such and such a one, or shall I wait until he nods to me?

Leontophon met him on the crest of his foolish dilemma: he was standing on the threshold, fingering his beard, still uncertain as to whether he should stay outside or come in. "Where is this meat?" said the veteran of Thebes, omitting all formal greeting.

156

He presumed upon the conspiratorial fellowship as persistently as the Cyprian muted it. "Since Agamemnon rode out, do you know how many times the dogs that he left here to see to his Citadel have been given meat? Nine times." He held up nine hairy, bony fingers.

"The meat is in there. Take what you want of it. I will provide the wagon." He looked at the angry face, a spare triangle thrown into disorder by the empty socket with its drooping eyelid. The temples were ridged with thickened veins, and years of rage showed in those ridges and in the single small affronted eye. "But it was not about the meat that I wished to have words with you. I have been told that the Captain of the King's Guardsmen—"

"Has jumped out of the bull pen? So he has, and gone eastward in a chariot with the first light."

"That happy chance"—he strove to control his annoyance at having his words snatched out of his mouth—"has left the garrison without a captain, and it has come into my mind—"

"To give me the post?"

The annoyance swelled into downright exasperation. "To ask my queen and my lady whether she will be gracious enough to name you to the post."

"Oh, she will be gracious enough. I have no doubt of that." The single eye narrowed; there was something obscene about it and the way it implied that the disabled warrior of an old campaign and the queen's favorite knew each other's thoughts all too well.

"She will dispose of that honor where I see fit," said Aegisthus sharply, and realized at once that he was making a fool of himself. Who else among the six with whom he shared his intentions could be set over guardsmen? Not the Cyprian—he was too young and soft. Not the Overseer of the King's Copper Mines—he must be left in his place to control six hundred brawny and desperate slaves. Not the Keeper of the King's Archives or the son of the Chief Priest of the Lady—neither of these had ever held a sword.

157

And not the steward of Clytemnestra's old aunt—a man wily enough in council but so burdened with fat he could never scale a wall.

"I trust you will see fit," said Leontophon less truculently, "to ask my queen and my lady to name me. It is a post I have coveted these ten years. It is no easy matter to take orders from a pig with the heart of a fish and the brain of a bird. Furthermore, who could better serve your purposes?"

"One who squandered less of his strength chewing on his grievances and used more of it in the winning of other men. But let it rest. You were the one I thought of first. Only, see to it that you make yourself a good name with the garrison. I have heard that they call you Old Vinegar behind your back."

"So they do." He walked over to the hearth and slapped the carcass of a spitted lamb so hard that it swung. "To come to them with such a present will not be a bad way to make a beginning. Look at this"—he struck the roasted beast again—"almost whole, scarcely touched."

It is not that he means to insult me, Aegisthus thought. It is not that my disgrace is salt to his meat. It is merely that he—like all the others except the Cyprian—is a coarse man molded out of dull and lumpy clay, incapable of sensing another man's disgrace. . . . Whereupon, while Leontophon walked back and forth and gloated over the rejected bounty, his host fell to wondering whether all who pledge themselves to shed blood in a time of peace are bound to be coarse men. All the butchers that he could call to mind at the moment had coarse hands. . . .

"Do you know what I have been thinking?" said the veteran over his shoulder. His voice was companionable now: he had begun to congratulate himself on the proposed honor, he was willing to show some measure of gratefulness. But all that was too late, so far as Aegisthus was concerned. He let himself down into a chair, feeling the returning assault of weariness and disgust.

"What?" he said in a flat voice, staring at his own hands and wondering whether loose joints and a habit of cracking them constituted coarseness.

"With things as they will be—with the garrison securely with us—we need not wait. The king and whoever comes with him—we can strike them down the moment they set foot in the palace," Leontophon said.

He entertained the proposition briefly; it was not without its merits. Since Agamemnon was certain to bring some of his warrior-companions with him, the conspirators had resigned themselves to a wait of several days until the guests would have departed, no matter how the dangers of betrayal might be increased by such a delay. But even though Leontophon's proposal would eliminate that delay, something made him hostile to it—his present exhaustion, his unwillingness to reconsider scores of details and change a good half of them, his numbing conviction that Fate would settle the affair in his favor no matter how he arranged it. "There are eight of us in the business now, including the queen and myself," he said in a testy, twanging voice. "Add to that enough soldiers from the garrison to butcher the guests, and you might as well take the whole Citadel into your confidence. No. Put it out of your mind." He had seen a flaw in it and he was glad—glad to find his dull brain working apace, glad to put Leontophon down. "Those who come home with him will be princes and leaders of armies and rulers of citadels. Will you embroil us with a dozen cities? See to it that you make no plans, see to it that you do nothing but follow what is already laid down, or you will entangle the rest of us in your foolishness."

"As you say." He came back from his wanderings, pulled up a stool to face the chair in which Aegisthus had settled himself, and sat down with his scarred and knobby knees apart and his hands hanging between them. "I take it then that the plan remains exactly as it was, except, of course, for the change made necessary

159

by what came to pass last night over there"—he jerked his head in the direction of the palace.

"What do you mean by that?"

Leontophon did not answer, only let the lid of his good eye droop indolently so that his face seemed now to be either half asleep or entirely blind.

"What change are you talking about?" He said it harshly and contemptuously as though he spoke to a madman or a dog. For the first time he realized that he hated this man and all the rest of the six, yes, even the Cyprian with his fleshy back and his oiled curls.

"Why, the obvious change," said the veteran of Thebes. "She will have to go, like her father and any of the others that remain here with him—any armor-bearer or groom or concubine."

He envisioned the *she* of whom Leontophon spoke—saw her as he had seen her across the street yesterday in the red afterglow of the feverish sun. Clytemnestra had been bitterly wounded by her arrogance: one large tear had made a snail's trail down her powdered cheek at the sight of the thin rebel in her poppy-colored finery. He, on the contrary—for all his pity for the slighted mother —had felt an almost unmanageable desire to laugh, and to laugh without spite. True, at that early hour he had been convinced that those who starved on her wretched hospitality would come to him afterwards to dine; true, he had not as yet guessed how deep a cut her insolence could make in his pride; true, he had suffered since through a sick and shameful night. Yet now, strangely, it was that evening image of her which stood in his mind: a lean mare rearing up and whinnying at a lion—senseless, ridiculous, and brave. His turgid blood had even stirred a little at the thought of what a time her husband would have to tame her. And, turning away from her to lay a comforting arm around the waist of her mother, he had thought: The girl was right, she deserves a better master than Asterion. . . .

160

"Surely you see it," Leontophon said. "Unless she is cut off, you and my lady can never rest secure—"

"Because of a girl?"

"Because of a girl who has the loyalty of the folk."

He was on the point of saying that the folk were no concern of his, that Fate set them to one side as though they were so many tame fowl, that the will of the folk could never impinge upon the will of a son—even a bastard son—of Thyestes. Then he bit his lip and shook himself and sighed. Nobody in Mycenae, least of all the beloved, knew what news a cousin had brought him from Corinth. Nobody in Mycenae knew or would ever know that he had not forged his own life, that he and his life—womanish, passive—had been beaten into their shape by Fate. "Give the folk a month or so and they will forget her," he said.

"That is not my opinion, nor the opinion of the rest of the six. Not one of them left this hall last night without saying to me that the princess must be cut down with the others—yes, and the prince also, if he should return, if he is not dead."

"Do you think for an instant that Clytemnestra would agree to the murder of her own children?"

"Must she agree?"

The small single eye had opened again and was looking at him steadily. Since it was a single eye, he could not be certain, but he thought that it was mocking him as a dependent child. "She is not stupid—she will find out," he said.

"From whom? From one of us?"

"Do you have the insolence to imply that *I* would tell her? Am I a child who cannot hold its tongue?"

"Far be it from me—"

Yet he knew, in spite of Leontophon's protest, that this one and his five companions-in-slaughter had reason to think of him in exactly those terms. Wanting always to be close to her when there were others in the room, uncertain of every plan until it had

161

gotten her express approval, unable to sleep until he had laid his head or his hand upon her moist voluminous breasts. . . . He stood up and shook himself again, this time in self-loathing. "Do as it seems fit to the rest of you where Electra is concerned," he said. "If you are afraid of the girl, then murder her. The queen will hear nothing of it from me."

Leontophon stood up and nodded. "Shall I be the one to take her?" he said, staring one-eyed at the painted floor and tapping his fingers against his thigh.

"No. Assign her to the Overseer of the King's Mines."

"I am as dependable as he is. I could take her."

"Do you *want* her?" He spat it like venom into the veteran's face.

The hairy fingers stopped tapping. "I wish to be of service to you in every way I can," he said. A flush came up into his face, and the ridges in his temples were more marked than they had been before.

"Tell the Overseer. Go first to him and then to the garrison. I will send the meat to the sally port. It will be there tonight."

When Leontophon was gone, he stood for a long time near the hearth gazing at his own hands—long, loose-jointed, white. Something—he had no idea what—impelled him to crack his knuckles. Shall I crack them, or shall I refrain? he asked himself. It seemed better to forego what was, he supposed, a vulgar habit; and he started quickly for the stairs, thinking to go up and bathe away the sickly sweat of the night. But at the foot of the steps he stopped and slowly, thoroughly, loudly cracked each of the loose joints. "Murderer, butcher," he said on the way up; but he did not know whether he was accusing Leontophon or himself.

THIRTEEN

TO THE WATCHMAN in the tower on top of the Holy Mountain, the Spring Festival had meant nothing more than a basket of gifts brought up by one of the palace guardsmen. He was richer thereafter by a block of dried figs, several slices of choice cold meat, some cakes sticky with honey, a garland unsuited to solitude and a bald head, and a bag of tea. The tea he valued most, since the princess Electra had sent it to help him in his sleeplessness, even though—having brewed and consumed a bag she had sent up on a former occasion—he knew that it was quite incapable of inducing sleep.

His days were longer now and harder to bear. The sun went down in misted red and befooled him time and again: a pool reflecting the sunset, a clump of trees whose delicate leaves took their color from the crimson source of light, the afterglow shining between two scrub-covered crags, deceived him into believing he saw a fire. He was forever laboring up the ladder and through the trap door onto the roof to take a second look; and always before he came down again he felt his mortality manifested in the fierce and uneven beating of his heart. How would it be, he asked himself, if I were to die up here? Who would find me and when? Would I stink? Would they have to hold their noses when they carried me down and thrust me into my grave? Whereupon his attention would be drawn to the poor man's cemetery on the slope: he had watched it with unflagging care ever since the day of strange snow when the princess had come; he had kept a tally of the burials—there had been sixteen—on the wall with a piece of charred wood.

Through the day of the Feast and two days thereafter he wore the garland that had come to him in the basket. He set it rakishly on one side of his head in a wry mockery of piety: so much empty time, so much empty space, such constant pondering on annihilation had somehow drawn the life not only out of him but also out of the gods. When he prayed to the Lady he spoke shortly, impudently, as a small boy might speak to a half-despised mother. He challenged the Horse to demonstrate his bragged-of power by speeding the weary business on the other side of the eastern waters. Because his throat was sore with the constant drift of yellow dust that came through his windows, he cut off all communication with Poseidon—a mean god, a miserly god, tight-fisted with his rain.

He had intended to eat his gifts sparingly so that they might cheer him during a long stretch of evenings, but at the end of two burdensome days he saw no point to his delay. In anger, with a

164

show of anger even though there was nobody to witness it, he flapped out his linen cloth and laid it on the floor in front of his leather cushion and spread it with all his plenty, meaning to devour everything at one meal, half in greediness and half in spite.

There was much to be devoured, and he ate slowly, not to savor the food, not to guard against the pounding and the tightness in his chest, only to kill as much time as he could. He sat down at sunset, finished off the bread and meat by twilight, chewed on figs and cakes through the afterglow, and went to the window only when the sky was dark enough to show the stars. And there before him, burning on a furze-covered headland that looked like the back of some great crouching beast, was the signal fire.

Or was it? Was it truly? He had expected to see it there for so long, he had put it there so often in his imagination, that its actual appearance held for him no surprise, no exhilaration. What he saw on the headland was nothing to change the shape of the world; it could not add one day to the tally of his life; it was only a stream of flame going up slowly through the hot and heavy air; it was nothing more or less than a fire.

Stupidly—for he should have gone up at once to kindle the pile of sticks that had long lain ready in a copper cauldron on the roof of the tower—stupidly he stood and stared at the distant blaze, noting the shape of it as if the shape were a noteworthy thing, trying to endow it with some significance. It meant that Troy had fallen—one more city to be added to all the others that had gone down under the torch since men had built cities on the face of the world. It meant that Agamemnon had triumphed—one more victory to be added to the hundreds that had been celebrated and forgotten. It meant that he could go down and live in the Citadel again—but now that the time of his release had come he could only ask himself what he could look forward to in the Citadel.

He took a small coal from his tripod and placed it in a pan. He went up the ladder and out by way of the trap and set his sticks afire at once—they flared and crackled wildly, they had lain in the dry heat so long. All that he did and saw and heard, even the great shout that went up from within the Cyclopean walls, were things foreknown; they had no more substance in actuality than they had had a hundred times before, visiting him in sleeping or waking dreams.

Torches began to appear, scattered at first, then more numerous, then so numerous as to merge into one great serpent of yellow light writhing along the main street. *That* he had not foreseen, and it entertained him for a little: he wondered whether Clytemnestra walked at the head of the procession, whether the princess Electra followed her, whether the Master of All the King's Messengers thought it better policy to walk shouting through the streets as though he had never had a queen for a bedfellow or to stay within doors, hiding his sorrow and minimizing his shame. What a night it would have been for the boy, had the boy been there! But he had neither appeared nor made his place of hiding known, so the bearer of the basket of gifts had said.

The night mist thickened slowly between him and the streaming light. Every evening during the last two moons the air had been heavy with this same oppressive mist, and tonight it subdued the yellow of the torches and brought out the red, so that within an hour the high street of Mycenae seemed to be running with blood. Clots of fire gathered in the main court of the palace. A wash of firelight ran down the palace walls. The cries of victory continued to go up, and he wondered whether an uninformed ear would have been able to distinguish between them and those other cries sent up inside the crumbling Trojan walls.

Something—perhaps long staring at the moving light, perhaps the unaccustomed abundance of his evening meal—made him sick at the pit of his stomach and so vertiginous that he had to turn his back on the Citadel and sit on his leather pillow on the steady earthen floor. All light, even the meager redness in his tripod,

166

troubled him now; and he closed his eyes and thought how for the first time in years it would not be wrong for him to sleep at night. But the possibility of sleep was taken from him by their cries, their chants, their paeans of victory borne up to him through the still and heavy air, and finally he cursed them all. "Like children," he said to the empty and unanswering dark. "Like children, all of them, and fools. Troy is down, and the king will bring home a few spoils and lay them in his treasury, where they will rust. Troy is down, but who will be saved by that from plague or drought or famine or the afflictions of old age? Troy is down, and it is nothing. A hundred years hence, not one whose sleep was broken by these shouts but will be shut up in the everlasting stillness of his grave."

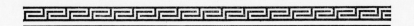

ONE

IT WAS WELL for the folk that they had burned so many torches and consumed so much wine on the night of the signal fire. No additional days of rejoicing were appointed by the queen, and Io waxed and waned eleven times before their hero-king came home.

Once the walls of Troy were down, much still remained for his doing: hecatombs had to be sacrificed in thanksgiving to Poseidon and the Horse; the allies of the Trojans had to be disarmed, reprimanded, and numbered for the tribute; the booty had to be divided, the ships repaired, the wounded healed, and the dead given

171

appropriate mounds of honor on the windy plain. By the time all these things were accomplished, the war-beggared autumn was far gone, and much of the Achaian host saw fit to live off the stores of the vanquished until spring. So those who waited in the Citadel had long to wait—waited until the victory was soured by time like milk left standing in a pail in the sun, waited until they thought twice before condemning the faithless queen who was like them in at least one respect: spoiled by waiting too long.

As for Clytemnestra, she grew visibly older as the year moved on toward spring. Her shoulders hunched forward unless she reminded herself to draw them back, and purplish pouches too large and dark to be powdered away appeared under her eyes. The folk said among themselves with a scornful kind of pity that she had more than enough to worry about: her husband's return hanging over her head, her daughter grim and close-mouthed and refusing to look her in the face. They would have been amazed to know how seldom she was occupied by these worries. What moved into her mind whenever she let her weary bulk down onto a couch or a chair was—and she knew it well—a madwoman's fantasy, a strange belief that ever since the night of the Spring Festival the palace smelled of fire.

Summer and autumn had not dried out that smell for her, winter had not blown or washed it away, and now it was spring again and the odor still clung. Unreal as it was, it nevertheless brought up a short old-womanish cough out of her chest. It set her to wondering how the ruins of Troy smelled under the strengthening sun, whether the bodies of beasts and men still putrefied among charred beams and tumbled stones or were only inoffensive bones by now—curiously jointed bones of hand and foot, clean rib cages through which the winds from the sea could pass. And often of late the cough had caught her where fire had never been: at the house of her aunt, at a banquet given by one of her few partisans, in Aegisthus' chamber after a bout of their fierce new-fashioned love. Along with the coughing came something else: a threat of suffocation, an inability to draw her breath all the way in, a wrenching spasm as if the hand of a god had gone through her flesh and were squeezing her heart. "I am sick," she thought, "in mind and body I am sick. It may be that I am sick unto death." But she spoke to no one, least of all to *him* about the persistent smell and the annihilating pain. He had troubles enough of his own.

Troubles that he did not heap upon *her* rounding back, troubles that she could not even have guessed if they had not shared the same couch or if she had still been able to fall into a deep sleep. Awake, he was as he had always been—casual, cheerful, busy with the king's affairs, but never too busy to send some present to her, a wreath of flowering myrtle, a perfect pomegranate, a little carved bottle of Egyptian perfume. They talked less eagerly than in the past, but that was as it should be. What occupied them both was a matter too monstrous to be tossed back and forth in words; and if they waited for it together, their knees touching, their fingers intertwined, they waited for it in silence. It was only in his dreams that he betrayed his suffering, turning from side to side, whimpering like a little one, growing sometimes so hot that she thought a fever was eating him and sometimes so cold that she sat up and listened for his breath in fear that he was dead. In the old days, whenever she had not slept because her desire had renewed itself, she had reached down for the source of her pleasure and the seat of his life; and it had always leaped into throbbing fullness at her touch. She had less commerce with it now, since he had sworn he would not send her big-bellied to receive her husband; and, lying awake, unsatisfied and yet without longing, she would grope downward now and again to test him, to spy on him in his sleep. What she found undid her: it was such a thing as one finds on an infant boy—flaccid, insignificant, capable of no spasm but the spasm that drew it back-

173

ward from her seeking hand. And she knew what no other knew: that he was changed and rapidly aging; that the face he wore before the world was no living one, was the dead mask of his former face; that he played assiduously and to exhaustion at being what he had once been—a virile, wily, self-reliant man.

It seemed to her in those months that her own mind had undergone degeneration: when she was not thinking of the acrid smell or waiting for the return of pain, she struggled with questions that were either futile or of no consequence. What, she asked herself, will Agamemnon think if Orestes is still absent when he comes? What will he think of the girl, brown as brown clay from walking the Citadel and the fields and the lower town in order to save herself the sight of me? What spice was it that he could never bear in his soup—mustard, cumin, celery seed? And then wildly, between inordinate weeping and inordinate laughter: What does it matter what he thinks or what he cannot bear, inasmuch as he is to be murdered when he comes home? Word came to her by returning warriors from across the eastern waters that her lord had taken as his war-prize Cassandra, the daughter of king Priam of Troy; and a witless fury of jealousy took hold on her, a fury that was not wholly shaken off when she assured herself that the nights those two could spend together were numbered and few. She found herself wondering whether she should have a new skirt and jacket made in which to welcome him, and then remembered—grinding her fists into her temples—that the burial would be longer and more stately than the celebration of his return; and some scruple as senseless as her other thoughts kept her from imagining how she would clothe herself for his burial.

When spring settled green and deceptively moist on the parched land, she knew by weather and rumor that the black ships of the Achaians had unfurled their sails and were moving westward, but she did not truly believe it: the coming of the ships, the disembarking on the shore of the homeland, the slow triumphal progress through village and city and field and wood—she saw it all in her mind's eye in harsh color, sharply outlined as if against a violently blue sky in pitiless sun, but its very clarity took it out of the real world, turned it into a series of events in a dream. And when Aegisthus told her that he would provide the meat and wine for the feast, she looked at him in confusion and said, "What feast?"

"Why, *the* feast. The one we spoke of in my garden last year on the day of the Spring Festival."

It was the first time in many weeks that he had made mention of the business, and she felt hot blood come stinging into her cheeks and saw that he had gone as white as whey. "Oh, yes, of course," she said, putting up her hand and picking a piece of lint from his dark robe. "I have not forgotten. It is very kind of you to offer the meat and drink."

The morning of the day of Agamemnon's coming was bright with a sun that scorched the eyelids and garish with hyacinths and anemones. A messenger came early from the king to let her know that he would be arriving a little after noon—only the time of his coming, nothing more. Taking the clay tablet that carried his sparse message into her hands, she felt her anger flaring at the niggardliness, the affront. Five words, she thought, only five words, and after all those years! Five words for the wife who bore him a son and two daughters. Five words for the woman who cared for his property, received the accounts of his overseers, and kept his slaves in hand! And the morning was far spent before she saw the madness of her righteous wrath, before she established in her muddled brain that she was not the silent endurer of his abuse, that she was on the point of taking vengeance for her slights. The habit of submission or the inability to believe in what was to come about—she knew not which—made her dress herself in the sort of somber splendor he approved, made her take part in wreathing the columns and strewing ivy and myrtle over the pavement of the

175

main court, made her say to herself repeatedly as she stood waiting in the entrance of the great hall, "Show no hurt, and speak softly and graciously to all his friends, especially to his concubine."

There was a shout as loud as distant thunder in the crystalline air: he was passing through the lower town. The Steward of the House, standing at her left, smiled and put his finger up to take a tear out of the corner of his eye. Her daughter, standing at her right, breathed out a long, shaking breath. She threw a covert glance at the girl and blamed herself for sending her upstairs to take off her scarlet rebel's robe and put on something more appropriate. The substitute was grey-blue, pale as an early morning sky and suitable enough; but it emphasized the sunburn, made the young woman look like a lean wanderer out of the Egyptian desert land, except for the startling lightness of her eyes and hair. And again, as the thunderous sound seemed to break now in the very court, the queen wondered: What difference does it make whether his daughter stands before him in red or blue, since within a few days he will be carried to his grave?

"They are at the Lion Gate," said the Steward.

"The Lion Gate?"

For, since she had seen him riding out of it under the two standing lions, she could visualize him coming in the other way, and with the image came the conviction of reality. He—Agamemnon —her husband—her deceived husband whom her paramour meant to kill, was entering the city and moving through the packed crowds of his cheering folk. She put her hand under her left breast, anticipating pain, and her daughter looked sidewise at her out of sea-grey eyes and mocked her with a slow and knowing smile.

She could hear, or she imagined that she could hear, the wheels of three or four chariots rattling over the stone street of the Citadel. Blessed Lady, most merciful Lady, is it possible? she thought. What shall I say to my king and my lord, whom I have rendered

176

up to be slain? And while the hard hand closed around her heart, the rattling ceased. "They have dismounted, we will see them in a moment," said the Steward. "Thanks to the gods that we have lived to set eyes on him again."

The king was the first to come up the ramp, dark and almost naked, having put off the gear of war, striding in the pride of his manhood, sinewy and hard as stone, burned red-brown by the sun and made leathery by the winds of the eastern plain—black-haired, black-browed, black-bearded, with the remembered shaggy blackness on his chest. Fear and pain came at her both at once, so that she would have doubled up in his sight if she had not caught and wrung the Steward's hand. His sandals were soft and soled with leather, but it seemed to her in her exigency that he was iron-shod, that he begot sparks and a sharp and threatening sound as he approached her over the paving stones. He kissed her on the forehead, not in tenderness, only to make plain to her and to the bystanders that she remained the mistress of his palace and his queen. The smell of his body, wet with the sweat of the journey, was at once acrid and aromatic; his kiss was like a brand pressed briefly on her brow. "I have brought another with me, the daughter of a vanquished king. Torment her not. She is not like the rest of us. From her youth she has been possessed by a god, and now she is mourning for all her kin," he said. Then, as a thirsty man turns from figs to water, he turned to his daughter, drew her forward, kissed her on the eyelids, and clasped her round with all his might. Pain, fear and pain—and now also the old rage, to see his copper-colored arms around the girl, to see his burning copper face against her bronze-dark face.

"Where is Orestes?" he said, drawing back at last.

"Unfortunately absent on a journey, my lord and my king." It was the Steward who had answered. "Come in out of the sun and we will speak—"

But his sentence was torn by a high, wild cry.

177

Was it I who screamed unknowing in my agony? the queen asked herself, and saw at once that it was not she but his other one. Face to face with her now—since the king had stepped over the threshold—stood a tall young woman, gaunt and white, running wild fingers through the strands of her straight red hair.

"What is it? What is it, Cassandra?" Electra said.

"No, now, do not be troubled," said a fat old woman coming up beside the mad one and carrying in the curve of each arm a swaddled infant. "The god is in her. He will go forth. Soon it will pass."

The queen found enough breath to say, "Come into the house, daughter of Priam."

But the daughter of Priam, though she did not shriek again, did not move a step. In exhaustion, in a kind of sullen resignation, she stared at the threshold with great greenish eyes. "How can you stand where you stand, my lady and my queen?" she said in a voice hoarse with shrieking.

"Why? What is the matter?" asked Electra.

"Are you blind? Do you not see it? The blood on the threshold. You are standing—all of you, all of you—up to your ankles in blood."

"Follow your master into the house," Clytemnestra said, more sharply, since it was plain to her that the two infants in the fat woman's arms could only have grown from Agamemnon's seed in Cassandra's womb.

The thin hands left off their combing and came down first to her hollow cheeks, then to her milk-swollen breasts, then to her skirt, brown wool, brown mourning for father and brothers dead. "Who will hand me over the blood?" she said. "I cannot bring myself to put my feet into the blood."

"Here, I will help you over," said Electra, holding out her hand. 'And the two went in together, and the nurse followed them, and the Steward entered also to look to the needs of his lord, and the

178

queen stood alone in the doorway, waiting as it was required of her to greet the others who came up: her husband's charioteer Eurymedon and some thirty men-at-arms with shields and swords.

The charioteer Eurymedon—copper dark like her husband—had also put off the trappings of war and ridden through the lower town and the Citadel in nothing more than sandals, a loin cloth, a wide bronze bracelet, and a triple necklace of turquoise and gold. He had gone away a lad and returned a man and a hero. His body, oiled against the sun, had a lion's power and a stag's grace; his eyes were pale brown; and his hair waved pale brown and luxuriant back from a hard, manly, flawless face. He has had many women and forgotten them all, she thought. Whether he sleeps alone or with another, he rises without regret, strides away to congratulate himself and anoint himself, to look at his perfect flanks in the first light of the sun. . . .

"My queen and my lady," he said, taking both her hands and bowing his brow against them; and the homage and the male fervor that he indicated in the gesture seemed to her expert and spurious.

She talked vacantly then with Eurymedon and a few of the others who had come up behind him. They told her of some who had returned with honor and booty and some who lay under mounds on a foreign shore, of this one and that one whose faces their names would not summon up for her. It was a strange sensation—it made her feel that she was floating out over the trampled greens on the paving stones—to realize she cared not at all which were reckoned among the living and which among the dead. Pain had departed, making way for fright. Blessed gods, what could have come over her that she should have left father and daughter together without her eye upon them? A few words from the girl, and he would know, and here she stood listening to their empty chatter. . . . "Come," she said without thought, cutting rudely across the smooth deep voice of the chariot-

179

eer, "why should we stand in the noonday sun? There is coolness and wine and a little food inside."

The room's shadow after the dazzling light made it impossible for her to know at once whether she had already been betrayed. She stood confused in the familiar place made alien by those who had entered it before her. Should she go to the long table to serve out the food, or had Electra insolently taken her place? Should she start for her chair of carved wood and ivory close to the throne, or had the daughter of Priam usurped her chair? She blinked many times before she could be certain that all was well: her husband sitting on his throne and beating the arms of it slowly, rhythmically with his closed fists, the Trojan princess standing erect and motionless as an idol beside one of the pillars, the Steward boning and flaking a big fish behind the marble table, her daughter on her knees before a heap of pillows and looking down gravely at something—at what?—at the twin children, unswaddled now and pale as ivory, their curled hands in their mouths, their downy round heads shining with the pale red of their mother's hair.

"What have you borne to the king of Mycenae, daughter of Priam?" she asked in her most gracious voice.

Eurymedon looked up at her and away again, as if he had an ear for the most perfectly modulated falseness. The Trojan princess did not answer, seemed not to have heard, was staring down in a madwoman's wonderment at her own long and high-arched feet; and Agamemnon only smiled a jovial and somewhat fatuous smile.

It was Electra who answered, still kneeling above the children, her hands clasped behind her as if to keep herself from touching that which was too beautiful to be touched. "One of each, my mother. A boy and a girl, come forth together. And what the one does, the other does also. Look how they suck at their hands."

The queen came to look at them; and as she came they turned

toward each other, brow to brow and fist to fist, as if they could feel the approach of an enemy. Their position reminded her of something that begot anger—at first she knew not what. Then, standing above them and smiling falsely down upon them, she saw that they had arranged themselves like the two beasts on the Lion Gate, beasts sacred to the Lady and symbols of the house of Atreus. Is it an omen? she asked herself. Do the gods intend to sting me with the knowledge that these will reign when mine are dead? She bent closer to them, and it was as if they could sense in the air some poison that she was exuding: they whimpered and slobbered, and Electra lightly, fearfully, tenderly touched their feet.

"Ah," said the fat woman, "they are hungry, the poor little things."

"Cassandra!" said Agamemnon in a brazen voice.

The Trojan princess did not turn, only dropped her head until her chin rested on her chest.

"Have you forgotten the babes? They want the breast."

"Yes, my lady, yes, my love, you must feed them now," said the slave, tugging at her mistress's hand until she seated herself against the pillar on the floor, still without raising her head. And she remained so, like a seated image of Io carved out of whitish stone, while the slave arranged her arms to hold the children, and went and brought them to her, and set the boy to the right and the girl to the left breast. The queen was amazed to see that the sweet sucking did not ease the captive, that the tears flowed from her eyes as freely as the milk flowed from her nipples, that not the slightest light of pleasure or relief passed over the half-open mouth, the thin cheeks, the large and desolate eyes.

"And now that we are out of the sun and at our ease," said Agamemnon, "tell me how it is with my eldest son."

Electra looked up from the two hollows that the little ones had left in the dark cushion. "He is on a journey, my father," she said in

181

a mild and conciliatory voice. "When it is brought to his knowledge that you are with us, he will surely return."

And what has come over her? thought Clytemnestra. Does she shield me here in my great hall so that she may take a keener pleasure in accusing me when he and she are alone?

"Where is he staying?"

"I do not know, my father." The girl stood up and walked over to the pillar against which the daughter of Priam rested her back. She was not looking at her father; she was staring down at the two round heads, whose vulnerable crowns could be seen, veined and mottled, through their silky red hair.

"You do not know?"

"No," said Clytemnestra, surprised that her voice should be so steady. "She does not know, nor do I. He went without a hint to any of us."

The king sat upright and looked at his daughter, his fists motionless now on the arms of his throne. "And you—where have *you* been that your skin should be the color of mud?"

"Nowhere, my father. To the graves of the ancestors in the round cemetery. To the watchtower. To the shops in the lower town."

"Why all this wandering?"

"I have been restless."

"That can be mended."

"Whatsoever is broken can be mended by the hands of my father." But she said it flatly, as if to deny that it carried any threatening overtones.

"I have chosen a husband for you, but we will speak of that later."

"Whenever it pleases my lord and my father. Only let it wait until my brother—"

The air was rent again by the voice of the Trojan princess. A cry of mourning—such a loud "Ai!" as sounds behind a bier

182

being carried to the tomb—issued from her, and a great sigh pulled the nipples from the sucking mouths, and the infants echoed her wail.

"Blessed gods!" said Clytemnestra.

The stranger lifted a contrite face. "Let my lady and my queen forgive me," she said in all humility. "It is not I. It is the god's voice that comes forth out of me. It is the god who grieves—"

"What troubles the god?"

"That the bridegroom should sit at table with a sword through his back and his mouth pouring blood over the venison—"

She knows, thought Clytemnestra. She knows not what she knows, but she knows. . . . The infants continued to howl and to seek blindly after the breasts. The Steward, as much at ease as if he had heard nothing but another complaint about the lack of rain, began to hand around plates heaped with flakes of fish and rusks of warm bread: the first to the king, the second to the queen, the third to Electra, the fourth to Eurymedon.

"Excellent fish," said Agamemnon coolly. "She says a god prophesies out of her mouth, and there were many in Troy that believed her. Myself, I do not believe her. She prophesies nothing but death and blood."

"Do not grieve, daughter of Priam," Electra said. "Too much grieving will curdle your milk."

"What difference does it make, gracious princess?" She looked somberly down at the two infants. "Take them, take them. Who would suckle those who are about to perish?"

"No, now, you have spoken more than I care to hear," said the king between mouthfuls of fish. "Hold your peace or we will send you hence and lock you in a room alone."

"Take them, nurse, and I will hold my peace."

It was Electra who took them, and quickly, since the thin arms of the daughter of Priam had gone slack and the two infants were in danger of rolling onto the floor.

"She will be quiet now, Clytemnestra," Agamemnon said, as if he were speaking of a hound that had no understanding of the speech of men. "She will give you no trouble. A threat will seal her mouth. She will become as docile as a lamb if she is threatened with any one of these three things: solitude, fire, or the dark."

"I have prepared a plate for the daughter of Priam," said the Steward to the king. "Shall I bring it to her, my lord?"

"Yes, surely. Give her to eat and she will eat."

"Here, I will take it to her," said Clytemnestra. The dangers inherent in every moment, the madwoman and her prophecies, the presence of the husband whom neither war nor the years had softened in the least—all these had so shaken her that she wished to test herself, to prove to herself by crossing the room that she could move with self-possession and grace. I am not afraid, I am not dizzy, I am not in pain, she kept telling herself as she walked. He suspects nothing, the girl has not betrayed me yet, I need only to keep hold on myself—

"Aegisthus!" said her husband, and she stopped and almost dropped the plate some four paces short of her destination. And foolishly, for nothing—it was only that her paramour had come to pay his respects to the king, and Agamemnon had shouted a hearty welcome to him where he stood in the blinding brightness near the open door.

TWO

IT WAS VERY STRANGE—so the princess Electra told herself—
that what was foreseen in thought and what was acted out in
reality could be so different. In the time before her father's return
she had harbored only one thought: to tear out of her life the
ugly and intolerable thing that had come into it when she had
seen her mother go veiled by night into the house of Aegisthus.
The sole way to be delivered of the loathsomeness that befouled
her days was to let it out in words, to pour a confession of it,
as if it had been a sin of her own, into the ears of the king; and
her whole being had strained, awake or asleep, toward the time of

the telling. But now her obsession had lost its hold upon her on the very day when relief was in sight. All through the hot long afternoon when Agamemnon sat again on his throne and beat the arms of it with his powerful fists, she had not once felt the old desire to tell rising in her like vomit, stinging her throat and tainting her tongue and lips.

Another matter—a matter wholly unrelated to her mother's hideous doings—had come to the forefront of her thoughts. She was obsessed, yes, but not with the thing that had made her flesh turn cold and begin to creep. What held her now was the pair of infants, as helpless, as perfect, as achingly beautiful as the unborn rabbits lying in the slit belly of a she-rabbit that the cook had shown her long ago: creatures exquisite and doomed, creatures about whom nobody cared, creatures destined to become terrible morsels—as tender as the ones Thyestes had taken into his mouth—in a savory stew.

All through the afternoon she had seen nothing but them and their mother, the poor captive. It had been one thing to hear Aglaia tell in the round cemetery how conquerors dealt with conquered women; it was quite another to think that her father—sitting before her sinewy and naked except for his loincloth—had struggled with this thin, fiercely grieving, god-possessed young woman and taken his will of her, paying no more attention to her shrieks than he paid here to her prophecies. And if the mother was to be pitied, how much more pitiable were the children! They could starve to death if no one was at hand to tell her to put them to the breast, they could roll out of her arms onto the floor if nobody caught them, they could lie for hours in their own excrement unless somebody lifted them out of it and restored them to their clean perfection.

And their beauty held her as much as their helplessness. She could never look long enough at their round heads shining with silky red-gold hair, at the delicate and almost invisible tracings of their eyebrows, at the curve of their cheeks and the clear demarcation of their pale lips. At first she was in awe of them and clasped her hands behind her, fearing that she would touch them too hard in her avid delight. Then, once she had been called upon to catch hold of them, she found in herself an amazing measure of skill and gentleness: she could feel the flawless softness of their flesh and enjoy it blamelessly; she could bend over them without harm and breathe their breath, a mingling of the smell of hyacinths and the smell of milk.

Only with a conscious effort was it possible for her to turn her attention from the children to the other matter. All through the day she had to keep reminding herself of what had once been a sharp and continuous pain like a thistle stuck in her heart. I must tell him, I must find some way to be alone with him and tell him, she thought. It is shameful that he should speak with Aegisthus as with a beloved friend; it is unbearable that he should let her sit beside him on the throne, never knowing that he shares his seat of honor with his betrayer. . . . Yet these things were so remote that she had to keep goading herself into pondering them. How is it with me? she asked herself. Have I not sworn that I would tell him, and sworn it twice, once before the ancestors and once before the gods?

After the evening meal, when the children had been carried off by their fat nurse, and the gaunt green-eyed captive had gone upstairs behind them, it was easier for the princess to keep her attention fastened on the business of the telling, but no easier for her to envision it. In the past she had conceived it one way and never thought that it could be otherwise: they sat in the great hall, they two alone, he on his throne and she on the floor before him, gazing earnestly into his face. In those fancies his face had always been grave and sorrowful and he had listened wordless to her tale from beginning to end; but now that he was here she could no longer imagine it so. His face was neither sorrowful

187

nor grave; either remembrance had deceived her or war had transformed him—the face that looked carelessly upon her and her mother and the many guests who came to offer congratulatory speeches and suitable gifts was as hard as diorite and as impervious.

Nor could she believe any longer that he would hear her out to the finish. He heard nobody out—to listen long to any voice except his own plainly drove him into uncontrollable irritation. He snatched other men's words out of their mouths; his fingers tapped in impatience on the arms of his throne; it was as if whoever approached him were another fool come to talk fool's talk in the din of battle, to ask fool's questions over the ring of sword on sword. Harsh, peremptory, acutely aware of the preciousness of his time, he told them all off one after the other, taking it for granted that he knew more about herding than his chief herdsman, more about trees than the Master of his Orchards, more about metal than the Overseer of his Mines. His voice rasped with uncalled-for exasperation above the other voices. And how could she bring herself to claim the attention of this brusque master of men, to force what she had sworn to say upon this overbearing marshaler of hosts?

Listening constantly to that driving voice, she tired early. The small coolness that came with sunset did not mitigate the heat in the great hall, lighted as it was with torches and crowded with visitors. She rejected wine, and her throat and tongue grew so dry that she could scarcely speak; she took a little of it, and her whole body was drenched with a debilitating sweat—sweat that was the more embarrassing because of the courteous attentions of her father's charioteer. Wherever she went he followed, standing so close to her that he must breathe the hot moist smell of her, must see the pale blue cloth where it turned grey from clinging to her skin. Besides, she could take little pleasure in his attentions, aware as she was that he would have given her scant notice if Iphigenia had been about. "Will you have more wine? I could bring it to you," he said. And she was long in answering that wine only oppressed her on so hot an evening: his eyes drew and held hers by their strangeness—they were brown, flat, and peculiarly expressive like the eyes of a deer; and his sunburned nakedness, muscular and spare, forced her to think of what lay beneath his loincloth, worked upon her against her will with a subtle and tyrannous power.

"Perhaps my lady and my princess would find it less oppressive out in the court—"

"No." She had said it too quickly, too sharply, and she could think of no way to make amends.

"Does my lady know my name? I ask because she has not uttered it, not once, through this whole evening."

"Certainly I know your name. The valiant charioteer of my father is called Eurymedon." And at once it seemed to her that she had gone too far in the other direction, had moved directly out of curtness into too much graciousness, doubtless making herself foolish and cheap by offering a compliment that he would not value from one whom he was attending only out of duty.

"Then shall we sit on a bench awhile?"

"All the benches are taken." She had jerked back to the curtness, the rudeness. She could not talk to him: she was distracted by the sun-gilded hair on his long hard legs, by the brown mole on his red-brown chest, visible through another tangle of hair. "If the charioteer of my father will forgive me, I will go up to my couch. I am very hot, very weary—" She stopped short again, wondering whether he would think she was asking for his sympathy.

"Certainly. May the Lady give you a peaceful night."

"You also." She could not bring herself to conclude it with his name.

"I will see you tomorrow. And the day after tomorrow, and the day after that." He lifted her inert hand and kissed it, and she

189

thought what other hands he would kiss with more relish once she had relieved him of the burden of paying court to Agamemnon's daughter. "We will have time for talk in cooler and less crowded places. Again, may you have a blessed sleep."

Halfway up the long staircase she looked back, but not at Eurymedon. She had reminded herself of her vow, and she examined the crowd below her to see whether her mother was brazen enough to join her paramour under her husband's eyes. But they were not together. Aegisthus—he seemed even more unmanly in comparison with the naked charioteer—stood near the throne in lively conversation with the Keeper of the King's Archives; and Clytemnestra had left her station at Agamemnon's side and was standing alone in the doorway as if she were in need of air. Her face—seen at an angle and at a distance—was so thickly painted that it looked like a mask. A mask of pain, thought her daughter: the eyes wide open and motionless, the painted lower lip caught between the teeth—a mask of age and pain.

That image remained with her, was not dispelled even when she stopped in the hall, amazed to see that the fat nurse was drowsing in front of the door of the room reserved for visitors, fearful to think that Cassandra was alone in there with the little ones and might roll over on them and smother them in her sleep. It was her mother's image more than Aglaia that she saw in her own chamber. She talked vaguely while she pulled off the damp and clinging clothes and bathed the sweat away, scarcely knowing what words passed between her and her slave.

"Have you been alone with your father, my lady?"

"Alone with him? No . . . There were at least fifty in the room. . . ."

"Then you have not spoken with him?"

"A little, a few words—"

"I mean: You have not *spoken* with him?"

"Oh, concerning *that?* No, there was no occasion. . . ."

190

"Perhaps you will decide not to speak—"

"Why not? Because of the captive? Give me a towel. She is certainly to be pitied, the poor captive. . . . No, let my hair alone, my head aches. She is to be pitied, of course, but that has nothing to do with it. I have uttered an oath, I have sworn it to the ancestors and the gods."

"Yet my lady did not set the day, did not say when she would speak—"

"No . . . Not as I remember . . . But it makes no difference. Whatever words I used, the gods and the ancestors knew what was in my heart."

"Still, if my lady has not *uttered* it . . ."

"Take away the lion skin—it is too hot for any cover. If the men can walk naked in the great hall, I can lie here alone in my nakedness."

"As you wish."

"Go and sleep. No, wait a little, Aglaia. Let your door stand open—"

"If you are uneasy, I will sleep at your door."

"I am not uneasy. Only, it came into my head that the little ones in the room with the captive might whimper or cry out, and you have sharp ears."

"Sleep in peace. I will surely hear."

But, although she had been relieved of the worry over the children, the vision of her mother remained with her and she could not hope for a peaceful night. Sleep did come upon her, but it was more tormenting than lying awake: empurpled by some fever in her blood, shaken by the fierce beating of her heart, thicker than the dank air of the real world, so thick that it seemed to her that all which happened in her dreams came to pass in a world filled with the steam arising from a tremendous and horrible black kettle of simmering stew.

What came to pass? First, a procession went moving through

191

the tepid and discolored atmosphere, a procession of the ancestors, the thirsty ones, risen from their graves in the round cemetery, with their gold funeral masks hiding their decayed faces, with their glittering garments of delicate cloth grown threadbare here and there to reveal a blackened sliver of hanging flesh or the blue-white shine of a disjointed bone. Since their names had been forgotten for so many generations, she could gain no power over them by calling upon them, she could not exorcize them by speaking their names. What names came into her head would not serve, would only infuriate the dead, because they were animal names, names for cows and goats and dogs. One of the thirsty ones, dressed in black all spangled with golden cuttlefish, drew close enough to whisper some dreadful thing in her ear, and she awoke, calling that particular wailing corpse by the name of a kid that she and her brother had loved and curried and ornamented with silver bows. "Do not touch me," she said, unable to stifle the words even though she was wide awake and saw the room. "I will do what I have said."

She sat up, drew up her knees, clasped them round with her arms and set her chin against them, trying to think of things that might give her serenity. There was no noise from the room where the captive slept with her children; the welcoming was over and the palace was quiet; there was no sound anywhere within. Now and again uncertain lightning flickered violet over the familiar objects around her—the fireless tripod, the shapely ewer, the lion skin rolled up at the foot of her couch—and hollow thunder sounded far away, as though some great rock were being rolled down the slopes of the Arcadian hills by the hand of a god. Gods . . . she had sworn also to the gods . . . and now she saw, not the persons of the divine beings, but their hands. Perfect, enormous, and eternal—bland and hateful in their everlasting perfection—the hands moved in upon her, one with a thunderbolt, another with a strung bow, another with a serpent; and their flaw-

192

lessness was such that she knew it was useless to pray for compassion: compassion was a thing that none of the gods could know. "Take away your threats," she said in a whisper. "Whatever I have sworn, I will accomplish." The hands disappeared, and closer lightning cut across the room, and she wondered whether it had frightened the two infants, how the sleeping body of Eurymedon would look revealed in such a glare, whether the flash had roused her mother out of her sleep. Her mother—where was her mother? Not, surely, in her father's chamber, in her father's bed, under the weight of her father's body, knowing the thrusts of her father's desire? That was possible, though she had never thought of it; a warrior come home might kindle at the thought of a wife's remembered body, might even feel called upon to make use of it in a kind of ritual of return, much as he broke a loaf of fresh bread and tossed a bough of apple-wood into the fire. . . .

But no, the thought was intolerable. She set her teeth into her knee and bit so hard that she tasted blood. That he should take Clytemnestra in ignorance of who had possessed her before him, that he should imagine he sealed his happy homecoming by going into the degraded womb that had known the seed of Aegisthus— it was horrible, and the more so since she could have prevented it, could have gone to him and said such words as would have stopped the driving voice and stilled the hands that beat upon the arms of the throne. The lightning flashed again, the thunder rolled again, so close now that the foundation stones of the palace seemed to shake. "I was most blameworthy to put it off," she said aloud. "I will do it soon." The niggardly sky flung down a handful of rain, and she lay back and listened to the isolated drops, listened until they ceased and she slept.

And now again the gate of dreams was opened and another apparition visited her, single but more terrible than all the holy and awful dead. It seemed to her that she walked in a thicket in the Arcadian hills, a thicket so dried by the endless drought that the leaves above her head were yellow as leather and hard as bronze and the earth under her feet was shifting sand. Something approached her and she stood still and watched it come, her legs bereft of power to move, her tongue sticking to the roof of her mouth, her throat so dry that she could make no sound. What advanced between the blackened trunks of stony trees was the body of her mother, headless, floating toward her like a ship. The head—it was crowned with a high burial crown of beaten gold—the head was held like a votive offering, stiffly, between the two hands. The face was the face that she had seen from the staircase, heavily painted, wide-eyed, with the upper teeth sinking into the lower lip. The neck, neatly severed, dripped a few drops of blood. And the voice—not out of the mouth but from somewhere behind and above her—a gibbering voice like the voice of a bat speaking among the desiccated boughs, said: "The wife of Atreus—she whom Thyestes took—she was bound hand and foot and flung into the sea, but those days are past. Now the offending wife kneels down and offers her head, and her head is severed in one instant by the sword."

The bonds of sleep were snapped and she sprang from her couch, drenched with sweat, cold even in the stifling heat, still unable to utter a sound. "He will kill her if I make her doings known to him," she thought; "he will kill her, and I will see her severed head as I saw it in the dream. How is it with me that I never thought of it before?" She knew then what a difference there was between her father as she had envisioned him in his absence—an idol washed smooth by her tears—and her father as he was and as she had seen him tonight. Agamemnon as she had imagined him would have heard her out with a bowed head and a stricken face, would have wept long with his shamed head leaning on her breast, would have sent the offenders into merciful exile in Egypt or Crete, and would have comforted himself thereafter with the ministrations of a beloved child. But he who had sat upon the throne in the great hall and assailed her ears with his brazen voice—he would stop short of nothing, would look unmoved upon a severed head, would send out messengers on the day after the burial in search of a beautiful young bride.

She could move her legs—the paralysis of the dream was passing from her—and she went and stood against the high window sill. The storm was over, but morning was still far off; all she could make out was the black glossiness of wet leaves here and there between the dull black bulks of roofs and walls. "Where are you?" she said, knowing only after she had spoken that she had addressed her brother. "Surely you will come to me now, seeing how it is with me here. If you do not come soon, I must think that you have forgotten the love that was between us or that you are to be counted among the dead."

Resting her elbow against the sill and her head against her hand, she strove to envision him, and her strivings increased her weariness and brought her into that borderland between waking and sleeping where it was hard to distinguish what had been conjured up from what had been sent by the gods in a dream. There was a shout—or was it more thunder?—and she stood near the Lion Gate and watched her brother ride into the Citadel in a chariot. He wore a cloak that she had embroidered for him, a green cloak bordered with silver olive leaves, and she thought in her heart: Truly, he must love me still or he would not wear in his triumphal procession a thing I made for him with my own hands. The chariot stopped very close to her, so close that she might have touched him by reaching out; and, like all royal warriors returned in triumph—though he had been to no battle, had never even worn a sword—he dropped his cloak and stood in his loincloth to show his manliness, his honorable wounds, his princely body worthy in due time to sit upon the ancient throne. Whereupon there was another joyous shout, but she herself fell to weeping because his delicate and blameless person was not as it had been—his arms were the sinewy arms of his father, his chest was the matted, sun-darkened chest of Eurymedon. He turned and smiled at her, but his smile also had changed, had lost the old easy gallantry, the old innocence, so that he seemed to mock her with his curving lips. "So you, too, have deceived me," she said, weeping. "Where was it, my brother, and with whom?" He did not answer, only nodded and passed again into the blackness— dull black wall, wet black shimmer of trees. And though the long standing had left her so exhausted that she was forced to go back to her couch, she did not dare to close her eyes again that night.

THREE

IN THE GRIM MORNING, with a grim heart, she bathed and dressed herself—no need to call Aglaia, no need to go in finery to her father, no need to paint the mouth which, at long last, must tell. The corridor was grey and empty: the fat nurse had doubtless gone downstairs to satisfy the cravings of her belly. The lamps were burned out, and their wicks gave off an oily smell of dissolution. The day halted, ashamed of itself, behind the eastern ridges; soon it would be dawn, and her father was always up before the light.

Yet she was drawn aside, diverted from her straight march to-

197

ward the moment of revelation by a sound behind the captive's door. The children were whimpering, or at any rate she thought they were whimpering; and half unwilling she opened the door and quietly stepped in. The room was fine and high, and even in the hesitating light gave off its glints of splendor: deep dyes of scarlet and shadowy blue, gleam of silver in ewer and mirror, the brown-grey of the skin of the hare—scores of skins stitched together to make a rug and a coverlet. Under the coverlet on the couch lay Priam's daughter, her red hair trailing onto the floor, her face an awesome mask of mourning even in her sleep. On the rug in the middle of the room, directly in the path of such breezes as might come in by the single window, lay the two infants, brow to brow and knee to knee. It was well with them; if they had whimpered they had done so in some dark amorphous dream that had passed over them as fleetingly as the shadow of a cloud. Still, though they had no need of her, she knelt down beside them, so close that she could breathe the smell of their humanity. They were soaked with urine below—the length of linen that had been put under them to spare the rug was sopping wet to her touch.

The strong unreasoning love that had bound her to them last evening took hold on her again. She blew lightly on their crowns, stirring their fine hair and thinking she might gently waken them; she made a low sound that should have been singing but came out harsh as the creak of a rusted hinge: she had not sung since the night Orestes had given her her father's ring. That ring, she thought, I will soon be giving back to my father, before I tell. . . . Yet the children, so breathed upon, had turned on their backs in their sleep; and she looked with wonder at the place where the birth-cord had been tied and severed and at their sexes—the soft inward fold and the protruding bud. And while she looked the sun rose, as it was bound to rise no matter what black business it had to shine upon. For the moment it shone on the children and unsealed their eyes; nor did they look at her in fright, only in a deep, steady wonder as though they thought: Look what a thing the gods have put upon the earth, how strange! And the boy held up his hand and closed it around a lock of her hair.

She looked over her shoulder and saw that Cassandra was still asleep. She lay in the deepest part of the shadow, as the children lay in the brightest part of the light; and it seemed to the princess Electra that here on her left hand lay all joy, all life, and there on her right all grief, all death. For an instant, so kneeling, with her head pulled down and sidewise by the boy's fingers, she felt a division in the world: the ancestors, her mother and Aegisthus, her father and all the heaped dead on the Trojan plain lay in the greyness with the poor captive; and she herself and Orestes and these children and hundreds of others born and unborn and struggling at this moment toward their lives lay in the rain-washed brilliance pouring over the window sill. But I must get up now, she thought, I must put away his little hand that holds me here, I must get up and go to my father and set myself on the dark side of the world. . . .

"Ai!" It was the cry of mourners. The Trojan princess, waking, had uttered it.

"Be comforted, daughter of Priam," Electra said.

"You also, gracious daughter of my master." She sat up, and the hare-skin coverlet, folding backwards, revealed her emaciated nakedness. Her skin was beautiful, of the color of milk and without a blemish; but every rib showed, and her swollen breasts were unbelievable between the protruding ribs and the knobby collar bones.

"The little ones are wet."

"Yes, so it is, every morning. I will dry them, though it is useless, useless. Look how he thinks to hold on to his life by your hair! He will go, he will go, no matter how hard he holds, poor thing." She began to weep and dried her wet cheeks with a handful of her hair. "And the fat louse has left me nothing—nothing to dry them with—"

"There are napkins in the chest. I will get them."

"Here?" Quite naked, the Trojan princess had come from her couch and opened the chest and dragged out enough napkins to serve twenty infants. Yet, having done so, she left them on the floor, kneeled beside Electra, and began to dry the girl as she had dried her own face, rubbing her red locks over the child's haunches.

"No, now, Cassandra, that is not the way."

"Not the way? You are right. I never know the way if the way is now and of this world. You do it. You dry them. There are the napkins—it was foolish of me to take out so many. Two would have been enough. Who knows that they will need anymore? Who knows how soon this little fountain"—she pointed at the pale and perfect bud—"will go dry?"

"Why do you say such things?" She caught the pointing hand and held it to her cheek. She tried uselessly to fix the wandering glance.

"Have I done wrong? Will I be punished? How should that be? It is the god that speaks. Go and tell my master your father to take the flat of his hand to the face of the god."

"No one will punish you here, daughter of Priam."

"Ai, for Priam my father! Ai, for my mother and my brothers and my sisters! Ai for the city that burned as this napkin would burn, burned in from the edges and crumpled into a piece of black on the face of the world." She snatched the napkin from Electra, spread it out on the rug before her, and fluttered her fingers around the edge of it, evoking the image of fire.

"In time the Trojan princess will be haunted by it no more. In time the vision of it will depart."

"Will it? Will it? Like a scene painted out on a wall? Ai! If only it could be taken from before my eyes. But no, it will not be so, there is not that much time."

200

"A year, two years . . ."

"Ah, come now." She nudged the princess with her elbow as though they were sharing some bawdy jest. "A year, two years! Say a moon, a day, an hour. Darkness is over me and mine, and over others too—many will carry the food of a feast cold in their stomachs to the cold tomb. But you will neither eat nor die. After long mourning, you will be comforted—"

"Cassandra!"

"Ai, how is it with me that I should have done it again? Do not tell it. Give me the little ones, they are dry enough." Still naked, she seated herself on the rug, cross-legged and dull, as she had seated herself against the pillar in the great hall; and Electra, feeling a vast yearning in her own flat chest, set the infants in the curves of her arms and gently pushed them forward until their seeking mouths fastened upon the breasts.

"I will stay with you only until you have fed them, and then I must go," she said.

"But why do you hurry? If you go or if you stay, the gods have established it, and it will be all the same."

"What will be all the same?"

"Why, as you know very well, the blood and the death masks and the wailing. The crowd for the tomb—ah, such a crowd of them. It is well for the kings of Mycenae that they have builded such mighty tombs."

"You have seen too much of death, daughter of Priam." Kneeling there in the sun, she was grateful for its warmth; she took up the soaking linen on which the little ones had slept, and folded it, feeling their warmth still upon it, inhaling the living smell of it, hard put to it not to press it against the spot where yearning opened like a wound in her chest. "You must rest," she said.

"Rest? Oh, yes, that, surely. But it will be a long time before the gracious daughter of my master will rest. Listen!" There were footfalls in the corridor, and heavy breathing. "It is the fat louse,

201

stuffed to the chin. Now, there is one that will bleed like a pig. Only, let it be between you and me. Go if you must and do what you must, even though it will make no difference. What is, is, and what will be, will be."

The nurse, entering, caught Electra with the soiled linen and made a great to-do about providing warm water for washing her hands. She washed them in haste, without another look at the infants. Already the sun had come up, round and burnished, into the grey-blue beyond the window. Death masks and tombs had conjured up the ancestors, and she went as quickly as if they were in pursuit of her down the long stairs.

There was, in fact, good reason for her haste. If she had thought to find him alone—she had often come upon him eating his solitary meal in the great hall before he had sailed for Troy—she was already too late. He and her mother were both there, eating at the same table as if there had been no war and no adultery; and some twenty of those who had come back with him were up and ready for the hunt: their quivers and arrows lay on the stone benches, and their bows and spears were set slantwise against the wall. Her mother smiled and nodded to her but did not raise her heavy eyelids—something in the blank countenance from which all lines had been painted away convinced her that what she had feared most had actually come to pass during the night. Her father bade her a hearty good morning, and Eurymedon leaped from his seat to ask her what he could bring her—curds, honey, a bit of excellent cold roast, some of this fine hot bread. She seated herself beside her father at the table, uncertain of what to do or say. It would have been possible to invite him to walk with her in the main court and to speak to him there without delay; but to do it in a place where there was only the usual cheerful bustle seemed outrageous. Let him eat his food, she thought, and stifled the realization that last night, when she had let him have his night's sleep, he had lain with Aegisthus' woman, thereby defiling and disgracing himself. . . .

"Surely the princess will want *some* morning nourishment," Eurymedon said.

"Yes, I am grateful. No meat. Only a little honey and curds—though surely I could get them for myself."

The charioteer went lithe as a cat across the room to the marble table; and her father's eyes, which had been fastened on her, deserted her and followed the charioteer.

"He is very comely," said Clytemnestra.

"Exceedingly so," said Agamemnon.

Electra nodded, but only grudgingly. He *was* exceedingly comely, with his sinewy body showing almost as plainly through his thin grey huntsman's tunic as it had shown in his nakedness last night. But it struck her as unseemly that her father should concern himself so much with his comeliness. It made her father seem old to her, old and capable of the strange doting that those who had fought their best battles will sometimes bestow upon the young.

"Twice he was wounded," said the king.

She did not listen to the history of his wounds, she only made herself appear to be listening; and when he had brought her plate to her, when his hard hand came into the line of her vision, she could only wish that things were now as they had been in the old days when it had been Orestes who had brought her curds and honey. She did not touch the plate, only stared at it and longed for another hand—hairless, childish, companionable to the touch.

Talk was going on at several little tables set up for the guests. At her own table they spoke in a desultory way of tributes and spoils. Her father told her that he had brought her earrings, bracelets, and a curious pair of sandals whose straps were studded with gold and coral, but she did not wish to see them—she only wondered why he did not name the gifts that he had brought for

203

Orestes. Eurymedon asked her whether she would ride out with them to the hunt, and she shook her head. There would be no hunt, nobody would ride out: as soon as her father had pushed his plate aside she would walk outside with him, and in the court under the strengthening sun she would discharge her vow. She ate little and tried to remember some mad thing that the poor captive had said concerning her eating; she bore with patience the fact that her father had signaled the steward for another helping and recalled distinctly the weary voice saying: "But why do you hurry? The gods have established it, and it will be all the same. . . ." Her mother busied herself with the duties of a hospitable wife, going once to make the rounds of the small tables where the visitors sat, filling her husband's goblet, and offering Eurymedon wine. To her daughter she did not speak, and the girl was glad of that: to refuse to reply was unthinkable and to make easy morning talk with one whom she was about to betray would have been sickening hypocrisy.

Then all at once, with his second plateful barely touched, her father stood up and wiped his beard and turned to her, smiling. "Come, my daughter. It is a long time since you and I have walked around the main court together," he said.

It was not easy for her to hide her agitation. They were chiding her, the fleshless ones, the thirsty ones. They were whispering among themselves in dry voices how she must be nudged and shoved into the business, how she had no heart to move of her own accord. With her head down, like a person who expects to be scourged from behind, she followed her father toward the open portal; and when he laid his arm about her waist she had to tell herself that she need not shudder, that she was not being encircled and squeezed by the arm of one of the terrible, mocking dead.

Yet here outside was the broad day in which the little ones had sweetly wakened. Here were clumps of laurel and paving stones grown fresh after even a meager rain. Here, beyond the parapet toward which they walked, was the wide vista of which the condemned were deprived forever—faithless and defiled as her mother was, she had pulled the weeds from the loose earth in the great laurel tubs, had watched men and beasts laboring in the fields below, had drunk the sweet waters of the spring Perseia, had felt on her cheeks and forehead the moisture of the mist. . . . They stopped at the parapet and stood against it, looking down. Nothing could avert it now, nothing but climbing to the top of the Cyclopean stones and leaping into the gorge below.

"My father—" She said it haltingly, closing her eyes against the life-giving sunlight.

"My daughter!" He had mistaken her breathless beginning for an expression of happiness at his return, and he clasped her so tightly that she thought her ribs would snap.

"I have a thing to tell you, such a thing that I—"

"No, now, Electra, let me speak first. There is that upon my heart which will choke me unless I utter it." She knew that he did not guess. Joy—a foolish, almost besotted joy—came incongruously into his dour face; and her own face betrayed her dismay so that he looked at her sharply and said, "Surely in my absence you were not so heedless as to give yourself in love."

"In love? With you gone, my father, and Orestes also, I have been alone in this house with such trouble—"

"Yes, yes, yes. I have thought of it often. Believe me, I was not unmindful of it. Though you marry late, you will marry well. You could not ask for a more valiant and comely husband than Eurymedon."

"Eurymedon?"

"Surely you cannot think of a worthier man—"

She could not answer at once, could only think that she would have been better served by one who was less manly and less worthy in the world's sight. This one with his hairy body and his hard hands filled her with a sick fear. And then, too, he would be forever taking himself off to the hunt, off to the war, off to the couches of fairer women. Gazing out at a horse running in the green fields beyond the gorge, she suffered beforehand the loneliness that would be her portion—the loneliness and the endless assaults upon her pride. "Father, how can I marry him?" she said at last. "How can I marry him, when my mother—"

"I know—your mother thought to give you to Asterion. But that was a piece of foolishness, and you will hear no more of it. I spoke to her of Eurymedon"—he took too much pleasure in saying the name, he let the name linger on his tongue as though it were the juice of summer fruit—"and she is gratified."

She *would* be entirely gratified, Electra thought, turning her lowered head aside to hide an uncontrollable malicious smile. If I were married to him at once, if my mouth were stopped up with his hard kisses, if he took me away tomorrow to his city with what I know locked up in me to be forgotten until after she and her paramour are dead, she would indeed be entirely gratified.

"As for myself," said Agamemnon, "when he put the matter to me yesterday evening, I felt as if a weight of bronze had been lifted from my chest."

"Am I so poor a bargain? So plain, so strange? Did my father think he would never find a bridegroom to take me out of his house?"

"Oh, come, you jest. If you are not his peer in comeliness, you are his better in station and in wit. You will give him fair children and high hopes—"

What those hopes were, she saw all in an instant, and they stung her more bitterly than the harsh and honest weighing of her worth. Oh, absence and the years had changed him even more than she had thought yesterday while she listened to him work upon others as he was working upon her now, snatching their words off their tongues, refusing to listen to any voice but his own. On the other side of the eastern waters he had taken his charioteer for his son; he had so far forgotten his son that he could encourage Eurymedon to hanker after what was the birthright of Orestes. "Oh, no," she said, catching hold of the parapet, wounding her clutching fingers on the stones. "I cannot marry, my father. I cannot go out of this house in a bridal procession until my brother has come back home."

"But that is unreasonable—"

"How, how?"

"They tell me he has been gone now some fifteen moons. Who knows whether he will ever return?"

Could he imagine it? Could he utter it? She looked at him openly with accusing eyes.

"Many here feel that he is dead," he said, "and I have no other heir. Nor am I likely to get another by your mother, since she is growing old."

She stared at him aghast, and he, quite unmindful, stared at his domain stretching green and golden before him. A sprouting field was crossed by the shadow of an eagle: cruel bird of good omen, bird of harsh kings and hard gods. The fire of revolt against earthly and unearthly powers flared up in her—she kept her face turned from him because she could feel it burning in her eyes. If I could outsoar the eagle, she thought. If my spirit could pass with the eagle to the holiest of all mountains where the immortals sit, unheeding and imperturbable. If I could ask them: Is it just in a king to forget his son, give his daughter where he will, beget children on the body of a mad captive? . . .

"As matters stand," he said, still looking out over the undulating vista, "you and yours are all that I can be certain of in my heart—"

False heart, doting heart, fickle as the heart of the lightest of women, she thought. For such a heart, am I to call the sword down upon the neck of her who bore me and nourished me with her milk? She put back her head and saw the landscape

207

beginning to turn like a slowly spinning wheel before her eyes. No, she could not tell him, not now; and nausea and the taste of vomit rose in her mouth at the thought of another haunted and tormenting night.

"What is the matter with you? Have you been stricken with some sickness?"

"No, my father. Height makes me dizzy."

"You are as white in the face as one of the dead."

"I will be better soon. Only, give me a little time to consider what you have laid before me. I cannot say either yes or no all in a moment. Perhaps my brother will come in a few days—I hope he has only been waiting for my father to return. But if it is my father's will and my mother's. . . . Only give me a little time to think."

He turned her around, put his arm about her again, and began to walk her slowly toward the big tubs of laurel. She looked at the carefully weeded earth around the gnarled roots and heaved up a great sigh. "Forgive me, my father. I know you strive after the best for me, and I am sorry to draw back from what you offer, even for a little while," she said.

He laughed a short laugh—knowing, relieved, and satisfied. "I see how it is, my daughter." He drew her close again and patted her bony side. "You are a virgin, and it is only to be expected that you would be fearful. But that, I assure you, is nothing to be afraid of. The first time, a little pain, and after that, much delight."

"Must I speak with him?"

"With Eurymedon?" She heard it again, his fatuous pleasure in the name. "No, no, I will see to it myself. Today on the hunt I will take him aside and tell him he must wait. It is not a small thing that he waits for. Take your time. Take your own good time."

"I am grateful to my father."

"Only, how is it that you grew dizzy standing at the parapet? I remember, when you were a child, I held you by the hand and you walked along on the very top of it. In the old days you never complained of dizziness."

They had stopped just short of the threshold and were looking straight at each other. If he was pleading with her to remember the old days and to accept his charioteer for their sake, he was pleading uselessly: she could find no soft childish thought still stirring within her, she knew that the last vestige of her childish love for him was gone. "Many things are not as they were in the old days, my father," she said, and turned her back upon him, and stepped before him into the hall.

FOUR

DURING THE WHOLE TIME her husband and daughter stood talking near the parapet, queen Clytemnestra conducted herself according to the demands of her queenliness. None of the twenty-odd guests could have seen that their hostess was disturbed: she seemed only to have been liberated to greater mobility and vivacity. Taking Eurymedon by the hand and drawing him with her, she went from group to group, sending greetings to one man's wife and children, exclaiming over another's scars of battle, promising another to find a husband for his sister and still another to send wine and ointments for his father's new tomb. Nor could anyone

210

have taken her indrawn breath at the sight of the returning two for anything but the cough into which she transformed it. "There they are, we must go back to the big table," she said to Eurymedon, as if she expected only more of the easy talk they had been having before the interruption.

Electra entered first, and it was impossible to get from the young woman's face any hint of what had passed. With her head still slightly lowered and her face as motionless as the face of an image, her daughter walked without looking left or right toward the foot of the stairs. "Sit down, my friend," the queen said to the charioteer, but did not take her own seat and could not force out another word until she had fixed her eyes upon her husband's eyes. Nothing showed there—not the dreaded thing, at any rate. He thrust out his lower lip and made a mild and offhand gesture toward their daughter as if to signal to his wife: "What would you expect of our girl except skittishness?" Then he settled back in his chair and began to eat again. "In time," he said to Eurymedon. "The others leave tomorrow, but you must stay for your answer. All you will need for the answer you want is a little more time."

And then, from the stairs, halfway across the room, her daughter's voice addressed her. "If my mother does not need me here, I will go up to the children. For the rest of the day I will do nothing—nothing whatsoever—but busy myself usefully and innocently with the little ones."

"Certainly. Do whatever you wish, my dear child," she said, and broke out into a heating and reddening sweat, and let herself carefully down into her chair for fear she would crumple and fall.

All that passed thereafter had for her the sweetness and serenity of her unexpected relief. She sat at the head of the table, her elbows on the marble top, her fingers lightly supporting her temples, while the others, ready for the hunt, took up their weapons and started for the door. The sound of their going feet was for her the receding of terror. The removal of their spears and bows from the wall was for her the removal of the executioner's sword. The slaves clearing the table and restoring perfect seemliness to the room were to her mind priests and priestesses washing away guilt with water purified and blessed. In the relative quiet—the slaves of an irascible man walk softly—her furious pulse subsided, the sweat dried on her skin, and she knew herself to be thirsty; ever since yesterday morning she had felt only repulsion for food and drink. She took up her husband's half-empty goblet and drained it, finding the taste as delectable as the taste of fruit she had eaten as a child. "Ah, blessed Lady!" she said aloud, and fetched up a long, loosening sigh.

"So it is, my queen and my mistress," said the Steward of the House from the opposite side of the table. He was drying a large silver serving dish, and he glanced up at her and smiled. "They are home from the wars and gone to the hunt, and the house is at peace and the heart of my lady is at peace."

"Even so."

For a space that seemed to her then and afterwards one of the most blessed times in her life, she fell to imagining that it was indeed so. She held her husband's goblet in her hand and thought how much she had dreaded his invasion of her body and how last night she had submitted to him without the old resentment and had had from his directness—after long moons of elaborate toying —more pleasure than she had ever known from him before. She thought of the long open day, free of the cares that had harried her in his absence: she thought of the lightness and pleasantness of such tasks as would be left to her—to spin the fine wool, to look to the herb beds in the garden, to walk down and chat with the Master of the King's Orchards, to test with her fingertips the hardness of the ripening fruit. And summer will come, she thought, with yellow globes in the dark green leaves; and

212

autumn will come, with olives lying purple in the grey presses; and winter will come, with a red fire on the hearth and nuts in a silver bowl and goblets of honey-sweetened wine. . . . All that came about in the great hall was a delight: as if her eyes had never before beheld them, she looked at the dishes being carried away, at the pattern on the painted floor emerging sharp from under a damp cloth, at the paintings on the wall growing brighter in the sun. "Ah, blessed Lady," she said again, and let her head down, and pressed her cheek against the marble table top as though she were a drowsy child in Lacedaemon. Dreams and remembrances and hopes moved through her mind, and time was suspended, and she tasted, still waking, the healing powers of sleep.

"My queen and my lady—"

It was again the voice of the Steward, speaking tentatively. She raised her head and pushed back her hair.

"My lady has a visitor."

"A visitor?" She thought how fine that word had been in her father's palace, carrying with it the promise of courtly attentions and news from faraway places. But those days were gone, and he who stood on the threshold held out his hand to her in a fervid gesture that tore the web of frail, reconstructed innocence. It was Aegisthus, and with the sight of him came the ingrained slyness: the Steward will go, the slaves are gone, we will be alone; my daughter is besotted with the captive's brood, and will be, as she herself has said, "usefully and innocently" occupied upstairs.

He came and sat by her at the long table, in the chair where Eurymedon had sat. "Was he with you last night?" he asked, and she laid one hand flat and palm upward on the marble as if to say: What do you think? With the other hand, she went on holding the stem of the goblet, a silver one ornamented with small raised lumps like those on the back of a toad. "Well," he said, stroking her loose fingers, *"that* you will not have to endure for very long."

She refashioned it in her mind in an effort to convince herself that she had endured it. But since you have made me a woman, she thought, not lifting her eyes to him, you cannot expect me to abhor the weight of a warrior's hard body on my chest. . . .

"When do they go home, Clytemnestra—the visitors?"

"Tomorrow." She said it lightly and then found herself shuddering. If they were to go forth tomorrow, then tomorrow evening —it struck her as so mad, so preposterous that she dropped the goblet with a clang and straightened and stared unbelieving into his face. The Steward came and took away what she had dropped and wiped up a little pool of reddish, sticky wine. Is it possible, she asked herself, that blood is to be spilled here, that I will sit in this same chair and watch a dagger being thrust into the back of him who knew me and gave me my children? Tomorrow evening? Can that be?

"All of them?" asked Aegisthus now that the Steward had withdrawn from the table and was leaving the hall.

"No," she said loudly.

"No?"

"No, not all of them, I mean. Eurymedon"—the name was like a reef thrust out in deep water toward a drowning man, and she clung to it—"Eurymedon will stay. He has asked for Electra. So there is nothing to be afraid of where she is concerned—she will not speak. She told me so this morning—as well as she could, seeing that she was speaking aloud to me in a hall filled with strangers. She will not tell—I know she will not tell."

He looked at her in puzzlement, with his bald brow furrowed. "Our worst threat is removed, then—at least until we can act tomorrow," he said.

"Tomorrow? But why must it be tomorrow? If she accepts him —and I would be willing to swear she will—she would not want to ruin her marriage by putting her mother to shame. She will let him take her off to his own citadel and never open her lips."

"Could you risk that?" he said to her somberly, pressing his

knee against hers under the table. The contact called up no prickling ardor, only the realization that she had belonged to him as
though she were his slave and belonged even so to him still.

"It would be a small risk, Aegisthus. She is so——"

He went on as if she had said nothing. "For if you can risk it,
I cannot. You have been so afraid of her that you have forgotten
all the others. What of Orestes? What of our fellows in the conspiracy? What of palace guardsmen and slaves? Do you think that
you can hold back the workings of Fate? What will be, will be."

"Tomorrow night?"

"Tomorrow night."

She looked about her wildly, pushing back her hair. The room,
without changing at all, had changed utterly. The room had a
yellowish fever, a fever that would end in death.

"For if we wait one more night than is necessary," he said, "you
and I and the other six of us could be taken in our sleep and
given before morning to the executioner. All of which you know
well, so it is foolish for me to tell you. Say to the king by tomorrow
noon that, since his guests are gone, his servants and companions
here at home claim the honor of providing him with a small and
private feast. I will bring the wine and meat—tell him that also.
And say that my steward will come to ease the burdens of your
steward——"

"Can I say such things?" She was amazed to have uttered it.
It was a question she had meant to address only to herself.

"Can *you* say such things?" He smiled feebly at her, he tenderly
mocked her. His arm, slight and bony of late, moved closer to
rest against her own richly rounded arm showing white between
the splendid bracelets. "I have never had any fear concerning
that, and I do not intend to worry myself now. Whatever mortal
woman has done or can do on this earth, that you can do also.
You will do it, and I and the others will do all else that remains
to be done. Thereafter—tomorrow night—I will sleep in peace

for the first time in many moons, and I will sleep with my head on your breast."

"And what of Eurymedon?" She knew that it was a fool's question, yet she could not stifle it. The young man was good to look upon and in the freshness of his strength. To hurl him down among the thirsty ones was like putting out the opening eye of day, the morning sun.

"Oh, come, surely you see how it is," he said, taking up her hand and playing with her fingers. "Am I to leave him to flee to his own citadel and raise a host against us? All that might be a threat to us—your husband's charioteer, his concubine and the infants he has begotten upon her—must be dealt with in a single hour. Otherwise, how could we ever sleep?"

She did not answer. Her hand went limp in his and she stared at the floor and asked herself, this time in silence: Can it really be? Will they all be slain like beasts with their muzzles in a manger? Will I sit at this table even as I am sitting now, and look down even as I am looking now, and see runnels of blood?

It was as if he had seen her thoughts. "In a year or two it will be as if it had never come to pass. Time will remove the sight of it from before your eyes," he said.

"Yes . . . Summer will come, and autumn will come, and winter will come. . . ."

There was madness in her voice, and he heard it. He closed her slack hand between both of his own and chafed it. "You are mortally cold, but we will warm each other," he said.

"So I hope. So I have always believed from the beginning. . . ."

But they had come so far and changed so much since the beginning that neither of the two could speak or look at the other. She laid her face upon her arms on the death-cold marble table; and he rose and left her so, pausing only to touch her faded and disordered hair with his lips.

216

FIVE

ALL THROUGH the hot and restless night the princess Electra
kept telling herself that she would be more at ease when the
visitors who had sailed back from Troy with her father had gone
their ways. It was true that their presence gave the place a cluttered
and unruly look: they slept in the great hall and under the echoing
galleries; their bedding, wrinkled and bundled up into irregular
rolls or untidy squares, seemed sordid lying about; their war-loud
voices recounting exploits on the Trojan plain made her feel as
if the struggle was not yet over, as if they prolonged it in their
thought and speech out of a strong distaste for peace. Some of

them, she was pleased to learn, were planning to leave after breakfast, but even so it was hard for her to walk among them, to bring choice dishes to the little tables at which they ate, squatting on their haunches like warriors at bivouac; and at noon, though there were only half as many to be served, it was harder still. When the last man of them has crossed the threshold, she told herself, it will be more as it was in the old days. I will help the slaves store away the coverlets and hides, I will work hard and weary myself with running up and down the stairs, and after that I will be ready to rest. But when every weapon had disappeared from its place against the wall and every piece of bedding was closed into a chest in an upper room, she found herself still incapable of peace.

For much was left—indeed, everything that actually tormented her was left. The three who had been the real cause of her distress remained inescapably present and were the more unbearable since they could no longer be lost in a crowd or dealt with according to the rituals of hospitality. Her father, her mother, Eurymedon—face to face with them now, she felt her spirit taking on the numbness of the avenging ancestors in their tombs; it was impossible to talk anything but trivial talk, it was impossible to make any spontaneous movement without being betrayed into hypocrisy.

If her father put his arm about her shoulders, she thought, "This is the arm that subdued the poor captive." If he spoke, her ears were assailed by the harshness of his voice. If he fell into a meditative quiet she could not bear his face in either of its two aspects: hard dominance or fatuous self-congratulation. When her mother spoke to her kindly, thanking her for her labors, she thought: "It is not that you are grateful. You are cringing before me and fawning upon me, and you will cringe and fawn until the day you die, always looking at my brow or above my head." As for her suitor—if he had been hunchbacked or harelipped or halting in his speech, he would have been more acceptable. "Liar, fraud and liar," she kept saying in her heart, "bring me no more pillows for my back or footstools for my feet. We would fare better with each other, you and I—we might even find a way to live out our lives under one roof in quietude—if you came to me with the truth: that you do not love me, that it will be difficult for you to lie against my angular body year in year out, that you are willing to pay such a price for a citadel and black-hulled ships and good horses and warehouses loaded with scented oil and fine cloth."

Since her childhood, whenever she had been called upon to be a hypocrite—to kiss her sister Iphigenia at a public ritual, to walk hand in hand with Orestes' little Hermione, to tell a lie to protect another—a strange affliction had come upon her: she had felt as if a great copper cauldron, suspended upside down in the air above her, were slowly being let down over her head. This fantasy was often accompanied by pain, a clutching pain at the back of her neck, as if some unearthly hand grasped her there and kept tightening its grip until her whole neck and head ached so violently that she was afraid of vomiting. The pain was upon her now and must be noticeable to all the rest of them. She revealed it by the rigid way she walked, by the queer way she turned her body from the hips toward anyone who said her name. And along with the pain came a more humiliating trouble: her thoughts seemed to congeal like melted fat cooling into one disgusting lump, and she felt as stupid as an idiot. So it was with her and so it remained all through the afternoon. The others moved restlessly around the great hall, but she went the smallest possible distances, stiff with the pain and afraid of colliding with some object hidden from her by the imaginary copper cauldron. The others talked vivaciously—or was it feverishly?—and she could think of nothing to say but "Indeed?"

As the afternoon waned, the awareness of hypocrisy, the realization that she would never be able to step out of it, and the persistent pain all seemed to be transfused into a pervading disgust. She shuddered in her spirit as children shudder at a scuttling rat; she found the room dim and ugly as though it were clouded with mist or divided from her sight by a scum over her eyes. At last she stood up and excused herself on the grounds of sleepiness—if she was to enjoy herself at her father's feast, she said, she must go to her chamber and doze a while. They let her go without protest; very likely they were relieved to be rid of her and her peculiar silence and rigidity. On the way upstairs she remembered with a wrenching of her heart how her brother had always seen her affliction coming on, how he had gone upstairs with her and drawn the curtains and strewn pungent herbs on the tripod and laid a wet folded napkin across her brow. Aglaia would have done as much for her, but she did not want Aglaia. "Go away, let me alone, all I want is quiet," she said, and lay a long time on her couch, straight and stiff as a corpse, until the seizure began to pass.

It had gone on so long that little time remained for dressing when she sat up and shook out her hair and knew that she could move again without bringing on a wave of pain. She remembered then that all day she had not been with Priam's daughter and the little ones, and she went down the hall and opened the door.

Cassandra was already dressed for the banquet. In a robe of saffron linen, intricately stitched and pleated, she sat motionless in a chair, staring down at her infants who lay on a pillow at her feet. Since she was a slave, she was not permitted to wear a necklace, bracelets, or a crown; but she had taken her abundant hair—from the roughness of the result it was plain that she herself had done it—and coiled it around her head in a kind of red-gold disorderly coronet. She looked up and nodded shortly to Electra when she entered. It was as if she had withdrawn, not so much from their brief relationship as from all the world.

"The daughter of Priam is fine and fair tonight," said Electra.

"Only let me set my hand here and there to the crown that the gods have given her, and she will be the fairest woman at the feast."

"Oh, yes, the heifer brushed sleek to be led to the altar—"

"A touch here at the side, only a touch—"

"Let it alone! Do not lay your hand upon me."

"Wherefore?" She asked it in wonder and in wounded tenderness.

The greenish eyes, abnormally large in the emaciated face, gave her one look of love and then went blank. "Who knows but that what is upon me now carries a contagion? We have touched often, you and I. It was enough. Besides"—she put her long fingers to the imperfect coil—"I think I have arranged it very well, better than you could, Mycenaean that you are."

"You have arranged it very well indeed. May I sit down on the floor here beside the little ones?"

"No!" The word came out of the captive like a cry.

"No? But I only wanted to touch them—"

"You have fondled them, I have fondled them, and now the time for fondling them is past. Surely you can turn your back on them as well as I, seeing that you never carried the weight of them nor shrieked at their coming forth nor gave them to suck. Ai! How my breasts ache!"

"Have you not suckled the little ones? They will be restless while you sit at the feast."

"Restless they will not be. They will sleep and want nothing. Why do you concern yourself?"

"Because I—"

"Love them? Oh, do not love them, let them alone." And then, in a casual voice, as if she were quite sane and had been talking the trivialities of sanity with another sane young woman, "What will you wear?"

"At the banquet? A dark blue skirt—"

221

"Studded with many golden trinkets?"

"Yes. Unfortunately, too many."

"That is well. What else?"

"A jacket of black linen—an open jacket. My father's charioteer will see that my breasts are no bigger than water cups."

"Would I could give you these!" She smote her bosom, swollen with milk. "Sour as curds—smelling of curds will I go down into my tomb—"

"Cassandra!"

The green eyes mocked her, and the wry mouth also mocked her, repeating after her in a jibing voice, "Cassandra!"

"When will you be finished with death?"

"When death has had its fill of me. Go now and let me alone."

Affronted at last, she turned and started for the open door. But on the threshold she was stopped by the voice saying passionately: "The princess is kind and gracious and has given me much consolation—I would not have her depart from me thinking it was otherwise. May the gods deal with the princess as kindly as the princess has dealt with me. May a hand be held out to her in her time of desolation, to help her step over the river of blood. Say no more to me, neither here nor at the table. That which has been between us is enough."

A kind of dull grieving came upon her then and remained with her while she bathed and dressed. At the head of the stairs, she felt the grief turn into disgust—what a shabby crowd her mother and Aegisthus had called together to meet her father down there; and at the foot of the long flight the disgust turned into outright fear—it was Leontophon, the new Captain of the King's Guardsmen, who met her and took her by the hand, and for some unfathomable reason she was afraid of Leontophon. It only worsened her state to remember that she was responsible for his rise in fortune: if she had not held the Spring Festival, if she had not worn an indecent poppy-colored dress, if his predecessor had

222

not been drunken on her wine and encouraged by her flaunting of her body and her assertion of her power, this one would not have been an honored guest in the palace tonight. His single unresting eye was distressing enough in actuality, but she had a remembrance of seeing it float, out of its socket, across one of her evil dreams. As for his hand—she could not keep herself from wiping her fingers on her skirt once she had gotten them out of his grasp. His hand was hideous, hairy, and so big-knuckled as to seem misshapen; it was hot as with a fever, yet it left a moisture on her palm that no amount of wiping could remove.

"I will not be able to eat," she thought, looking at the lamb on the spit and the ostentatious plenty on the table. And indeed when the charioteer Eurymedon came to offer her a fine morsel of salt whitefish she had to force herself to swallow it. She felt as if she were something weird and inanimate—perhaps a jug to be used for slops—yes, a tall black jug with an opening instead of a mouth, an opening into which she unwillingly thrust the scrap of fish.

"It seems," said Eurymedon, "that I am not to sit beside you."

"No?" She heard more distress than she had intended in her own voice, and she saw his face brighten at it. Plainly, he had not been turned away from the glories of wide-wayed Mycenae, not even by the sight of her childish breasts.

"No. You are to sit at the other side of the table, between the Overseer of the King's Mines and the wife of some other dignitary whose title I have forgotten. But afterwards we can walk a little in the court, if you wish. It will be cool. There may even be rain tonight. The wind is blowing in from the eastern sea."

She wished that she could walk out of the hall and into that wind with its sharp smell of salt and finny creatures. There was something distasteful about the whole occasion. Nameless apprehension made her stupid, and her every encounter somehow went wrong. She forgot people's names, collided with slaves, could think of nothing to say but banalities—and all this under her suitor's eyes. Silence suddenly fell upon the group, and she was as agitated as if some curse had turned them all to stone. It was nothing, of course; it was only that they were respectfully holding their tongues to watch her mother and father coming hand in hand downstairs. They were a regal sight, descending slowly, draped in somberly splendid garments of such colors as one sees in late autumn on the backs of large flies. The kingly he and the queenly she were followed at a proper distance by the concubine walking alone, and her face was awesome. The charioteer took Electra by the elbow and said in a whisper, "What has befallen the daughter of Priam? If she were not moving, I would take her to be dead." And truly she looked like a walking corpse, her eyelids so far down that her eyes showed only as watery slits, her flesh so wasted that the death's head seemed to be pressing out against the skin, her thin lips folded one against the other as if they no longer had need to drink the air. And this face was the more fearful because, for all its moribund look, it wore a fixed and malicious smile.

Aegisthus came in, followed by his Cyprian steward, who carried a silver tray heaped with thin slices of venison.

"There is one thing I wish your father would make plain to me before I go forth from this palace," said Eurymedon, still whispering and still holding her by the elbow. "He must tell me wherein the virtues of your uncle lie and how he has come to hold so high a place in your parents' hearts."

"Aegisthus does not please you?"

"No, now, how could he please me?"

"He has a very lively wit."

"Does he truly? I would have thought a man of his kind— aging, bald, loose in his joints, with a scraggly beard like the beard of a sick goat—would have to be altogether witless to wear such a garment. Hyacinth-blue scarcely becomes him—"

"There is no color that becomes him." She was unreasonably hot in defense of her enemy to this alien piece of male flesh that held her too hard and too long. "Therefore it is all one—he can wear whatever color pleases him," she said.

Yet, now that Eurymedon had brought her mind to bear on Aegisthus' ugliness, she could not keep her eyes from him; and her uneasiness was increased by what seemed on his part an equal uneasiness. It was a small business to direct the few guests to their seats, yet he made much of it, pointing first at each guest and then at the place assigned to him, as if it would be a crucial matter if somebody were to find himself in the wrong chair. His motions were more rigid and jerky than usual, his twanging voice seemed on the point of quavering or breaking, and the little jests and compliments he addressed to each of the banqueters were strangely lacking in tact and taste.

Her mother, though her face was impassive under her tall crown, seemed to be sharing the discomfort of her paramour. Seated at the head of the table on Agamemnon's right—the space on his left was reserved for their dear cousin—she remained motionless with her elbows on the board and her plump hands clasped above her plate, clasped so hard that the knuckles showed white. "Can she think that I would accuse her here?" Electra wondered, and was so disturbed that she did not hear her own name, though Aegisthus had apparently uttered it repeatedly and was pointing with a desperate kind of emphasis at her place between the Overseer of the King's Mines and Leontophon's wife, an insignificant small woman who was overburdened with trinkets and whose strong perfume mingled disgustingly with the smell of roasting meat.

"Where is your husband?" Electra asked. "I thought I saw him here a moment ago."

"Oh, yes," she said, fidgeting and blushing under her paint. "He was here, he must have gone out, he will come again soon."

For some incomprehensible reason, Electra kept looking for

225

him to come in from the courtyard; but when he appeared it was not at the main portal but at the head of the long staircase that led to the upper floor. She stared at him, dragging her palms over her skirt, and found it strange that he, too, should have stopped up there to rub his ill-shapen hands on his thighs.

From the beginning the little occasion went infelicitously. After everybody was seated and Aegisthus in his hyacinth-colored robe had subsided beside the king, there was an unfortunate delay: an unseemly disagreement broke out between the Steward of the House and Aegisthus' overweening Cyprian. The Cyprian contended that the great door should be closed because a dank wind was blowing in from the sea; and the Steward of the House insisted that the door stand open—only on the bleakest nights of winter was it the habit of this household to shut the door. The argument grew loud enough to silence all chatter at the table: the Overseer of the King's Mines listened to it avidly, as did Aegisthus; slaves stood behind the gesturing pair of stewards, fixing shamed eyes upon the smoking dishes waiting to be carried to the board. Finally the queen turned on her own servant in exasperation: "Oh, shut it, shut it. What difference can it make?" she said. "Shut it and let us eat in peace."

But once the high portal was closed and the hall was robbed of the grey evening light, it became obvious that the torchbearers who lined the walls tonight were far too few. The king took the blame upon himself: he had been long away and had forgotten how many bearers were required on a night of feasting; still, it was no matter, no matter—fair women, like stars, shone brightest in the dark. But not one woman at the table considered herself fair, and the worn epigram only made the female guests more prickly and silent. As for the males, two of them—the Overseer of the King's Mines on Electra's right and the Keeper of the King's Archives, sitting between Cassandra and Eurymedon—took no part

226

in the conversation. It was as if they had just quarreled with each other; both were gloomy and preoccupied.

The first course was the venison, brought from Aegisthus' house and therefore served by his Cyprian. It was excellent meat, done with a savory sauce, sliced very thin and sprinkled with flakes of dried parsley. But once it was on her plate the princess Electra could not bring herself to touch it; the very sight of the pinkish slices brought on apprehension and disgust. She was also troubled by the fact that Eurymedon, sitting directly across the board from her, took such a large serving and went at it with such gusto. Her father also, chewing on a slice of it, moved her to acute distress. What is the matter with me? she asked herself. Do I think the meat is tainted? And, looking covertly around the table, she encountered Cassandra's eyes. They were wide open, but there was in them neither light nor luster. It was with Priam's daughter as Eurymedon had said: if her left hand had not been slowly moving around the rim of her plate, it would have seemed that a corpse had been seated in her chair.

"Ai!"

But it was not the concubine who had uttered it. Who, then, had cried out in mortal grief or pain? And why were the Overseer of the King's Mines and the Captain and Aegisthus out of their chairs, standing behind the other guests?

"Ai! I am stricken a mortal blow!"

It was her father. He struggled up and crashed forward and downward onto clanging silver and crystal. Aegisthus stood behind him—Aegisthus had dealt him his death from behind. And not her father only. There, on the other side of the table, Eurymedon's mouth gushed blood onto his dish of venison, and Priam's daughter had crumpled over her plate, and above and between them, with a dripping dagger in his hand, stood the one-eyed Leontophon. The Overseer of the King's Mines was rising from his place beside

227

her. I also? Electra thought. Is his weapon for me? Whereupon the Steward of the House darted between them and then tottered there with the point of a long dagger thrust unbelievably through his bloodied white girdle. "Oh, flee, my lady," he said, gasping and clutching at the protruding blade. "Flee, flee!"

She fled, but not toward the closed door against which the Cyprian stood, imperturbable and smiling. As though the infants had been flesh of her flesh, she ran up the long staircase where Leontophon had stood wiping his hands before the serving of the venison. Down the long corridor she ran, to the room of the captive. And there she found what she had foreknown: the fat nurse lying on her back on the floor, spurting blood from her belly, and the two little ones flung one across the other, their throats slit, their mouths open to show their toothless gums, their eyes staring at nothing as awesomely as they had stared at the world.

"Ai!" she said quietly, striking her forehead. The Steward's blood was on her naked flesh where her jacket stood open. "Ai!" she said again and took the blood upon her fingers and stared at it and wept. Footfalls sounded on the staircase, and another voice —her mother's? Aglaia's?—shouted "Flee!" She remembered that there was a back staircase leading from the upper corridor into the slaughtering pens outside, but she could not take it at once. "All this," she said aloud, "this and all that downstairs is on my head." She kissed the round crowns of the infants, avoiding the soft spots, thinking that life and thought no longer pulsed beneath the sagging tissue of the skin. "Yes, gone," she thought, "and at my doing. Why should I flee? It would be better for me also . . ." But nevertheless, hearing the footsteps closer now, she fled.

There was nobody in the corridor, nobody on the back stairway, nobody in the slaughtering pen—only some geese that let out the fierce shriek that she could not utter. They fluttered around her in the darkness, pecking at her and smelling of dust. "Yes, tear me, rend me," she said into the wildness of their wings. "My father is dead, and the little ones, and the poor captive, and the charioteer, and the fat nurse who stuffed herself for the sacrifice. All these are gone because I held my tongue in spite of the gods and the ancestors. Aegisthus had them murdered, but I am the real slayer. The blood of them all is upon my head."

SIX

IT HAD NEVER occurred to her that the wall of the Citadel—bulwark against any invader, strong so far against even the legendary offspring of Heracles—could be as cruel as a noose to anybody whose enemies were inside. The Lion Gate and the sally port were the only two openings, and they would certainly be watched by Leontophon's men: the guardsmen would be waiting in the thick damp blackness there with orders to cut her down. But if escape through either of these exits was impossible, what was there for her to do? It had begun to rain; the enormous hand of Poseidon threw a few large drops in her face and made urgent sounds in the empty streets as if the whole lightless city were telling her in whispers, "Go! Flee!" She stood still, unable to tell whether what she heard was the beat of raindrops or the fall of pursuing feet. And while she stood she thought of the sole way to get over the wide battlements and down onto the path that led to the lower town.

Of all the buildings in the Citadel one only, the King's Granary, stood close to the wall. She conjured that circular mass of masonry out of her memory, she envisioned its vine-covered sides and remembered the outside staircase that wound around it as a snake winds around a staff—wooden steps going all the way up to the roof, a flat roof that jutted out a little over the ancient Cyclopean stones. That way would be hazardous: once she was on the roof she would have to risk two leaps, a short one from the top of the Granary to the top of the wall, and another very high one from the wall to the pathway on the other side. That second leap —she must not think of it, the drops were coming down in torrents now and she could not tell whether she was being pursued— that second leap might break her bones. Well, that would be as it had to be; the first thing was to find the Granary, to recognize it by the glossy leaves that clung to its stones. Fortunately it was close to the palace—she found it soon, groping into its leafy veil. But the darkness was still so thick that she could find the stairway only by the impact of her foot against the bottom step.

And now her fear of her pursuers was transformed into a fear of falling; her eyes were useless, no sense could serve her but the sense that lived in her skin and the knowledge that, if she kept grazing the stones and the leaves with her left shoulder, she would not step off the stairway and plummet to the cobblestones below. She fought down the images that could confuse and undo her: her father heaving up in his final agony, the cold white crowns of the infants, the Steward's girdle with the blade and the blood. But I am doing very well, she told herself—and almost did very ill indeed, almost lurched to the unprotected right because something had collided violently with her head. Stand still, do not stagger, wait until the blackness no longer dances with silver slivers of pain. It is nothing, it is only the roof extending out a little over the stairs, a few more steps and I need climb no more. . . .

But once she had dragged herself up and was lying on a graveled flatness that smelled of dust and rain, she felt too tired to move, she could only lie still and stare out toward the palace from which she had taken flight. Far down in the blackness a torch, red and sputtering in the downpour, approached and paused and wavered. That was her death down there—she did not dare to wait. She went forward on her hands and knees until her seeking fingers found the edge of the roof and her eyes, more accustomed at last to the dark, saw the faint grayish glimmer of the Cyclopean stones below. She stood up, took a deep breath, and leaped, and down there her feet struck more vines and sent some creeping creature—a snake? a lizard?—slithering off in fright. I must rest a while here before I take that other terrible leap, she thought; I must rest and take off this soaked, dragging skirt, this jacket, these heavy necklaces and bracelets. . . . She lay on her back on the top of the wall, and rain came down, colder now, and went in runnels into her ears and through her hair.

It came into her mind then that she could not strip herself of the trinkets or the sodden clothing. It came into her mind—more unnerving than the thought of the approaching torch—that what she had on her back was all that she possessed. So long and only so long as this poor treasury would last, she could buy meat and bread, sleep under a roof, warm herself in front of a fire. After that, when she could pay no more, she herself could be sold to the murderers, doubtless at a good price. Her poverty, her weakness, her danger broke upon her one after the other like violent waves, beating her down. She knew the smallness of her hoard, the frailty of her thin woman's body. She knew that she was orphaned and worse than orphaned, that her father had been slaughtered at her mother's will, that her brother was gone and would not dare to return, that she was left bereft of the help of men and given up to the fury of offended gods. "Ai!" she said, and turned on her face and lay wildly weeping, with the rain like lashes at her back and the leaves bruised under her beating hands.

Voices—two torches, both of them coming closer—and voices. She must not put it off, she could not wait. She crept on her belly to the edge of the top of the wall, dragging leaves and tendrils with her, hurting her breasts on the enormous stones. Here, here was the edge, as far above the earthen path as her window in the palace was above the street. She could make out the pale bloom of weeds growing on the strip of ground between the wall and the path. If I hang by my hands and let myself down, she thought, the distance will be less. . . . But she could get no sure hold on the slippery stones and wet vines; she hung by her hands only for an instant, and then her fingers betrayed her. She hurtled down and fell backward with an impact that seemed to break her consciousness, her flesh, her bones. Twice she rolled over in the weeds; and even after she knew how it was with her—everything jarred but nothing broken—she could not rise. A terrible shuddering seized her: her teeth clattered against each other, her arms jerked and she could not force them to be quiet, the sinews at the backs of her knees were unstrung.

Then, with the fresh moist smell of the weeds rising around her, she had a sense of things stopping, of imminent evil slowly withdrawing. The shuddering ceased, the voices trailed away, the rain no longer fell. She stood up, heartened, and stepped onto the path, thinking that her strength had been renewed, that she could easily run down to the lower town. But her ankles and knees and thighs ached so hard that even to walk was difficult, and the path was slick with mud. She followed it slowly, tentatively, down along the west wall of the Citadel, down and down into crackling brush and

233

stinging thicket, down the steep slope into the gorge where the little stream, black and sleek as a serpent, gurgled at her feet. On the other side of the shallow water—it was cold, it had bitten painfully at her sore ankles—the upward slope of the gorge was cleared of growth: the folk had chopped down every tree and bush for firewood. It was with the folk that she thought to find shelter and sustenance. Their huts—low squares of mud brick thatched with brush and dried grass—showed themselves as soon as she reached the top of the ravine. There were no lights in the window openings, no torches in the wandering, muddy paths that served for streets; but by now her eyes, like the eyes of an owl, could pick large masses out of the dark.

She had visited many of these houses on the day when she had gone to buy what she stood in need of for her Spring Festival, and she remembered with a melting heart that the folk had dealt generously with her then. But now? How would it be now if she knocked at a door in the black of the night and asked for shelter? Who would recognize her royalty, soaked and bespattered and scratched as she was? And who would let her in if she told the truth—that she was in flight from a new king on his throne? King Aegisthus . . . Aegisthus, king of Mycenae . . . Agamemnon is king of nothing. . . . Kings whimper and thirst with tanners and woodcutters in the country of the dead. . . . The slippery street onto which she had wandered smelled of dough fried in rancid oil, of sweat and filthy woolens, of dried dung and greasy broth. . . . We have both been flung down, my father, you to the dry country and I to this, and which of us is in the sorriest case, I cannot tell. Ai! My legs ache and cannot carry me. Ai! My mind is as dull as an idiot's. Who but an idiot would wander back and forth, round and round, likely to startle a dog into barking, likely to rouse the whole town?

She turned off at the next hovel she came upon, walked up two sagging steps of wood, and knocked twice on the door. Nobody answered. The house stared at her through windows vaguely lighted by a small fire inside. The house was impervious—she began to beat at the door wildly with all her depleted might. She was still beating when the latch was undone—she followed the door, still beating and sobbing, as it moved before her into the dim, ember-lighted room. A man—gaunt, bald, and strangely familiar —stood in her way with a club in his hand. The sparse furze of hair over his ears, the club and the hand that held it, were all leprously white, dusted over with flour: this was a miller's room— in the room of this same miller she had seen the measure run over for her brother Orestes' sake. The man dropped the club and took her by the shoulders and turned her round so that the dull light of the fire fell on her face and her soaked ugliness and her shame. "My lady and my princess—it *is* my lady and my princess," he said.

She nodded, wordless. It seemed to her that her heart was leaping in her throat and fluttering there like a bird.

"Why has my lady come?"

"Not to buy—to beg—" Crazy laughter, uncontrollable, came out of her, and she let her head drop until her forehead touched his hairy, floury chest. "My father is dead." She heard her own voice speaking and knew it to be the voice of a child. "My father—"

"The king?"

"Yes, he is dead. Aegisthus slew him—"

"Aegisthus? So?"

He believed it. He had heard rumors, he had thought of it before. "Yes," she said, tottering against him. "Aegisthus stabbed him in the back, like a steer at the manger, helpless. He is dead, and also Priam's daughter and her little ones, and also the Steward of the House and the king my father's charioteer. Ai . . ." This time the word of mourning came out of her on a shaking sigh. She straightened and looked at the gaunt miller. And now that she bore herself like a daughter of the house of Atreus, he took his fathering hands from her shoulders and stared at the strip of earthen floor between them, white as if Poseidon had strewn it with snow.

"And my lady the princess has fled from the palace? She does not trust the queen her mother?"

She put up her hands and rubbed her eyes in puzzlement and weariness. Had her mother consigned her to the slaughter along with the others? What woman's voice had shrieked at her to flee? She did not know, could not remember, had been too wild to tell. She flung her left hand out in a gesture of ignorance, and there was blood on the wrist, and the miller saw the blood.

"Surely he did not set upon you also?" he said.

"Yes, one of them set upon me, but the Steward of the House came between and bought me this wretched life with his death. Would I were lying with the others in the palace. Would I were—" She broke off, ashamed. It was not meet and proper that the royal ones should grieve before the folk who died of plague and starvation, in battle and at labor in the fields, like the innumerable cicadas whose voices cried from the trees and then grew fewer and at last were no more. "This blood that is on my hand—it is not from *that*. No blade touched me. I let myself down over the wall, I fell into weeds, I came to the lower town through bramble thickets. I have a few bruises and scratches upon me. Otherwise, it is well with me—well at least with my flesh and bones."

"What will my lady do?"

She sighed again and sank her teeth into her lower lip. She did not know what she was to do, and she could not bring herself to think. The dull fire, his spare and simple face, the recollection of his former kindness, and his touch—all these had led her to believe that *he* would do the puzzling out. "Hide—hide at least for this night," she said.

He closed the door behind her, put the latch down quietly, and

motioned her toward some rags and worn leather pillows that lay
before the fire. Sinking into the bulky, sweat-smelling mass of
stuff, she knew that his body had just risen from it. It was his bed
—he was giving her his bed. The fierce realization of her loneliness broke upon her as she sank down, raising a cloud of flour.
Lie here with me, stranger, she thought. Lie here beside me and
hold me through the night. For I am stripped of my royal heritage
and orphaned and hounded by the ancestors and threatened by
the gods, and there is no more strength in me than there was in
the poor prisoner, and I have such a sickness in my vitals, such an
aching in my bones. . . .

He came and stood above her, his head bent, his dusty face
half buried in his scrawny hand, his thumb sinking into one cheek,
his bent fingers into the other. "You can hide here as well as in
any other house," he said. "My wife is gone forth for this night
only, to look to my daughter who has just given birth. Tomorrow
she will come again."

"There are those who may follow me—"

"If my lady's enemies should come in search of her, I will hear
them and rise up from my watching-place at the window and put
her into a great basket and cover her with rags and flour."

But I must not use him in his blindness, she thought. I must not
devour him in my need as all the children of the house of Atreus
have devoured the folk. "There are none in the palace to defend
me and many to make an end of me, yes, and to slaughter any
man that holds out his hand to help me," she said. "All that were
my partisans are in the dry country, save only my brother, and
he is gone these many moons, nor will he return now that Aegisthus is on the throne. Also, I have offended the immortals—I have
forsworn an oath I made to both the ancestors and the gods."

He sat down on the floor, cross-legged, at the narrow window
and remained there long in thought. The warmth that his body
had left in the rags and pillows was gratifying and sustaining.

Under the poor covers, she took off the wet clothes and stripped her arms of the heavy bracelets. Her eyes ached and the dull red of the fire began to blur; she floated on the boundaries of sleep.

"As well here as in any house," he said again. "Tomorrow we will see what can be done. It is wisest to wait out the night."

Sleep drew her over. She was a child, drowsing before the fragrant fire in the great hall, turning and sighing against her father's chest. "Give me a little water. My mouth is dry," she said.

And the voice that answered her taught her where she was and what she was. Her father was a corpse, and her heart had mocked and belittled him while his life was yet in him. Her brother—if indeed he was still on earth in the light of the sun—would not return. She lay in a mud-brick hovel at the charity of a miller—a miller upon whom she had put the necessity to risk his life for her sake. "My lady must sleep without water. The ewer is empty. Would she have me fill it outside in the middle of the night? Would she have me rouse the dogs? Let her keep her silence now if she does not wish to bring her enemies down on this helpless house," he said.

SEVEN

WITHIN TWO DAYS the fat nurse who had come over the water with Priam's daughter and her little ones was put into a shallow grave in the poor man's cemetery on the slope under the watchtower. Within three days the Steward of the House was laid away with modest rites and seemly gifts in the tomb of his family outside the Cyclopean wall. But five days went by before the royalty of Mycenae and Troy were carried with the necessary pomp into the regal sepulchers; and even though their changing bodies were splendidly covered, even though the infants were wrapped up in gold beaten into foil and the faces of the king and his concubine were hidden under gold masks, the wait was much too long.

The royal tombs of Mycenae, vast hollows hewn into the belly of a mountain, were almost inaccessible. Atreus had built the last of them, a chamber shaped like a beehive opening up at the end of a long passageway cut straight into the mountain rock; and it was this passage that caused the sickening delay. In fear of mad or godless thieves inside the Citadel, in even greater fear of the return of the avengers of Heracles, Atreus had ordered his builders to dig far in and had commanded that the whole corridor should be filled up with earth packed hard, earth that would have to be dug out before the door to the sepulcher could be unsealed and the rooms could be used for other burials.

Packed hard it was: the folk and the royal slaves who labored at it said that either the long drought or some malice on the part of the immortals had almost turned it into stone. They went at it with picks and shovels and gave themselves no rest. They talked endlessly about the hideous changes that were taking place in those who lay in rich trappings over in the great hall. It was a dreadful thing to lie unburied. He who lay unburied was neither a king nor an ancestor—he was an abomination. They stopped in the digging to sniff the air and imagined that even at this distance, with the massed Cyclopean stones between, they were breathing the taint of dissolution.

What was imaginary in the dank passageway to the tombs was actual in the palace. Queen Clytemnestra sent for jar after jar of perfumed holy oil, but no spice scent nor flower scent could overcome the clinging odor; and in the end she knew that death could not be made to smell like spice and flowers, that spice and flowers from this day forth would smell to her like death. She could not flee the bodies: this was royal decay and made an undeniable claim upon her respect and solicitude. To abandon the corpse of the bitterest enemy, so long as it was a royal corpse, was to affront

240

the gods. Day and night she stood in the great hall where the heat of sunlight and the heat of torches hastened the melting, the falling away; and most of the time she stood alone.

Later, she thought, I will ask *him* why he did not stand with me. Later I will mock him with his weakness, will tell him how, though he was man enough to cut down the living, his manhood deserted him when it was a matter of watching with the dead. . . . He sent word to her that he was sick. He had a friend point out to her that it was doubtless better for her and him to remain apart until after the burial—a foolish excuse, since everybody was conducting himself as if the holocaust had been a tragic accident. The first time he showed his face he could not bring himself to stay longer than a moment: he went out choking and white and ready to vomit, pressing his hand over the pit of his stomach as she kept pressing hers over her heart.

The pain there was violent and recurrent; sometimes it seemed to her that she herself was one of the dead, that her sagging cheeks and breasts were dissolving like wax, that her mouth gave out the odor which her nostrils breathed in, that this sleeping on her feet was a form of going forth out of the world. Then something—a draught of goat's milk, a fresh wind touching her face—would convince her that her death was different from the others' deaths, that hers would pass. The passageway will be cleared out, she told herself. They will be carried forth and shut away. I will walk in the orchard with the light falling upon me through the blossoming trees. Blessed blossoms, blessed light . . . But when she dreamed herself there, with the white absolution over her head, she never thought of *him,* she always saw herself walking there alone.

Others came and went, leaving their gifts for the dead: every table and bench in the great hall was loaded with offerings—a fortune to be buried with carrion. With the arrival of some of these visitors, a strange transformation would come upon her.

They behaved as if she were merely a widow with a widow's grief, and their gifts and consolations stirred up a false sorrow, and she found herself on the point of falling on their necks and shedding an ordinary widow's tears. But she did not indulge herself in such mawkishness. She was not a woman bereft—she was a murderess who had released herself from an intolerable captivity. And by the fourth day she had grown so contemptuous of these lapses, these softenings, these healing lies that she had turned her face into a thing of stone.

On the fourth day she saw that this temporary death of hers was about to come to an end: *he* arrived along with his Cyprian steward—she was forever expecting her own steward to look to this or that, forever forgetting that her own steward was dead— *he* arrived and asked her approval of his arrangements for the funeral. It was late afternoon when they came, the worst time for the stench, and a time when sight also was affronted. As the light became oblique in the inward reaches of the room, the corpses became more grisly: a web of shadow descended upon them and clung to them; it was as if cobwebs had settled down upon them— it set her to wondering whether a colorless mould grew on the dead in the graves. *He* placed himself with his back to them, and she smiled maliciously at that and at his hand going to his nose, his stomach, and back to his nose again. "There will be a long procession," he said. "All the Mycenaean court, and then you, and then—then those—and then I, and after me the slaves to carry all—all this—"

He had never before faltered in his speech; always she had taken pride in the readiness of his tongue. She stared at him with narrowed eyes and said to him through a mocking, scarcely moving mouth, "And it will depend upon the way the wind is blowing which one of us gets the worst of this stench, you or I."

He looked at her quickly and looked away again. His ears at least had not lost their old sharpness for overtones. "I know how it is with you," he said in appeasement. "Day and night I think of nothing else. After we have—have put them away tomorrow, come to my house—"

"I do not believe I will do that." She uttered it coldly, with dignity.

"No?"

"No. I will not have it said—not of me, at least—that I fled a stench which I raised up. We will wait—it will be no great cost to me to wait—until my palace is acceptable to you. Then you will come to me."

He looked at her wretchedly and said nothing. It was she who went on with it. His Cyprian was standing nearby with a tablet bearing the list of the court mourners, but she cared not at all who heard her in her bitterness. This at least she had bought with the slaughter: the right to speak out, the right to lie and connive no more. "Have you named my daughter among the funeral guests?" she said. "Where *is* my daughter? Last night when I was standing as you stand now—but I was turned around the other way—last night I looked too long at the captive, and it seemed to me that I was lying in her place—"

"You?"

"Yes, I myself, with Orestes stretched out on my right and Electra on my left."

"May I be accursed if I—"

"Oh, you are accursed as it is. Both of us are accursed—"

"May I be accursed if I have touched so much as a hair on the head of either one. They are the fruit of my beloved's womb—"

"True, true, the last fruit, the only remaining fruit. Never think that you and I will raise up others. I am dead in my belly, dead beyond the giving of life. As for you"—she raised her voice in disregard of his begging eyes—"I do not think *your* loins are altogether untouched."

And he, too, careless of the Cyprian, said, "Accursed I am,

and used by Fate, and sick unto death with this, and hopeful of nothing except that in you I may find rest—"

"Rest?" She laughed, and the laugh was loud and obscene in the presence of the corpses. "What rest can I have or give, seeing that I have sat through such a banquet and stood in such a house of corruption? Go—take your Cyprian with you and go—his stomach is as squeamish as your own. Let them be buried according to whatever plans you have made. I care nothing about their burial. Ants that feed on their dead fellows are more reasonable than men. I cannot keep a proper face with thinking how laughable it is that slayers should be so ceremonious over the dead hulks of those they have slain."

He went—she did not see him again until the morning of the funeral. Her weariness was beyond enduring. The returning pain in her chest made her left arm feel as if it had been hewn out of granite; in four days and four nights she had not taken the sum of one night's sleep; and when she was awake she had scarcely been off her feet. Exhaustion, horror, and contempt for the deserter had so worked with her that the court, waiting for her before the palace, could easily take her for a widow distraught. In the shrill scream of funeral pipes, she could make what sounds she chose, she could speak to herself unheard.

The sky was pitiless in its brilliance and its empty immensity. She muttered against the sky because its blueness gave the brown robes of the mourners a purplish cast, as though they were on their way to a festival instead of a burial. She muttered against the sun that showed her in her ravaged state; she muttered against the wind that would not stir, would not blow the clinging cobweb of decay back into *his* face. The long procession of the well-born moved in front of her and she reeled after them, stumbling as if she were drunken and uttering whatever came into her head. "Curse you," she said to the many who had kept—and who hoped to profit by—their silence. "Move on, keep your faces front. If

244

you turned and looked and saw what this has done to me, you would cut me down and set some other on the throne." She cursed the Lion Gate as she passed beneath it. "Are you here," she said to the standing beasts, "to remind me that what stinks behind me rode through your shadow in glory a few days ago? Would you were broken, would you were pulled down, would you were smashed by the hammers of the avengers of Heracles!"

Beyond the gates were the folk, bowed and with muffled faces, and these also she cursed, these also she consigned to destruction for their rigid ritualistic grief. "Ai!" they said repeatedly and in a maddening rhythm; and the smell of their sweat was sickening —life itself was mortality, living gave off the smell of death. . . . Something flew through the air behind her and startled her. She thought it was a wild red bird and turned her head. No bird—an anemone thrown by one in the crowd onto the bier of Agamemnon —a red anemone, large and feathery and fringed, the color of revolt, the color of a certain scarlet dress. Only the girl could have thrown it, none among the folk would have dared to throw it. And the girl also she cursed as she moved forward between the two files of walking and chanting folk: "The gods dry up the marrow in her bones, the gods dry up the moisture in her womb, for it was she who goaded me to this, it was she who pushed me up to the neck into the stench of this."

They went on, carrying the noise of pipes and wailing voices to the riven mountainside, to the opening of the passageway to the burial chambers of the house of Atreus. Here at the entrance there was a wait: the Chief Priest had come out of the tomb to meet them and to say the words of comfort ordained to break the sudden unbearable hush. He said them accurately, though he was old and weak in his mind and his voice cracked now and again: "Ai, for those who depart out of the light of the sun. Ai, for those who follow them to the tomb and without them go back home. Yet man is mortal, and fortunate is he who has satisfied his ancestors and his gods and is brought in honor to a seemly place of rest. . . ."

There was more, but she did not hear it. Behind her, around the bier of Cassandra and the infants—she had quite forgotten that bier—there was some stirring. It seemed to her that she had heard the metallic crackle of the gold foil that encased the little ones, had heard it before she heard the quick multitudinous drawing in of breaths. It was true—she *had* heard it: a figure cloaked and hooded was reaching through gold into corruption, was giving to Cassandra's children such little pottery figures of divine guardians as poor folk always buried with their little ones. "What is this?" said the Chief Priest, startled, staring. And the queen said, "Nothing. Let her alone."

For it was she and no other. The hood had fallen backward. The hair had been cropped. It lay short, like an athlete's, around her narrow cheeks. Her eyes were at once insolent and craven. Insolent for *him* and me, her mother thought, and craven before the ancestors and the gods. . . . "Ah . . ." said the folk, and then, themselves craven, turned it into "Ai!" and gazed at their own sandals as if to show that they had seen nothing of what had come to pass.

"Will you come in now, my queen and my lady?" the Chief Priest said.

"Surely." She took his old arm and knew that she could not lean upon it. Indeed, in his witlessness he had thought to lean upon her; and the two of them halted and staggered through the darkness and the shadow, through the great door, unsealed at last, into the tomb.

ONE

THE YOUNG MEN had been on their way for a long time, so long that they had lost count of the days and could not hope to find themselves again in time until Io, long absent from their black nights, showed her two horns again above the unpeopled woods and hills. In space, too, they were not sure of themselves. Dream visions had warned them both—first Orestes and then Pylades—to use the least traveled paths on their way from Crisa to Mycenae. The messages of the gods were inscrutable: why they should have to hide themselves now that the walls of Troy were down and Agamemnon had returned to his Citadel they did not know.

Yet the young men had obeyed their dreams and were not sorry for their scrupulousness. The highroads were hot and dusty in late spring; and they made their way through places where perhaps no man had set his foot before—through forests of pine and plane, over green beds of fragrant needles, out onto ridges where the sky opened up into blue innocence crossed by clouds that looked like lambs down into untilled fields where the fresh winds blew the weeds now westward, now eastward, shaking the yellow mustard flowers, turning the scarlet blooms of the anemones.

They went on foot, of course. It would have been foolhardy to take a chariot; no wheels could have gone over the land through which they passed. They carried on their backs skins filled with curds, wine, and dried venison; and to these they added mountain water, cress and wild celery, and certain harmless and savory roots. They took pleasure in their shared solitude, in the sound of their own voices in silent places, in the sight of their shadows falling before them over the flowering weeds. The shadow of Pylades was longer than the shadow of Orestes: though he had not been old enough to go to the war at the time of the marshaling of the host, he had turned in the interim into a warrior without a battle. He was spare as an eagle, hard as a rock, burned brown as a nut by ceaseless walking and working in the sun. It was a small court, small and poor, the court at Crisa. And if the family that inherited its palace wanted fruit and flour and wine and yellow oil from the olive press, they themselves had to go half naked into the orchards and the fields to help during the time of harvest and the time of sowing. Pylades—though he was of princely stock, being the son of the sole sister of Agamemnon and Menelaos—Pylades had less trouble than his cousin Orestes in disguising himself to look like one of the folk. The time on the road had increased the illusion: his straight black hair had grown down to his shoulders, and his beard—untrimmed but blue-black and lustrous—covered the lower part of his face.

When now and again they met with any others—gamekeepers, messengers, sick men seeking help at a shrine or desperate men in flight—it was Pylades who did the talking, giving his voice a peasant twang, moving his hands in wide gestures as a village dweller would. And not once in all those days had their rustic disguise been held in suspicion. All whom they encountered believed what Pylades said: "We are two shepherds from Crisa, dismissed by our master because a third of the flock was carried off by foxes and eagles. We have heard that Agamemnon is come home to Mycenae, and we are bound for the Citadel to see if we can find work with the Overseer of the King's Herds."

The ease with which he told this lie amazed his cousin Orestes. Perhaps, the exiled son of Agamemnon thought, the secret of it was something like a beginner's luck in a game of chance. Pylades lied so well because he was a *fresh* liar, reared in a court where it was never necessary to lie to save one's skin, where, in fact, one's skin was never in jeopardy. In Crisa, the mother loved and served the father, the father loved and sustained the mother, and love from both of them, intermingled, came constantly to the child. It was ample love; there had been enough to take care of him also, the frightened traveler without a hearth fire of his own. In Crisa, everything was simple, everything was easy. He could say what he liked the moment it came into his head, without asking himself, "Which of these bitter contenders am I likely to offend?" And this workaday directness gave a kind of authenticity to the few deceptions made necessary by a complicated world.

"I cannot stay here—this is the first place where Aegisthus will look for me," he had said to the father on the day of his arrival. And the father, assuming a shrewdness not overdone through daily use, had smiled and answered: "But you were foolish to come in

251

the first place, and for that very reason, you must remain. Aegisthus will think that you would never come to your aunt—you are not fool enough for that—so he will look in a dozen other places before he seeks you here. Therefore you can stay in safety —not, of course, that we will not make ready a place for you to hide in, if rumor should bring him here."

Crisa . . . He could not think of Crisa without feeling the ache of loss, a palpable gnawing emptiness as if some starving creature crouched in his stomach and ate at it from within. Pylades could leave the place gladly enough: he had seldom left it before, and he meant to return to it soon. But he, Orestes—when would he see it again, its hall of state so small that the comforting fire in the middle of it cast a ruddy blessing on all four of its walls, its floors and benches haphazardly strewn with pillows and rugs, its visitors clomping in at all hours with clots of mud on their sandals, its lord cracking nuts with his strong fist for himself and for everybody else, its mistress never called upon to strike a pose, always at peace in the pose the gods had assigned to her—a grave presence on a stool, spinning wool in front of the fire?

"Our palace is not proper to live in," he had said once to Pylades, who had looked at him in wonderment: the palace at Mycenae was known through the land for its comfort and magnificence. "What I mean is: It is not suitable to *live* in—"

"Is it cold? Are the drains corroding?"

"Oh, no, no, no. It is warm enough and every drain in it works just as it should. I only mean that, as a place to *live* in—"

"But if it is not a place to *live* in, then of what use is it?"

"It is well enough for giving banquets, for receiving ambassadors—for all that manner of thing—for a feast, or—or for a—"

He had ended it stammering, for a strange thought had come into his mind, a thought he could not utter even to this most pleasant of companions, the thought that the great hall in his own home was best suited to the pomp of a funeral. . . .

252

They stopped in their walking, both held by the same sight: a marsh grown over with delicate grass. Blue-eyed grass they called it, for when it was in blossom as it was now, it broke into thousands of minute flowers, flowers of so pure and unearthly a color that they seemed like fragments dropped from the morning sky and left to float on earth. "Marsh country," said Pylades. "This marsh, and then Nemea and then another marsh that mingles with the sea."

"Nemea is not far from Mycenae?" He put it in the form of a question because almost every observation of the sort he had made on this journey had proved inaccurate. *He* knew courts, policies, intricate intrigues, dark secrets; but Pylades knew the face of the land.

"Not too far off," said his companion. "From Mycenae to Nemea was an afternoon's stroll—or so they say—for Heracles. But we are not demigods, and seeing that we are mortal and weary and the sun is close to the zenith, my thought is to indulge our weariness and rest."

Though Pylades spoke always of "our weariness," Orestes knew well enough that the prince of Crisa had not been weary once in the course of their journey. It was *his* knees that felt as if they would buckle, *his* heart that pounded in his chest, *his* pale back and arms that grew feverish and blistered in the sun. That feebleness had not always been with him. It had entered into him along with the daemons of chills and fever when he and the good old man—buried now in a cave near the palace of Crisa—had been in flight from Mycenae; it had assailed him now and again in the time of his exile; and he had never been sure that he had not invited its return. To lie on a couch of sickness in Crisa was to lie suspended in a warm bath of love; and it was as if he had cunningly taken from the mother and father there what he had missed at home. He was ashamed of that, yet he smiled secretively to remember it: hot milk sprinkled with spices, bread pulled into small

253

bits and put into his mouth as into the beak of a pet bird, the softest covers, the most yielding pillows, the glow of the carried lamp shielded by his aunt's plump hand: "Oh, have I awakened you? I did not mean to startle you. It was only that I was anxious for you and felt a great need to see how it was with you. Go to sleep, go to sleep. . . ."

"Whatever you decide in your kindness and your wisdom, my cousin Pylades," he said.

His companion looked at him out of the corner of his eye, plainly hearing in his voice some echo of the old debility. "This is not a place where a man should be taken with chills and a fever," he said. "Near Nemea there is an inn—a poor inn but a clean one. If we walk northward, we will miss the depth of the marsh, and then we may eat and rest a little in that Nemean inn. Think of it —hot porridge and fresh bread!"

He did not think of it. He thought with loathing of the palace at Mycenae and managed to distract himself from that by conjuring up the narrow, earnest face of his sister Electra. *Her* he would be glad to see—unless, of course, she too was changed and tainted; everything was changed or tainted sooner or later. Suppose they had given her in marriage to Asterion. Suppose she was with child, pear-shaped, coming on heavy feet to meet him. Suppose she had discovered the thing that had made him flee and had herself taken flight. . . . It was impossible to bypass the marsh completely. Every now and again he would find himself up to the ankles in oozing mud and would be hard put to it not to shiver. He was not so much afraid of an onslaught of his sickness as he was of being afraid.

His cousin, striding along beside him, cursed the ooze. "It is truly wretched here," he said, as if he sensed the fear of fear and wished to do everything possible to allay it. "It is enough to make any man shudder: cold underfoot and in the shade, and hot— roasting hot in the sun."

254

"Are we near the inn?"

"Is my cousin tired?"

"No, not in the least. It is only that I would be grateful if you would look at me to see whether I am still a creditable shepherd, before I come under other men's eyes."

The prince of Crisa stopped, stepped in front of him, and scrutinized him from top to bottom. It was pleasant to see Pylades against blue sky and far-off floating islands of blue-eyed grass. He was lean, but with a healthy leanness, as if his mind had told his flesh not to burden him too much. He had long arms and long legs whose only curves were bulges of muscles. The tendons showed plain and strong through the dark, tight skin of his neck and his hands. His smile was slow and grave: it came only of itself, he never made it come. The shape of his eyes was strange, somewhat like the shape of an almond; and the eyes themselves never ceased to startle and delight Orestes. They were of a clear pale brown, and they knew no cloudiness, no veiling, only a certain shyness. They would look steadily and then dart aside, like the eyes of a stag encountered in a wilderness.

He looked at the "creditable shepherd" and then nodded. "Well enough," he said, "well enough." Then, with a freedom that nobody else but Electra had ever used toward the sacred person of Agamemnon's sole son, he rumpled the tawny hair, lightly slapped the beardless cheek, turned on his heel and walked toward something that looked like a beehive on a horizon shaken with the light and heat of noon.

It turned out to be the inn, that beehive—a big square shed roofed over with stubble and dried grasses. There were fields around it: the ooze of the Nemean marsh seeped to the surface here to nourish patches of cumin, barley, and crinkled parsley. Peasant girls, with their skirts bound up so high that their legs showed bronze-colored in the sunlight, called to them old phrases of banter and invitation, so long in use that they no longer had

255

any actual force, could provoke nothing but laughter and equally ritualistic replies.

The inside of the inn was shadowy, smelling of simple and decent cooking, and flecked here and there with vague bits of sun that came through the gaps in the thatch. Aside from the plump innkeeper, who welcomed them with busy hospitality, bringing them basins of cool water for their hands and feet, there were only three others in the big square chamber. A sunburned lad of twelve or thirteen sat in a corner, cutting and trying a reed pipe, and two huntsmen were squatting at a low table near the far wall. Their gear stood out sharp against the unpainted stucco: two long bows, two quivers, two leather bags over which the necks of dead partridge hung, dripping blood on the reed-strewn floor. Orestes chose a place not too close to the huntsmen, and Pylades asked after their fare and did not forget to lay out three little copper beads to show that, vagabond shepherds though they were, they could pay for whatever they would eat.

A pleasant sleepiness settled upon Orestes. Later he remembered it as more than pleasant, as a condition that was close to bliss. The simple food ordered and expected—pease porridge and a cut of roast fowl and bread and yellow wine—became in recollection food fit for the tongue of a god. He looked at his companion through drowsy eyes and found him good, reasoned that Fate had not cheated him in sending him forth if he had been paid for his exile with such a friend. Even the necessary return to the palace at Mycenae had ceased to gall him: perhaps *she* had given up that shameless business with *him* now that the king had come back; perhaps the blackness and the stench of it had not even touched his sister in her innocence; perhaps, as age came on and the blood grew cooler in his mother's veins, she too would be content to sit spinning, happy with the kisses that a passing husband or son or daughter pressed on the top of her head. Had it been so once, before the coming of Aegisthus? He was too sleepy to think, he had been too young to know. . . . He smiled back at the un-asked-for smile of Pylades; and the lad in the corner tried his reed pipe and ornamented the stillness with a silvery thread; and the two huntsmen—doubtless minor lords from their quiet voices and from their dainty ways with their fingers and their food—had finished eating and had begun to talk.

He did not listen. It was from a sudden stiffening of the face and body of Pylades that he took his signal for the end of bliss. "What is the matter?"

Pylades shook his head and tilted it, almost imperceptibly, in the direction of the huntsmen. They were—Orestes noticed it for the first time—father and son.

"Dead," said the son.

"No, come, now," said the father. "How am I to believe it?"

"I have heard it twice—once in the house to which we went for water, and here again in the kitchen from the keeper of the inn. Ask him and hear it with your own ears when he brings the food to these others."

Orestes said with his lips only, "Who is dead?"

"Wait," said Pylades, "I did not hear, I am not certain. Wait, we—"

Their innkeeper came and set the meal before them. But the blessedness had gone out of it: it was poor food on poor crockery. Round yellow dots of grease swam on top of the soup, and the rim of the bowl bore the print of the innkeeper's thumb in a dirty green.

"Innkeeper," said the huntsman's son, "tell my father that which you told me in the kitchen."

The fat fellow straightened and set his fists on his hips, and began his story. He was loathsome now in his obesity and his self-importance. Fully, sparing no detail, he told what he had had on good authority: how the queen of Mycenae now shared the throne with her paramour; how the king and four or five others had been stabbed from behind at a banquet; how Atreus had built the burial places so fine and so far in that now they must pay for their pride: five days—five, mind you—the corpses had lain stinking in the great hall at the palace, waiting for burial.

"Ai!" said Pylades, beginning to get to his feet. "Let us depart from this place—"

"No, no." In matters such as this, the prince of Mycenae was the knowledgeable one. "We must eat a little of the food, we must show no concern. If Aegisthus is indeed on the throne of the house of Atreus, then surely he will have sent out to look for me."

The boy in the corner had cut his reed to suit his taste. He played on it mournfully now. Though he had never seen Agamemnon and had probably never laid eyes on the glories of Mycenae, he played what could be taken as a dirge for a dead king.

Orestes lifted the bowl of porridge and drained off half of it, peasant fashion. It was dreadful, the business of swallowing against an urge to spew up. Once he choked and got some of the stinging, loathsome stuff into the passages of his nose; and even then he did not allow himself to sputter or cough, but set his hand to the meat and stuffed it into his untasting mouth and followed it with large chunks of bread.

"A whore," said the father to the son.

"Very likely. And yet who knows?"

"Who knows what? Who knows but that his own woman—"

The rest of it was lost because traders with bales and baskets were coming in. "Eat a little, Pylades," Orestes said. "In the name of the blessed Lady get a little of it down, so that nobody will guess." And the prince of Crisa, unused to taking his food along with terror and bitterness, did what he could—which was little enough.

When they came out of the darkness into the early afternoon, the sunlight was almost blinding. The bare-legged girls had gone from the fields, and the fields were too shimmering green, the sort

258

of lustrous, poisonous green to be found on the backs of lizards or the markings on snakes. There was a grove, and they went grim and unspeaking toward it. There was shadow, and they lay down in it, Pylades on his back with his legs drawn up and Orestes on his face at full length. He wept, tearing the grass up by the roots; but it struck him that he wept ritually for something far away in which he had no part. His tears were like the dirge played by the lad at the inn and he wept the more, stung by the knowledge that he could not truly weep.

"Ai!" said Pylades, and added at once out of his harsh honesty: "I never knew your father except as a great warrior and a king. Therefore I will not tear my garments or the grass, but will only grieve that one who cast so long a shadow should have been taken from the land."

The dead man's son saw that long shadow, armed and crowned. The warrior of flesh and blood who had been murdered at meat by his wife's paramour was less real than that shadow. A king alive is barely a man, and, once dead, becomes entirely a king. The huntsman back at the inn had a son who would lament loudly over his grave; Agamemnon, the king of kings, lay in a royal sepulcher, and there would be no wailing, nothing but circumspect and dignified rites at the sealed entrance to his tomb. Here, too, in the grove north of the marsh of Nemea, mourning was measured. To speak of one's own needs and dangers in the light of the same sun that had shone upon the revelation would be an impiety; so the two young men, having no more to say concerning the dead, grieved in silence until dusk. Then it was Orestes —Pylades would never have thought of breaking the muted mourning first—who asked "What shall we do?" and admitted that he had been pondering the question while he wept.

"Perhaps we should turn back and hide again with my mother and father," said the prince of Crisa.

"Perhaps we should. It would be wiser, doubtless. But then again . . ."

"Let us sleep here and be refreshed before we make our decision. Here we are safe. No man would try to cross the Nemean marsh in darkness. Tomorrow we will have clearer minds for it," said Pylades. And almost at once the two of them turned back to back and pulled their cloaks up to their chins and fell asleep.

TWO

YET ORESTES could not rest, and suffered in his sleep certain
muted afflictions. It was cold in his dreams—the chill of the marsh
night came through his skin and pervaded the room to which
longing had drawn him back: the ridiculously small great hall
where he had known his first unbroken peace. All that were there
were sleeping, the mother nodding over her spinning, the father
drowsing over his lapful of unshelled hazel nuts, Pylades on a
bench among rugs and cushions. He himself could not sleep because of the chill, and he stretched himself out in front of the
hearth, yet strangely enough he was on the bench beside Pylades

too, for it was possible with a little turning and twisting for him to gather warmth from Pylades' shoulder and knee. Ah, he thought, to lie here forever! What does a man want more than a roof and a little food and a good companion?

As if in answer and somehow to rebuke him, a girl-child was suddenly there in his arms—the little Hermione. "But I am not yet ready for you," he said, putting back her pale brown hair from her heart-shaped face; and she replied: "No? That is a pity, my betrothed, for in Argos also the waters are bitter and the fires burn low. Helen spins, and goes early to the couch of Menelaos, forgetting Paris. But is that love? And when shall I find love?" He did not answer; indeed there was no need for him to answer. For the girl, with her soft hair and her arms and legs like the peeled branches of a young tree, was gone out of his arms, and he did not know whether to shrug or to weep. Then I will shrug and rest, he thought, and pulled toward him a rug made of the hide of a lion, which was also strange in Crisa and vaguely troubling, since the skin of the lion was reserved for the uses of the house of Atreus and could cover nobody but a member of the royal house. . . .

The hide was on his couch, in the palace, in the Citadel. It was the darkest hour of the night, and the most silent hour, too, so that, sitting up and listening, he could hear the almost inaudible footsteps. She came to him, his sister Electra came to him in the sweet and terrible core of the night, on her bare feet. She sat at the foot of his couch, a vision and weightless. Ah, blessed Lady, he thought, choking on the spittle that had gathered in his throat, am I to take it from her bodilessness that she was one of the slain? But she looked at him mockingly, spitefully, as if to tell him to put such foolish thoughts out of his head. "Is it well with you, my sister? Are you still in Mycenae?" he whispered, and felt Pylades turn aside and heard him sigh.

"I am still among those that walk on the earth and see the light of the sun," she said. "But I am utterly bereaved. Our father is dead, and what can I hope to have but poison at *his* hand or *hers?* You also—you have betrayed me."

"Once, only once, with a peasant girl at the Feast of the Harvest, and that was nothing. Perhaps it was because I did not love her and came down upon her quickly, as an animal comes upon his mate. And then again, perhaps it is that men make too much of that beforehand, so that the little it really is becomes even less. Give me your hand. I would rather have your hand."

But she withheld herself, she clasped her hands together and wrung them. "Dead he is, and you cannot mourn for him," she said.

"Can you?"

"Mourn for him? Perhaps not. He was long absent, and a king of kings. Do not, at any rate, stint your tears in the belief that the measure will be filled up with tears of mine. I am heavy, heavy, heavy—"

"With child?"

"No. I have not betrayed you. I am heavy with sorrow, and heavy with terror, and heavy with loneliness."

"Where do you abide?"

"Come, now," she said aloud, and her grey eyes narrowed and her mouth twisted with scorn. "I have looked for you up and down the palace, and in the lower town and on the hillsides where missing men are sometimes found in unhallowed graves. Look for me as I have looked for you, and you will find me."

"Are you gone forth from the Citadel?"

Her eyes opened and flashed sea-grey upon him. "Do you reprove me with it—you who took flight and left me behind with the two of them?" she said. "Blessed Lady, men are what they are, there is not one of them who can be leaned upon. Ai, ai . . ."

Her wail was transformed into the bark of a distant jackal. He sat up—terror propelled him into actuality and the dank marsh-

263

land night, and his sudden movement wakened Pylades. They were where they had lain down together, in the solitary grove. A faint network of boughs quivered in the wind above them, black against a paling sky, hard against the moist softness of paling stars.

"What is it, cousin?" said Pylades.

"She has been with me—here and in Crisa and in the palace at Mycenae—"

"Who?"

"My sister."

"Which of your sisters?" For in Crisa they had spoken so little of Mycenae that Pylades could think that Iphigenia might visit his sleep.

"Electra. Who else but Electra?"

"Did she speak in this dream, your sister Electra?"

"Yes, she spoke. She bitterly reproved me. And truly she said no more than I would say myself, truly she was just. Oh, I did ill—ill—ill—" He bent his forehead against his knees, he rocked back and forth on his haunches in self-recrimination. "I did ill to leave her there with the two of them alone."

"Perhaps you should have brought her with you." The voice did not accuse him; it was merely meditative.

He felt his face flush up. Long ago, in his childhood, he had heard the king and queen of Mycenae name this same cousin as a possible embarrassment, an unwelcome suitor who must be turned away because of his poverty, yet dealt with circumspectly and courteously because of the ties of blood.

"She also," said Pylades, "could have dwelt a while with us in Crisa."

But it unmanned him, it brought him close to tears to think of Electra in Crisa. He kept his silence, knowing that his voice might shake, and conjured up an image of his sister in the firelight of the humble room. She sat by the mother, helping with the spinning. Her long, sun-browned hands were busy with the carded

264

wool, and when the father crossed the room to give her some shelled hazel nuts, she could not take them—he had to feed them to her as if she had been a bird, putting them one by one between her lips. . . .

The stillness was heavy between them, and to his shame it was the unwanted suitor who had to break it. "Yet I am foolish to say that you should have brought her. How could you have brought her in flight through the unpeopled stretches of the land—a delicate maid?"

"Oh, she is not delicate."

"No?"

There was disappointment in the voice. Once, long ago, Pylades might have heard the name and dreamed a little over it. Perhaps it was painful to him, even now, to attach something not delicate —some being with brawny arms and hard, overwhelming breasts —to the remembered name.

"I mean: she is not delicate or womanish in her spirit. Her body is slight, though she is tall enough. I meant only that in her spirit she is steadfast in a time of danger and strong to bear burdens. I leaned upon her all my days—she is not as delicate as I."

"Come, Orestes, lie down and pull your cloak about you. Whether we turn back to Crisa or go forward to the Citadel, we have a far road to travel. If the fever came upon you here in the marshland, I do not know what we would do."

He lay on his back and stared at the stars caught in the net of twigs and branches, but he could not put her image from him, nor did he dare to close his eyes. Where was she? What danger stalked her? The dagger, coming at her in the dark? The looped rope twisted about her neck? Even now, this instant? And if he slept she well might visit him again, saying: You have walked back to Mycenae at your ease, my brother, stopping at inns to eat, stopping in groves to rest. For the remainder of the journey you may come as slowly as you like—I no longer stand in need of you.

They have laid me in the tomb of the house of Atreus, where I fester among the other festering dead. . . .

The jackal made his coughing, barking sound again, eastward where the ridges were turning ashen grey in the first of the light. "May the gods strangle that beast," said Pylades. "Now I will be wakeful, waiting for the next time he barks. Now I will never be able to sleep."

"Nor I. Let us talk a little."

"What was it we spoke of before we lay down?"

"My sister Electra."

"Yes. Is she betrothed?"

"She was not bound when I went forth. Unless those two have given her, she is still free."

"Did she speak at all concerning that in the dream?"

"Yes." He put up his arm and covered his eyes against a sudden image of the peasant girl, her skirt pulled up, her legs parted to reveal rawness and coarse black hair. "She said that she had not —she said that she was still untouched."

There was another long silence. The beast on the far ridge was still, and it was possible that his companion had suddenly fallen back into sleep. But he could not put the peasant girl out of his thoughts, and he heaved and sighed, and his cousin heaved and sighed and said with seeming carelessness, "Is she fair?"

"I do not know. To me, she is fair enough." His voice was cooler and more guarded than it had ever been in his speech with the prince of Crisa. "I mean: it would be difficult for me to say, since it is as if the gods had made the two of us out of the same shaft of sandstone. Every man is inclined to love himself, and she is very like myself."

"Truly? The same eyes? The same hair?"

"The same." It had come out of him curtly: the daylight vivacity in Pylades' tone had begotten a rasping irritation in him, and he could not pursue the subject with proper courtesy. The

266

uneven ground beneath him hurt his back, and he shivered and was afraid that the chill was coming on.

Pylades took his own cloak, warm from his body, and cast it over Orestes. "Not that *I* think of her," he said without bitterness. "What is Crisa beside Mycenae? What am I beside the daughter of Agamemnon?"

Oh, it is not *that,* Orestes thought. If an embassy were to come from the king of Egypt to ask that she be given to his eldest son I would suffer from this same unquietness. . . . He laid his hand upon his cousin's arm and said, "Crisa is so much better than Mycenae in my sight that I wish we might turn back and I might abide there for the rest of my days."

"Then we will not be turning back at sunrise?"

"No. How would that be possible after the reproof she uttered in the dream? I must go and look for her. So much at least is her due. Only the gods know how long and hard she has searched for me."

"My cousin need not justify himself at such great length. I set out with him for Mycenae. Nor did I say when we came out of the inn that I would not go on. If it is his wish to go to Mycenae, then he will go to Mycenae and I will come with him. But now let us get what little sleep we can."

Orestes lay waking longer than his companion. Something—the bark of the jackal or the strange, rank smell of the marshland—brought the matter of the stinking corpses back into his mind: he had heard once that it was terrible to catch the smell of a jackal's breath, that a jackal stank of the rotten meat it fed upon. It occurred to him also that the food he had eaten in the inn still lay in his stomach; and he gagged on it and swallowed against it many times before he could overmaster it. By this time the sky was pale and touched with a faint rosiness; the stars seemed to grow larger in it, like swollen shapes showing through water; and the net of boughs rocked and trembled in a wind that smelled of the sea.

Soon it will turn warmer, he thought—not yet, but at least the air will grow no colder than this. I have lain through the worst of it; yes, and he also—he who had no need to come with me and might have slept out this night in Crisa under a warm coverlet. . . .

And gratefulness and remorse prompted him to return the cloak; he laid it over the long, sleeping body of Pylades. Why have I wounded him? he asked himself. Not, surely, because I could wish to see her led off to the marriage couch of one who owns such and such a number of sheep and oxen and copper talents and fields of grain. . . . Yet the nameless rancor stirred in his flesh and made his earthen bed unbearable; and the ridges were red and the dew was gathering on his face before he fell asleep.

THREE

IN THE DAYS of the early summer of that year it was rumored that a lion had come out of the Arcadian wilds. In the Citadel the rumor was repeated with curiosity and awe: a generation had passed since the king of the beasts had come padding on soft and terrible feet out of the west, and therefore the lion was surely a foreshadowing of some great upheaval—an upheaval likely enough considering the unholy, illegitimate, and nerveless condition of him who wore the crown. But in the lower town where there were no Cyclopean battlements between the listeners and the roar, the lion was a lion. There, shepherds came home haggard from sleeplessness with their flocks, men were put on guard among the thickets and in the woods, and women counted their children before they bolted their doors for the night.

Another dry year was taking its course, in spite of the extraordinary festival given to Poseidon, in spite of thousands of prayers sent up privately to the blessed Lady, who usually dispensed nothing but love, yet who might, in dreadful need, be called upon to give generating rain. The crops burned in their youth in fields that were cracked as if an earthquake had heaved beneath them; all the wells except the spring Perseia were brackish and had a metallic taste; and the clouds of dust that went up from the earth made the setting disk of the sun and the rising disk of the moon as red as if they had been washed in water stained with blood.

In those weeks no ambassador from a foreign court could have recognized the princess Electra. Indeed there were whole days when she could scarcely be said to know herself. Much of the time she wandered solitary in places where others dared not go, since —being herself of the house of the lion—she had no need to fear the lion. It was said among the folk that if she and the beast should meet, the beast would stand on his hind legs and put his forepaws on her shoulders and lick her face. For her the coming of the hateful tawny one was a peculiar kind of blessing. The sandals, the bracelets, the gold ornaments that had weighted down her skirt on the night of the slaughter—all of them had been paid out for bread and meat. And now her sacrosanct position in connection with the lion had given her, just when her stores were exhausted, a new worth among those in the lower town. She and she alone could go into the uncultivated fields to dig up baskets of the roots that men ate in times of famine; she and she alone could go into the wooded stretches to gather twigs and break off the dried branches they needed for their fires. "Treat her well," said the men to the miller, "for without her, what would we eat?" "Nourish and sustain her," said the women to the miller's wife, "for if we had her not, the ovens would be black and we would have no bread." As for the children, there was between them and the stranger who lived among them a brazen bond. If one of them called out that she was in sight, the rest of them would run out of the hovels and stand at the outermost limit and call to her and watch her approach, bent almost double with the load of twigs she had lashed to her back or carefully balancing on her head the basket of roots.

When she was among the children, she knew herself for what she was; but the time she spent with them was very short. Worn to exhaustion by unaccustomed labors, she spent half her time in sleep; and between her sleep and her waking there was small difference—her sleep was haunted by her work, her days were haunted by her dreams, and sometimes it was impossible for her to know what was a dream and what was an actuality. Once while she lay among the rags in the miller's hut, she closed her eyes and became the lion. Gold-brown, glistening, reduced to bone and muscle by anger and hunger, she had been going on an errand of fury, meaning to crouch and make a leap over the wall into the Citadel. Thereafter, when she tore the roots with a screeching sound out of the drought-hardened ground, she would repeatedly let herself be the lion. In the lion's body, she strode by night into the sleeping palace, overturned the marble tables, trod out the fire on the hearth, sent the carved chairs crashing onto the painted floor. In the lion's body, she went up the long flight of steps, shaking the staircase but making no sound, and found them on their couch, sleeping entwined, the loathsome spindly one almost lost in the loose embracing flesh of the aging woman. . . . Or, suddenly remembering at her tasks what ill she had thought of her father while he lived, she would pass again into the lion and go up the side of the hill that housed the royal tombs. There, standing near the marker already half covered by drying grass, she flung back her head and uttered such a cry of rage and remorse and desola-

271

tion that the dead must have heard it in the dry land and come back for a little to their rotting bodies to whisper how she was to die, since certainly she would never be forgiven.

She wrestled with another confusion. As there were days when she did not know whether she was a human being or a lion, there were other days when she was in doubt as to whether she was a woman or a man. Her hair was cropped and she wore a boy's straight brown tunic cut off above the knees; and, since her breasts had grown sore with all the reaching and bending, she had bound them down flat with linen bands. So, seeing her image in water or at the bottom of a copper cauldron, she would think how, if her brother ever returned, nobody would be able to tell the two of them apart. "I am not his sister," she would say to herself, wrenching at the dead branches. "We were born twins, both boys, and our hands were clasped in the womb, and we came forth hand in hand."

Hand in hand, in her waking and sleeping dreams, they went in the blackest hour of the night up the path from the lower town to the Citadel. Hand in hand, they walked to the sally port—sometimes they fell upon the guards and killed them, and sometimes they found the guards asleep and went past them soundlessly, two erect and narrow shadows, so close that they seemed actually tied together as two beasts are bound shoulder to shoulder to the same plow. By devious ways—every time she thought of it, they took a different way—they came to the palace, and entered and crossed the great hall, and climbed the stately stairs. There she would cut off the image, not out of fear—she knew no fear, and not out of compassion—she spat upon compassion. "What happens *then*," she thought, "I will not spoil with imaginings. What happens then, I will save until it happens and I can see it as clearly as I saw my father heave himself up from the board with his death in his face."

It came upon her now and again in the harsh red evenings to

272

play out those fantasies of hers with the children of the hovels. Once she got down among them on all fours and shook her hair as if it were a mane and roared and pawed the earth with her hand; and once she called herself Electrion and spoke in a deep voice and insisted that they address her by the changed name and refer to her as "he." But on both occasions the little ones were frightened and wept and the older ones moved away from her as if she carried some contagion and looked at her slantwise out of the corners of their eyes. Noting this and having nothing but the children with which to soothe her weariness and stifle her remorse, she saw to it that in the evenings she was always herself. She tied a bit of rope around her waist to make herself seem womanishly girdled, and she even went so far as to take the flattening bands from her chest.

There was a day when the sun was so violent that even those who depended upon her told her not to expose herself to the heat. Worn out and tremulous with gratefulness for the dour kindness of the folk, she stayed in the miller's hovel in a dark corner among the heaped rags. It was unlikely on such a day that anybody would come from the Citadel to buy flour; and if one did come, unless he looked sharply, he would take her for an idiot boy groveling in the filth and powdered over with the flour. It was good to lie so, in misery and abjection. Lying so, she could punish herself with her own fists for the hard thoughts she had harbored against her father while he still lived—she pushed and ground her bony knuckles into her thighs, her breasts, her belly swollen for lack of food. "Ai!" she said in her thoughts, addressing him sometimes as the strong and kindly one on whose knees she had sat as a child, sometimes as the war-hardened one who had shouted and beaten the arms of his throne, sometimes as the vague, masked piece of corruption onto which she had thrown a red anemone. "It was I who deceived you, it was I who gave you to the murderers and thrust you into your tomb. How was it with me, when I was a

273

young woman and a princess, that I took less pity on your honorable wounds than on the pain that showed in *her* face? How was it that the oaths I swore to the gods and the ancestors were washed out of my thoughts? With what water did I wash them away?" And, asking herself that question, she raised her hot hand to her sun-blistered face and found that her cheeks, her mouth, her chin were wet with tears.

She consigned the whole of that day to mourning, and would not eat of the broth that the miller's wife brought to her, would not even rise to empty her body, though her need to relieve herself pressed upon the small of her back and dragged her vitals down. It was dusk and the room was red with the fire of dusk when someone crossed the threshold and asked for a measure of flour. The voice hung in her vacant mind and became a memory. It was Aglaia's voice, and the discovery so caught her that she cried out, and the nurse also cried out, partly in recognition and partly, doubtless, in unbelief that this scarcely human thing could be what she had pampered and washed and fed.

"My lady and my princess!"

"No, now," Electra said, "she is a friend!" For the miller had seen a long-dreaded instant turning into reality and had reached behind him for the knife he always kept at hand. "She will not betray us. Let her alone." And she got up and came and stood before Aglaia, near the board, in an oblique ray of the setting sun, so that all might be made plain at once: the cropped hair, the short tunic, the bound breasts.

"How I have searched!" said the poor old woman. "How I have searched for you! I have been here three times and never found you. Where in the name of the blessed Lady have you hidden yourself?"

"Here." Her speech had grown as short and rough as the speech of the folk. Though there was no love in her, she offered an em-

274

brace since an embrace was called for, and withdrew the offer because to touch Aglaia would be to cover her with flour—flour that could be carried back to the Citadel as a sign of her hiding place.

The nurse stood before her, shaking the bony hand that covered the lower part of her wooden face. "Do you know? Do you know how it is at the palace?" she said.

And suddenly that voice became the voice of reason and pity, speaking in the round cemetery, begging her to have mercy upon her mother and all women, to swear no oaths, to keep the cruel thirsty ones and the impervious immortal ones out of the affairs of mortals who had enough to suffer as things stood. The seed of pity—had it so grown in her vitals that she had kept her silence in spite of the wine she had sent through the holy earth to wet the parched animal chaps of the dead? Rage tore up in her. Rage made her voice loud and rasping, like the sound of the bronze drill driving through stone. "Yes, surely, I know how it is in the palace. We know all things here. The rugs and pillows stink of five days of corruption. Upstairs, the she-dog whom you taught me to pity lies with my father's murderer, and they kiss and bite and tickle and laugh aloud as they please. Whoever steps over that threshold must step wide—it runs with blood."

Even as she said it, she remembered the captive who had cried out that she could not get across that awesome stream, who had asked for a hand to help her step over it. She felt her own hand, as it had been—still smooth, still cool and pliant—taking the white emaciated hand. She saw, over Cassandra's shoulder, the fat nurse with the infants, one in each arm. And she saw also the delicate rounds of their heads—vulnerable, tender, crowned with fine-spun reddish gold.

"Forgive me, I blame you unjustly," she said to her nurse without ceremony or deviousness, as a shepherd might speak to a maker of wheels. "It was no doing of yours that I held my tongue. It was something that came upon me when I saw the captive and her children." Like the shepherd, like the wheelwright, she did not utter the rest; she suppressed the words: I was melted in the stony core of my being by pity and love.

The old woman—for she also had changed in the time between —wept and closed her hand convulsively over the brown veil that fell across her shoulder.

"Are you wearing that mourning," Electra asked, "for Agamemnon your dear lord?"

"For two, for two. For yours and for my own—my husband."

But her husband had gone forth with Orestes, and if she could know of his death, then she might also know—

Plainly the nurse had seen the fierce hope flare up in the marred face, for she shook her head. "No news, no news at all, my lady and my princess—"

"Then how do you know—"

"Because he came to me in a dream, ashen-grey, with his hand over his heart."

"Did he say nothing?"

"His jaw was bound. I could not hear it clearly, whatever he said. Only, when I wakened, it seemed clear to me that he wished to tell you that you should flee."

"Because my brother is dead?"

"I do not know. How can I tell, when his mouth was properly stuffed with thyme and cumin—"

"Then Orestes is dead."

"I could not hear, I do not know. All I know is that I have been looking for you to tell you I will flee with you, wherever you choose to go."

She did not answer. Her heart seemed to swell and fill the emptiness between her ribs. It rose into her throat, so that she thought it would choke her to death. Struggling with this wild heart, she

276

looked at the miller, who had been standing there with the two of them all the while.

"Look," he said in his dry and croaking voice, "go with her. It is not that I wish to rid myself of the danger, though the danger is great."

"I know that, father."

"Then go."

"But I cannot."

Aglaia broke in, laying her hand on her mistress's chest. "There are many courts that would give you refuge," she said. *"She* is ailing and without her *he* is like a piece of straw, he can be blown away at a breath. Go to your father's sister in Crisa. Go to Helen and Menelaos in Argos. Go to Aulis, to your sister Iphigenia. Only go, and I will come with you."

"What is the profit? We will be slain on the way."

"Dye your hair with the juices of roots. If I did not know you, who would know you? We will come safe to some hiding place, and you will cleanse yourself and eat and sleep, and the flesh will grow again upon your bones, and the sores on your face will be healed, and the gods will see what you have suffered and will give you forgetfulness and rest."

"The gods see nothing." She pushed the nurse away and went apart from them both to sit among the rags. "You see, I am here and you cannot move me," she said. "I will not go forth until those two that clasp and kiss are rotten corpses in the light of the sun, until they have lain five days side by side in corruption, and have had their fill of each other. I will wait here—here in Mycenae where the deeds were done—until I drop without life in a field or a thicket. For blood has been shed, and I am in guilt for the shedding of it, and I must pay the price of it, blood for blood."

"My lady and my princess—"

"Why do you call on her?" said the miller. "She has forgotten that she is a woman and of the royal house, and it will profit her

277

nothing to remember it. Go and let her alone and come no more. She is beyond saving. With you and me, it is still otherwise for a little while, and I would not have a slave of the house of Atreus shorten my days. Do not haunt my hovel, to bring them down upon me, or you will come to know that this knife has a double edge. Come no more."

FOUR

"MY QUEEN and my lady will be glad to hear that the heat is somewhat less."

It was the clever Cretan who said it, she who was responsible for painting regal serenity into Clytemnestra's face—a task that grew more and more difficult with every moon. The queen glanced at the pots that held the red juice of berries and the white chalk powder. Not ten days ago, she thought, they were filled to their brims, and already they are almost empty. I have come to wear a mask as thick as the masks of beaten gold that are laid over the faces of the dead.

279

"Will my lady look upon herself?" asked the Cretan, holding up the polished silver mirror.

She looked and nodded and forced a smile that threatened the exquisite handiwork. Poor girl, she thought, she labors and I spoil it. Under such painting, I ought not either to laugh or weep. . . . She remembered then that the Cretan had brought her good news of the weather, and said that she was glad indeed; but whether she was truly glad she did not know. Sorrow, sickness— a malaise of the spirit, a malaise of the body—these were with her constantly, and if she could not try to ease them by sighing over the heat, she would have to find something else over which to sigh. *He,* of course, was the trouble closest at hand; and she rose in her loose morning robe to go to him, to fret over him, to contend with him. She could see from her window that a table had been set for them in the small court, close to the tubs of laurels, on paving stones wet with another feeble sprinkle of rain; and her anger began to burn properly: it was *he* who had ordered the morning meal to be brought out there—he with his covert urgency to get out of the palace, always to get out of the palace, as if it had not been scrubbed and scented from cellar to roof, as if some last vestige of what she had stood in for five days still clung to the curtains or waited to breathe out at him from the walls. It was childish; the air was actually sweet with the light dampness that had come during the night—so she told herself as she walked down the stairs.

If she had found him waiting for her in the great hall, her anger might have been appeased. But he was not to be seen either there or in the lesser court; and she knew that, if she demeaned herself by looking across the cobbled street, she would see him in what he persistently called "his own garden," weeding "his own flowers," gathering some of "his own herbs." She moved to the table and sat down at it soundlessly. If she made her presence known, he would come at once, and she wanted the grievance of a long wait. Before her, in the middle of the table, was a nest of ivy and myrtle, at the center of which he had doubtless laid a gift for her, something chosen from the spoils of Troy—a ring, a brooch, a curious unset stone. She sneered and did not look at the morning's gift. The morning's gift was more often than not an apology for what had been withheld at night. Their strange new loving had gone the way of the old; he gave her no more now than she would have had from a little one hiding its eyes against her from a malevolent world.

She waited, furious, motionless, allowing herself not so much as a tapping of her fingertips. A slave—accursed idiot—drew his attention by opening the door to ask her whether she wished to be served. She watched him come, spindle-shanked, grubby with his digging, into the bluish morning shade of the laurels. She gave him the common morning salutation, no more, no less. Why did he deck himself out in olive green? The color made him look more sallow, more pinched and withered. And it came upon her, as he offered her the same terse greeting, that he might well ask himself why she decked herself out in hyacinth blue—an aging, thickening woman, painted past recognition, supporting on the edge of the table two yellowing elbows and two pendulous breasts.

At once, as though he were indeed a child undelivered by last night's sleep from yesterday evening's terror, he began to talk of the lion: let her believe him or not, as she pleased—with his own ears he had heard it roar. Early this morning he had been over there among his laurels—

These also, she said drily, jerking her head back toward the plants in the silver tubs, were his laurels—

Why, he asked, must she put meanings upon every word that came out of his mouth? Why must she be forever stopping him in the middle of an utterance with insinuations and accusations? The subject of his speech was not laurels but the lion. He had

281

heard it roar with his own ears—less a roar than a howl, wild and filled with lamentation. A peculiar, half-bestial, half-human kind of roar.

"Perhaps you dreamed it. Sit down, the slaves will be coming with the food."

He sat down hard and winced because he had jarred his back against the carved chair in his exasperation. "I did not dream it. I tell you, I heard it not an hour ago, while I was pruning—those laurels over there. Would you have me believe myself mad?"

Since she was close to believing as much of herself, she took cool and condescending pity on him. "Oh, no," she said, making her voice airy, partly to reassure him and partly because the slaves were crowding the table with the food—food that neither of them would be able to eat. "Very likely you did hear him. The Cretan said this morning that a maker of harnesses came up from the lower town last evening and told the kitchen slaves he had seen the lion yesterday around the time of noon."

"Seen him? Where?"

"How should I know?" It was said lightly, almost blithely. She had no fear of the lion: to be afraid of a lion seemed to her a relatively blessed state. One might run from a lion, hide from it, board a vessel and go out onto the wide waters where no lion could come. But what escape was there from what went on within—the conviction that one's heart would grow to twice its size, would press and press, would finally leave no room for the drawing in of breath?

"It came from the eastward side," he said, and added much more in the way of particulars—these days he was obsessed with, drove her mad with, particulars. He seemed to believe, like some ignorant peasant, that if he could describe a thing minutely enough he could describe it out of significance. She ate—not to appease a hunger that she did not have, only to show her contempt for his particulars.

And he also ate, to indicate that he could do as much as she, never ceasing meanwhile to add more and more detail: how the howl had taken on for him the sound of the cry of mourning, how it had seemed to come sometimes from the northeast, from the region around the tomb of the house of Atreus, and sometimes from the lower town—

"Wipe your mouth," she said. "You have a crumb of bread in the corner of your lip."

He was as furious at that as she had intended him to be. He clenched his teeth, flung down his napkin, and glared malevolently at her across the untouched nest of greens. "Tell your Cretan to paint you less. I cannot see your face for the chalk," he said.

That cut laid her open to the old tenderness. Ah, blessed Lady, she thought, allowing the tears to make snail-trails down her whitened cheeks, where is it gone, where is it gone—our love? What have I in this world? Nothing. Nothing save him alone. Ah, if he would get up and come and kiss me now, if he would stand behind me and stroke my shoulders and press his mouth upon my head. . . .

A slave came with another hot loaf, though they had scarcely touched the first one; and when the intruder was gone, she reached across the table and touched his wrist to beg for peace.

Whereupon, with peace satisfactorily established—for him at any rate—he harked back to the lion. This maker of harnesses who had seen the beast—did the slaves in the kitchen know his name? He would go, he would go at once and ask them. And, if he succeeded in learning who the fellow was, he would go down there and discover whatever he could. He got up, jarring the table, and started for the palace.

While he was in the kitchen, she robbed the nest of myrtle and ivy, trying to comfort herself with the thought that every evening he went over to the storehouse to search the Trojan loot for some-

283

thing that would give her an instant of delight. But she knew that his primary reason for going was to breathe air other than the air of the palace, that he stayed apart from her as long as he could, that this giving of presents had become a loveless ritual, a child's game of which the most stubborn child must eventually grow weary; and these thoughts led her to another bitter thought: that it was Agamemnon who had taken the great store with which *he*—no soldier and truly now a lesser man—entertained himself between the evening meal and sleep. She did not like the ring that he had found for her. It was silver chased with circles of the new black metal; and that metal seemed always to her an ill omen, since there was a belief among the guardsmen that from this same black metal the avenging offspring of Heracles would fashion their indomitable swords. . . . . She must wear the ring nevertheless, and grew still more angry with him when she found that the only finger it would pass onto was the smallest one. Her hands were fat—fat and yellowish at the knuckles. She hated them and longed to hide them, yet she must leave them bare and obvious on the table in order to display the ring.

But when he returned he did not see it. He had changed his soft shoes to sturdy sandals and had brought a pair of walking shoes for her—he knelt and fitted them on for her, remembering to kiss her knees. Hate and devotion so wrought with her that she did not know what she wanted. Let him embrace me, she thought. No, let him take his craven mouth from my flesh. I will not go with him—why should I spoil the cool of the day by walking among the stinking folk? I will sit here in the moist air, in the shadow of the laurels. No, no, only the gods know what thoughts will hound me if I sit here alone—I will go with him, I will talk to him of the lion on the way, I will indulge him in his fear and give him all that is left in me to give, a little tenderness.

But on the road they did not speak at all: he fell out of driven speech, which was the way with him of late, into impenetrable

284

silence. His face was drawn into a mask of wretchedness and waiting. Perhaps he was listening for the lion, perhaps he was actually imagining that he was hearing it roar. Now that there were no words to distract her, she also fell into secret watching, measuring her breathlessness, conjecturing the weight and the size of her heart. The town impinged upon this inward brooding with its smells and its ugliness. A little of her rage was channeled toward the folk: Why had they all made their houses of mud-colored brick? Even in years when water was plentiful, had they ever washed their filthy bodies? How was it that the place should be squirming with miserable dogs when they were forever complaining that they had not enough to give their children to eat?

They were directed to the hovel of the maker of harnesses. It stank with a stench of its own that asserted itself above the other stenches: ill-scraped hides, with bits of blackened flesh still upon them, hung over a rope stretched between two poles—hides as malodorous as the inner rooms of a tomb. So it will be with all of us at the last, she thought; and then flew into a rage because there seemed to be nothing that he would spare her. Why had he dragged her here to breathe this air and be gaped at by these emaciated children and bowed to by these sullen, leathery women? They were glaring at the hateful fat that clung to her bones as though she had gotten it by snatching away their meat and bread.

He had his particulars, as many of them as he could possibly want, not only from the harness maker but from the women and children who were voicing their own terror: by the time they had uttered all of it, the beast had grown to twice the size of the one Heracles had slain in the Nemean marshes, and had been endowed with eyes as red as embers and muscles to lay low twenty young men. Why these details concerned him, she did not understand. She thought sourly that *he* would not be meeting the beast, that the beast was dreadful to him only as a portent, and that a scrawny animal would serve as a portent quite as well as a mag-

285

nificent one. Thinking such thoughts, she let her sight rove angrily around the circle of folk who had gathered about them; and her eyes stopped, felt as if they were being drawn out of their sockets toward another pair of eyes—narrow, arrogant, and the cold grey color of the sea.

She almost said the name aloud. She knew that this person was her daughter Electra, though all she saw was cropped hair, a boy's flat body, a blistered and demented face. And wildly, to distract his attention from the mad, fierce, vulnerable presence that stood its ground and dared him to look at it, she began to ask questions of the women, advancing upon them so that they would step backward and hide that one whom he must not see. "Is there water in your wells?" she said. "What do you stand most in need of? What can we send you from the palace? Dried meat? Figs? Bread?"

They told her, having moved enough to obscure the insolent figure. She could not tell whether he had seen it, had not the courage even to turn her head until she heard a scratching sound behind her and knew that he was listing their needs on whatever he had found at hand: the sound was the sound of a pointed stone scraping across a shard.

"Meat," they said, and he echoed the word.

"Ointment to help against the bites of wasps and flies." He repeated it and wrote at the same time. And while he wrote the presence detached itself from the others, glared insane defiance at her, bowed from the waist as one of the folk might bow, and disappeared up a narrow alleyway. It was only then that the queen could bring herself to turn and look at his face.

She found no sign that he had seen; but then, he was very shrewd, he might well have seen and decided to keep his knowledge to himself. His voice was steady; some of the old twang came back into it whenever he said what he wrote: linen to use for bandages; seed to plant next year because this year's crop would yield no seed; milk for some of the mothers who could not drink the bitter water and whose breasts had gone dry as stones. . . . He wrote, his head tilted to one side; and his voice and the way he held his head conjured up a recollection:

In the great hall, long ago, when every closeness had still been precious to them because their times of touching were few, the court had gathered around her to play the game "If only," and he had been her recorder, standing at her side, daring every now and again to let his look merge with hers. Since then, how he had changed, how he had withered! The hand that scratched the list on the shard with the pointed stone—she stared at it, saw it through an accession of sudden tears—was slack, veined and speckled, scrawny and old.

"Enough now," he said to the women, dour again, already weary of them and this distraction. "I have no more space to write in. We will know what other things to send down to you, the queen and I." Throwing the stone away and tucking the shard into his wide belt, he turned his back sharply upon her—he went before her over the narrow path cluttered with rubbish, never turning back. He had forgotten her for the first time, had left her to follow as well as she could, and the great, sick heart within her softened like a lump of beeswax left in the sun, and she did not have the wit to invent a devious question to betray him into revealing whether he had seen what she had seen, even though she knew that, if he had seen it, he would pursue it to the death.

They did not speak until the lower town was well behind them, and then it was she who broke the silence, speaking of love out of her melting heart. "I was thinking how there was a time when we could meet only in secret, when we considered it a blessed thing if we could stand a few paces apart."

He did not answer. He looked at her blankly, and she knew

that the sounds she had made with her lips and tongue were of no more account to him than the clatter of wheels on the cobbled street.

"I was thinking how once, when we played 'If only' . . ."

"That is a foolish game."

"It is indeed."

"Everything they said concerning the lion could not possibly be true. I have seen lions, dead and alive—there is no lion of any such size. As for the maker of harnesses—he especially is a scoundrel, or perhaps he is mad. Red eyes, he said. There never was a lion with red eyes."

FIVE

BUT HE HAD NOT really been brooding on the lion. His mind—he thought of it these days as a locust, taking astounding and unpredictable leaps, settling now on one worry and now on another—had jumped from the lion to the girl. She had been there, no doubt of that. Her actuality could be established by the difference between her person as he had seen it at the edge of the crowd and as he had imagined it—clean-skinned, clear-eyed, dressed in scarlet linen, the topmost tier of her hair crowned with a golden dove. Only Fate, working more subtly than his visions, could have wrought such a change: the body so thoroughly unsexed that for

289

an instant he had thought he was looking at Orestes, the hair cropped and curling close to the sunken cheeks and temples, the upper lip and the chin marred by great white blisters, the eyes staring with the old insolence at the loosened face of the chattering queen.

The queen still chattered. On the way home and afterwards in the great hall where she established herself in a chair and constrained him to sit down with her, the two of them played one of those hateful games at which they spent more and more of their days. Sometimes the game was "the blame is less mine than yours," sometimes "I love you more than you love me," sometimes—as it was today—"I know that you know more than either of us will admit." He had no mind left over for such thrusting and parrying. The room oppressed him: the stench was still in it, no matter what she said. He could not impose quietude upon his body; he had to get up and walk back and forth, back and forth, talking about the lion and thinking meanwhile with breath-choking horror about the girl.

If Clytemnestra would only stop her talk, he might be able to push himself beyond the immediate terror, might plan like a sane man what steps he should take to protect himself. But he was given no peace, nor any promise of peace: her old aunt, the Overseer of the King's Mines, the Chief Priest of the Lady and his daughter and son-in-law would be sitting down with them at the evening table. And in the interim, with shrewd deliberateness, she caught him at the beginning of every piece of reasoning, sent him upstairs to get some ointment for fly-bite, sent him to the kitchen to tell the slaves not to overcook the kid, sent him across the room to bring a pillow for her head, a footstool for her feet. Putting the footstool into place, he saw that her ankles were swollen to half again their usual size, and he made a mental note that she must be pitied, made it as feelinglessly as he had recorded that the folk needed dried meat. "Blessed Lady," she said, "I am fearfully tired." And he answered that it was no wonder, seeing that they had walked so far; and he wished while he said it that she would go elsewhere and fall asleep.

He walked the brightly painted floor of the hall, and wherever he walked, he felt that the girl stood behind him, glaring at his hunched shoulders and spindly legs, exulting in and sneering at his restlessness. Well, glare, he thought in a kind of madness, glare your fill, and I will glare back. Fate has made you almost as ugly now as I. Feeling Clytemnestra's look fixed upon him, he made a roundabout tour of the splendid chamber, stopped to examine some drying greens in an alabaster vase, picked up some strewn pillows and laid them on a bench, and seemed to settle quite by chance in the one place where he could hope to feel secure—on the tall throne. I am here, and I can outface her, he thought. But her mother said in a false flat voice that he was sitting far away and behind her, that she could not see him without twisting her neck.

"Why must you see me?"

"That is a sound question. Why should I want to see you with such a look on your face?"

"What look?"

"As though you had seen the lion. Or perhaps a spirit raised from the dead."

"If I displease you so much, perhaps it would be better for me to go forth out of the palace."

"Go—go—go. Who stands in need of you here? Go and watch the young women sitting in the courts. Go and play with the spoil that Agamemnon brought back from Troy."

"You speak often of Agamemnon these days."

"Does that surprise you?"

"Yes, a little. It seemed to me that you were more taken with his charioteer."

291

"Never give either of them a thought. They are both dead and buried."

"Did you lie with one of them, thinking of the other one, the night of the return?"

"If I did, you should not grudge me. I have had little enough of that since."

"I will not stay to have my weaknesses thrown in my face."

"Who asked that you stay? Go. Why should I deceive myself: it is better with me when you are gone."

But it was not better with him when he had made his wished-for escape. He had no place to go. He only maddened himself by eyeing the young women sitting in the courts: they were so many pieces of flesh that did not stir his member. They stared at him curiously; perhaps there *was* some revelatory look in his face—self-contemptuous, hang-dog. He straightened, told himself that he was king of Mycenae, decided to pretend that he was making a kingly investigation of the Cyclopean wall. He kept close to it, bringing his hand down upon it now and then as if to test the soundness of the monstrous slabs, bruising the ivy that fell over it in green cascades. Ivy survived all things and covered all things. A time would come when ivy would cover him also, and the blood and the stench and the unstirring nights would all be as if they had never been. . . .

Amazed at this thought and pondering it numbly, he came to the sally port, where six guards, unhappy to see him, scrambled after the pieces of their game of chance. A wooden bench stood against the wall and on it, eating from a bowl of curds that rested on his scarred red knees, sat Leontophon, the Captain of the King's Guardsmen. And he continued to sit, even when his king and his lord stood before him, continued to work his jaws and to swallow, to put out his pointed tongue and lick his colorless lips. "What news?" he said shortly, not as to the king of kings, but as to a fellow-conspirator.

292

"I have a thing to tell you." He stared at the shut and sunken eyelid; he could not bring himself to fasten his look upon the single eye, which had of late made him sick at the stomach, so sick that he had feared he might spew up his food.

"Sit and tell me."

"I do not choose to sit, and I cannot tell you here. Put away your food and take your haunches from that bench and walk with me while I finish my circuit of the wall."

The Captain rose with an exaggerated respect which turned his compliance into insolence. They walked together, Aegisthus still bringing the flat of his hand down upon the stones, still preserving the illusion that he was inspecting the wall. What did I mean to tell him? he asked himself in one of those spells of numbheadedness which came upon him often of late. About the harness maker who saw the lion? No, of course not, about the girl—about the girl hiding in the lower town, waiting for the appropriate time when she can pass into the Citadel and hide in the palace and come stalking up the stairs to our sleeping chamber with an avenging dagger in her hand. . . .

"Has anything gone ill with you?" said the Captain.

"No. Why do you ask?"

"Because you are grey as a stone. It would be childish of you to fear this much-talked-of lion. I myself have never heard him. I do not believe that he exists."

"He exists. Never doubt it." His voice was hateful and belligerent, though he did not know why—he had ceased altogether to concern himself with the beast.

"Very well, then, my king," said Leontophon with the same mockery of respect, "he exists."

"But it was not of the lion that I came to speak with you."

"No?" The single word, uttered in the rusty voice, implied more than it said. There was a note of resignation in it that suggested: What now? What new piece of madness?

293

He is entangled in my guilt, thought Aegisthus, and I will see to it that he is entangled also in my terror. He stared straight at the hard, sightless profile—the eye was on the other side, seeming to scrutinize the wall. "Electra is alive and in the lower town. I myself saw her this morning."

The face remained unchanged, and a new fear crept upon him, driving sweat out of the palms of his hands. What dumbfounded him was a thing taken for granted by others. Others knew and whispered together about matters of which he was kept in ignorance.

"Is she truly?" said the Captain after a short silence.

"You knew of it—you knew—?"

"Very well, then. Let us say I knew of it. I heard it as a rumor, and I dismissed it as a rumor."

"You heard it, and you never made mention of it to me?"

"Why should I have made mention of it? It seemed to me that you had enough to chew upon without it. What harm can she do —a solitary girl without power and without gold? Can she raise an army and march against the Citadel?"

His palms—he rubbed them together—were slick with the sweat of fright. He saw in an instant that Leontophon had no cause to fear what horrified *him:* the girl with the dagger coming up the staircase by night. If he and Clytemnestra should be found some morning with their throats slit ear to ear, the Captain would be none the worse for it. Indeed, the Captain's case might be given a turn for the better thereby; he had the guardsmen in his command and could bribe them with the spoils of Troy to seat him on the throne. He waited until the realization had sunken down and been immersed among all the other terrors. Then he cleared his throat and let his hand come down hard enough to be bruised on another of the stones. "I will have her cut down. See to it that she is cut down, and see to it quickly," he said.

"But wherefore? What is to be gained by that, except the anger

294

of the folk? She threatens nobody—she is said to be mad. They say she cries out like a beast at her father's tomb."

"Mad?" His horror was multiplied. He had guessed it himself, staring at her marred and arrogant face, and from that guess had sprung the terror which had submerged his worry over the lion. If she was sane, she would be restrained by fear of her own death. But if she were mad, her mind would not go beyond the instant of vengeance. There it would stop in a kind of crimson ecstasy.

"Mad," said Leontophon, "mad and helpless. Therefore I have not troubled my lord and my king with it. Therefore it seemed better to me to let the matter rest."

"And to keep me in ignorance? Am I not ruler in my own Citadel?"

"Who has gainsaid you?"

"To hide a matter from me is worse than to gainsay me. No man of mine shall know what I do not know. Make an end of her —yes, and make an end of her brother also, if he should return. When you have done it—and you yourself will do it—bring me her father's seal and signet, which I saw on her hand this morning—" He broke off, aghast, remembering the big ring hanging on her finger. Mad she was. What better proof of it than that she should wear that ring in a public street? "The sooner it is done, the better it will be for you," he said.

"I have not uttered any word that should lead my king and my lord to believe that I would delay. Only—" The Captain turned and faced him, and they stopped within sight of three young women—pieces of flesh as sickening as plucked pigeons—whispering among themselves over the fact that they were actually seeing the king. "Only, I have put more of them out of the way than any of the rest of you—more, in fact, than all of you put together. Look, now—the charioteer, the daughter of Priam, the two infants—" He counted them off on his stubby fingers. "That is four, and if I am to add a fifth, I mean to be paid."

"Paid?"

"Surely. My lord has the key to the storehouse where he keeps the spoils that Agamemnon brought back from Troy. My queen and my lady would give me nothing for cutting down her daughter —that I know—no matter what daemon may have gotten into the girl and addled her brain. Therefore, it is fortunate for me that it is the king and not the queen who holds the key."

Aegisthus turned a little aside and rested his back against the wall. The ivy—the all-obliterating ivy, lay cool against his cheek. How was it that he had not thought of her? Why had it not come once into his mind that the dagger which cut down the girl would also put an end to their sick love?

SIX

"IS IT TRUE that you are followed, my daughter?" the miller said.

She did not answer at once. She sat beside him on the doorstep and stared into the wan evening, into a sky veiled again by a false promise of rain. She thought how she had meant to tell him herself, how it would have been more just, more befitting a daughter of the house of Atreus if she had been the one to utter the word. But she had not told him. Twice now she had sighted the single eye peering at her out of the crowd, and she had not told him; and the third time—so some malevolent ancestor whispered in her ear—would be the last time, the termination of everything, including her great weariness. . . . She picked at the dry skin around her fingernails, and said in shame, "Yes, my father, I am followed. I have been sought after these last three days. Leontophon, the one-eyed Captain—it is he who follows me. And certainly you do not wish him to follow me here. It was wrong in me that I should have stayed so long. Now I will depart."

It was in her mind as if she had acted upon the word. She saw herself rising—a princess still, even in a dirty brown tunic. She saw herself going, straight as a measuring stick, up the filthy alley that led to the end of the lower town. And she was surprised to find herself still on the step, still picking at her fingers, when the miller said, "Before the blessed Lady I swear it—I would keep you with us if I could."

"I know, father. I know."

"I am old, and yet I cling to my life—"

"That is only as it should be. We cling to our lives—" It was stupid, it was halting, in her own case it was not even true. Out of her coldness—these days, with a brief respite from the heat, she often found herself mortally cold, as though the wind of death were blowing through her bones—out of her coldness rose the only warmth she knew: the hot red tide of self-contempt burning in her cheeks and stinging in her eyes. "I would not rob you of your life or of anything. You have let the measure of kindness run over many times for me. So I will go now—" She rose and straightened her belt. She gazed down at the top of his head. She had never chanced to see it before, and she wondered how much of the grey was age and how much was flour. She struggled, too, to put down an impulse to kiss the powdery crown. Mad, weak—he was a dour man, he wanted her to take herself off, he wanted no kiss. "Thanks, good father. Thanks and farewell."

"But wait a moment, my girl. I would not have you go forth unfurnished. What will you have to take with you?"

"A knife."

"A knife?"

"Yes, father. That two-edged knife that you keep behind the board. When I am gone, none will come in search of me, and you will not stand in need of it so much anymore."

He looked at her, peering. Then his whole body sagged and he sighed. "The knife you will have, since you ask for it. Also a skin of water, and a few cakes of bread. Also figs and dried meat."

"No figs. No meat." She could not eat of them; they were unholy, having been sent down by the two of them from the palace. She would not lie dead with their hateful bounty in her bowels—their bounty was worse to her than corruption.

"Well, well, as you say, my daughter." She had thought that he might give her a little respite, might tell her to stay at least through the night. But plainly he could not trust her determination, and she did not blame him: her determination belonged to her sanity, to those times when she dwelt in the world; and a word, a dream, an image could send her out of the world. He rose and stepped behind her into the hovel from which she was already exiled. "As you say, the knife. Yes, here it is. Some water—wait, I have a fine, sturdy skin. Of our four loaves I will give you two—"

"No, my father. One is enough."

She stood in silence while he walked about in the shadow behind her. Her knees were unstrung, and she longed to sit, but he would take her sitting down to be a faltering of purpose, and she could not bear to expose herself to further shame. She looked at the misted sun and thought how tomorrow the world's weather would mean nothing to her. That knife, which the miller doubtless thought she meant to wield in a futile fight with the Captain —that knife she would plunge in here, just under the band that flattened her breast, between this rib and that one. It was easy to discern the place, skeleton that she was; at the first touch she could feel the beat of her heart. . . . For it is better, she thought, to die by my own hand than by the hand that cut down Cassandra and slit the throats of the little ones. And if I myself do it on the hillside above the tombs, my father's bones will know of it, and he will accept me as a sacrifice and forgive me what the gods and the ancestors cannot forgive.

"Here," said the miller, coming behind her and putting the skin of water over her shoulder on a hempen sling. "And here are the loaves, I have wrapped them in leaves for freshness—" He tucked them under her belt. "And wait, here also"—he put a copper bead into her hand—"in case it comes upon you to want some meat or to take a couch at an inn."

"You have been kind to me, father."

"So you said a moment since, and once is enough."

She longed to come up close to him, to encircle his bent neck, to embrace him; but she knew that the sight of her back was all he desired. "Farewell, and prosper," she said, and started up the winding alley; and the alley was unreal and her going was unreal because she had sent her mind on before her. A dog barked and jumped around her knees, wanting petting, and some children called to her from the doorway of one of the hovels, but she did not answer. "Mad again—she is mad again this evening," said one of them, and went in and closed the door.

She walked slowly, like one who goes in a procession behind a bier. The sun, pale and watery, was scarcely visible in the dusky grey sky when she left the cluster of hovels; there was no light but a faint coppery afterglow when she found herself at the southwest corner of the Cyclopean wall. Why have I come here? This is no place to do the deed, she thought, and knew that—somewhere between the thickets behind her and this wall against which she stopped to rest—she had lost her courage, she had decided to wait until morning, to give herself one last night's sleep. There were also other things around her that she wished to give herself: moist air free of the stench of crowded life, the cool trailing of the ivy over her dry skin, the sight of the upper windows of the inn outside the wall—windows that showed as squares of the palest yellow against the faded sky.

What else? What else? She closed her eyes and mourned that she would die a virgin. Most grievous of all it is—so ran the old saying—to descend into the dry country without having lain upon a couch in the act of love. She had not wanted it, she did not want it now, yet she pitied herself that she had not had it. Had she been a good daughter to her mother, she might have had Asterion. Had she been a true daughter to her father, she might have had Eurymedon. But as it stood, she had had neither; and those in the land of the dead would mock at her, coming among them as she must without knowledge of love, with shorn hair and with bound breasts.

She wept freely, without any sound and without any effort. Tears ran over her face, and she raised her hand to dry them and found the little copper bead still where the miller had put it, pressing into her palm. But look, I have this, I can buy myself some small thing, she thought like a child who can be comforted by a trifle after long weeping. What shall I buy? Wine—wine at the inn with the beautiful pale windows. How long has it been since I have moistened my mouth with a goblet of wine?

Nobody was on the road, yet she kept to the wall, going somewhat faster now through the whispering stalks of weed. She knew that the zenith of her sanity and courage was passed—the road was all downward. The weeds spoke in lost voices:

"Come, let us feed the white horse," said Orestes.

"You cannot have it, it is mine," said Iphigenia.

"If you could only come to think of me also as something human," said Clytemnestra.

"What a wit you have—the mind of a seer in the body of a girl-child," said Agamemnon.

The door of the tavern stood open—a large room, almost unpeopled, smelling of burning firewood and wine. No lamps were kindled here as yet, since the hearth fire gave light enough. She came to the darkest end of the board, and laid her copper bead upon it, and did not raise her eyes to the face of the innkeeper.

"Red or white wine, my lad?" the innkeeper said.

"White."

Here and there others drank at low tables, but she did not wish to look upon them either. To be in a vast place, to hear voices and see no faces—it was for her a kind of pre-enactment of how it might be tomorrow when she would stand unknown and alone among the other dead.

"That is a wicked knife you wear in your belt," said the innkeeper, faceless.

She made no answer.

"Will you barter it? I will give you three more goblets filled to the brim."

She shook her head.

"What is it with you? Are you deaf and dumb?"

"No. I need my knife, and I have had enough."

She knew as she turned from the board and started toward the door that she had had more than enough. The floor seemed to turn like a slowly spinning wheel beneath her. The wall, firelit, shifted and wavered; and it was only by the sternest effort that she got outside. There, in the oblong of light cast onto the dried grass by one of the upper windows, she put her hands to her temples and pressed hard—there was a roar as of an angry sea in her head. And over the roar, voices again, two voices:

One said, "But what if we are recognized and taken?"

And the other, the voice of her brother Orestes, said with rueful merriment, "Why, then we are done for, unless indeed a griffin . . ."

It was kind of him, she thought, to send me the recollection of the griffin. Perhaps he remembers me and tells me that it is not a fearful thing to die, not so fearful as I think. Perhaps when the

302

knife goes in, the spirit flies out, and a griffin comes to bear it away, over the beautiful islands, over the wine-dark sea, even to the island of Crete where the air is sweet with the drying of petals and the brewing of ointment. Sleep well this night, Orestes, for your kind thought, whether you sleep in a far country or wait for me among the dead. . . .

She had walked in her pondering as far as the northwest corner of the Citadel. There, where the wall made its eastward turn, there was a kind of shabby wilderness where the weeds were strewn with shards from broken vases and with bits of rag. She breathed deeply, unable to tell whether her madness still drew in the fragrance of the ointment vats of Crete or the scrub was yielding a real scent from its sun-withered blooms. Lovers had lain here many times—the weeds were flattened—and she let herself down to sleep her last night's sleep. Once, only once, did she start out of her rest, wondering whether an actual voice could have floated down to her from the pale window of the inn. No, no, she thought, I am mad again, as that child said at the door of the hovel. But tomorrow I will be sane—I am always sane when I first waken— sane enough to do what must be done at the tombs.

SEVEN

NOBODY IN THE garland stall outside the inn was in the least surprised that the two young herdsmen from Crisa should ask for ivy
and myrtle properly twined to ornament a stone above a royal
sepulcher. They were rustics, and rustics were always pious. Their
town was one of those small righteous places where there was
scarcely a day when some ancestor was not being presented with
a wreath, some god was not being remembered with a branch of
apples or a handful of green wheat. Furthermore, since the two
had made it generally known that they were seeking service with
the king's flocks, it seemed only circumspect that they should leave

304

something on the hillside to propitiate the former king: many of the calves they would be tending if their journey proved felicitous had been in the bellies of the heifers on the red night when the tally of Thyestes had risen above the tally of Atreus.

So the folk in the garland stall said among themselves as they watched the narrow backs moving in the direction of the kingly tombs. It was early, and the day was not yet tainted by heat and the meanness of bargaining—the day was pale and golden, windy and crossed by shadows that were violet and blue. The young men also had a sunrise air, as if they were about to begin anew. What would they do after their new beginning? Little, very little. Deliver the cows, prod the bulls, carry the newborn calves over their shoulders, peel willow switches, make love, breed children, break the honeycomb and let its treasure run over their tongues. Very little, but such was life; and on so fine a morning, cool after long heat, life was enough.

"They suspected nothing," said Orestes, shaking back the rough piece of cloth that covered his hair. There had been no juices with which to color that hair, and its tawny lion's hue had revealed itself through every application of ashes and dust. Now the wind moved it, made it tingle at the roots, begot a prickling in his scalp; and he did not know whether what he felt in his hair and in his heart was fear or joy.

"Keep your hair covered, in the name of all the gods," said his companion.

"We will meet nobody."

"Are you mad? We will meet many. It is milking time."

He smiled and did not point out that Pylades was thinking the thoughts of little Crisa in Mycenae the great: the lands of the line of Atreus were broad; the lowing herds were making their shambling way through far-off woods; and the lovely shadows would be gone by the time the carts laden with the milk jars would come clinking toward the Citadel.

305

He had given Pylades the garlands to carry, and that young man kept holding them out and looking at them with contempt. He had said earlier, and justly enough, that nobody in Crisa would buy such dried-out garlands for half the price. But Crisa was well watered and kept its green even in these years of drought, and Mycenae was high and stripped of trees and surrounded by thinning, shabby stretches of wilderness—even the hillside that was crowned by the funeral stones of the royal dead showed more earth than blade or leaf. Starting up the slope of it, he strove to down excitement and call up sadness. My father is dead, he told himself, my father's body lies somewhere under this ground I walk upon, my father is falling away to nothing under his war-gear and his funeral mask down there in the dark. . . .

But all such thoughts could conjure up nothing more than a mild earnestness. They could not even blot out the beauty that showed itself from the top of the barren sacred place: the little clump of plane trees to their left trembling dark green in the bluish light, the faraway Citadel at their right so magnificent that he had to turn his head to see how the sight of it worked on Pylades —all those polished stones and columns and façades shining as if they had been washed in liquid gold. It was my father's Citadel, he thought, and tried to brood in a seemly manner at least upon the death of a great king. Yet the broad, high space where they had stopped engendered the realization that time also was vast, that Perseus had founded the city, that Atreus had raised its battlements and buildings to this tall splendor, that kings come and go, that perhaps there were more kings mouldering now under the earth than common men walking in the light of the sun.

He got down on one knee, took the garlands from Pylades, and draped them around the as-yet-uncarved funeral stone. Later— when men had forgotten Agamemnon as he had lived, angered and shouting and striding—later a stonecutter would picture him here as men had wished him to be: riding under the Lion Gate and blessing his people with an outstretched hand and a fatherly smile. Then it would be easier for all who came here, including his son, to give him his due in tears. But now it was possible only to utter the ritual words, and even these were feeble, bereft as they were of their meaning since they were spoken by rote and were poor rivals for the thoughts that ran along with them in his head:

Will we find her at the palace? Can she have fled? Would they have locked her in some chamber, so that she does not come forth to look at the herds and to feed the horses bites of sweet cake as she used to do in the old days? If she does not come to us where we will be dwelling in the wooded places, can Pylades go and seek her without being recognized and taken? I will draw him a plan of the palace, small, with a sharp stone on a piece of black pottery. I will go over it with him, and he will commit it to his memory against the day when he—

He did not come to the end of either his pondering or his prayer. Both were broken off by a hoarse cry issuing from the mouth of his cousin; and he sprang up and saw, not ten paces behind him, Pylades and another rushing together with bright daggers in their hands. One fell, and it was not his cousin. One fell at full length on his back with a sound that must have reverberated through the tombs. One whom he did not know lay dead on the sparsely covered slope, grotesque because he had fallen downhill and seemed to be thrusting up his big coarse feet, and because he stared at the wide sky with a single eye.

Pylades stood near the head of the corpse and stared with a kind of sick amazement at his own fingers, which were dark with blood. "I have killed him. He is the first that I have ever killed," he said.

"Who is he? Where did he come from?"

"Do you not know him?"

"I? Not in the least. Where did he come from?"

"Out of that clump of trees. But if you know him not, why should he fall upon you?"

307

Orestes looked down at a great gold medallion, lying quiet on the unbreathing chest. "He is the Captain of the King's Guardsmen —Aegisthus' captain now."

"Aegisthus' captain? Well, I have driven the soul out of him." He shuddered and wiped his bloodied fingers on his thigh. "Without thought I took my dagger and thrust it in—and then he fell—"

"Fortunately. Otherwise, I would have been the one to fall."

"Yes, oh, yes, I see that, my cousin. But he is the first that I have ever sent into the dry country. Cover his eye—take a leaf and cover it."

There was no leaf at hand. He took the cloth with which he had covered his hair and tore off an end of it and let it fall onto the glaring, one-sided face. They were known, then, they were followed; he had barely come away with his life. If this one did not return to the palace to say that the deed had been accomplished, another would come in his place. "Take hold on yourself and help me," he said. "We cannot leave him here, we must put him out of sight. Perhaps we can hide him among those trees."

"Bury him there?"

"We have no time for burying." He kept his voice hushed and reasonable, reminding himself that it had not been he who had thrust the dagger in. "Go apart, and wipe your hand on the grass. I myself will drag him to the trees—it will be easy work, it is all downhill."

But the dragging was not easy, even though he tried to tell himself that what he dragged was an unfeeling corpse, and did not once allow himself to look behind. The lifeless hand by which he pulled was still warm enough to feel like a living hand; the corpse would not slide but came bumping over the knobby earth; and he could not keep from wondering whether livid bruises were appearing on its back and head. The six or seven plane trees that made up the little grove were set so far apart that they gave small shadow, and the dead Captain looked as fearful there as he had

308

looked on the hillside in the full sun. As soon as Pylades came—still white in the face, but steadier—they decided between them to tear down some branches and tent the body over with a thatching, not that such a covering would keep off the jackals but only because they could not leave the place without some act of piety. The thatching was almost complete when they heard a sound and turned and saw that a single person was walking slowly up the hillside to the memorial stone.

Who? Who? He leaned against the trunk of the outermost plane and shielded his eyes and stared at the figure. Who? Himself, yet not himself, yet in this wild instant of recognition dearer to him than himself. She came with her head bent, as if her weariness weighed like a stone on the nape of her neck. She came haltingly, and stopped to look at the blood and the trampled grass, but as if such matters concerned her not. Her face, beautiful to him in its blankness and its emaciation, was burned the pale brown of a dead oak leaf. Her hair, cropped and unruly, caught the sun and flared tawny as a lion's mane. Changed as she was—transformed into a dark and tormented woman while he had tarried in Crisa—she was his sister and his beloved; and he had an aching emptiness within his chest that would be eased only when he held her hard against the vacant place.

"Blessed Lady!" said Pylades, grasping him by the arm, "is it you, my cousin, or is it she?"

"She, she!"

She disappeared briefly behind a shoulder of the hill and appeared again close to the top of it, near the marker. Her hand groped about her person for a little as if she sought something, knowing neither what nor where. Then the long brown fingers grew purposeful and pulled a knife out of the hempen girdle around her waist, and laid it on top of the stone. That, he thought, is for shearing off a lock to give to the dead. I too should have done it, but I forgot, and look at her fair hair—she has shorn it away lock after lock, she has given all the warm length of it to the dead. . . .

She knelt and put her forehead against the marker. "Blessed Lady!" said Pylades again. "They have dressed her in the rags of peasants and harried the flesh from her bones. How was it that the two of us remembered her not and lived at our ease in Crisa? How shall we ever comfort her? Come, come."

She was still at her prayers when they came up behind her. Their feet made a rustling in the dry grass, and she turned with something pitiful and craven in her face—she shrank as if she feared a murderer yet meant to give herself up freely to be slain. It was long—his heart beat loud and slowly for several counts— before her knowledge broke in her strange and vacant eyes, before she sprang up and turned and clasped him cheek to cheek and knee to knee. Her mouth tasted of fever and the salt of tears. "Brother, brother! I thought you no longer walked in the light, I thought they had buried you long ago," she said.

The presence of the funeral stone restrained them, and he saw that this was well: the storm of sorrow within her might not break free at once, she might hold it in, she might spend it later in quieter accessions of tears. Gravely, he made his cousin known to her, and gravely she took the offered hand, darker than her own, and looked straight into his pitying eyes. They sat down on the ground at the spot where the shadow of the marker stopped, and softly, as if in fear of disturbing the dead, sister and brother told each other what had come to pass. Trivial things crept into the story and lengthened it—a dog in the lower town, an herb-tea brewed in Crisa, blue-eyed grass floating on the Nemean marsh, the strength of wine swallowed after a long fast. But these irrelevant matters served a blessed purpose: they slowly became the actualities and all else gave way to them as the images of a nightmare give way to familiar objects in a sunlit room.

They had recounted much and had been sitting for a while in

silence when she asked about the bruised grass and the blood; and, once Pylades had told her the whole of that story, including his own sickness and the partial burial in the clump of plane trees, she startled them both by leaping up in exultation and saying, "Take me there. Let me see."

"It is a terrible sight—why should your eyes look upon it?" said Pylades, also rising.

Her face twisted in bitter laughter and then seemed to crumple before an assault of tears. "Oh, if you knew—if you knew what my eyes have seen!" she said, and fell upon his neck. And it was he—the compassionate stranger—who held her through the real violence of her grief, stroking her heaving back, calling the daughter of Agamemnon a poor rabbit, speaking to her as if she were a sick child.

At Crisa, Orestes thought, they are skilled in the craft of comforting, and strove at once to strain the sourness out of it, to cleanse his gratefulness of the taint of mockery. If in Mycenae they were skilled in the craft of murder, then who was he to jibe at the healing arts of Crisa? It should be enough for him that she came out of his cousin's arms consoled and should speak no more of running like a Fury to look upon the corpse of Leontophon.

Mycenae or Crisa, Crisa or Mycenae—it was this that they weighed in the balance through the rest of the morning, while the gravestone reabsorbed its shadow and the sky took on the burning blue of noon. To go to Crisa, to abandon the Citadel, to leave the score between Atreus and Thyestes forever as it now stood—this was Pylades' counsel; and Orestes was drawn to it, even though it was his Citadel that his cousin proposed to leave behind. It was to Electra more than to him that the plea was addressed: she would gain thereby a new mother and a new father; her flesh and her spirit would be renewed in a peaceful house; she would lack nothing that a woman might want—for what does a woman want more than wool to spin in the quiet evenings, and a warm bath, and a soft couch, and good food at a cheerful table —these and love?

By the time he fell silent, her gaze had wandered from him and was fixed on the knife that lay on top of the marker. Almost as if she had not been listening, she started up again and took the knife and thrust it back into her girdle, forgetting—or so Orestes thought —to shear off the lock for the dead. "Kind cousin, good Pylades," she said, standing above him. "I cannot go forth, not while those two lie side by side and mock what lies here under our feet."

"Your father knows in the dry country what you have suffered. He will ask no more of you."

"That may be so, but I ask more of myself. In the lower town, I was seized by a madness. There were times when I did not know whether I was a woman or a man or a lion. I was mad and could take no food and knew not whether it was winter or summer, morning or night. While those two live, how can I lie down without the thought that on the morrow I may well go mad again?"

"Truly, my sister?" said Orestes, but it was foolish to ask it. He had known it and hidden it from himself at the first sight of her; he had known it by her bent neck and the blankness of her face. Also, there was the blade. . . . "Give me the knife, I will carry it," he said, and Pylades sighed deeply, but nodded and spoke no more of the place of peace.

Still, even those who are ruled by the mandates of the cruel dead may yet find life—so the three of them thought, walking down the slope away from the stone. They would have to beg and starve and hide and connive. She would have to find new linen bands to bind up her breasts. Io would wax and wane innumerable times before the waters of Crisa would slake their thirst or a couch at Crisa be spread for love. But it was a fair day, and the road was broad enough for them to walk three abreast, holding each other's hands. Between the emaciated hand and the hand of Orestes there was an urgent clasping, but with the other, he knew,

312

she was drawing sustenance from the compassionate stranger. And if there was pain in his awareness that she was no longer wholly his as in their childhood, he could feel the first stirrings of release at the thought that a time might come when they would move serenely apart, when they would be given the heart to say "Farewell, my sister," and "My brother, farewell."